THE JADE CAT

THE JADE CAT

Suzanne Brøgger

Translated from the Danish by
Anne Born

THE OVERLOOK PRESS
New York

First published in the United States in 2009 by

The Overlook Press, Peter Mayer Publishers, Inc.
141 Wooster Street
New York, NY 10012

Translation of this work has been supported by a grant from
the Danish Literatue Centre, Copenhagen

Cataloging-in-Publication Data is available from the Library of Congress

Printed in the United States of America
FIRST EDITION
1 3 5 7 9 8 6 4 2
ISBN 978-1-59020-230-2

KATZE'S BOOK

THE MEZZANINE

Tobias was the man of the world and Otto the stay-at-home. That's what Otto had believed all of his life, and he still believed it on New Year's Eve in 1940. The table at Gammel Mønt 14 was laid with the gold-edged plates from the sideboard. Marie, short in the leg and large of bosom, had followed two generations of the family from Rosenvænget to Gammel Mønt. She took charge of the preparations as usual. Or almost. The Director had – in spite of her resistance – insisted on making the mayonnaise for the lobster himself, his feet up on a stool on account of his thrombosis. Marie had known the Director since he was a boy and she was a slip of a girl.

Tobias and Katze were giving a New Year's Eve party, a white-tie affair. Only the petit bourgeois expected guests in white tie and tails. Dinner jackets were worn only at everyday gatherings. It should be noted, however, that it wasn't that Tobias minded what "one" did or said. He did only what suited him. It was Katze, who had married into the Løvin family, who upheld the formalities, hectored the family into line, and who suffered.

Tobias, like every other Løvin, was a born after-dinner speaker, but he surpassed them all in wit. The unvoiced conviction of the family was that Løvin – always spelled with an ø – was a particularly fine name because it followed the pronunciation of the French "e", and thereby the Løvins were loftier than mere Levins. It should surprise no-one that the Løvins were born speakers, for named after Lion they were bound to roar. Conversation at dinner was always carried on at full volume, whether about politics, social matters, business or gossip. The Løvin family put ordinary gentiles to silent flight.

To outsiders there was something threatening about the way they bellowed at each other. It was as if they were concealing some terrible secret. Katze regarded this shouting as uncouth. The Løvins were well aware of their gift for eloquence. This was not a family which, when it came time for a toast, drew scripts from their inside pockets or their handbags. With a Løvin, it was always improvisation and esprit. And that was especially Tobias' talent.

The Løvin family was as assimilated as one could imagine. They considered the ghetto Jews to be humble in the *wrong* manner. Ghetto dwellers were the sort who said quietly: "Well, there's nothing to be done." But there was always something to be done about it – as Li, the eldest daughter, maintained – and the Løvins knew what. To the day of their deaths, the Løvins all insisted that it was simply unthinkable for one of them to be victimised or carted off to a concentration camp. The idea of a Løvin in striped concentration camp uniform would be as absurd as a tiger in pyjamas. "A Løvin would rather kill himself – after first shooting a German!" said Tobias' daughters with one voice – or rather, they will be saying it soon.

On the New Year's Eve in question, Tobias rose to his feet, attracting his guests' attention with a discreet tap on his hand-cut Russian glass. He had set the table himself, for Tobias was the connoisseur of celebrations. Earlier in the evening, at about eight o'clock, the air-raid sirens had begun. The bell of the old Copenhagen Town Hall clock had just struck twelve. Tobias pulled out the gold pocket watch he had inherited from Papa and put it on the table; then he picked up a pile of gramophone records. The guests expected them to be old favourites significant in ways that Tobias would explain, but instead, to the general astonishment, he dropped them in a shattered heap behind his chair. His game was that each guest had to find in someone else's broken shard a piece that belonged with his own. This was how they would identify the partner they were to kiss at the stroke of midnight, the New Year. Very witty and very elegant. Very Tobias!

Meanwhile Katze sat at the opposite head of the table, in her long mustard-coloured crêpe de Chine, seething. She smoked too many Craven As, but she had good teeth and good legs. She had sex appeal too, unlike that common cow fru Fonnesbeck, soon to be kissed by Tobias – a racing certainty. Glenda Fonnesbeck was a fleshy woman with white skin and freckles, set hair and buck-teeth. She even rinsed her hair copper since that was supposed to be more refined than dyeing it. She was married to Buller, a small, round, bald fellow whose only interest in life was the price of coal and coke and who was indifferent to his wife's escapades. Katze often and bitterly remarked that they could by now surely stop inviting those dreary people, couldn't they? But Tobias, who had been forced to give up his position as Director General of Vacuum Oil in the Baltic countries when the Russians arrived, planned to start afresh from Gammel Mønt. He might set up a sales agency; he had already had his letterhead printed, THE VULKAN CO. LTD. Tobias calculated that Buller, with his knowledge of the Danish market, might be a great help. When the war began, there would unquestionably be a demand for fuel. Besides, wasn't Glenda Katze's best friend?

Katze always pronounced the "l" in Glenda with scornful emphasis so that everyone could hear how degrading it was to know her. Although they were naturally on first-name terms after a friendship of more than 20 years, Katze could never be a close friend of anyone who boasted of having "a sensual disposition". Good God, the woman was simply wanton. A street girl. Katze had never been like that. She came from a good family and she had been christened Katarina after the Russian empress.

Katze surveyed the guests with condescension. Her blue eyes were clear, no hint of bloodshot. She hadn't drunk too much yet, and she smiled sweetly at one and all. Her perfume was Guerlain's new Mitsouko and she wore Helena Rubinstein's vermilion Dark Diva lipstick, which left blood-red marks on her Craven A butts. When she saw Glenda taking a cigarette from her pearl handbag, Katze offered her a Craven A from the silver mug on the table.

There was Otto, the nitwit, searching for a sliver of song. He was very sweet, the only Løvin who had accepted Katze with real kindness, even siding with her against Tobias. Otto had supported Katze's decision to buy tea towels when Tobias favoured investing in lobsters and prawns. It wasn't that Katze took any particular interest in tea towels as such, but when it came to maintaining Gammel Mønt 14 in unstable times, she knew where her duty lay. And what store could she set by Tobias? At the end of the day, what was he really *worth*? What use was he when the Buick broke down on a gravel highway in Lithuania? How much use was he altogether with his long, manicured fingers that could manage nothing more intricate than a Havana cigar or deck of cards?

Otto's wife Titta, a Monies before she married, searched in her well-bred way for a matching fragment of gramophone record for her own. She was no wet blanket, even in her dinky collars and puff sleeves. With her neat black curls, ivory profile and long red, claw-like nails, it was as if – heaven help us – she had just been painted in miniature by Fanny Falkner, last wife of Strindberg. With her masses of money and sugary smile, Titta had gone to finishing school in Switzerland and won a beauty contest in Hornbæk, where she was also the tennis champion. How boring and predictable it all was! It had taken her years to land the easy-going Otto. She had been a visitor at Rosenvænget since she was a girl and she had set her cap at him, but somehow she had failed to penetrate his defences. Finally she threatened to marry someone else. And she did! This marriage – which had at least borne fruit in the person of her son Ib – had of course been a mere misunderstanding. As soon as Otto caved in, she ran away even from Ib whom she deeply loved but was forced to sacrifice so as to be able to marry Otto, who wouldn't tolerate competition in the form of children. After their marriage Otto changed not at all. He conversed only in brief, clipped utterances: 1: Whisky with ice? without ice? 2: Will we be bombed, or not bombed? 3: Shall we play seven or *vingt-et-un*? All the same, he was invariably sweet to Katze, and Katze wondered what it must feel like to secure the man you loved. Katze had done that herself, of course, in a way. But still.

Mama, old Sara, Papa's widow, sat with her head shaking and a net over sparse blue hair. Everyone had been afraid that she would get up to speak and go on about Papa's memory. She had only been a widow for two years, and she was a tireless speechifier – but, exceptionally in the family, she needed little notes to jog her memory. There was always the risk that she would recite from memory a long poem by Heine. But now old Sara sat perfectly still. She was remembering the obituaries of her husband, "fine man, fine Dane", that had also extended praise to her: "At no house in Copenhagen was the Christian Yuletide celebrated with more splendour or devotion than in this Jewish home."

Mama gazed through her grey cataracts and thick spectacles at the guests wandering about with their pieces of broken records. She was too fearful of forgetting the point of the game – finding a kissing partner – even to open her mouth. Not that she was a prude. Georg Brandes, who had been a guest in her childhood home and later at Rosenvænget, had been provocative enough for his time. But, as Nathansen wrote in his book about him, Brandes was above all passionately truthful and uncompromising in his belief in the freedom of thought. Robert Storm Petersen had attended Papa's funeral too, and Storm was certainly not boring. But this . . .

Marie came in and whispered a question in Katze's ear: should she serve the coffee? "As you like, Marie," Katze replied absently. She and Marie were both born in 1900, and they had known each other for two decades.

Katze looked sceptically at Palle Gaustrup – known as Gaus – the young financial genius Papa had hired and welcomed into the family. Otto had met him in the United States; later, Papa had installed Gaus, as if he were one of the family, in Tobias' old rooms in Rosenvænget. Even though he was in evening dress and had no eye patch, there was something piratical about Gaus. True, he was only a shoemaker's son from Horsens, but he had married a great deal of money in Norway. Aud, his wife, had gradually gone blind and was loved by everyone except Gaustrup, who carried on with the housekeeper for the whole world – save his wife – to see.

Katze looked at her children with a strange fear, as if they were strangers to her. Balder, Liane and Rebekka – whose side were they on, hers or Tobias'? And how would they get by in Denmark with their German schooling from Riga? Men considered Li the attractive one, with her fair-skinned, indolent limbs and her amber eyes. They all said she looked like Greta Garbo. Li was Tobias' favourite, although he would sometimes fly into a rage over her tantrums. Tobias was not religious, but he did

7

religiously believe that one should be happy and positive; he despised whining and moping (Katze's speciality). And if the slightest thing displeased her, Li could make everyone's life a perfect misery by not speaking for a fortnight.

Rebekka, the youngest, was the most beautiful by the standards of classical Jewish beauty. The two sisters spoke German together, whereas Balder – who had just passed his examinations at a Danish boarding school – vainly reminded his siblings that they were no longer in Riga.

Balder was spineless, Katze thought sorrowfully, just like her father. Who or what had crushed him? Why had he turned out like this? Male weakness embarrassed and aggrieved her. Perhaps it was because Tobias went to Tivoli to amuse himself with that bitch Baby Zornig just after she had given birth to Balder. Still, she couldn't deny that Balder, her firstborn, was the best-looking of them all. "Beau Løvin" they called him at the maternity home, the handsome baby born under the sign of the Lion, but there wasn't much of the lion about him now.

Years later, after Tobias became the Director General of Vacuum Oil in the Baltic countries and they had moved to Riga, Balder was sent to school in Denmark. It had been necessary so as to ensure him a successful future, but Katze was against it. She could still weep at the memory of sending such a little boy away. Or perhaps it was the atmosphere at Rosenvænget that had destroyed Balder's confidence? Had Mama's strictness and Papa's vagueness shackled him? Was he teased at school about his red hair and big nose? He had high spirits, but not an ounce of self-belief. And in a way that was strange. It was obvious how a woman, dependent on her reflection in a husband, could lack self-confidence. But a man? It contradicted nature.

And Liane? How had she turned out like this? Surely not because they had spent a night in a brothel during the flight from Riga? Was it there Liane had been ruined? They hadn't been able to find a hotel throughout the drive across Germany because there were notices everywhere saying *"Juden nicht erwunscht"*. Li had sex appeal, like Katze herself. She could get any man to move mountains for her, without even asking. It was simply a power she possessed. But how would she use it?

And Rebekka . . . the youngest and Miss Know-It-All. She was definitely the most intelligent of the three, the youngest and the one who would go furthest. But Katze worried that Bekka might spoil her chances with her arrogance.

"Li is enchanting!" Glenda said across the table to please her friend.

" I worry about Bekka," Katze said without thinking.

"But why? She is clever at school, hard-working and sensible!"

"But where's the good in that, when you can't get a man?"

"Well, there *are* other things in life," Glenda said.

"How would *you* know?" Glenda chose to take Katze's remark as a compliment.

"A woman who can't seduce a man troubles me," Katze went on.

"But why shouldn't she be able to seduce a man? She has such a lovely face."

"You don't seduce anyone with a lovely face," Katze said.

"You've no right to take such a pessimistic view of your own daughter," Glenda protested. "Besides, there is such a thing as a *mind*!"

"Indeed, and you would know all about that!" Katze laughed.

In the meantime Gaus and Li had matched their records. Katze watched them heading for the drawing room. But her head was full of Tobias and Glenda and she wasn't aware of their escaping the party.

In the stairwell, Gaus gave the daughter of the house long kisses. He seized her hand and they flew down to the mezzanine. Liane could hear the sound of her taffeta skirt between her thighs. Gaus told her that he had keys to the brokerage office. In there, he said, he could kiss her much better, for he just couldn't get enough of her. So they made love on the writing desk, cushioned by heaps of share certificates and exchange bills. Liane, who had never tried it before, was very flattered. She knew that she had sex appeal, but it had never paid such dividends until now.

"Do you think your wife noticed anything?" she asked, at once anxious and hopeful.

"Aud is as blind as a bat, you know that."

"Blind people can feel more than others. Beethoven . . . "

"We're not going to talk about him now," whispered Gaus.

"I'm glad I'm no longer a virgin anyway."

"Anytime you wish!"

"There probably won't be another time," Li said sharply.

"Always at your service," Gaus said, buttoning his trousers.

"If anything happened to my father . . . "

"What d'you mean?"

"If the war . . . "

"No matter what happens, you can always count on me."

Li relished the excitement of nobody knowing what had happened in the mezzanine. She hadn't planned it that way – Gaus was the one who wanted it. But his feelings didn't much concern her. Later on, when all sorts of terrible things came to pass, Li would remember that New Year's Eve on the writing desk – that she had been with the only man who during the Occupation drove to Asserbo in a taxi when others couldn't even afford bicycle tyres. Gaus certainly had personality.

While Li was lying on the stockbroker's desk, Rebekka was gripping a fragment of a record, triumphant in her certainty that her father had its mate. Bekka rejoiced at the way he had let the whole pile of records crash to the floor. In his munificence, her father had made a sacrifice to the God of Waste. Unlike most women, Bekka was never one for housewifely nagging about money and budgets. Stinginess might be a feminine trait, but to Bekka it was old-maidish and the last thing on earth she could stomach. It was impossible to imagine Zeus counting the drops of gold in rays of sunshine or Thor saving energy on lightning. Masculinity must be forceful and generous, and those qualities must be *abundant*, and for these qualities, in spite of his excess, her father was the man who most brought her happiness.

Strange that Tobias had still not stolen a kiss from that dragon Glenda. Instead he carried his piece of gramophone record to Katze and kissed her: "Happy New Year, my treasure." They had both found a piece of "I never had a dream come true".

2

THE CANDLESTICK

K atze didn't feel like dwelling any longer on the photograph of New Year's Eve, 1940, and shut the album with a bang.

"Men are riff, women are raff. Human beings are riffraff."

When you entered the great patrician building and took the ramshackle lift – a narrow wooden box, with folding doors and windows, hanging from an iron chain forever threatening to snap – you wobbled past the mezzanine. That was the most exciting floor because there was only an iron grille and you couldn't get out. The mezzanine – the very word signalled something mysterious and ambiguous, and the grille suggested something suspect behind the respectable nameplates: CORN OFFICE and STOCKBROKERS. Were they real firms? Involuntarily, you felt the urge to go on up to three.

Once the door with its stained-glass panes had gleamed. It had been decorated with holly and a Russian Santa Claus in December, and the brass plate with Director Løvin's name in italics had been polished. The Director's overcoats still hung on hooks in the hall, though he was long since dead. The red silk domino, his fancy dress outfit, still hung in his wardrobe. Katze could not bear to throw his clothes away herself, for in spite of everything she had loved him.

The window of the guest cloakroom occupied Katze's full attention. In the Løvin family, it was bad form to say toilet, especially if you spoke with an aspirated "t" like shop assistants and servant girls. It was called the WC, and Katze always said "water closet" in English. Or Debbie, who came from the gutter in Borgergade and metamorphosed into Lady de Bath, called it the "powder room". Katze put her dry martini – without vermouth – behind Aunt Mudde's hand-painted flower-patterned lamp. She had a strong sense that her husband had re-incarnated himself as a white dove, and there he was behind the pane on the window cornice. Hush, hush, she had whispered for several years after Tobias' death, tip-toeing into the cloakroom to greet her husband, the white dove. It had settled onto the cornice outside Gammel Mønt 14 as if it knew Katze's motto: "The whole world may pass away, Gammel Mønt will always stay." She would cling to that motto. Wasn't she, indeed, the one who had stayed in Denmark during the war and kept the house open and the firm going? Not that oaf Tobias, who had fled with his tail between his legs.

Under a crystal mirror, there was an old chest from their time in Riga on which were displayed Russian miniatures of snow scenes, sleighs and sable furs. The inside of the chest did not smell of mothballs but of dead silk, for silk can die just as pearls do. There were live silks among Katze's old gowns, one of them a pleated tomato-red dress in rich crêpe de Chine, a black Chanel dress from the '30s; a dove-grey Chinese cloth embroidered with dragons that laced up at the sides to let the naked flesh peep through. The most daring one – and only Katze knew whether she had ever worn it – was a transparent creation with a deep back, two long, wing-like trains, and a sophisticated neckline cut so low that the breasts were provocatively apparent. Katze kept this delicate garment because it had belonged to Angelika, a Swedish countess and an old friend, who had been born in a castle, wore hats as wide as windmills and had been divorced five times.

Beneath the arch between the drawing and dining rooms stood the Russian altar candlestick that Katze had bought from a Latvian Jew – probably stolen from an Orthodox church. It stood one-and-a-half metres tall. It had been one of a pair, but the other one had been turned into a lamp. Katze, who was sensitive to matters of *bon ton*, had shaken her head at its fate when Rebekka returned from visiting a Hungarian school friend's house and reported the presence there of the silver lamp. On such occasions, Katze would assume a particular expression: with the merest twitch of her lips, she managed to impress good taste upon Rebekka. Katze always kept the candlestick in a prominent position. It had a yellowed, dusty candle, but it was never lit. It gave the impression of something sacred and stood in its place guarding against . . . what? Well, against bad taste, because at least it had never been turned into a lamp.

In the dining room, next to the samovar, the sideboard was laden with gilt-edged plates and silver salvers. Above the sideboard hung a painting of a Jew fleeing with a bag on his back. Katze had bought it just to help the poor Latvian painter. In the dining room there was also a portrait of her father-in-law, "the administrator", known as Papa. When he introduced the art of advertising in America, thereby making Denmark's biggest daily paper the most profitable one, all the newspapers called him "one of Denmark's leading sons". All these so-called leading sons – whether they became brewers in Chicago like Max or publicists like Papa – could be traced to the founder of the Danish Spirits Factories, Isidor Løvin – *aqua vitae*, the water of life.

3

PERSONALITY

The same phenomenon that makes "the family" so intolerable when you are young is precisely what makes it so fascinating when you are old: that concentration of karma, of memory, and skeletons in the cupboard.

The primary task of the family is to convince its members that they are magnificent, unique, absolutely special. Not every family manages this perfectly, for it needs a divine progenitor. In this respect the Løvin family was blessed, for its own origins were in Isidor's eldest son, Maximilianus.

In the American biography of him, Uncle Max, a Jew with aquiline features, looks down on his creation and observes: "It is good." It is not by accident that he "observes", but in Maximilianus' case, the heavenly light was indistinguishable from the limelight that invariably surrounded him. According to the book, he never sought that limelight.

However essential, it's not easy to have a god in the family. You can boast about it, but you cannot derive any serious benefit from a divinity so close to home. Divinities need death and distance.

Max was flamboyant. At once divinity, scholar, inventor, healer and celebrity, he cast a golden lustre over all other Løvins. Max was the blossom and fruit of the family, but also the worm in the apple. In fact, he used the same description whenever he was complimented in his old years on his youthful appearance: "Yes, on the outside I look like a fresh red apple, but inside I am rotten." Incidentally, it is worth noting that the idol of the family was hostile to it: "God chooses your relations but, God be praised, you choose your friends yourself," Max said. He had another side to his personality: he had sympathy for vipers. Even when he fell into a nest of them, he never tried to fend them off. He was faithful, honest and unselfish in all things. He was not religious *per se*, but he had such a high regard for the female sex that he more or less established a new religion to worship it.

Gods – whether born from thigh or forehead – descend upon us from primordial mists. Max descended upon the Løvins in 1859, as the god Bacchus from the mists of spirituous liquor. This does not mean the god was intoxicated; on the contrary, he was conceived by an alchemist who could transform potatoes into spirits. So it was that, from the moment that he was born, he inhaled intoxicating elixirs. Later in life, Max attributed his unusually robust health to the fact that the vapours of aquavit had humidified his cradle. His father, an impoverished Isidor Løvin, hiked into Denmark from Poland with a pack on his back and wheels on his feet. As the son of a poor gold-wire drawer and trimmings maker, he grew up with 15 siblings in a modest weaver's workshop. For dinner they had mashed potatoes as the principal dish, potatoes for pudding, potatoes for supper with dry bread and – when times were particularly bad – herring and syrup. When people fought over every cold boiled potato, it is logical that their ultimate goal in life should be an alchemical one: transforming potatoes into spirits. And so, with a talent and affinity for science, Isidor let the recipe ferment in his head. In 1838, with the permission of the Danish king, given in person, he left his birthplace – where Copernicus too had been born – to settle in Aalborg. There he founded the Danish Distilleries and, with the aid of an advanced European distilling apparatus, he invented the fusel-oil-free taffelaquavit, a brew fit for the royal table.

There is no doubt that Max's father, the tribe's patriarch, had an incandescent soul as well. On bidding farewell to his fatherland, he knelt down with his travelling companions and said: "The first one of us who eats *treife* will be strangled."

Isidor Løvin ate kosher all his life and observed the Sabbath most strictly. Isidor had brought Emilie Wasserzug – called the "water-wagon" by Katze – from Thorn to secure himself a proper kosher-bride. To her husband's dismay, she gave all her sons Scandinavian names. For as immigrants with an accent, Emilie must have known that Danish names would serve best: Max, Louis, Erik, Frederik, Arthur, and Emil.

By the next generation, they were thoroughly assimilated. Max's brother Erik converted to Christianity, was baptised, obtained a royal appointment as consul and corn merchant in Odessa, and rose in the ranks of freemasonry. Like the big businessmen of the day, who considered it their duty to be patrons either of the arts or the sciences, Erik Løvin underwrote a number of polar expeditions and even had a stretch of the North Pole – between the 86th and 88th parallels of latitude – named after him.

Isidor's sons, distillers and brewers, remained fairly true to the family heritage. Emil sold hops and malt and became a millionaire with a palace in Rungsted. Arthur, the joker, taught England's population to drink lager, which he himself had invented. He always took a thermometer with him to restaurants, and took the temperature of every glass of beer. He could also tap out a polka in several octaves on the piano – with his nose. It goes without saying that all the Løvin sons opposed Prohibition, though naturally this was the only area of politics that interested them.

Among these princes of Denmark, one might easily overlook Max's sister Rosa, but we shall come to her later.

The Løvins *wanted* to be Danish, and, regardless of where in the world they were, they *became* Danish. But this was not to last. Stop, said Hitler. Are you the person you believe yourself to be, or the one others say you are? The Løvins did not believe they were Jews until the world insisted. They were technically Jews, but in their own style. "The law" they used as a yardstick for success or fiasco. The fact that none of them had been in prison indicated to the family that life had gone well for them.

Max set the rare example of one who was simultaneously rebellious and successful. He detested the social etiquette laws of the 1870s, "affectation". With genuine shame, Max regarded his poor mother's velvet boudoir as pure kitsch, a social climber's attempt to be cultivated. His father's behaviour also embarrassed him. He was mortified, for example, every time his father opened a box of Havana cigars, passed it round for the guests to smell, clapped it shut and gave them cheaper ones to smoke.

It was not surprising that Max's generosity was his distinguishing characteristic. He was the one who invited and paid for his guests and who organised parties for others. Perhaps that is how he indemnified his sense of shame. Perhaps he had to compensate for his parents' tight-fistedness. But he was not sentimental, he was happy-go-lucky.

At Aalborg Cathedral School, Max befriended a shepherd boy (who later became a doctor) because he found in him the authenticity his parents lacked. The boy taught Max a timeless lesson: those who have gained riches may still be poor, and *vice versa*. Max and his friend were democrats, their toast was "Schleswig back to Denmark", and they fantasised about a poetic world without class differences.

Max's success, however, was built on the twin foundations of sadness and anger. As the eldest son, Maximilianus assumed he would take over the Aalborg factory. With this objective in mind, he dutifully obtained a doctorate in chemistry from Marburg University. He even wrote songs and arranged festivities for the factory workers. But his interests were passed over when Isidor sold the distillery as a limited company and used the proceeds to build a mansion at Sohngaardsholm. Worse still, Max had fallen in love with a noblewoman, a Miss Heiberg, who came from a family of intellectuals. But since he did not inherit the factory, he was not permitted to marry her, and so he went to the United States and became an American citizen. Miss Heiberg, adored as she was in a variety of social circles, followed him across the Atlantic and married him there. When she died, a list of her previous admirers was found among her papers, with the annotation: "And then she took the most foolish of them all, Max."

In Chicago, after the obligatory setbacks, he founded a brewers' institute, which he named the Løvin Institute. He introduced the first pure yeast culture into America, then identified the source of the typhus epidemic which was killing hundreds of people at the time. Milk bottles being washed in the polluted Lake Michigan water was causing it. Max's advice on hygiene was published in all the newspapers. However modest these accomplishments may seem, to Max it was as if he had saved the whole world.

There was nothing false about Max. On heathland in Jutland, as a contribution to the Rebild celebrations on July 4th, he built the Hørgdalshuset, which he instituted as a bridge between Denmark and America. Above the entrance he had a question branded into the wood: "Are you genuine?" It was an echo of his lifelong disgust for all affectation. But his genuine nature did not mean that he disliked irony. On the contrary, when it rained, Max would say: "The sun always shines in Hørgdalshuset." If things did not go to his liking, he was never resigned, but merely remarked: "Ah well, you can't always be in the Garden of Eden. Even there things went wrong." As a god, he would be the one to know.

When he found it possible to buy back his father's estate at Sohngaardsholm, he established the Danish-American archives there. Then, as a tribute to Abraham Lincoln, he built a log cabin, where Max's close friend Knud Rasmussen presented him with an American flag. Max conversed as spontaneously with presidents and kings as he did with farmers and woodcutters. He seemed to attract the light, but he equally enjoyed the shade.

He was not himself an outstanding scientist, but he understood how to run a laboratory and was motivated by high ideals. As the technicians said at the Carlsberg Laboratory: "Although Dr Løvin knows all about the secrets of the fermentation process, he is still more interested in the human fermentation process than in the chemical one." He was not well-read, but he still canvassed to raise the standards of Chicago's Public Library. Above all, possessing that rare combination of magic and stop-watch precision, he was successful in the role of organiser and producer of festivals, banquets, campaigns and exhibitions.

He sailed between Denmark and America 94 times and thereby spent nearly three years of his life on the Atlantic. He led a double life between the two countries and two wives. For, as the male members of the tribe put it, Max, "like every Løvin worth the name, had a mistress on the side". In fact, with his enormous vitality, Max managed to live ten lives in one, all without his wife. The much sought-after Miss Heiberg was out of her husband's life the moment she embraced it.

When he underwent a cataract operation at an advanced age, the old wizard, as he had come to be called, invited nine nurses to the Strandmølle Inn, but after dinner he was so tired that he allowed himself to be taken back to hospital, while paying for the nurses to have fun at Tivoli.

There was some irony about Max's death. The cosmopolitan, a man who all his life had moved through so many big cities without suffering so much as a scratch, met his end following a traffic accident out on the heath. He suffered nothing more serious than a broken thigh in the collision with a horse-drawn vehicle, but tradition has it that, as soon as the son of Bacchus lay down and the fire that drove him could no longer ignite, he lost heart, caught pneumonia and died.

Maximilianus had one real weakness: He had never been able to hide his feelings. He had no trick with cunning. He was fond enough of friends but he loved the truth more. This ensured that he was a personality. In turn, this was what the rest of the family tried to emulate.

Every god leaves behind him an unwritten law, and Max's was: Thou shalt be a personality. But what is this personality to comprise, and what must it achieve? Little by little this became irrelevant. Where good Christians chose the humane virtues above personality, the Løvins agreed unanimously that the code word was *attentiveness*. While proper Christians humbly prayed: "Give us this day our daily bread," in the Løvin family they asked: "Give us this day our daily dose of solicitude – we'll see to the bread ourselves."

As the banality of quotidian life was considered the worst of crimes, it should be no surprise that someone in the family would decide to commit a proper crime. In the service of a higher cause, to be sure, to conform to Max's unwritten law.

"Would you like salmon or prawns?" Katze remembers Max asking her at the Phoenix Hotel. She hesitated for a long time.

"Then you won't get anything at all," he said, closing the menu. And Katze laughed, entranced.

4

THE MESSAGE FOR GARCÍA

Papa Løvin, administrator and publicist, had wanted to study mathematics at university, but his father had forbidden such an extravagance, and so instead he trained as a pharmacist in Randers. Spirits and medicines – booze and drugs, in other words – are the source of the tribe's well-being as long as it doesn't go off the rails. Papa then emigrated to America to emulate his brother Max, but also – more pressingly – to flee his fiancée, Sara.

In Chicago, the white city, Papa was hired as a bacteriologist in Max's laboratory. He always remembered the World Exhibition of 1893 as a high point in his life. There he discovered the new power of advertising and all the great advances like the tabloid press which he, *miserabile dictu,* later introduced to Denmark. He even seized on a new invention: the zip fastener. He tried to import this novelty to Denmark, but to no avail. Papa, the publicist, was a man ahead of his time. Such was the family characteristic, for good or bad, mainly bad.

Because Papa couldn't live in the shadow of the great personality, his elder brother, he returned to Denmark and started working in the publishing house Gyldendal, under Peter Nansen. One would think that a publishing house is a strange workplace for a bacteriologist, but as a publicist he established several periodicals. He hired the most daring writers of the time who, through their profession, knew how to spread the essential "viruses" to the greatest effect. Papa swiftly acquired the taste for importing Anglo-Saxon best sellers. He bought A.E. Milne's *Winnie the Pooh*, and had a famous article translated for the American market, where it sold like hot cakes, as well as several hundred thousands of copies as a gift book in Denmark.

The little book which made such a big impact was called *The Message for García* and was based on a tale from the Spanish-American war in Cuba. A message had to be delivered to García, the leader of the uprising, who was somewhere – no-one knew where – deep in the jungle. A young private soldier was dispatched to carry the message to García. The story never reveals García's identity, or why he needed the message. What was the message? We have no idea, and the point is that we should not ask. Not even the hero of the story asks these questions. He fulfils the one necessary duty: to deliver the message to García. The soldier was considered a hero, not so much for his physical courage and his ability to penetrate through a fearsome jungle, but for his moral fibre and his integrity.

What worked in Papa Løvin's best-selling publication failed in real life, where the message to García never got through. After the Bolshevik revolution and the Nazis' rise to power, it was impossible to have any faith in the idea of a "world order" or even in individual relationships. From then on, whenever anyone was asked to deliver a package, he would never know if it contained a bomb or not. Ever since Mussolini, who ensured that the trains ran on time, and Eichmann whose trains have become a symbol of the uttermost barbarity, no-one can dispatch the Message any more. No-one dares to take responsibility for the Message without having first enquired into the recipient's identity, the package's contents, the expected profits and the worst-case losses.

So today it seems strange that Papa Løvin could sell 50,000 copies of *The Message* in one week. And yet, he was even invited to take over at the Berlingske newspapers, the leading Copenhagen papers, which he administered with a liberal hand for the rest of his life. They said he was so good and generous that he had to be a Jew.

Before the world war, he bought a magnificent villa in Rosenvænget. The architect Helweg Møller designed the library where Papa housed his rare book collection and his autographed first editions. The author Johannes V. Jensen, who had been in Chicago researching his novel *The Wheel*, became a friend and regular visitor. In the garden, which was large enough to be a park, there was a pool with a great fountain.

But the administrator was not a garden lover. While his wife Sara supervised the rose beds, he nestled in the library. The rest of the time he spent at the newspaper office or with his mistress, whom he had installed in an apartment near Pilestræde – like every other authentic Løvin. One cannot blame the administrator and publicist for hiding from his wife, for she was too strict, and he had married her by accident. Sara came from a good family from King Solomon's Pharmacy in Bredgade, and her doctor father had won fame in the fight against the cholera epidemic. That was all very well, but it was not enough to induce him to marry her. In an absent-minded moment, he let her lure him into taking a walk in the garden. Behind a hedge she gave him a kiss, on the mouth, then took him by the hand and pulled him into the living room, where she announced that they had a little secret that *he* would really like to share with the family. Since he was a gentleman, he had no choice but to declare their engagement. He had never cared for gardens since that day. In fact, he went all the way to America chiefly to escape Sara, but a telegram soon caught up with him, saying: "Arriving Chicago, track number so and so".

In Chicago, Sara gave birth to their children and from that time on, they were Papa and Mama. There were no problems with the eldest. Tobias entered the world prematurely, as if he couldn't wait for the new century. He was born on a kitchen table during a heat wave. Soon, he was decked out with long curls in pageboy style and lace dresses, as was the fashion. During his first few years, his pet name was "Ester", because Sara had wanted a girl. Though he was a spoiled boy, he had a fiery temper – he was after all the grandson of the man who had founded the Løvin dynasty and invented Danish schnapps.

Along with his small head, large ears and gigantic eagle's beak, Tobias had inherited arrogance that earned respect even when he cheated or teased. He didn't take much notice of rules. He made his own, and his own became the rules other people lived by. Tobias, then, was also a personality. He was – in accordance with the Løvins' secret handbook – flamboyant. Otto, who was born a year later, died at once, no doubt at the prospect of living in Tobias' shadow. Which was why the second Otto, the one who survived, always claimed that in reality he was dead and buried in Chicago.

5

DRAGON SEED

Katze reeled round the apartment. She was wearing an old
kitchen smock, its seams fastened with safety pins, sticking
plaster, even clothes pegs. She wore shabby red plastic slippers.
She crossed her arms under her breasts to alleviate the soreness
of the shingles that she complained of to her visitors.

She had covered the Danish Empire furniture in the drawing
room with pale yellow silk. Yes, *she* had done that because *she*
was the one who looked after Gammel Mønt 14, and everyone
else could go to hell. The gin and vermouth bottles stood on the
Czar's silver tray, *her* tray, come by way of her connections with
the Russian court, of course, while the others all snored and
thought of nothing but what Jews always think about: sex, sex,
and sex.

Tobias had read all the books of that hog Henry Miller which
had been translated – needless to say – by a Jew. He had even, as
if she were some kind of idiot, tried to hide them from her. The
large mythological paintings above the sofa and the bookshelves
were peopled with Norse gods, all facing away from the artist.
Katze studied one backside at length. "A fine example of a man's
behind," she said aloud. It called to mind the lithe shape of one of
the young law graduates who had just been hired at the office.

Beneath the divine buttocks were kept the remnants of the
Rosenvænget library, now no longer of any great value. "Don't

you read *newspapers*, Miss de Thura!" Papa had once said to her, as if he were referring to the Holy Scriptures. Now she regarded his library with scorn. That fool Thit Jensen – Good God, how could the woman dream of teaching men anything at all with legs as short as those?

And Edith Rode, who thought she was so clever. Katze took one of her books from the shelf to remind herself just how stupid she was. *The Art of Living without Philosophy*, Heaven help us! On page 88 there was a chart to show compatibility in husbands and wives: 1. Is the couple on the same intellectual level? 2. Do they like spending evenings quietly at home? 3. Do they like each other's friends? And so on. Ten questions and Katze had answered No to them all. The heart is broken, Rode's chart concluded. Katze had underlined that with ten thick lines. Elsewhere, because the book was about being happy, the author had written that everything passes. Katze now scribbled "rubbish" and "drivel" on every page she read. She didn't *want* to be happy. Once she might have, but now all she wanted was to be *truthful*.

Katze took another gulp of her red Aalborg schnapps. She sent no loving thoughts to the drink's inventor. Katze couldn't be bothered to put on an act any more. "Have you ever met a woman who completely changed her expression and tone of voice when a man came into the room?" Glenda! Katze wrote in the margin.

Katze stumped to her bedroom, where she had fashioned a world of her own under the influence of Dostoevsky and Tolstoy: "All happy families are alike, all unhappy families are unhappy in their own way." How true. She also kept the Bible on her bedside table – books of substance. All the same, Katze believed that the Bible should be banned. The chosen people! Who did they think they were? "Surely it can't mean that people must come to hate their fellow men through reading this book!" Katze had written on the title page: "A book written in hatred and for revenge. It will create anti-Semitism for as long as it is permitted to be in print." Then, for safety's sake she had added: "Of 240 million Mohammedans, only two percent can read and write. Ugh!"

All references to "unclean" women stirred Katze's fury, and she wrote that those passages should be omitted as unworthy of the Bible. She loathed the oriental tradition of cutting a woman into twelve pieces, and undoubtedly identified with the woman condemned to death by stoning. "Poor wretches," she had written in the margin.

Every time she came to a passage about the Jews blowing their trumpets with joy, Katze would snarl, "Foolish infants!" And yet, though she hated the Bible, Katze entirely agreed with it. She underlined all the curses in the Old Testament, page by page, as if they were her own, as if she herself were the last Court in the land. Thus she sent a greeting to Sara, her mother-in-law, comparing her to the camel: "No soul, no understanding of fellow creatures, stubborn in the extreme, cunning and spiteful." She cited her friend Glenda as saying: "I have been a good mother, even if I have had relationships with other men."

The Bible says that the faithless will perish in darkness, but Katze's experience suggested otherwise. She found that life was remarkably good to the faithless.

Katze recognised that her tears were self-pitying and triggered by alcohol, but nevertheless they relieved her. She too had been an idiot, after all. She should not have been so stupid, so ignorant. Yet how could she have been otherwise? She had been one of the cleverest girls at the convent school, and the nuns had impressed on her that she would grow to greatness. Whatever she drew, the nuns would look at it with awe and say: "You'll be an artist." When she wrote an essay, the nuns would pronounce: "You'll be a writer." They viewed her future in a fairy-tale light, probably because of her beauty, which enchanted them. When Katze played the Madonna at Christmas, the nuns didn't say, "You'll go to heaven." They said, "You'll go into the theatre."

Katze had long since detected the hypocrisy behind the nuns' holy façade. They prayed with their eyes half open, forever ready to catch a poor sinner in some trifling misdemeanour. The nuns at the French school had never thrown themselves on the floor streaming snot and tears, cursing God like Job, as Katze did throughout her life. That was why she had rewritten the Bible, for the Bible was the most terrible book she knew.

She also criticised the little booklet with gold lettering on the binding, *Rules of Life for Young Girls*, which was presented to Katze at her confirmation. She never challenged God's creating, guiding and sustaining power, but she did take issue with the Trinity. With thick, angry strokes, she assailed the idea of God's judgment and Jesus' death on the cross for our sake. She put a question mark beside "perish by suffering", as if she doubted it, and she scored two black lines beneath "the Peace of the Soul".

She chose her reading with care, remembering that "wicked books can give a false view of life, corrupt the heart and weaken the will". Had she been careful in her choice of friends and made sure never to do anything that she wouldn't want her mother to witness, even if her mother was blind? Had she tried to follow Jesus Christ and His blessed mother and practised the virtues of love, humility and self-denial? Had she learned to accept suffering and misfortune with patience, as coming from the hand of God? Had she mastered her natural coquettishness and dressed according to her station and avoided flashy garments? Had she lent a helping hand to the poor? Was she a ray of sunshine in her home?

The nuns' good advice was expensive, and Katze's parents were poor, down-at-heel patricians. What was the use of her forefathers building Hirschholm and Eremitageslottet* when now her father was a shop assistant in Magasin's gentlemen's clothing store and probably died of stomach cancer because he was so obsequious that he would hold in his stomach muscles whenever he sensed distinguished customers? The family whispered all sorts of rumours, and Katze's mother despised her weak husband, who always sat counting coins when he came home from the store.

Her ancestor from the island of Bornholm, a Kofoed, had once walked across the ice to warn of the attacking Swedes. Her mother, when she was young, had joined a women's group with the radical writers Agnes Henningsen and Karin Michaëlis. Since then she had gone blind out of contempt for her husband and regret over her wasted life. When she was in the kitchen, she shook her head all the time and murmured: "What can I have done to have deserved such a life?"

They were three sisters, Misse, Maja and Musse. Misse had been christened Katarina and she wanted to control her own life so she quickly dropped her pet name and became Katze. Musse was blind, like their mother, and fat as a cream cake, but she still found a husband by advertising in *Lonely Hearts*. She may have been as blind as a mole, but the man was a compositor at

* The Hermitage Castle

Berlingske Tidende and, although he was a Communist, the marriage was something of a miracle. Katze often wondered if, in the end, Musse had not been the happiest of the three. True, she had never had children, but her husband had the whole of the Soviet Union, and she had her cream cakes.

Katze didn't want to think about Maja. Maja was so nice and decent it made you unwell to think of her. She had married a senior clerk at *Berlingske Tidende*, as if that was anything special. She had boasted all her life that *she* had at least married a man who was faithful. So what? She didn't have a clue about love. It certainly had nothing to do with senior clerks and niceness.

Katze would never forget her sisters' reaction when she told them about her "accident". And with a Jew! Her father and mother had despaired over the disgrace that Katze had visited upon the family. At first her slow-witted father hadn't understood. "Don't you understand, you fool," her mother had said to him, "Katze is going to have a child!"

A child with a Jew! A black Jewchild! To a family that had once built a castle! The shame was devastating. From then on Katze was treated as a leper. And not only in the moral sense – they actually called her "nigger mouth". In the hall of the little flat in Dr Abildgaards Allé, neighbours shrank against the wall in disgust when Katze passed. How could she have been so stupid, she who had always been the loveliest and most gifted of the three?

But in the end really everything went quite well. Katze left school at 14 and took a secretarial job with High Court Judge David to avoid being a burden to her parents. She soon had enough money to buy a bicycle. It was during the First World War, and she was as slim as a greyhound, with long, elegant legs, chalk-white teeth, blonde hair and blue eyes. The most innocent and Nordic in all Copenhagen, or so she supposed. But why was she going to the Students' Union in the evenings? She just wanted to go out and to have fun. Oh, well, fine then. The war would soon be over, surely. But how innocent was Katze? Did she know that the Students' Union was the place where she could meet young men of good family? Did she really think the young men, Michelsen of the jewellers' and young Jørgen Birger Christensen of the furriers went there only to *look* at the girls?

Until the end of her life, Katze went on listing all the men that she could have conquered. And so why did she go home with Tobias Løvin, the young Mephistopheles with the small head, large ears and gigantic nose? He was by no means the handsomest or the richest. She had always claimed that she never gave any of her escorts so much as a kiss in a street doorway and always had enough money for a taxi so she could make a quick getaway if threatened. If this was true, then why had she gone with Tobias?

The fact was, she admitted, she had fallen in love. Head over heels, idiotically, in love. In a sense, she could never forgive herself for that one night when she lost control and shackled herself to the Old Testament. Not that the Løvin family were believers. But Katze was. She did not believe in Christ, that imbecile, but she had a lifelong battle with *fate*, which had caused her to weep so despairingly when she was young. But she wept over her happiness too. She wept because she loved Tobias, as well as because he was unfaithful.

6

THE CONSUL

Katze noticed that the sun's rays had bleached the Chinese silk dragon that Uncle Sophus had brought back from Japan.

All the Løvin men had lady friends. "We are very faithful in that respect," Uncle Otto would say. The men of the family didn't think of themselves as Don Juans, only as "charmers". And for a few of them to marry four or five times wasn't a crime, surely. Otto's partner in the pursuit of ladies was his uncle, the robust profiteer Emil, who had grown rich on the Great War. Emil laid bets on everything: the weather, ladies, corn and cannons. He called Otto several times a week – his wife was deaf – and then he and Otto waltzed out to play cards and enjoy the company of their lady friends. They did so because they had so much life in them. And their better halves could hardly protest against . . . life. Besides, the wives suspected nothing. At that time, women were old when they had finished having children – another of Otto's maxims. And it had to be said that the men did behave with decorum. They turned up at meals and attended parties and the theatre with their wives. A couple of nights a year they even let themselves be shoe-horned into evening dress to keep "distinguished" company, which the women insisted was necessary to preserve connections. When the women complained that the guests didn't seem to have enjoyed themselves much, the men replied: "Of course they didn't. Were they supposed to?"

So it was like a breath of fresh air when Maximilianus' daughter Gerda got married. Gerda was an opera singer who married – the first time – Carlo Edwards, head of the Metropolitan Opera in New York. The wedding was held at Uncle Emil's house in Rungsted. The festivities having continued into the small hours, the bride announced that she was tired and wanted to go to bed. "That's fine," the bridegroom said, "I'm off to the Adlon."

"That was Carlo Edwards for you!" they said afterwards in the family. A man who would go out on his own to have fun, alone, even on his wedding night: "The man was an artist!"

Katze wasn't so awe-struck. She padded into her bedroom in Gammel Mønt mumbling, "Men are riff, women are raff," and concluded as usual, "Human beings are riffraff." She thought of inscribing a note to this effect in the Bible, but she was too tired to hold a pencil. She had been at the office all day, and shortly she was going to lie down and die. She couldn't be bothered any longer. One day she would write her will. Quite soon. As she was on her way to bed, the telephone rang. Unable to regain the salon, Katze answered it in Tobias' bedroom. Not that she could care less which fool was calling. It was Glenda. It would be. When she first picked up, Katze was grumpy and threatening, as was her wont. Then, and for no apparent reason, she suddenly cooed "my dearest darling" in a honeyed treble – that was why everyone in the family called her "Bodil Ipsen" or "Clara Pontoppidan" – after the actresses – and "Russian princess" (when they didn't call her "Eeyore", that is). Seduced by Katze's affectionate tone, Glenda offered to come over, with a prawn sandwich because she knew how hard Katze worked at the office. But Katze didn't want the pleasure of her prawns, for she knew only too well the price that went with them: sitting and listening to all Glenda's complaints about her cancer and the rubbish about her long-dead admirers – the ones she deluded herself into thinking she had had.

"Ah, no, my lamb, you mustn't think of it. I'm going to bed at once. I've had a hell of a day."

"I can't understand why you keep on with that work, Katze – you're past seventy."

"How could you understand? You who have never lifted a finger in your life, my lamb."

"I'm only saying it for your own good. Why ruin your last years? Why not get the best out of them?"

"You've always been so good at that."

"When I think of all the men you could have had: Jørgen, Ole, Michael, Dietlov . . . And you just went on working! What have you got out of it?"

"Shingles!" Katze said, laughing in spite of herself.

"Ah, I can imagine," Glenda said, and then played her trump: "I've got lymph cancer. Now really, shouldn't I come over?"

But Katze pleaded to be left in peace and replaced the receiver with a sigh of relief. Tobias had died years ago, but she still believed that Glenda prepared food solely for *him*. Decades had passed and still Glenda went on persecuting her. Once they had competed for who had more sex appeal. Now it was who had more cancer. Glenda was way ahead with her lymph glands, so she really did have something to boast about. Glenda who took all her clothes off and hopped into bed even if she hadn't been invited to. Katze had never been like that. Not for nothing had all *her* admirers in Riga called her "the Duchess", for Katze could never be tricked into anything. As her admirer Kiko Lonnegan used to say: "You can cultivate Katze for years and years and you may never be rewarded for it." Katze remembered complacently what Edith Rode had written about cats: "They are beautiful and elegant and so distinguished. One is honoured by a cat's friendship. But you never get on intimate terms with a cat." Katze had often thought that was the reason English was the best language for love – it kept its distance. Katze saw herself sitting at the piano in the 16-room apartment on Kalpaka Boulevard in Riga, where she had had three maids. Kiko Lonnegan leaned over her while she played "A little kiss each night". She always knew five numbers. Mind you, how exhausting to play "Duchess" for a hundred years.

Katze cursed and went into her bedroom. That's where she kept all her memories of Riga and her precious keepsakes from the Orient – her uncle had been a consul in Japan. An album with a rosewood cover, porcelain decorated with gilt holy men. In the *escritoire*, she kept the letters, photographs and greetings she had received through the years. A card with a crown on it from the Czar's cousin and a note of greeting from George Kennan, when he was ambassador. In the same drawer Katze also kept photographs of Cousin Olaf, tall, handsome and masculine, a Nazi before Nazism was invented. He had "monkeyed about" with the girls when they were little. On the back of one of the pictures, Katze, in a drunken moment, had written "The Eagle".

Katze, who treasured the worst of things, wrote on the back of all the photographs, and obviously she had made some of her scribbles when the worse for wear. Her writing, usually neat and tidy, became wild as she scrawled out a death sentence. Venereal disease is attributed all round. Members of the family, friends and acquaintances, she divided between the clever and the stupid. As a rule, they are clever just after they are born, but they don't live long before Katze has decided to rip out their guts or give them syphilis. Bitterness or reality soon take hold – in short, the sexual instinct, and where that is concerned everyone fails, and dies. In Katze's book, it comes to the same thing.

She opened an album from Riga and turned the pages of photographs of all the people she had known there: "Dead, dead, shot, executed, murdered, gassed, gassed, gassed, dug his own grave and shot," she read the litany aloud with a certain satisfaction before snapping the pages shut.

Katze took out Uncle Sophus' letters from Kyoto. Yellowing packages of meticulous handwriting bound up with silk ribbon. When memories of Tobias' unfaithfulness and the Løvins' arrogance depressed her too much, she turned to Uncle Sophus, brother to her father, the poor Magasin shop assistant. Sophus had been a man of the world. *He* was an Aladdin, made of right stuff. He was a de Thura and not like those Løvins, who thought the whole universe theirs of right. Uncle Sophus, who had been Danish Consul in Yokohama, had a suitably large turban which more than compensated for all the lions in the family she married into.

Katze had not been alive when Sophus' letters were read out in Fredericiegade in the 1890s. When she was born in 1900, she had, it seemed, internalised the fairy tale, and it gave her the courage to see life as something potentially great. Perhaps that was the reason she dared to go to the Students' Union.

"Denmark is a little country, and sometimes it is good to live there – but how insignificant it is compared to what one finds abroad," Sophus wrote. How right he was, Katze sighed, thinking of the legion of her foreign admirers.

Yes, the Danes were quite simply an insignificant nation. So insignificant that they can never grow into a great one, heave and tug as one might. The Danes have a passion for envy and for comparing themselves with one another. That is what holds the country together. They have no capacity to imagine anything outside Denmark, anything comparable. If the Danes see something that doesn't resemble them, it must not exist! Katze thought that the Germans had a different type of greatness. Nonetheless, it didn't do to utter that aloud, even though *she* had known the right Germans: the Baltic Germans, whose lineage could be traced to the proud old orders of chivalry.

When Uncle Sophus set off – with a crew-cut, a trim moustache, and audacity in his blue eyes – he viewed the world as bathed in electric light. He saw progress! In Marseille, there were electric eyes and electric smiles in the alleyways; everything was far removed from the muddy twilight of his homeland. In his letters, Uncle Sophus described heavens hitherto unimagined. On board the steamer to Japan, he was still so Danish that he sent the menus to his parents, knowing how Danes prized food above all else. Once he had ventured into the wide world and experienced French cuisine and French lifestyle, he realised why he had so often shaken his head over meals at home. He wrote about Malaysian prawns as big as plates and about colours so vibrant that they would never be seen in Denmark.

In a letter marked "to be opened on Christmas Eve", Sophus wrote to his mother:

> This time I'm not writing from the office but from the hotel where I am being entertained both by the numerous disturbers of the peace and also three elderly Japanese ladies who sit beneath my windows to discuss their affairs. I must tell you, dear Mother, that there's nothing to separate the weaker sex in the oriental and the occidental parts of the world. Here too they love to have a good gossip. It's a shame I don't know enough Japanese to understand what they are saying, but I am pretty certain their conversation involves their servant girls. When I say that they are sitting beneath my windows, you mustn't think they are sitting on a bench, because this would seem unpractical and unusual to them. They are sitting, as everyone does in the East, on their haunches, which looks a bit comical to European eyes.
>
> On the whole, the Japanese have many amusing

peculiarities. If a man wishes to show his respect, besides bending double in a bow, he accompanies his peculiar words with a sound rather like the one you make when you slurp your soup. Priceless. It's less pleasant when the Japanese attempt to eat like Europeans. Now and then the better off Japanese come to the hotel for a European meal. If the cuisine is Western, the Japanese's method of consuming it most definitely is not. Apart from the amusing way he employs his knife and fork – accustomed as he is to eating with chopsticks – his slobbering, sucking of teeth and loud belching after each course is anything but civilised. These people have certain boorish habits and their table manners are in general, typical of their character.

Katze relished the thought of the shock that Uncle Sophus' letters must have been to his genteel Christian home. How would they have been redeemed from their suffocating self-satisfaction if their love for Sophus and the example of his exotic way of life had not liberated them?

They are certainly not strait-laced here, and if *you* are, you are swiftly shaken out of it by the constant presence of the Japanese. These fellows haven't the least sense of modesty. The wealthier ones walk about wearing only the light covering known as a kimono; the workers, porters and so on are stark naked, with a belt of sorts around their waist and a piece of cloth which hides only the bare essentials. Now, you mustn't blush too deeply, for if the Japanese ladies can put up with it in life, you can surely cope with it on paper. But I can hear you, dear Mother, exclaim: "What pigs, can't they put a stop to such things?" Well, the Japanese women are also in kimonos with bare breasts. They are a very clean race and you can meet with the ladies at the baths once, sometimes twice, a day. These public baths are a striking proof of a complete unawareness of modesty, for they are separated from the street by nothing more than a trellis. Inside the trellis, you can see a dozen naked women being hosed with hot water and rubbed down.

The Europeans maintain an absolutely French way of bathing out here – that is, you change into a swimsuit in cabanas and then, ladies and gentlemen together, all wade across the flat beach. Of course it's quite natural for a certain freedom to develop in a place where such behaviour, at least among the foreigners, isn't inhibited by police regulations or the like.

Sophus married a lovely American girl, Aunt Fanny, but we hear no more of her. At Skodsborg she always sat on the terrace of the cottage with her back to the sea. In Japan she had seen the floodwave come in during the earthquake.

No wonder Mudde had been in love with Sophus – her own brother. "I can understand," Katze wrote on the back of a picture of Mudde cuddling up to him with a reverent, almost pained, expression. The picture captures a hallowed moment in which the Japan-traveller consul looks merrily unconcerned.

On the back of a family group photograph Katze has written: "They are all thinking." It sounds a strange thing to say, but if you look at the picture carefully you notice the black hole into which they all seem to have fallen. They are huddled together – and quite alone.

*

"Be careful of the trams and the needles!" Aunt Sophie forever warned her daughter. "It's *two* minutes past nine, Mudde!"

Katze could still hear Mudde's mother's stern tones in Fredericiegade 14 when Mudde, who was grown up, arrived home two minutes late and went to bed in her child's cot. Poor Mudde, she had been kept on a leash all her life. First by her mother, later by embroidery. She did *petit point* for Magasin du Nord for 1.10 kroner an hour. When they encouraged her after 40 years to take a rise in pay, Mudde said grandly: "I wouldn't hear of it." And an old-age pension was out of the question.

When Katze considered her worshippers and all the debauchery she *could* have enjoyed, she felt like a veritable *femme fatale* compared to Mudde. Mudde would indulge in nothing more than her birthday party with hot chocolate, and then her two little rooms would be filled with other old maids all wearing false teeth and wigs. True, Mudde had rich women friends who took her in their cars for summer holidays – the great event in their otherwise uneventful lives. The friends spent most of the year planning and packing for the holiday. Nothing interesting ever happened to them, but they still wrote bundles of postcards.

When Mudde was 90 and could no longer manage the stairs in Fredericiegade, she had to move into a rest home. There she suffered an outrage that killed her: they asked her to sit at table beside a *postman*. Mudde died of dismay. After she died, no-one could think of a single memorable thing she ever said.

Katze couldn't help crying when she turned up a letter from her cousin Mary. In 1918, when Katze had been pregnant for a few months, Mary writes from the Wedelsborg estate: "I'm sorry you're feeling depressed, little Cousin." To cheer her up, Mary wrote of a dream she had had of the two of them travelling round the world. "Probably we won't be able to afford black servants, but could you think of taking some secretarial position in Ceylon or Singapore? I expect we'll need to get some work en route." The year after Katze was married, Mary died of Spanish flu. She was only 19.

Aunt Olga, Mary's mother, was the most talented of the de Thura family. When Katze was about to be married, Aunt Olga gave her 500 kroner, but Katze's blind mother was adamant: "Give that money back immediately! You received it under false pretences!"

Katze took the tram to Blågårdsgade and returned the gift: "It was under false pretences."

"We knew that perfectly well," said Aunt Olga. She ended up in the madhouse because she knew too much.

Katze stood in her living room in ski socks, tears running down her cheeks, trying to find the shares she had inherited from Mudde. One day perhaps they would be valuable. Her luck was bound to turn soon, before it was too late.

She thought of little Elle, who never waited for anything or anyone. "Why are you sitting and knitting?" Elle said once on a visit to Riga while Tobias was off on some adventure. "You, the most beautiful woman in Riga, sit here waiting!" The exclamation had impressed Katze. Even though little Elle was a Scala chorus girl, one of those who walked down a staircase wearing nothing but a flower you-know-where, Katze never thought of her as a "street-walker". She had something irresistible; she had sex appeal. She had what the great courtesans had and which is beyond price: access to the world of men and power over them. She was married four times and could pick and choose among the very richest. Katze was convinced that Elle had also done it with women. She almost felt proud of having known a woman like Elle. It made her feel as if she had played a daring, albeit small, role in the fairy tale. "What are you sitting there waiting for?" And, my God, how right she had been!

In Katze's wardrobe there still hung dresses from Elle's time: transparent black crêpe de Chine with sparkling rhinestones, rows of furs, from grey astrakhans to sables – but she didn't wear those now. She preferred an old tweed Ulster, lace-up shoes and a turban. The cupboards were piled high with cashmere cardigans, night-gowns and lingerie that Tobias had given her over the years, probably to please her, but most of all because he couldn't bear to see her growing decrepit. Katze had her own way of punishing the world. "I haven't any friends, thank God," was her motto.

She glanced at the book with the de Thura genealogy, the mansion of Hirschholm and Eremitageslottet. Tobias had no claim to think of himself as anything special. He hadn't even been able to pass his examination at the Polytechnic! He had planned to cheat his way through it, and even at that he had failed, the idiot! He bribed Miss Krabbe to deliver the exam questions in her gold bag with a note to the porter's wife. Tobias would then snatch the envelope. "There should be a letter for me." Unfortunately for that fool Tobias, the porter's wife was ill that day! The Løvins were nothing but a bunch of lecherous goats. All the same, she would always, when a Jew was mentioned, say, "one of ours".

They were married just after the Treaty of Versaillles was signed. They had no idea that the world was already ruined and that Western Civilisation had been effectively destroyed. They had to live – and they lived – like every other generation: moving forward, regardless of whether the world was beginning or ending. They never doubted it was beginning . . .

She heard a knocking sound from above.

7

ATTEMPTED MURDER

The noise was still going on when she reached the bedroom – right above her bed. A porn club had moved in on the fourth floor. No such club existed, they said. She was paranoid, they said. But Katze knew what was what. It had started up again. They were tearing the walls down and making an outsize brothel. They certainly didn't have planning permission for that. This had been a fine establishment at one time, and now they were wrecking the ceiling and, if no-one intervened, it was going to come down on her head. She buttonholed the criminals and demanded to see their credentials, but they simply called themselves "photographers". Any fool could be a photographer – it was just pressing a button. Katze had no doubt that the woman, with those ferrety little, black, Jewish eyes, was a madam. She complained to the building management too. She hadn't worked in a solicitor's office for a hundred years for nothing. But what was the use when the caretaker claimed to know nothing about it? He was probably a client up there himself! Katze wasn't born yesterday. The banging started again.

The situation reminded Katze of the evening she had knocked on the door of the study in Niels Brocks Street, where she and Tobias had lived as newlyweds. She knocked at Tobias' door when he was playing cards with that bitch of a Baby Zornig they had met at a fancy-dress ball. The gentlemen always drank Dom

Perignon, and the ladies blackcurrant liqueur. While all the other women tried to outshine the dinner jackets with their pale blue satin and powdered wigs, Katze was a Pierrot in a tight-fitting black dress, a little black hat with a long feather, and a white organza collar. She sulked. Baby Zornig was a pirate girl with a Napoleon tricorn. She and Katze had been the only ones in black. The black brides. Once again, Katze had to knock to get her husband's attention.

"I think the waters have broken," she said, for she was on the point of giving birth again. She knew that Tobias was having an affair with Baby Zornig, so she didn't like having to go to the clinic where she couldn't keep an eye on him. As a result, she didn't pay much attention to Liane, her first daughter, and it explains why her breasts were empty. She didn't give that nonsense a second thought: she though only of Baby Zornig, who wore very short lamé dresses with pearl fringes and carried a little gold handbag with a built-in powder compact. In 1921, Katze's dresses fell *below* the knee, thank you very much.

Otto and Emil Løvin's Hugo brought flowers to the maternity ward. The next day Hugo said to Otto: "You must congratulate me now."

"Why so?" Otto asked.

"I'm engaged!" Hugo replied.

"But why didn't you tell me yesterday?"

"I didn't know a thing about it yesterday."

Katze was disgusted with the bragging charmers, but she was fond of Otto. Hugo got punished for all his womanising, however. His women all dyed their hair baby blonde to keep his attention. The last one, who called herself Vips, dressed in her party best and all her jewels, swallowed a bottle of pills, and died on the balcony.

Katze emptied her glass and put it on the bedside table, right under "the brothel".

Hitler had just become leader of the Nazi party in Germany, and Li cried when she came into the world weighing only five pounds. She wept so bitterly, not like other infants, but with big tears as if she were saying: "I shouldn't have been born. This is all a mistake."

Each one of Katze's three children hated milk all their lives.

Years later, Marie, who looked after the children in Niels

Brocksgade, said of Li: "Every morning when she woke up, Li howled. Never have I known such a child. We were all quite helpless. Either she was smacked or locked in a cupboard – no-one had any idea what to do with her."

Li with her yellow eyes was the most difficult and puzzling. The eldest, Balder, "child of shame", with his red hair and big nose, slunk around, cowed by the girls. The youngest, Rebekka, had dark curly hair. She was the funniest and toughest and the one who needed the most attention because she had so many problems. Her legs had to be straightened with metal bars. Her crooked arms had to be put in a cast and she had to have surgery on her eyes, which were crossed. From very early on, the lives of all three children were absorbed by medicine, as if they, bewildered and unsuspecting, had been brought into life just to be cured.

Li screamed from the pain of an ear infection and was given bread and honey. Bekka was taken to hospital, but unfortunately came home again. Li suffered because so much attention went to Bekka. Li was nearly four years old, and Bekka only two. One day, as Bekka sat on the floor playing, Katze waltzed into the living room carrying a heavy gramophone.

"Lucky I didn't drop it on Bekka!"

"Pity you didn't!" Li said.

She was scolded, punished, and never forgot that moment. It is no mere chance that the Bible begins with fratricide. All siblings wish one another dead.

Li was beastly to Bekka because Bekka was the only one of the children who wasn't afraid of everything. She was extroverted, happy and energetic. When the girls lay on the floor drawing and Li gave Bekka only the nubby crayons, Bekka never made a fuss. Years later, Li felt guilty that she had been so unkind.

Li was a nervous child. One day Katze was playing "Frühlingsrauschen" and Li knocked over a glass of water. She was paralysed with terror for what retribution might be her fate. But Katze only said: "Was that you? But, good heavens, you should just *say* so."

That was precisely Li's problem: she could never say *anything*.

*

On a luxury steamer bound for America, Tobias wrote about

"little Solveig" and swore that there were no grounds for divorce on her account.

> She is eighteen. Sweet and lovely – and innocent. Well, I haven't verified it, but she is! We have had such a nice time together. I won't say we haven't flirted; in my usual manner, I made a few passes at her, mostly in a teasing way. For safety's sake, I should add that I have *not* kissed her – or anyone else. Hope you can say the same, because I have had some *very* horrible dreams. Especially the first night. It didn't help when, a day or two later, I heard a superstition that your first dreams in a new place come true. I *certainly* hope that this is not the case. For if it is, there'll be a lot of accidents when I get home. And we don't want that, do we?

Tobias of course must needs fail his first examination at the Polytechnic. Imagine cheating *and* failing! After that rather pathetic incident, he was a broker on the Stock Exchange for a year or two. He then changed jobs to become an advertising manager. Although he had a talent for advertising, specifically advertising himself, he had decided to go to America to pursue a possible job in an American company, Vacuum Oil. When he finally arrived, he was told the post had been filled.

"I don't care," he said, "I want it." And, sure enough, he got it. A man who could react like that was worth his weight in gold.

It was 1927. Katze was contending with Bekka's eyes, and the other two were jealous because they were *not* having operations. Tobias wrote letters full of references to movies, salted peanuts, milk shakes, iced water, canned food and electric cookers. No-one has maids in America, he told her, so everyone eats out of tins. One of his hostesses made him waffles on an electric iron, which Tobias thought was *very* smart. Katze thought that Tobias had allowed himself to be too easily impressed again. No doubt he admired the woman with the iron more than the waffle.

While Katze would be spending long days at the orthopaedist's getting Bekka's legs fixed yet again, Tobias was in New York, going to the cinema for 75 cents with symphony orchestra, choral singing, Roxy girls, and a ballet. He went to nightclubs with dancing partners for hire, and he described his pleasant company in the nightclubs:

There are none of the ladies you find in the Adlon or the Valencia. Mostly married couples or maybe engaged ones – more or less – but no single ladies. So I haven't danced with or even spoken to any of the little lasses you so greatly fear. After what I have seen thus far, I don't think you need be afraid of anything.

Sentences like that would drive Katze to distraction. Did Tobias' constancy depend only on the temptation he encountered? How could a man with a little head and big bat's ears measure the world according to his own tastes! Was he utterly devoid of modesty? Katze would tear letters like that into shreds. On others she scored through his sentences and often wrote "idiot" in the margin.

Her jealousy had plagued him from the start, but how could it be otherwise when he seemed willing to embrace all of womankind? His self-assured, shameless, easy-going attitude made Katze furious. Before they were married (in a headlong rush – they didn't even have any photographs taken), he had written all his *billets doux* on restaurant bills from the Bohème so that she could see that he was no economiser.

When things began to go wrong, he gave her some drops. In his letters he would ask if she had been taking her drops, have they worked? Worked! Silly ass, her son was already on his way! Katze wouldn't have dreamed of taking anything that could damage her firstborn! "My firstborn," she wrote on the outside of the letter. Katze found the letter announcing the outcome she had dreaded. Tobias had to inform his father.

My own little girl! Yes, now I have said it. It went, to come straight to the point, quite well. Papa was terribly kind and didn't utter one angry or wounding word, although he wasn't *overwhelmingly* enthusiastic. We sat there quietly and peacefully talking things over, and he agreed with me that we should get married as soon as possible. He wanted to think about it for a day or two without saying anything to my mother, and he said it was as well not to mention anything to your parents before we assure them that everything has been arranged. Having talked to him, I feel like a new and better person. The worst is almost over, and he has promised to

help me. Everything else will go well, don't you think? Little
girl!

Little girl and little mother: Katze was 19 when Balder was
born. She was old enough to know that she wanted to have her
child; no-one else was going to decide that for her. Tobias, who
was in his early twenties at the time, ended his letter by declaring
his love. But was it genuine?

So I don't think I have anything else to write this evening. I
love you, that you know. But if (and I hope not) you have
forgotten, I shall tell you a couple of million times more to
beat it into your little brain!

Some people need to be told only once that they are loved. Others
need to hear it a hundred times a day, and still they don't believe
it.

No, Katze didn't believe it. Their tenth anniversary was on the
horizon, but she still wasn't sure of Tobias. Sometimes his
assurances came in the strangest disguises: I hope you are still
faithful to me and not playing around too much while Father is
away. I myself am almost a little angel. With the exception of a
tiny bit of flirting (if you can even call it that) with a little 'dancer'
and Solveig on the ship. But she is not at all dangerous, since she
is – though unofficially – engaged in Denmark."

Katze's friend Elle, the one with the flower between her legs,
prodded her: "Your husband's in America having fun, why do you
just sit here getting bored?"

"How do you know Tobias is having fun, have you heard
anything?"

"Listen, no man holds back when he's offered something, why
should you?"

"What do you mean, should I . . . ?"

"Yes, of course!"

"But I have my children to think of!"

"You're 27, you won't be young much longer, then you'll have
all the time in the world to think about them."

"Well, I have been invited to the Adlon several times, but I said
no because I don't think it's right for me to go out when Tobias is
in America. People talk, you know."

"Poof, it's only the *petit bourgeois* who go in for gossip – the ones who don't have any fun themselves. You're too good for that, my angel. Don't cheat yourself of life."

"Oh, Elle, you put me in such a good mood. Why *should* I say no to everything?"

Katze got out her short black party dress, the one with the jet beads, and decided that she too was going to have fun. Tobias even encouraged her:

> So you've really been going out, have you? That's good to hear. The only thing that's made me a little reluctant to go out is that you weren't with me and were perhaps staying at home while I was having a good time. I can well understand you going to the Adlon, and I have nothing whatsoever against it. It is only a question of *with whom*. Of course, you may do what you think is right. I won't worry as long as you don't go in for too much of the strong brew. Kiss my three sweet darlings on their sweet eyes and save the most loving kisses for yourself, your Tobias.

The problem was that though Katze liked Jørgen Birger Christensen, Tobias did not. Tobias heard nothing from her for some time. As Katze herself admitted, JBC was about to snatch Tobias' cake. He was quite wild about her, but while Katze could see herself as an object of interest, flattery or desire, she was incapable of feeling love or desire herself. The children found their mother distant, completely absorbed in how much she was adored. She kept on telling herself that at least she loved her children, and she hugged them with her empty arms and unfaithful eyes.

One day, when they were visiting Papa and Mama in Rosenvænget, Balder and Rebekka were in the garden playing by the goldfish pool. Balder was towing a little sailing boat on a string. He was eight years old, and Bekka was four. Suddenly she fell into the pool. She lay there splashing about in the water, about to drown, but Balder never noticed. Katze spotted the catastrophe from the window and came running. Later, when they questioned the panic-stricken Balder about why he had paid no attention to his sister, he had no answer.

But he was not punished. That did not happen until the day he took his father's cigar and stirred Katze's powder box with it.

"What was your father's cigar doing in your mother's powder box?" Tobias roared, beside himself with anger.

"I don't know," Balder stammered.

"Did you have permission to touch your father's cigar and ruin such a fine costly cigar?"

"No."

"Why did you do it then, tell me!"

"I don't know."

"Did you have permission to touch your mother's powder box, may I ask?"

"No."

"What were you doing in your mother's things?"

"Nothing."

"Answer me, what were you doing in your mother's private things?"

"I don't know, I just wanted . . . "

"Do you promise never to meddle with your parents' things again?"

"Yes."

"So we won't say any more about this, then."

Balder was banished from the table and forbidden supper. Li envied him – she didn't feel like eating anything. She and Rebekka had a china doll with an open mouth. They had been feeding it for quite a long time. The doll had a big appetite, but after a while it started to get bad breath and one day worms crawled out of it. The girls were given a scolding. Liane cried. She had realised that maternal care was a position of great responsibility, but also dangerous. The food was rotten, just as once the breast had been poisoned, the empty breast she could no longer remember. Liane was pathologically fastidious, like her father. Balder and Bekka were fastidious too – it was almost a prerequisite for being a personality. The Løvins defined themselves by the things they did not like. Tobias "could not stand" fish, milky food and so on. All the same, the children were ordered to leave clean plates.

It wasn't difficult for the children to find out what was allowed and what was not allowed. Most things were not allowed. "Children should be seen and not heard." But it was hard to find out about food. When fat Aunt Musse came to visit, she couldn't keep away from the larder. The children seemed to grasp that she came from a slightly lower class. She had, after all, found her husband, a Communist with a flower in his buttonhole, through a lonely hearts advertisement. Although the children didn't know what a lonely hearts column was – or, a Communist, for that matter – they gathered that neither was very impressive. They could also hear their mother complain: "Imagine, Aunt Musse claims that when she danced with Tobias, he squeezed her and put his hand on her breast. How could one say such a thing! Imagine being so wicked!"

Katze did not say this directly to the children; it was something they shouldn't have heard. They did overhear it, however, and they failed to understand their mother's anger because Aunt Musse had always been so sweet to them. She enjoyed playing with them even though she was almost blind. She pretended that everything was "food". She called the buttons that she put on the table "burgers". They were quite different and not nearly as nice as the pearl buttons Marie had on the white blouse she wore when her fiancé came to visit. He worked at the sugar factory. They were sweet pearls, round and white, the most beautiful buttons in the world.

In the courtyard there were children noisily at play. Balder, Liane and Rebekka leaned out the window and asked if they could join in. But they were not allowed to because the children in the courtyard were "not suitable". One day, Balder and his sisters made a pile of their toys and threw them out the window to the other children, and for that they were severely punished. Why on earth had they tossed their lovely toys down to those brats? It was beyond belief! But the courtyard children were delighted, and from that day on, Balder, Li and Rebekka were very popular.

At Zahle's College, Liane was so terrified that she couldn't understand a word of what the teacher said. Li didn't understand that when the teacher spoke to the class it also included *her*. She was neither the one she believed herself to be, nor the one the others said she was. She wasn't anything at all.

8

THE MARRIAGE BED

On October 28th, 1928, the family set sail for Latvia on board the *Niedaros*. Tobias had returned from the USA to manage Vacuum Oil in three Baltic countries, and the headquarters were in Riga. His grandfather had originally come from the East with his fiery spirits, and now Tobias was returning there with another kind of inflammable material.

They arrived in Riga harbour in the morning. Problems arose as soon as they reached Customs: they were required to pay duties on every last vase and ashtray. Tobias said to the officials: "Obviously we must get this settled, I will give a luncheon." The Customs men downed ten schnapps apiece and after that there was no duty to pay. Riga was a divided town. On the one hand it was a backward peasant culture, and on the other an international, glamorous world of foreign diplomats, businessmen and spies, all busy sniffing out the novelties of the East. Estonia, Latvia and Lithuania had been independent from the Russian suzerainty for just ten years. The Soviet revolution was not long past, and everyone feared that it would spread through the world like a plague.

Diplomacy was conducted in a festive manner, with much socialising, cheap spirits and flirtation. Sex was another pleasant pastime, like golf or card games. Anyone who came from Western Europe or received a salary in Western currency was a millionaire overnight and a member of Riga's high society.

When it came to relations with the indigenous population, Westerners associated only with aristocratic Baltic Germans like the von Rönne, von Engelbrecht and von Drachenfelz families. No-one had anything to do with Latvians. They lived in a different world, one of black bread and lace curtains, of horses with nosebags and wreaths of flowers. Of oilcloth, home-made stockings and icons, wooden sledges, lice and shaven heads. If the Latvian women were invited to balls, with an invitation that stipulated evening dress, they arrived in their night-gowns with black teeth and with bows in their plaits, radiating faith and hope in a new and better world. As recently liberated serfs, they demanded a motorised future. The ubiquitous "Izvoztschiks", horse-drawn wagons with wheels in summer and runners in winter, were now being exchanged for motorcars. Progress couldn't go quickly enough and Tobias had arrived with the combustible stuff.

The country's great hero, President Ulmanis, walked around barefoot. Out on the boulevards were live horrors that he instituted. Half-naked, pinioned deserters were driven along in military columns to frighten and be a warning to the populace. Barefoot or not, Ulmanis was a formidable president where Latvian nationalism and independence were concerned. To the people, he represented a reassuring response to its fearful and well-grounded anxieties about Russia.

Before Tobias found a suitable apartment on Kalpaka Boulevard, opposite the Russian Orthodox cathedral, Katze stayed at the Hotel Metropol and complained of migraine and of all the bugs on the walls. That she could be asked to live in such a primitive country where, as soon as night fell, insects swarmed! At the same time, Katze's heart bled for all those downtrodden souls who – unlike the Løvins – did not pride themselves on anything, but endured their fate with dignity. Still, she fell short of loving them totally, for they also made her angry for living so wretchedly.

It was not much better when the family moved into their many-roomed apartment with porcelain stoves and – when they could eventually afford them – Caucasian and Persian carpets. Tobias found a governess, Ida, to teach the children German, allowing Katze to spend all her time in bed, a cloth pressed to her forehead, staring at the flies on the ceiling.

The Nuremberg laws of 1935 forbade sexual intercourse

between Jews and Aryans. "Flies on the ceiling" had become Katze's euphemism for marital cohabitation. She conceded that she couldn't remould Tobias, but she could deny herself pleasure and, in flaunting her contempt for him, obtain a certain power over him.

At the entrance to the apartment there was always a "*dvornik*" to whom one gave a couple of *santim*. On the ground floor, there was the Anatomical Museum, where Balder, Li and Rebekka stared at wax heads of children and at little foetuses preserved in formaldehyde and pockmarked dolls with wounds. They had heard their mother whisper that the rashes that disfigured these specimens derived from sexual diseases. The Jewish family Monastirski, who made a living by catering kosher food for parties and weddings, lived on the first floor. Then the children went on up the wide snail-shaped staircase with Jugend wrought-iron rails, and at last they were home.

The worlds of the parents and the children were kept distinct. Tobias managed three offices, one in Riga, one in Tallin and one in Kaunas, and was constantly travelling. When not attending receptions, Katze stayed in bed with stomach pains or headaches; or else she was busy catching the maids stealing soap.

On March 22nd, 1938, German Jews were forbidden to grow vegetables.

The children had their meals in the kitchen with Anette, the cook, and Betty, the maid, who filled up a deep dish with butter which they ate neat, topped with sour cream from the grocer. There was a special kind of cosiness in the kitchen, emphasised by the servant girls' eternal "*mach die Tier zu, es zieht*" in the Riga dialect – as if there was a warm animal in there which could not survive draughts. On the big iron stove, and with much juggling of the iron rings above the bright flames, Anette cooked memorable dishes, in particular a *boeuf stroganoff*. All their lives, the children referred to this recipe as if it were a Biblical text.

Nowadays we tend to associate servants with a humbler station in life. But in many of their school friends' homes, an ancient, shrunken *njanja* held absolute power; they had looked after the children from when they were small.

When Anette was dying of tuberculosis, she asked *die gnädige Frau* to bury her in her black velvet dress with the red rose. Fifty years on, Katze still wept over Anette's pathetic life.

Living their strictly regulated German existences in a German school, Balder, Li and Bekka did not have much time to study the foetuses preserved in formaldehyde on the ground floor. They went to the swimming pool – on March 22nd, German Jews were forbidden to swim – skated, skied, danced, did gymnastics, ballet, studied English and played the piano. They also sang *"Freude schöner Götterfunken"* at the orphanage with flowers in their hair. If ever a rendition needed to be a semitone higher, the teacher glanced at Li, who broke in with her perfect pitch.

To her astonishment, Li was adored by the opposite sex from childhood. She herself adored her friend Livia, who, as her name bore witness, was possessed of all the *joie de vivre* that Li lacked. When Li was with Livia, life seemed replete.

A boy in Balder's class started to write letters to Li. As time passed, the letters grew bolder – *"Willst du mit mir ficken?"* – but Li did not understand the proposal. When Katze and Tobias discovered the letters, they made a terrible fuss. They moved Balder's bed out of the room he shared with his sisters without explaining why. Only one thing was clear to all the children: there had been a catastrophe. They had done something – although they had no idea what – absolutely unforgivable and irremediable. And now Liane was fetched from school and from swimming.

Again without ever discovering why, the children felt how miserable their mother was. Her tears hung heavily in the curtains. Each time their father returned home, joy and festivity returned, but it was not long before this mood of celebration was met with reproaches, weeping and accusations. Something was out of tune.

From their earliest days, they had idolised their mother as beautiful, wonderful and adoring. Believing their father was very cruel to her, they pitied Katze. When they were away in the country and Tobias was preoccupied with the English ladies, Katze retired to bed with inflamed sinuses or some other mysterious complaint. They always walked on tiptoe, as quiet as mice. Father had sent Mother to bed, and now the children suffered. Then, as Li began to grow up, she gradually realised that Katze consciously pitted the children against their father by lying down and weeping.

Tobias had flirted with Katze's best friend Lilla and kissed her on the cheek. Lilla, who was an old-fashioned Norwegian type, said: "When shall we tell Katze?" Tobias was utterly aghast, for never in his wildest dreams had he imagined that she could take it seriously in *that* way.

"When shall we tell Katze?" Katze just lay there sobbing.

One day when Li was walking from school down Elizabeteila, she saw her father's blue Buick parked at the kerb. She was about to run to it, but stopped in time . . . In the car beside her father sat a fine red-haired lady whom she didn't know. Their two faces were very close. Li walked slowly home, not knowing what to think or say. She stood for a long time in front of the preserved foetuses and decapitated children's heads. Clearly, what she had seen was something she must not tell. She and her father shared a secret and no-one else must know. She suddenly felt delight at the thought of her father being admired. At home he was always being scolded and reproached for everything. It was only right and proper that her father should be with someone happy. And beautiful.

Later on, when Li was 16 and Katze became aware of her eldest daughter's yellow eyes, she wanted to confide in Li about the cause of their domestic misery. Balder's untimely conception, the rushed marriage – the whole story. Li only stared at her blankly as Katze narrated with the gravity of someone describing the decline of an empire or a vast, international scandal.

"So what?" was all Li said.

"What do you mean, 'so what'?"

"I mean, why was it so terrible?"

"Well, can't you understand that I could only be married on the condition that you, my children, were baptised!"

Li's expression didn't change. In Li's eyes, this earthquake was caused by sheer stupidity and ignorance – and by the genteel, middle-class conventions of her mother's milieu. To Li, Katze's attitude was ancient history. That was the difference between someone born in 1900, which was still the old century, and someone born in 1921, when you automatically metabolised the liberated '20s.

"That going to bed business has never meant anything to me, I have never felt a thing," Katze said proudly.

"Is that something to be proud of?"

"So you're on your father's side?"

"Besides, why sleep with a man if you don't feel a thing?"

"He was the one who wanted it. I was just in love. That's something quite different."

"It's not something different."

Katze looked at Li. Had she got herself into trouble too? She brushed the thought, even the possibility, aside, and went on dreamily: "To be fêted, flattered and admired by elegant men . . . that's something a woman can never get enough of."

In Li's eyes, that was a poor reward for a life of illusions. But the fact was that Katze was only happy when she was being admired.

"Any fool can sleep with someone," Katze sneered, reiterating the message that sex was not "the thing to do".

*

Li would happily have lured any woman in Riga into her father's arms, with the exception of Kirsten Inger Svendsen, known as KIS. She was Tobias' secretary and Li hated her. Fraülein Svendsen was always scurrying at the Director's heels in the most servile manner. When it came to her work, she was exceptionally conscientious and inordinately devoted, and she couldn't resist occasionally slipping a short Stuckenberg poem onto the Director's desk. Li found Kirsten Inger Svendsen completely absurd, and made no attempt to disguise her contempt.

One school holiday when Tobias and Katze were in Denmark and the children had been left behind in Riga, Fraülein Svendsen was asked to watch over them. It was not an easy task. They teased her in every possible way: hid from her until she became very frightened; pretended to have been kidnapped. Each time, Li was the instigator. But one day Li went too far when she poured Fraülein Svendsen's coffee into her saucer:

"Will you leave the table this instant!" KIS said severely.

"No," Li grinned.

Fraülein Svendsen had never been spoken to in such a tone, and she was on the point of bursting into tears. She shouted at Li to go straight to the bathroom and stay there until she was called for.

"I won't," Li replied calmly and quietly. The children, used to being chastised in a German school, recognised authority when they met it. Fraülein Svendsen did not possess any. Moreover, Li had remarkable inner radar that registered that KIS was a pretentious snob who believed herself to be an intellectual. But there was nothing at all in her personality to support her self-regard. She possessed none of the ecstatic inner life that she referred to constantly. Everything about her was false except, perhaps, her love for the Director, which only stoked Li's hatred further. Such an inferior human being had no right to love her father. The fine red-haired lady in the car was better than Fraülein Svendsen, much better. Li could keep a secret when it was a matter of being true to her father.

Katze sensed that Li had gone over to Tobias' side.

"I know you've seen your father," Katze said the very day that Li had spotted him with the red-haired lady.

"Yes."

"Why haven't you told me about it?"

Liane did not reply.

"Was it because you didn't want to upset me?"

"Yes."

Tobias had obviously confessed as much himself, and later that evening she heard him repeat it. By chance he had run into Madge today. Oh, so her name is Madge, is that it? Katze would rage and wail that Madge was the name of the witch in "*Sylphides*". Her father was in London by then. The red-haired lady was mentioned. Her mother just lay down and wept, but the children no longer took their mother's side, for children are always on the side of happiness.

Katze had to have an operation to correct an intestinal obstruction in Copenhagen, where flowers and a message were delivered to her private room by Crown Prince Frederik, who was in hospital at the same time. This royal attention did Katze a power of good. Her old stamina was returning, indeed she was even able completely to ignore Tobias' foolish remark, written in anticipation of her convalescence: "Be good! Glenda is a devil at getting others onto thin ice."

After Katze came back to Riga she was able to face life with renewed courage. She made use of her fresh energy to ring for the carpenter. She ordered him to saw the marriage bed in half. The carpenter, thunderstruck, stared at her: '*Ach, gnädige Frau, tue es nicht*!' he wept, but Katze was unshakeable. She had finally regained her willpower. Moreover she began in earnest to profit from Scala-Elle's sly provocation: "What is a beautiful woman like you doing sitting there waiting?"

She hadn't been thinking of doing anything, not deliberately, certainly not anything serious, only something light. The children had no idea that their mother had begun a flirtation or an innocent affair, but one day out of the blue she had given them a bar of chocolate. They were astonished. Never before had their mother given them a bar of chocolate. Of course they were pleased, but at the same time Li felt, without being able to explain why, the chocolate was given in the wrong way. Grown-ups were too busy sawing their beds in half and with their other such pastimes, to give a thought to the fact that Nazism had long ago insinuated itself as an educational norm in the German schools the children attended, and the Baltic Germans were yet more nationalistic and Nazistic than Hitler himself. If the children had ever seen what love was, it was through the colour that bloomed in the teachers' cheeks, and their shining, tear-filled eyes when they quoted the speeches of their beloved Führer.

Tobias and Katze did not understand why Bekka had grown so sulky and petulant when she was going out skating. Why did she all of a sudden not want to go? Why make such a fuss over nothing? Cheer up! But Bekka did not dare to say it aloud. She dared not talk about anti-semitism and everything she was forced to take part in so as not to be ostracised. "She stinks of garlic, you know what I mean . . . " they said eagerly, Gisela, Hannelore, Erika and Rosemarie with the long blonde plaits, about a Jewish classmate. That was before all the Jewish girls were sent away from the school to a separate one. The anti-semitic remarks would scarcely have been a problem for her if she had not discovered quite by chance that her father was Jewish.

They had never talked about it in the family. And it didn't mean anything anyway. It was not until Liane had happened to take home someone else's school report by mistake. She threw it away in disgust. She had touched a book belonging to a Jew girl. Her father, dismayed, took her on his lap and told her that he was a Jew. Then he said it.

At first Li didn't believe him. It couldn't be right. The one she loved more than anyone in the world. He also said that it wasn't anything they attached a great deal of importance to in the family. But why didn't they attach importance to it? The worst possible thing! And her father! Li was paralysed, unreal. Would she still be singled out in "Racial Knowledge" for her Aryan profile? Would the teachers and her friends – not to speak of Liane's worshippers – suspect that there was something hidden that wasn't *comme il faut*?

Li and Rebekka prayed that their father would not come and fetch them after school. That he would iron out his unmistakeable eagle's beak which was the very model of all the illustrations their class teacher continually warned them against. Once they had been disappointed that their parents never came and saw them in a nativity play or choral concert. But now they just hoped that – especially their father – they would keep well away. Their heads and hearts were divided.

Then one day Balder came home from the Kommerz-Schule with a popular Nazi emblem on his collar that he had swapped something for, and Tobias decided to send him back to Denmark.

*

Balder was to have a Danish schooling and live in Rosenvænget with Papa and Mama, who kept him strictly in order.

Mama's greatest passion was her morning dispute with the maid over what could be bought *most cheaply*: the excitement over who could better who in low prices! Mama had a definite view on how much water was necessary for a bath, and she had tied a knot in the bath-plug chain. The greater the privations she imposed on herself and others, the more her spirits rose. When Balder and a friend were out in the garden playing they made fun of Mama: "How can you be so extravagant, Balder dear. Whatever would your *Faather* say?" they mimicked in her old-school Copenhagen accent.

Papa, sitting in his library, where he always hid himself, heard it all and chuckled. Ever since their marriage he had instructed Mama to say as little as possible. He cultivated his bibliophile's passion and hid his newly acquired first editions from her severe gaze in the lining of his coat. Every summer he sent her off to Hornbækhus so that he could have the whole house painted, wall-papered and put in order. Mama thought it was lunacy to spend so much money on that kind of thing, but the grand-children loved the smell of fresh paint.

One day when Balder was at the Metropol cinema he saw Papa sitting beside a strange lady, with his head close to hers all the time. Balder didn't know what to do. What if Papa should see him?

He thought of leaving the cinema before the film started, but he didn't want to miss it just so as not to embarrass his grandfather. When it finished he left as fast as he could. But he had no way of knowing whether Papa had seen him. At the dinner table he didn't dare mention he had been to the cinema when he was asked what he had been doing all day. No-one said anything in the voluble Løvin family. But Mama always saw to it that Balder's hands were clean.

9

THE YELLOW HOOD

At the end of the swimming lesson season on the beach at Bulduri you had to swim across a stream. It was not the depth of the water that scared Li and Rebekka, but the seabed, which was full of mud and sludge. The year was 1939.

For the last summer the children spent in Riga Tobias had rented a majestic mausoleum of a villa in white icing. Pure '30s Hollywood. But it turned out to be a false paradise; there was no water in the swimming pool; the gigantic doll's house in the nursery had bars in front of it; and the windows of the house were fitted with gratings to prevent anyone from kidnapping the children, while the fallow deer and rabbits lived behind protective hedges. You were not allowed to pick any single flower, or walk in the surrounding park or go near the fountain, the gardener was on guard and always lying in wait.

The weather was breaking up and the cook and maid, Anette and Betty, quarrelled the whole time and refused to sleep together. Li screamed and demanded that Bekka should *knock* on her door and wait to be told to come in. And no-one wanted to go near Balder, who had intituted a new strategy for survival: he refused to wash.

Mama was on a visit from Copenhagen, which was her custom every second summer. The children laughed at her because she swam like a turtle, but she passed the time quite happily with a metre-high pile of newspapers, as the family always had. She did her needlework or went for long walks in her wine-coloured bathing robe, white canvas hat with its leather ribbon and her walking stick, which Katze thought sheer affectation.

Katze was never well, but she was particularly out of sorts in the company of her mother-in-law. Mama could not help reminding Katze of the "mistake" which the rest of her life was based upon. That Katze had been so very graciously accepted into the Løvin family, who in reality, of course, were nothing but a bunch of blacks and apes, even though they behaved as if they were all barons and world-renowned philosophers. But Mama herself was not a Løvin but a low Levin, and she had sailed clear across the Atlantic just to snap up the oh-so-weak Papa, who couldn't get far enough away to escape her talons. If there was anything that Katze found shaming it was the way in which women incessantly ran after men, their dependency. Mama had never let Katze forget that she, Katze de Thura, was dependent upon the Løvin family and upon Tobias' kindness. How humiliating to have to be grateful. Each month Papa paid her poverty-stricken parents' rent, and one of these days Papa was going to die, and then Tobias would have to pay for them, he who had *lowered* himself to marry her because she had got herself into trouble. "Bungler" was engraved on Katze's back for evermore! The arrogance of the Løvin family poisoned the air wherever they went, and Mama personified it extremely by her seeming independence of everything and everyone, convinced as she was in her innermost heart that the whole world loved her if only she condescended it a pleasant nod on her daily walk. Her servants at home in Rosenvænget, Marie and the housekeeper, knew better. They knew she was lonely and unloved. That was why the housekeeper kept up her legendary quarrel with Madam every morning, to cheer her up. But by the graces of God Mama couldn't take up the whole holiday house, and a drink or two helped.

One morning early, at about four o'clock, Katze and Tobias came home from a party with some friends from Riga. Kiko had gone a bit gaga after being hit on the head with a cricket ball. Several times over the summer he had hushed his dogs when they barked, and each time his holiday house had been emptied by thieves. They set about mixing drinks while they made breakfast and flirting in the kitchen in their white dinner jackets and evening dresses. They had decided not to wake the maids, when suddenly they saw Betty, wide awake, creeping off in a Salvation Army bonnet. Betty stared in horror at her employers and their guests, sitting on each other's laps drinking spirits at four in the morning. Tobias and Katze stared at Betty in equal amazement, she was obviously on her way to save the world, and when she had disappeared they started giggling and confessing to their friends that they hadn't had the slightest idea of the parlour maid's hole-in-the-corner, bonneted other life.

It was a hot summer, and it was the last summer. Ribbentrop and Stalin signed their non-aggression pact on August 23rd. The Baltic countries were sold to the Russians and the Germans bought themselves a breathing space on the Eastern Front. The girls' school was closed on September 2nd. All foreigners were to be expelled from Latvia and all the Germans were to go home. "*Alle Deutsche heim ins Reich*", the teachers rejoiced. Although Hitler Youth was forbidden in Latvia, similar youth organisations existed, and they were in high good humour at the prospect of going home to their kingdom and the beloved Führer. In no time 60,000 Baltic Germans were sent down to Posen and other parts of Germany and moved into apartments with fuel still glowing in the stove and warmth in the cooker. The Baltic Germans came offering "*Winterhilfe*" to their leader. The apartments and houses they moved into had mostly belonged to Jews, who "had left".

Ten years after the war and 20 years after the war, 30 and 40 years after the war, when Gisela, Hannelore, Erika and Rosemarie invited Rebekka to the class jubilee in Germany, Rebekka would always phone and say: "I can't come before I've got to know what you thought when you moved into the apartments where the stoves were still warm." But her school friends thought only that Rebekka had gone soft in the head. So Rebekka stayed where she was, as the strict book-keeper of the family. "I have total recall," she always said. While everyone else forgot or pleaded ignorance – "you can't live in the past" – Rebekka had determined to remember and to keep a record.

Throughout her life Rebekka relived the school "*Krippenspiel*", when all the girls with long fair plaits – Liane and Rebekka were the only ones with short hair – in a long column passed through the dark hall, lit only by the four candles in the Advent wreath hanging from the ceiling. Through the attentive crowd of spectators, on white stockinged feet, draped in gauze, with cardboard wings covered with glitter, and golden headbands with stars. You walked cautiously and held your taper with the greatest care so as not to set light to the angel in front of you. The pairs divided in front of the stage, one to the right, one to the left, to form a living backdrop like the chorus in a Greek tragedy. In long columns, two by two – but where was Lucie and was Ira with them? No, their surnames Aronson and Levin made that impossible. But all her life Rebekka visualised them in dreams in another column, grey shadows in rags and tatters, with no tapers in their hands and bearing another star. In the icy cold they pass in endless rows to another stage, where only death awaits them. Some to the right, to the gas chambers, the old, the sick, the children. Some to the left, the able-bodied, to the camp.

And when later generations would ask Rebekka how it could happen, and how was it possible, she invariably quoted the old Jew who answered her son's everlasting question – in Yiddish: "My son, you have not been tried." It referred to the Baltic, which had to be "tested" and to everything that would befall the world, and from which it would never recover. And for that matter it also referred to Bekka's own life. What did it mean to be "tested"? It was certainly something different from the red eagle stamp: "*geprüft*" – the signal that the authorities had started to open and censor letters.

Katze glanced through the cuttings of herself, Liane and Rebekka when they left Riga: "NO DANGER TO THE DANES IN LATVIA" ran the headline.

> "I only came home to send my daughters to Danish schools, When I have done that I shall go back to Riga, where my husband still lives," says fru Løvin, the Director's wife. "Of course, I shall have to change my plans if, as is unlikely, it should turn out that the situation suddenly makes it risky to stay in Latvia. But I certainly do not think there will be any question of that."

Katze wanted to return to Latvia because she wanted to be back with a certain man, and it was not Tobias. She had met Dietlof von Sachensollen. Elegant and all that, secret trysts in cafés, flattery, evergreens, butterfly kisses, increased self-esteem which had been minus nought at the age of 40. Dietlof von Sachensollen was big cars and beautiful walks, but not all that smuttiness. Katze was deliciously free of that, while she allowed herself to be adored, squired and entertained. And Tobias knew nothing, that was probably the most titillating thing about it. A close little foxtrot and an extra glass of champagne, dizziness and tantrums, swooning and waltzes. Katze wanted to be back on the carousel. But war had broken out, so for the time being she had to sit and wait and dream at the Pension Larsen in Kastelsvej without a krone to her name. When she was in Latvia she always dreamed of being back in Copenhagen, for she far preferred to eat at Nimb rather than the Schwarz. Now she was in Copenhagen dreaming herself back in Riga. Tobias tried his usual encouragement:

> Now your dream has been realised: Copenhagen with your children. Couldn't you – for your own sake – try to be reconciled to Copenhagen and the family? You know, a kind smile, instead of endless tart criticism, would be surprising and refreshing! I so much look forward to seeing my old friend, eternal love and young wife again. In spite of – or perhaps because of 20 years of marriage – I still love you and hope that, in the noise of the big city and the hurly-burly of the boarding house, you won't completely forget your old husband.

Tobias nourished a false hope if he believed that Katze would be reconciled with his family. Katze was never able to find a five øre coin to phone Mama. Tobias was horrified to learn that the family – instead of falling into each other's arms upon Katze's, Rebekka's and Li's homecoming – had come to blows. Katze and Mama actually drew blood, although Katze would never demean herself by recounting the incident. It is a forgotten wisdom that only the oldest man in a family can make peace between the women. Only Tobias could write to "the old warrior": "Don't forget that both you and Rebekka can be very provocative, irritating, arrogant, cocky and superior." Tobias did not write "*besserwissen*" in Yiddish, for he didn't feel himself to be a Jew.

If you wish the world were happy,
Then remember day by day
Just to scatter seeds of kindness
As you pass along the way.

But doggerel wasn't enough to restore peace. What was required was Tobias' physical presence. But he didn't dare pack his suitcase, for if everything went up in smoke in Copenhagen, he should hold onto his refuge in Riga.

Soon afterwards, a Morning Interview was conducted over the telephone with Director Løvin in Riga about his plans to secure a steamer for all the Danish residents' possessions. "The Danes want to go home," the headline read. "The Bolsheviks are coming, but Director Løvin intends to stay on. 'I have confidence in the government,' Director Løvin declares. 'The Latvian government is strong.'"

With the Russians at the gates and Legation Councillor Treschow, the ambassador, weeping on the sofa, Tobias took over. Like Uncle Max, Tobias was a mover and a shaker, and managed to save all the Danes, plus their chattels, at the last moment. During the evacuation, one of the Danes went mad. He screamed hysterically and fled to a psychiatric hospital where shortly afterwards he died, which all his countrymen considered a stroke of luck. Tobias spent his time in Customs, having his personal possessions examined, from pockets to socks. The new laws had come into force, outlawing the export of radios, gramophones and cars – everything, in other words, that the Russians wanted for themselves. If Tobias were sent back to Denmark, he would lose both his radio and his car, as well as the dog Karenina. He would lose a good deal that year, he suddenly realised, signing himself "Riga's Don Juan" as he tried to rescue the business – and his life.

He was still the get-up-and-go person he had always been. For several years he had been seeking a better post in the more civilised part of the world – not least out of consideration for Katze, who always complained about the dearth of culture in the Baltic. Among other things, Tobias – true to his origins – played with the idea of establishing a liquor distillery in Denmark, but the plan collapsed. Having no alternative to Riga, he was forced to be optimistic. Especially in those times, when it was dangerous to stick your nose out too far, particularly if your nose resembled Tobias'.

As always, he tried to lower the temperature, convinced that the German campaign was meant only to frighten people into leaving. The partial Aryan would stay, of course. And there were certainly some pure-blood Germans there as well. It had turned out that the first alarm that "the Bolsheviks will be here in two weeks" and "Latvia is to be under Russian rule" were bluffs by the German ministry of propaganda.

Tobias couldn't know the intentions of the Russians or the Germans, nor Katze's connection with Dietlof von Sachensollen, he of the monocle. Not yet. Not by name. Not definitely. While everyone else dropped Latvia like a hot potato, Tobias tried to stand fast – far beyond what was realistic. America was demanding prepayment for a cargo of fuel oil, and, even though it was almost impossible to comply, there being no currency left in the country, somehow Tobias succeeded. He didn't have a moment of peace, however, before the ships docked and the oil for the Latvian army made its way into the right hands.

Katze's innate jealousy raged on. Even though Dietlof von Sachensollen soothed her, still she couldn't help speculating about what was keeping Tobias in Riga. It certainly wasn't Madge, for he had written to say that Madge now lived in the little house she had bought when she went back to London. She wasn't with her husband any more. They were not getting divorced, but lived apart, "à la carte", as Tobias described it, which was obviously the way things were nowadays done. Despite the failing marriage, Madge still had enough money to keep her Rolls Royce, her chauffeur and three servants. It was a pity that Katze hadn't found herself an English – or German – millionaire; that way life would have been different from the Pension Larsen. If there were over 100 kroner left in the account, Tobias insisted that Katze spent half of it amusing herself. "We are not that poor yet." There were enough unhappy marriages about. He encouraged her to go to the Palladium with the children.

In November 1939, Tobias tells her how he went into a bar, full of frightful Germans, drinking and eating up the last of their cash. A Dane had shouted "black butchers' boots" at some drunken Germans, who had given them bloody noses and ended up in jail. Katze assumed that her elegant Dietlof von Sachensollen was not back in Riga, and she had no idea where she could find him. Tobias still knew nothing about her affair until one day he overheard a chance remark from one of the few remaining members of Riga society, that alerted him. "I have always distinguished what is fun and what is serious," Tobias wrote to Katze, "and of course you can take a dim view of fun, for actually one can do without it. So you can – if you are not living it up or flirting – reproach me for my irresponsible style of life. Sober living is to be respected, and so I do not reproach you for anything." Tobias then noted that all of Katze's old heart-throbs, the fur-trapper BC, Michelsen and Jørgen Schou, whoever they all were, they were a chapter in the past, and that Katze had always been faithful to him. Tobias just couldn't get used to the idea that Katze had a serious love relationship with another man, one that might endanger his marriage. Katze reassured him over the telephone while rejoicing at having frightened him.

The day in the café when she was with Dietlof and Tobias strolled past without noticing her, was the high point in Katze's life. Hitherto he had lived under the false pretence that he alone in the world had trysts. When he realised that Katze too had her own life, he exploded with the famous words: "I am a fool!"

> You are a terribly dangerous woman when you send sweet loving words over the ether or in a letter. Or when you, "à la woman", aim your delightful blue searchlight at some poor man! You are so hard to resist when you want something. And the worst of it is that you are always so convincing because you believe in it yourself for the moment. You are – to speak the language of today – a magnetic mine, so I can well understand how another man would run straight into it, even if it meant being blown to pieces.
>
> Did I tell you that relationships in Denmark were discussed at a board meeting and a man I didn't even know reported that you and I were to be divorced? I have also heard that I shouldn't be sorry to be rid of you. Because I was too good for you! After all, you who had been a barmaid! – they actually said that. Well, it was just laughable. But you can see how careful you must be. I asked D and A if I should crack down on the barmaid rumour, but they told me to leave it be. Despite your affectionate letter I find it hard to forget and to sleep.

Tobias wrote about Latvia, the survival of the marriage, and his beloved fox terrier Karenina, who had been traumatised after being caught in a butterfly net by an official dog catcher. Karenina couldn't walk properly after that, and Tobias' legs weren't particularly healthy either; he had begun to get thrombosis and the doctors had advised him to shelve his cigars. Tobias consoled himself with the thought that those doctors probably wouldn't live very long. In some families, only certain persons are allowed to be ill, while the others must stay well. With his blood clots, Tobias could checkmate the whole family.

All the embassies were ordered to close down by August 25th, 1940, at the latest.

> At 2 o'clock, right in the middle of lunch, Tallin telephoned to say that our business had been nationalised. Soon it will probably happen here in Riga as well. Unfortunately, I will be forced to leave, but we don't know yet whether we'll get three days' warning to close down or three months. Personally I hope for the latter, though of course I have been very disappointed in my bright optimism, so I am prepared for anything.
>
> We're getting blow after blow here: Karsten has come to say that money can only be released by application, and the salary list must be approved by the "Office Alliance". The leaders decided that our salaries were too high and must be reduced! The highest pay in Russia is fixed at 1200 lat. Now we'll see how it goes tomorrow. Life is full of excitement.

Tobias enclosed a list to remind Katze of things to buy him at Illum: Aqua Velva; Pepsodent; Williams talcum powder; Fast Brilliantine; gramophone needles that play 10–100 times.

The highs and lows of the letters reflect Tobias' luck at cards. He glosses over his losses, knowing that gambling gets on Katze's nerves. But he can't help mentioning the times he wins money at bridge because then he feels like the responsible provider. In 1936, he received a letter from the World Bridge Olympics, Rockefeller Plaza, N.Y., telling him that he and his partner were masters in their country. The worse Tobias' life went, the more he needed to play and the more risks he took.

Katze looked forward to seeing her husband again "in good party form", but on April 9, 1940 he wrote:

Thanks for replying about the kisses. It may seem strange, but to me certainty – however uncomfortable – is better than uncertainty. I would prefer to hear of "various things" from you than to be surprised by them, as I was the other day when someone said my wife looked so sweet in her yellow hood. "I saw her walking up and down in front of the Hotel Rome." That completely knocked me out! It was so public, the two of you meeting in front of the hotel – perhaps to go inside afterwards or perhaps simply to stroll – how should I know? But as it was, the off-the-cuff remark ruined my weekend. In front of the Rome . . . walking . . .! Can't you feel that I am slowly but surely going mad? Otherwise you'd better give me up at once.

You are still young and beautiful and charming, and you'll soon get married or find another sort of happiness. What can I give you other than a bare subsistence? As you admitted before your departure, you have never – since those first five days in Hareskov – been happy with me. I take it you mean that I have ruined the only happiness you ever had, and as far as that goes, you're right. So I advise you to consider once more what you want, whether you wouldn't rather be rid of me. If that happens, there is always the chance that, as you said so sadly before leaving, you would lose both your men. A telegram or letter will, no doubt, summon him to Copenhagen, if he is not already there. If he can give you the happiness which you – like every human being – deserve, you should take it – only not as my wife. For if I have not been able to make you happy in the past, I certainly can't now. The remnants of me aren't worth much.

Unfortunately I long for you so much and have often thought that, if I could only lay my head on your soft, white breast, I should be very happy. That which I – perhaps naively – thought was mine.

Well, I won't plague you with more today. I don't know if you have shown my letters to the children. If not, I don't think you should – I wrote them in an agitated and perplexed state of mind. I hope I shall soon be more sensible. Greetings to all, your T.

P.S. Just had the horrific news of the German occupation of Copenhagen. Hope you are all safe. A kiss to all my dear ones.

10

OIL IN THE MOUTH

The Russians entered Riga on June 17th, the day that Tobias saw an amusing film starring Danielle Darrieux and Douglas Fairbanks. He walked out of the cinema to find that Latvia no longer existed. It had become Latvian SSR, and it had only one flag, the red one. Even the day before, they had begun to decorate the town red, red, red, with Stalin's portrait in the middle. Everyone was very depressed, which was why he had gone to the pictures, and several of Tobias' friends and acquaintances had lost everything. You would be lucky if you were permitted to take a job in your own factory, for 500 lat a month.

During the summer of 1940, Katze and Tobias each lived under an occupation: Katze under the Germans, who had annexed Denmark on April 9th; Tobias under the Russians, who had seized power in Latvia by a fraudulent election. Under the Russian occupation in Latvia, the only way to obtain bread coupons was to put your checkmark in the right place on the voting slip. The Russians had promised the Latvian president, Dr Ulmanis, a free passage to Switzerland, but instead put him on a train for Moscow, where he was presumably shot, if he did not die en route of sorrow at the fate of his country.

Even though Tobias was still trying to maintain business relations with the Russians, Katze couldn't get back to Latvia. Tobias acquired a visa for the Soviet Union, where he hoped to get a job interview with Nafta, the oil syndicate in Moscow. Normally, the authorities never issues visas unless they thought that they could themselves benefit, he wrote, which made Tobias hopeful. But then Stalin started his open campaign against the Jews.

Katze couldn't remain at the Pension Larsen on Kastelsvej. She and Tobias were on the verge of dividing up their furniture, but whenever Tobias wrote to ask which pieces she wanted, she did not reply. Perhaps she still had a faint romantic hope that Dietlof von Sachensollen would reappear, or perhaps it was that she didn't want to take responsibility for the divorce. Or perhaps, a true female, she didn't indicate the specific items of furniture she wanted so that she could later complain about whatever she actually received.

Li had been sent to St Mary's Domestic Science School. Since Katze and Tobias believed that Li had more talent in the romantic than in the civilian sphere, they thought that a stint learning how to cook would be good for her. Then she would be able to offer her various husbands if not a feast, then at least a minimal bird's diet to peck at. She was now nineteen. She noticed that Papa at Rosenvænget suddenly showed her a new sort of attention. He would lead her into his library, take the first editions from his bookcase and place them carefully in her hands, inhaling all her deliciousness, as if her mere presence was for him an essential ingredient for life itself.

Her parents had always credited her with that indolent charm they called "sex appeal", which originates in the fear of not existing. She did not feel that this "appeal" had anything to do with her. When the handsomest boy in the class fell in love with someone, all the others did as well; that phenomenon had nothing to do with appearance or personality.

Tobias too had seen – in a photograph – that Li had blossomed into a nubile young girl. This made him happy, almost as if he were in love. Just looking at her made him happy.

All the other girls at the domestic science school at Jægerspris received opulent parcels from home. But Katze, more inclined to ostrich feathers and gold lamé, was not the parcel-sending type. However, for a month or two, a small brown paper bag had arrived with the laundry. The bag contained an apple. Li blushed with shame when she realised that it was for her! When Mama had learned that it was possible to send parcels for nothing with the laundry to St Mary's, she pounced upon the opportunity. Every week she sent the housemaid with a piece of fruit to Kastanjeallé where the laundry van went to Jægerspris. Li failed to see anything touching in the gesture, it was just embarrassing and cruel. Li could imagine nothing worse than stinginess or cruelty.

She put on weight at school. When Tobias saw her again, he observed that she had grown plump. After that, Li would give up eating for the rest of her life. That was Katze's opinion.

After the war, her parents concluded that the tuition money had been wasted. Li never carried out the daily tasks at the college and made her fellow students do everything for her. In exchange, while the others fried her rissoles, stirred her sauce and wrung out her dishcloth, she wrote their German essays. Her cookbook was full – not of recipes – but of book titles: *À la recherche du temps perdu, Ulysses* and *Point Counter Point*. Her spare time she spent writing letters to her father in Riga.

From the day she saw her father with the red-haired millionairess, an almost erotic "conspiracy" developed between them. Li was able to speak her mind. She accused Glenda of having always been in love with Tobias, and she told her that it was anyway a matter of common knowledge. Glenda became very upset. "Nothing hurts like the truth," Li said.

In return, Tobias gave Li fatherly advice:

> I can well understand that you liked the Finnish Volunteer the first evening he came to the house, but it still isn't very nice to break an appointment. I hope you are sensible and won't go and get engaged – or anything else – for the time being. Above all, you must be quite sure, and, as you are not yet 20, you can't possibly know what you are looking for, and I am sure that he is equally unsure. You can be absolutely certain that the first three times you are convinced that a relationship is serious, it isn't! So take care, my darling, and think it over carefully. It is so terribly painful when you discover you have made a mistake – which most people do. Kisses, Father.

Rebekka was sent to Zahle's College to prepare for university, like Balder, who was at boarding school. The Løvins considered

Balder's education more important than his younger sisters'; after all, one day he would have to have a job and provide for a family. But Rebekka's desire to learn and to acquire knowledge (preferably more than anyone else's) was irrepressible. She regarded it as her "typical Jewish characteristic".

It gradually dawned on Katze that she would have to find an apartment, otherwise the family would split up. In the midst of all the misery, she suppressed her whining and showed per- severance. Since the war had broken out and her children's lives were at stake, she became surprisingly efficient. She acquired a comfortable five-room flat with a maid's room: Gammel Mønt 14. Tobias wrote: "Furnish it in your own taste."

The Gammel Mønt apartment was the Copenhagen pied-à- terre for the director of Vacuum Oil, whose principal residence was a mansion in Jægersborg. It had become available because the director and his wife were getting divorced. After seeing two children's beds in the apartment, Katze – who as the years went by became firmly convinced that children and grandchildren were the only things that mattered in her life – despaired of going through with her own impending divorce.

There was something heart-breaking about moving into a divorced home, and the more so in this case since Katze had always admired the director's family and the wisdom of his wife, Anne-Lise. Nor was it very cheering to discover that the couple's firstborn, a boy for whom they had cherished such high hopes – not least that he would inherit the company – had almost suffocated in his own vomit and did later die of pneumonia in the apartment. His last words were, "I have oil in my mouth." Katze would later say: "That's what you get for trying to control your own children's destiny."

It was surprising that Katze, so steeped in the Old Testament and so superstitious, had dared to move there at all. But for the rest of her days she would regard this new home as her creation; the interior designer in her, who had always been able to make a palace out of a pig's ear, was delighted. She wrote to Tobias that Gammel Mønt 14 was the ideal apartment, and he hoped she was right. She loved making the curtains herself for 50 kroner apiece instead of buying them for 350. Katze even found a cleaner, though of course it wasn't easy to manage with just part-time help when you were accustomed to having two full-time maids.

Tobias understood very well that Katze felt lonely and missed a husband – especially after having had two over the past year. Naturally they had made a terrible hash of tax matters. They should really have consulted a solicitor. In any case, he would be ruined now. Wasn't it Uncle Max who always called them nitwits!

Tobias got hold of a floor plan of Gammel Mønt 14, and, on his own initiative, sent the furniture from the birchwood room, the piano room, the dining room and the nurseries, along with Katze's bed and wardrobe. He was far less attached to material possessions than Katze, and planned to move from the 16-room apartment in Riga to a small wooden house in Valdemara Street.

And then one day, Tobias decided to come home. His plans were immediately quashed. He woke up to discover double police guards on every street corner. Sealed railway carriages had been held in the station for several days. They were said to contain "food supplies", a gift from the Russian people to the Latvians. In fact the trains were filled with goods the Russians were sending direct to Moscow. Perhaps they were sending people too. Rumours were flying. Tobias' storekeeper wept at the prospect of taking over the management of the firm. Tobias heard the news from London over the radio that France wanted to make a separate peace. Peace was coming soon – but what a peace! Tobias advised his friends to sell everything, including silver. Each person was allowed to take out only a half kilo. Now everyone would need a permit to take clothes out too. Tobias wanted to sell their belongings, but what about Katze's dresses? He had already exchanged three of her sweaters for a down quilt, but he promised to bring back her white hats and her needles. He couldn't find her black petticoat anywhere. He signed himself "Tovarish Tobias" and congratulated Balder, who had just become a carefree university student in this frightful year of 1940.

The head office in New York approved of Tobias' attempt to make a business deal with the Russians and of his going to Moscow with Aloscha as interpreter. He had even been promised a meeting with Mikoyan. He made it to the Soviet capital, but on September 14th, 1940, he was obliged to write that "the dream of Moscow" had come to nothing. Like so many others, Tobias had suffered a defeat; the Kremlin walls were not to be so easily stormed. Tobias was disappointed because it was always unpleasant to lose and also because he would have dearly liked to carry through an arrangement for Vacuum Oil as one of the handful of foreign firms to operate in Russia. In another way, however, he was not disappointed. Moscow would be an intolerable place to live in the long run. One couldn't mix with the Russians because they either would not or could not mix with foreigners. That left the embassies, and despite all the rights and advantages they enjoyed, there wasn't a single lively one. Tobias also felt that all the diplomats carried on like gods who would never deign to mix with private individuals outside their circle. He would have been in a quite different situation if Katze had been with him and he had been able to rely on her brilliant talent. Tobias was sorry too that she wouldn't be able to see the town, for in many ways it was an experience – even if, ideally, a short one. He assured her that she would never tolerate living in Moscow, and neither would Li. But perhaps Balder and Bekka would appreciate it as much as he did. In Moscow, there wasn't a single well-dressed person to be found. Most men didn't wear ties; instead of hats, the women wore little berets; silk stockings were a mere dream. It was, quite simply, the land of proletarians. He had never seen so many poor people at one time. He hadn't seen a pram in ten days. The women carried their infants to work and breast-fed them in the street when they cried. The city was teeming and squalid – as if you had crammed all the inhabitants into one street. The shop windows were full only of fake goods. And the Muscovites were proud of all this! As one of the leaders said: formerly the aristocracy lived in the city centre and the workers in the outer districts. Now the whole town is a workers' district!

What delighted Tobias were the metro, the opera, and the ballet – and the ticket prices. Also, apart from cockroaches, there were no pests. He had only been bitten once by a flea, which died immediately afterward, "presumably from drinking my bad blood". The Russians had built a gigantic canal from the Volga to Moscow and Tobias had seen the terminus just outside the town. A whole palace clad in marble, with big mirrors and parquet floors. A playroom for children, if mothers who arrived by boat could not take them into town. A nurse in white looked after them, and visitors had to put on white sterile overalls before being allowed to enter this sacred space. Masses of toys, like a branch of Thorngreen's, animals and dolls of every size, games, and a switchback. Brand-new, and clean. There were no signs that the little ones had played in it for three years, but surely it could not be that it was only for "show"?

No, surely not. Tobias was reluctant to think ill of the Soviets, because, while he was still waiting for word about the prospects for Vacuum Oil, he saw Moscow as his last chance. Later, Katze found a letter:

> I concluded that I could no longer live in Denmark and decided to follow any course of action that would keep me away from there. The children can certainly do without me – and you too, as long as you have someone else. But I admit that sometimes it's sad being alone. Enjoy yourself as much as you can. I haven't forgotten you – I was about to say, unfortunately. When I think back over the past few years, I begin to see more and more what an incredible ass I have been. I really have, as you used to tell me, been a blue-eyed innocent and, as you claimed all along, I am no God. I have been egotistical and full of self-pity. But there was a time when my nerve failed, and then one writes silly things, which one more or less regrets afterwards. Now I think I am all right again, with the small shift inside me that I am poorer by an illusion and richer by an experience. Take care of yourself during the blackout.

The bridge clubs in Riga were closed. Tobias was back from Moscow, aimless. Katze explained away her yellow hood and restless pacing up and down in front of the Hotel Rome. She swore that she never kissed Dietlof von Sachensollen in a café or tea-room and certainly not on the street. She was furious at Tobias for taking her for a tart. God in Heaven, Katze was no Glenda! But through all the denials from the unimpeachable Katze and the insistent rumours still surfacing, Tobias grew even more crazed.

> If not in the café or in the street, where were the kisses given? For surely you don't kiss each other just once every two and a half months. Everything whirls around and around and seems hopeless, and at night it gets worse. I never before

remember my dreams as such a direct continuation of the day. When Betty wakes me, it is from a conversation with you. A conversation without answers, for I can well understand that you did not want to say anything about what you were really feeling because it would annoy me. So begins another long day, when I tell myself the whole time that I *must* pull myself together. Naturally the best moment is the arrival of your sweet letters, where I read both directly and indirectly how much you want things to be good and where you take pity on me – just as you used to do once a week when you had had enough to drink. I can't forgive myself for being such a gigantic ass that I did not deduce that when you did not – as you did in the old days – come of your own will, there *was* something wrong. How it must have tortured you.

The war apparently caused all the veiled forces pent up for so long to break out. Tobias couldn't prevent the World War or abolish censorship, but he tried to bring honesty into the marriage. He didn't want to excuse all the unpleasant things he wrote that Katze didn't want to hear.

If there is a rift in the lute, great or small, I think the only way to mend it is to talk things out thoroughly. And even then it is often doubtful whether it can be saved. But there is one thing that is absolutely definite: certainty, however unpleasant and bitter it may be, is preferable to half-truths. If a house attacked by rot or woodworm is to be repaired, it is *essential* to remove everything affected. If there are one or two worm-eaten beams in the cellar, they will crawl out at some point. Then the whole thing will crash in ruins and never rise again.

Perhaps Tobias confused the collapse of civilisation with the break-up of his own life. He sent Katze a poem by Henrik Ibsen, which couldn't possibly have cheered her.

The two of them lived in a snug warm house,
In autumn and in winter days.
Then the house burned down, in ruins lay,
And both of them were caught in the blaze.

74

For under it a jewel was hid
A jewel that never can be burned.
And if they diligently search it may be
They'll find it, and the lesson be learned.

But if they do, the fire-branded two,
Find the precious, fireproof treasure,
He never will find his burned-out faith,
Nor she her burned-out pleasure.

Heavens above, what a lot of high-flying nonsense! And what a pretentious way to behave! Mr Faithless! How could he tarnish her innocent trysts with all his grubby imaginings? He who had been unfaithful to her from the moment they married. But of course, she could have run off with Dietlof, for she was on the same wavelength as he was, and they could talk together. But that was something Tobias would never be able to understand. To Tobias, everything was sex and percentages – that was the Jewishness and the destructive element in him. Tobias had initially construed that her love for Dietlof was not 100 percent love, but 75 percent vanity. Later on, he had conceded that it was probably 75 percent love, with chocolate in cafés and kisses in doorways – "For you can't have been standing in the middle of the street in broad daylight!" How could he be so stupid! There were some things – a higher plane – that had nothing to do with percentages. No woman wants to be taken for granted. That was all he needed to know.

Tobias' excess of vitality exasperated Katze and prevented her from feeling any sympathy for him, although his thromboses had alarmed her. Otherwise that man never lay down. He was saturated with an egoism surpassing all decency. Katze never considered the fact that Tobias, like his father, always gave his staff what they asked for, that he had a special account in which he saved up any surplus from the firm for his employees. Katze called that greed. He fattened up his workers to gain popularity. Katze had no truck with Tobias when he drove out alone at Christmas with presents for the old and sick in the family. Løvins all of them, a rabble. Nor did she think much of his helpfulness, when in snow or rain he would pull up at a tram stop and say: "I have room for three passengers." Sheer vanity. In the hour of danger he thought only of himself.

Not long ago the fire brigade came rushing through Valdemara. The tower of the Ministry of War was in flames. In half an hour they succeeded in confining the fire to the tower. In February, Jensen ordered some cigars for me in Østergade. They are paid for. Because of the freezing conditions, however, they were not sent off. Then the Occupation took place with various export embargoes. Could you go in and ask if it isn't possible to get an export permit for this item, which was ordered and paid for before April 9th, and which is not for resale, but for my own use?

Look after yourself, my faith (-less? -ful?) old darling.

11

THE MAN IN THE BARREL

Katze had not heard from her beloved; he had vanished without a trace. Perhaps his wife had found out about the affair and he was afraid to face her. Or had it for him been just a fleeting and insignificant romance? Katze couldn't help wondering. Then a letter from Tobias arrived which confirmed Katze's feeling that a supernatural force was involved.

It had been suffocatingly hot. Tobias was out walking in the evening when a strange thing happened. He sat on a bench, Karenina exhausted and panting at his feet. Suddenly the dog started to growl, as she did whenever an enemy approached. Tobias looked round, but no other dog was to be seen. He hushed Karenina and glared at her, but she continued angrily to growl. Then he noticed an elegantly dressed gentleman walking along the beach towards him – white trousers, a dark jacket, a tie and a pearl. And a monocle. Dietlof and his wife had been turned back at the Swiss frontier and were living temporarily in a holiday house. Tobias was sitting beside the road – the same road that the man with the monocle travelled – but suddenly he turned off and vanished among the dunes. We hardly heard another word about von Sachsensollen, although Katze always claimed *she* did.

Things were beginning to come together for Tobias. The United States granted his colleague £1,500 so that he could go to

Palestine, but the man made a fuss; he thought the sum was insufficient and demanded £3,000.

On October 1st, a decree was issued stating that no-one was to occupy more than one room. Twenty people moved into the apartment below his, so Tobias told those of his friends who had lost everything that they were welcome to move into his flat.

The sight of Kiko and Bunty, his old party friends – "a little kiss each night" – turned out to be more than Tobias had bargained for. Kiko staggered around like a drunk and seemed to have lost his wits. When Bunty arrived, he fell to his knees weeping and groaned: "What have I done to my lovely Bunty? I've ruined our whole life for the sake of another woman and now she has given me poison because I won't marry her." Their house had just been confiscated, and Tobias did what he could to help them. He wrote to Li that Kiko had tried to commit suicide and that he and Bunty had several times had to keep him from jumping out of the window. Eventually they resorted to calling Betty to restrain him.

Tobias praised Balder, Li and Rebekka for their sensitivity and integrity, but, he wrote to them, some wounds cannot be healed no matter how tenderly they are nursed. The children spent all their lives silently longing to unite the incompatible. At this time they yearned to be back in Riga to relive their childhood summers when their father and mother were a little less unhappy. But Tobias rejected these hopes and wrote, "forget it", there was a war going on, and he would no longer have a car. How did they imagine it was possible to travel to Jurmala without a car! Besides, you have to be careful, you never know what might happen these days.

Bombs *can* go astray, thromboses *can* take unexpected turns. So today I'd rather – better now than never, and although I hope to live to repeat it many times – thank you three for what you have meant to me – both now and all my life. Usually I think it is the children who thank their parents, but I realise that I have more reason to thank you than you me. In every way, you are all better than I have ever been. That must be because you've inherited your mother's good qualities. Only one thing I would beg of you: be good to each other. Help each other when you can, and help your mother, too, and don't take advantage of her inability to say No.

Rebekka was studying for her entrance exams at Zahle's, and Liane had a job as a secretary in a solicitor's office. Balder, who still didn't wash, refused to have his hair cut and slept late. He had not yet pulled himself together to get a job because he was too busy kissing one countess after another and listening to jazz records.

Katze brought back Marie even though the Director wasn't there. But one thing she was bound to complain about: the "monkey-music" that Balder was forever playing. Katze expected that Tobias would soon be back too. It wouldn't be long before he had burned all his bridges, and perhaps she was glad of it. Without a man in the house it was lonely and, besides, she still loved him, the blockhead. She always had.

The curtain had gone up on the last act, and it was not a long one. Twelve years, nearly to the day – October 28th – after their arrival in Riga, Tobias left. On his last morning, he was out walking with Karenina, and came back to find a guard outside his office door and a couple of gentlemen watching the back staircase in the courtyard.

Tobias could not stay at the office now that it had been nationalised. There was nothing more for him to say. The commissar opened letters and telegrams and decided everything.

On October 20th he had Karenina put down.

He and Aloscha had brought caviar and fruit back from Moscow. Instead of keeping it themselves, they agreed to throw a little party. He invited all his colleagues. It was their first dinner with him, and their farewell party. Bunty was there too, as was KIS – they were both living in the apartment. When other people rang up in the middle of the meal, they were invited too. Between the caviar and the pears there was a steak. It was three o'clock in the morning before the party broke up.

Tobias managed to get home in time to celebrate New Year's Eve at Gammel Mønt. December 31st, 1940: the festive evening when he so elegantly dropped a pile of gramophone records on the floor and asked his guests to match the pieces. He found a new terrier and called her Vanessa.

At that moment, however, it was difficult for Tobias to call the tune. He couldn't show himself at the Hotel d'Angleterre or in other public places, not with his particular physiognomy, not after he had been on the front page of a Nazi newspaper caricatured as an oil magnate "whose forefathers lie poisoning the Danish ground water out in the Mosaic Cemetery". Even so, no-one expected anything would happen to the Danish Jews, but it was obvious that Tobias couldn't count on finding a new job. He hadn't done anything wrong, but the places where he applied simply didn't reply. One should not ask; it was "the times".

One person was glad to see the Director home: Marie. Her view was that Gammel Mønt was only itself when the Director was there, even if he was full of nonsense, which he always was. Marie, plump and high-bosomed, had her own jolly, slightly captious manner with the Director, though he could easily take the wind out of her sails, like the day he summoned her to the lunch table and asked for a step ladder. What on earth does he want the steps for? Marie wondered. But when she returned with them, he asked her to climb to the top step.

"Can you see the salt, Marie?" Ugh, that was embarrassing. How could she have been so silly as to forget the salt? She had never done that before.

"COFFEE!" roared the Director a little while later, lest anyone doubt who was the boss in the house. That day Marie didn't mind, because she was cross with herself about the salt. At other times it amused her. The roar felt nice and safe.

On May 15th, 1942, German Jews were forbidden to keep pets.

Every day, when Li had finished work at her solicitor's office in Vimmelskaftet and prepared to go home, a German soldier would be waiting for her, ready to play the gallant escort. She spoke German as though it was her mother tongue and had idealised everything German throughout her childhood and adolescence, particularly the opposite sex, so she felt quite at ease talking to him. It was impossible for her to see the Germans as enemies. One day in Rådhuspladsen, where the townspeople had gathered in silent protest against the Occupation, German soldiers drove at them on their motorcycles, frightening people, to demonstrate who was in charge. One of Li's silk stockings got muddied. She did not understand what had happened – how could German soldiers be so boorish!

She was in her element when the German soldier was

escorting her home. She sensed what Katze had always referred to as sex appeal. She grew familiar with the soldier and told him, with complete disregard for danger, that they were Jews. She did so just to shock him, but he didn't turn a hair. They mostly talked about jazz. Li liked risky things, when they didn't involve too much effort. She was the only Løvin who lacked the gift of the gab. She proved her existence through shock.

And music. She had always played an instrument, but swing music was something else. It was sexy in a new way. At the Blue Heaven, where Svend Asmussen played "Ring them Bells", she had met a lanky boy who explained to her that swing was what made the whole world go round. It was not just Leo the Lion, Ingelise Rune and Kai Ewans, but the way she walked, the way she smiled with her eyes – everything about her was swing. It don't mean a thing if it ain't got that swing. Jas himself was a swing buff with his high-heeled shoes, hat and piano. Happy-go-lucky. It was his Resistance effort, the polar opposite of goose-stepping and cold baths. He had just taken his finals at the conservatoire, and they had gone well. Well, that is, except for his striking one wrong note, a crucial one, in the Polonaise in A major. Technical hitch.

Jas had perfect pitch. In his eagerness, though, he couldn't hear Li's quiet resistance. He was in love. He followed her like a blinded young stallion and used every nerve in his body to interpret the smallest indolent movement in her body or the smile in the yellow eyes. "It's not 'cause I wouldn't, and not 'cause I couldn't, it's just because I'm the laziest gal in town." When something displeased her, she squinted until her eyes turned white. His adoration irritated her. He was rather ridiculous, just as everyone is who is in love. But then he sang to her.

> Mad with joy
> I'm happy as a baby boy
> With another brand-new choo-choo toy
> When I marry sweet Liane.

With her yellow eyes, she smiled at his ardour and his joy, but she never dreamed of marrying him.

Tobias and Katze didn't consider Jas a great catch. In the summer of 1943, when the hopeless relationship had gone on for

18 months, they decided to move the object of Jas' passion, along with the rest of the family, to Tisvilde. But Jas followed, becoming a pianist with the Tisvilde jazz band. If the piano wasn't available, he took the bass or the guitar. At night, he slept in a barrel. He had found an extraordinary one, which might once have served as a dog kennel, near the Løvin property. The barrel was his place of retreat and his favourite place to sit and ponder. He decided to save up his money for smart clothes.

Li was not the only attractive Løvin; the whole family was blessed with good looks. Jas saw Li for the first time at Gammel Mønt 14. He had never seen an apartment like that before, with its heavy silver, carpets, and paintings of naked gods and oriental silk dragons. In the middle of the living room stood Katze, wearing a bright red dress with a diamond brooch, and red lipstick. She was 40. If he hadn't been in love with the daughter, he would have at once fallen for the mother, but he did not hold many cards with which to pique Katze's interest. She could play the piano herself – any fool could. Jas had no serious education, and worst of all, no family name of interest.

When he woke up in his barrel, Li crept out to see him. After all, he was great fun. She found the lanky creature stretched out on the ground with his lower body and long legs under the open sky. As soon as he saw her yellow eyes, he stretched out voluptuously on the grass and sang with a thick morning voice from inside the barrel.

> I want to buy a paper doll
> That I can call my own . . .

Li laughed. This was a bit different from a German school. It was tender and moving, like the time when Karenina had puppies.

She experienced the first fright of her life when Jas invited her home to his parents. On Amager. Sundholmsvej. As soon as she saw the nameplate on the door, Li sensed something was wrong. Jas had told her his surname was Theisner, but the nameplate read Theis-Hansen. Li felt ashamed, mostly because Jas seemed embarrassed.

His mother was welcoming; she was making a grand feast in the kitchen, as the Danes do, since they make food the foremost ingredient in life. The mother even talked about the various little hot dishes, while Liane stared at her, incredulous. Food was not something one *talked* about. Not in that way. But perhaps it was just to hide everything Li was supposed not to notice. There were only two living rooms: the red room with the piano and the finest book in the house, *Hellas*, placed at a slant on the crocheted tablecloth; and the dining room where Jas slept on the sofa. Li stared at the kindly lady with her large bosom, big pink mouth and false teeth, tucking with big lusty mouthfuls into the peas and carrots in mayonnaise. Li gaped in despair at all this pleasure; she had no idea what to say or do. Jas kept the conversation going with one crack after another. His father, an attendant at Sundholmen, the shelter for drunks – his cap with its badge hung in the hall – didn't contribute one word. Perhaps all the food was meant to camouflage the fact that he was nothing to boast about.

After the visit to Sundholmsvej, Li was inclined to ignore Jas' declarations of love. He called her his thoroughbred and his silken doll and his little dolly-bird. But Amager was too alien for her, not because she was a snob, but because she needed something strong, something she could respect. She thought about Gaus. He, too, was a social climber, but he could always do what he liked with her. Since the New Year's Eve when she had been liberated from her virginity in the stockbroker's office, she had been seeing Gaus regularly. He bought lingerie for her and demanded she put it on in his office as he sat behind the desk observing her with a cigar in his mouth. He could make her walk across the room in the new lingerie and sit on his lap. With Gaus, she was free to think what she liked. She was not in love with Gaus, but she was impressed. And perhaps slightly in love with the effect she had on him – that she could make a man who had everything lie groaning and moaning. Jas had no power over her, he merely reinforced her own powerlessness.

But when people can't work things out for themselves, world events can sometimes do it for them. On August 28th, 1943, a state of military emergency was declared, and by October it was clear that the Jews could not remain in Denmark. How strange that seemed! For Tobias had never regarded himself as a Jew. It is true he had not been baptised, but neither had many Danes. He was not religious. He ate lobster and prawns and pork chops and roast pork like everyone else. He did not keep the Sabbath; he celebrated Christmas. He had allowed his children to be christened without discussion. What more could you expect? Nonetheless, he was a Jew.

Thanks to the marriage of Tobias' delightful cousin Henriette to a German, the Løvins had good connections with the German embassy in Copenhagen. From there they heard the warning that would save the Danish Jews. It was a secret message from the naval attaché, C.F. Duckwitz. It spread like wildfire in different versions through the town, from family to family. At the Løvins', the word came by telephone from the manager of *Politiken* in the form of an invitation to bridge. "We need two men on Tuesday evening." That meant there was no room for two persons on a fishing boat. The "invitations" came in consecutive messages as places became available. The first one was for only one place. "I'll have that!" Aunt Titta chimed immediately. Uncle Otto stared at her. Everyone was speechless. They felt Titta's fear to be pure selfishness, but this was not the time to quarrel. Over many years Glenda would – just for fun – repeat Aunt Titta's famous "I'll have that" so Titta refused ever to see Glenda again.

Naturally Tobias needed to leave first. His very presence in the town exposed him to mortal danger. A family council convened at Gammel Mønt 14. Should they all go to Sweden or should some stay on in Denmark to look after the family interests and take care of Tobias' new dog, who had already devoured one of Li's Peter Sørensen shoes? Only one was safe to stay – Katze. She would look after the apartment. Gammel Mønt must not fall into the waiting hands of the Germans! Katze appointed herself in charge of ensuring that her family had a home to return to when the war was over. She would also try to carry on Tobias' fuel business so they would have an income to live on during the war, and perhaps even after it ended. It could not last long, surely. They would probably be home in a month or two, certainly for Christmas.

The thought that all the children would leave her and go with their father brought out primordial strengths in Katze. She felt like a lioness who discovers that the male has grabbed one of her cubs, whereupon without hesitation she sinks her teeth in its neck and carries it back to where it belongs – with *her*. Meanwhile, she would send the male an icy glare. She had read all this in a lion report entitled "A Mother".

Katze was torn apart in her solicitude. Would all the children prefer to be with their father? She stared at them as if they had become strangers to her. She did not think of Hitler's decree, or that, as half Jews, they too were in danger. She thought only that they would desert her in favour of something better. She was already jealous of the flight. Those who fled thought they were really something. She looked at Li and saw she was crying.

"What's the matter, darling?" Li sniffed. "Nothing will happen to you and Bekka and Balder. They won't take 'halves', you know."

"What do you know about it?" Bekka said.

"That is what the decree from Werner Best says."

"Dear Mother, do you really think the Commander-in-Chief of the German forces will consult as they turn around? The Gestapo will make a clean sweep, infants and the infirm, whole and half, and they are doing it all over Europe already."

There she goes again, Miss Know-It-All, Katze thought. Bekka was totally on her father's side, but of course that was natural with her dark complexion and dark eyes. It was different with Li, fair-haired and bone-idle. Would Li really pull herself together enough to flee? And throw herself into darkness and uncertainty – not to speak of all the trouble?

Li ran weeping into her mother's lap.

"My darling girl," Katze was weeping too.

Throughout the discussion Tobias had gone on working at his crossword puzzle, a cigar in his mouth. He hadn't said a word.

Katze reminded him that Vanessa had fleas and it was very hard to get hold of a tooth comb in present circumstances, so what should they do, how on earth would she catch them?

"With a lasso," said Tobias, without looking up.

*

It was decided that Liane should marry Jas, who was an Aryan – and thereby a kind of life insurance.

"But I don't love you," said Li.

"That doesn't matter, I love you enough for two!" Jas said.

Li was flattered, but then she came to her senses: "You can't do that."

"What can't you do?"

"Love for two."

"I can!"

Li looked at him. She saw his good heart. His warmth. But she also saw he was flighty and a little bit stupid. He was simply too lightweight. She ought to have a man with real weight, a man like Gaus.

"Mother, is it possible for people to get married without loving each other?" she asked one day, when mother and daughter had come home from their respective offices and were sitting with their feet up, each in her armchair with all the newspapers on the footstool. Tobias had gone to his club for the last time. Li needed to talk to her mother about her innermost, confused feelings, but she didn't know how to ask, and Katze didn't know how to answer. She couldn't say that she had never loved and still didn't love Tobias, for then her whole life would have been meaningless. Moreover, it would not be true, for she did love him, the idiot. Nor could she say that she loved a man who was about to run away from her. Despite the fact that Katze didn't think about much else than who loved whom and why and to what degree, she could not give an answer. Li felt again that she and her mother were very far apart.

Li's unvoiced question in the erotic sphere pained Katze. Not only because she blatantly suffered from a sex phobia – which she tried to keep to herself, just as she concealed every other phobia – but because she was afraid of pointedly emotional questions, particularly when they came from her children. And so she invariably wriggled away from them. For Li this was the greatest let-down of all, but she did not acknowledge her pain. She swallowed the disappointment without feeling more than a kind of anaesthesia. She just had to continue loving her mother, especially for as long as the war lasted.

"Have a drink," Katze said, going to the silver tray and pouring a vermouth for Li. "Here, make yourself comfortable, darling, put your feet up, that's right. Would you like a rug?"

Li felt as if her mother were tucking her in. Perhaps she should marry her mother rather than Jas. She couldn't stop crying.

"Women always cry when they are going to be married," Katze said.

"Do you mean that?"

"Now we're at home, that's what matters. The others can cut and run." She noticed that Li was still crying.

"Is there someone else?" Katze asked, trying to change an

unbearable situation into a romantic cliché.

"What do you mean, 'someone else'?"

"Someone you love?"

"No," Li replied.

*

It was Gaus who saw that they all got to Sweden safely. He divided up the Løvins by installing them in various apartments where they were to live "underground" until they could escape. He had 18 Jews living in his holiday house at Asserbo.

With his walking stick, Tobias made his way through the woods near Vedbæk with Titta and Otto. It was after curfew, and they had waited for the onset of darkness. Glenda's husband, Buller, helped Tobias by carrying his little suitcase with his dinner jacket and a packet of playing cards – sensible luggage when you think of the long waiting times a refugee suffers. Being a refugee consists of waiting and nothing much else.

Titta was so frightened that she fell over tree roots in the woods; she risked giving them all away with her stumbling and her constant little cries of fear. The enchanting Titta, the beauty queen from Hornbæk, had never encountered discomfort. Now, suddenly, there was uncertainty about her life. She didn't understand it, and she thought of all the lovely preserves standing in jars in the apartment. What would happen to her preserves?

Every time she whimpered, Otto gave her a hard tug. It was late in the evening, and she was scared to death. The cutter was ready for them; they would be placed at the very bottom of the boat with doped babies and small children. Titta needed pills of her own. She couldn't bear sitting in this cramped position and was about to perish from claustrophobia. The coastal police guards had been bribed. Just before they departed, they heard steps on the deck overhead. Boots. They had been discovered. Titta was on the brink of screaming. But Otto beat her on the head and put his hand over her mouth. She couldn't breathe. Tobias thought that everything was immaterial now.

From his underground hideout, he wrote to Katze, maybe his last letter. What do you write when you are to be parted, completely unprepared, and don't know whether you will ever meet again?

October 1st 1943. My own darling. Well, when you get this
we shall presumably be on our way. Don't worry about me, I
will manage well enough until we meet again – within a year,
I hope. The only worry I have is for you and the children, but
I think you will manage at least for a couple of years with
what we have now.

To start with, I advise you to sell my fur coat and the carpet.
The coat is coming apart a bit in the sleeves. Let Bang repair
it and ask if he can get it sold for a reasonable price. You
should get roughly 6–7,000, or at the least 5,000. The
carpet should bring in 7–8,000. Gaus will probably be
interested, so if you get an offer, don't sell before you ask him.
If you get these things sold you'll have 12–13,000 kroner and
that should see you through for 14–15 months. I have given
Gaus power of attorney to deal with my accounts. Three of
the bank books belong to the children. You must keep
Balder's in reserve for him. He has to find himself a job soon.
If Li stays, she can have hers cashed for what she needs. You
can keep Rebekka's and use it for her studies, but don't allow
her to manage it herself, as she might feel dizzy over so much
money and use a few hundred kroner for clothes. Given the
present conditions, I don't think she should do that. She
wants a shirt blouse. I think there's a blue one, slightly worn
in the sleeves and colour, in the left-hand wardrobe. She can
have that. On the right hand side, there are a couple of white
shirts with double cuffs, they are worn too. She can have one
of them. But *not* the dress shirts with collars attached.

You should give all the money you get to Gaus, who gets
interest on it for a higher rate than you get at the bank.
Furthermore, you will not run so much risk if the various
accounts are seized. The interest on 10–12,000 kr. a year is
500–600 kr. and that will cover all your gas and electricity
and telephone bills, so you really must do this. I have already
spoken to him about it, so he might be hurt if you don't.
He will no doubt surprise you one day with a nice sum
of money. So long as he is with you, you can be sure that he
will do everything for you and the children. If all goes well,
I shall of course be glad to have some of my clothes in
Sweden.

Finally, there's the wine. I reckon it's worth 14–15,000

kroner. You should try and sell it. There are 24–25 bottles of burgundy, you should get 25 kr. for five or six bottles of ordinary red wine – 10 kr. Five bottles chateau vintage 30 kr. Whisky, two or three bottles 60–70 kr. Cognac, two or three bottles 60–70 kr. Port wine, two kinds, 15 and 25 kr. – one is a vintage wine. Original French vermouth 25 kr. Gin (original English) 30–40 kr. and up in your hat cupboard a large bottle of Cointreau. I think you should sell all the original wines. Then with some of the money, buy some Danish Cognac-Whisky-Gin so you have something in the house for guests.

One more thing. I didn't get hold of a new tap for the heating apparatus. Do it. For whether you keep the room or let it out, it is good to have it heated. (I should wait with the letting as long as possible.) If the worst should happen and they take Mama's money, I hope you will take her in until I come home. Likewise I am sure she will help you if necessary. But above all, stay with Gaus. He is managing Mama's, Otto's and my money and he will see to it that you are never in need.

Well, my darling, till we meet again – not goodbye – for I am sure we shall be together again within a year. Don't overburden yourself, you will manage very well until then. Here – or there. Take care, beloved, and thanks for everything you do for me and the children.

Your – and always your – Tobias.

12

RAZOR BLADES

"Oh dear, how spiteful and vindictive people are when life could be so nice and happy," old Sara said. Mama was 75 and blissfully unaware of everything going on around her. Gaus had her admitted to Bispebjerg Hospital under the pseudonym fru Hansen. The hospitals and the Resistance movement worked together. When the doctors asked her: "How are we today, then fru Hansen?" she invariably replied: "Why am I lying here? There's nothing wrong with me, and my name is *not* fru Hansen." She always added a saying that she had adopted after Papa's death: "Goodness gracious, I can look after myself. I can see and hear, walk and sleep, so I have much to be thankful for."

Mama was supposed to have been with the people who were fleeing from Gilleleje and who were caught in a hayloft by the Germans. She too lay waiting in the hay, but for some mysterious reason, she was tipped off by a student and managed to escape while the others – including her relatives – were sent to the concentration camp at Theresienstadt. After news of the catastrophe spread, Gaus found Mama in Hillerød, walking along with a confused look and a Persian lamb fur over her arm. The bow on her hat, which should have been at the back, was at the front.

Balder distributed Resistance newspapers, and Rebekka dyed her hair red. Before they got across the Sound to Linhamn, they had to spend a night in an undertaker's on Dragør Island.

Rebekka nourished a secret hope that Tobias would weep with joy at their reunion: "God bless you, you got across alive." She imagined that it would resemble the scene in *The Forsyte Saga*. But when they finally arrived in Stockholm, Tobias said curtly: "What are you doing here?"

Camp beds and sofas were made up in Aunt Rosa's reception and dining rooms. Aunt Rosa was Uncle Max's sister – in a way, she too was one of "Denmark's leading sons", except that she was a daughter and almost forgotten. Almost forgotten, that is, until she turned up as the guardian angel. They could stay with Rosa for the time being. When she contemplated all the possible mishaps, Rebekka decided that it was a miracle that the whole family, save only a few, was together again. She found it incredible that she had relatives almost everywhere with whom she could stay. All those with relatives in Sweden were immediately released from the transit camp and sent off with money for train journeys. When Bekka heard her father's customary salutation – "What are you doing here?" – she felt immediately at home.

They tried to tell Tobias about the flight, but he only grumbled, without taking the cigar out of his mouth, "Was it really necessary?"

A fortnight later, he went to the Stockholm railway station to meet his mother. When Mama saw her son, she burst into tears and sobbed that it had been so terrible. She wanted to talk about the hospital, fru Hansen, the hayloft, the student, the fishing boat, the crossing, the claustrophobia, Helsingborg, the refugee camp, but Tobias stopped her: "Never mind all that, we'll talk about it later. Your hat isn't on straight."

*

War broke out between Katze and Glenda in October 1943. Katze didn't understand how their relationship had deteriorated so much, but it did increasingly irritate her that Glenda gave her no credit for her work running Tobias' fuel firm, Vulkan Co. Ltd.

As time passed, Katze became a veritable Terror of the Accounts Department. Finding errors, to her, was life and death. She could spend days going through columns of figures the gentlemen had miscalculated. It was always Katze who found mistakes, Katze who ensured that everything added up in the end. But to her great chagrin, Katze's efforts never made any impression on Glenda, who had lovers and who went regularly to St Luke's Clinic, wearing a pale pink chiffon night-gown, mascara, rouge and hair curlers. Curettage, stillbirths, abortions, bacteria, inflammation – all of these were par for the course in Glenda's dissolute life. Afterwards she would recuperate at Store Kro, the country hotel.

Glenda's attitude to Katze's redemption, cross and martyrdom – her work – was, "Why does she bother?" Glenda had secured herself Buller, a fat, bald man who provided her with a high standard of living in Stockholmsgade. He was only interested in the stock market, coal and cigars and couldn't care less how his wife amused herself as long as she organised lavish cold buffets and card games, fun and entertainment at home. In which role, Glenda was never idle. She knew how everyone liked their roast beef; she knew how to get meat in Dronningegården and cakes in Østerbrogade. Katze called her "the cook" – the most scornful term of abuse she could devise.

Katze didn't learn how to cook until the Occupation, because she had had Marie. But now she only had her three days a week. Marie had to look after her husband as well. He worked at the sugar factory where both the first and second foremen were disciplinarians. Katze felt she was becoming quite handy in the kitchen, but it was still degrading. How naive women were to believe that beauty made them attractive! Katze had seen through that ruse long ago. She knew quite well why Glenda was so popular with the opposite sex. It was simply because she was, to put it bluntly, a cook and a tart.

Katze had of late become unreliable in the social sphere. She stopped going out in the evening, claiming that she had to wake up early to go to the office. If she did go out, because of the blackout and curfew she was obliged to sleep at Glenda's and the next day she would inevitably have a headache. That was no good when she had to be reliable in the matter of figures. Glenda found a new lover called Birger, and she, graceful as a cow, wanted Katze to admire her sex appeal! Instead she earned Katze's disgust: "Women's tomfoolery!"

Katze wanted to be admired for managing for herself and earning money for the rent, but that achievement left Glenda cold. She had always admired Katze for her sex appeal, but now she scoffed at her as a drudge. A chance remark led to the outbreak of war. Between bids at the bridge table, Glenda let slip a comment about Katze being a rotten mother. Katze rose from the table and left.

For a long time, Tobias wrote to Katze at Glenda's, but, with this dispute raging, Glenda didn't dare accept the letters that showed his return address, and Katze had no wish to collect her mail from Sweden if it entailed going to Glenda's. And when she or Li did go to Stockholmsgade to fetch their letters, Glenda could never find them.

Katze did miss Glenda, and that was probably why she chose to write to Tobias in Glenda's name. Given the censorship in occupied Denmark, one had to write under pseudonyms. Sometimes she wrote as Li Theisner, her daughter's married name. It grew hard to distinguish between mother and daughter. To make it difficult for the enemy to pinpoint the family's location, everyone had a new name. Balder was Peter, Titta was Anna, Otto was Axel, Rebekka was Trille, the wife of her father Tobias, who had now taken the name of Max's son Henry, Captain Henry Wiinblad.

> 18/10/43 Met Henry Wiinblad the other day, he would like a word from you. Send him a greeting at his apartment. The address is the old one: Bellmansgatan 22 B.

Captain Wiinblad wrote that he would very much like to be there to celebrate her birthday on October 30th with a bottle of bubbly and one of burgundy, but he doubted if he could get home on that day. So he sent her silk stockings and lingerie – plain and elegant, just to Katze's taste. She would wear them on the day they met again . . .

Katze told Captain Wiinblad that her husband and son both had their shirts with collars attached, and that she herself still had some with loose collars. The war raged over the heads of all those who fought to save their collars.

"Unfortunately it is quite right about Mama's cousin" meant Theresienstadt.

Most of the letters were marked with the censor's discreet pastel-coloured calligraphy in pale blue or eggshell yellow. On the back of the envelope, the censor stuck a strip in German:

KONTROLLIERT. Or even KONTROLLERET if it was something the Danes had conceived themselves.

In fact the Danes were obliged to hatch many new tactics. All those who changed their identity during the war had to invent fictitious lives as well. "If Uncle Lauritz comes, tell him to bring warm clothes, for it is much colder here than in Copenhagen," Captain Wiinblad wrote. They fled in light clothes and felt the cold in October; it was freezing in Stockholm. Luckily, Katze's friend, Elle – the one with a flower between her legs – was married to a real captain who arranged for the shipment of goods. Katze packed suitcases for six people. Aunt Titta's list became famous. In addition to ski trousers, she wanted "the cerise-coloured party shoes" and a matching suede handbag. "My Schiaparelli evening dress, the black one with a stole with gold embroidery." Tobias wanted razor blades most of all – there weren't any in Sweden. He also asked for 14 ties, 19 pairs of socks, five of silk pyjamas, two evening shirts and a dinner jacket. Katze refused to send the jacket: "I want to keep a bit of you at home." That turned out to be a sensible decision because either the clothes turned musty while they were in damp suitcases waiting for a ship, or they were stolen. Katze was particularly annoyed that two pairs of Rebekka's new shoes from Peter Sørensen had mysteriously vanished. People had become so unreliable.

The censor could not have failed to realise that, in October and November, many Danes in Sweden wrote for winter clothes to be sent! In this instance, he politely contented himself with covering the notepaper with his pale calligraphic marks. As time passed, people developed an ironical relationship with the censor: "Well, I had better stop now, we don't want to exhaust the censor," Trille wrote. A certain style emerged where it was no longer possible to distinguish between political censorship and emotional self-censorship, between authority and repression.

Tobias couldn't conceal his longing for Glenda's cooking. To understand his torments, it is important to remember the First Commandment in the Løvins' Bible, which concerns beef, bridge and burgundy: thou shalt not drink milk. According to the culinary bible, it was permissible to put cream in sauces – the more the better, and to mix mother's milk and blood. But one must always use cream, not milk. In Stockholm, however, Tobias had to put up with potato cutlets with runner beans in milk sauce.

A Løvin demanded no more than that the food should resemble that served by the cook at Rosenvænget. Mama asked only for a soft-boiled egg for lunch, for that was what she had always had. She loved her daily egg so much, but now she could get only one a month.

Tobias reported that some of his friends had been to a sanatorium to get slim. He couldn't understand why because, in times like these, weight loss was inevitable, voluntary or not. When Katze heard Tobias was getting thinner and thinner, she wept and warned him: if he didn't eat, he would fall ill. Katze lived for the day when she and her husband would be together again. If Tobias didn't go on living, Katze didn't want to either.

*

As early as October 19th, shortly after his arrival, Tobias occupied himself. He wrote to Kruse, the minister at the Danish legation, offering his skills in the organisation of Danish refugees. He pointed out that he was familiar with the refugee situation and that he had helped to evacuate the Danes from Lithuania. If the office preferred younger workers, he could propose his son and daughter – both students of modern languages.

There was no reply to his letter. So, for the time being, he had to settle for helping his wife keep the fuel firm in Copenhagen alive, which was a difficult task since there were no longer any goods in circulation. Enquiries and orders were huge, people were crying out for charcoal, but Katze couldn't even get enough for her own family to live on because all the charcoal was sold on the black market for 2.50 kroner a kilo. She couldn't advertise: with a whole family of refugees, she had to keep a low profile.

Katze always wrote about the business. She talked mostly about figures. Glenda, on the other hand, often gossiped in letters to Tobias about his wife. In October 1943 Katze replied under Glenda's name:

> Then there's Glenda. She has sown her gall and wormwood and sent it to you. I went to the St Luke's Clinic several times with flowers. First she kisses one man, and then along comes another one. What flirting! I certainly felt her insolence, and Birger's too. I have heard about all the low things you claim I've done. I've clearly been weighed and found wanting, so I

won't ring any more. I'm not even curious enough to want to know what the rumours are. When allegation confronts allegation, there's nothing to be done. I withdraw. She started to insult me brutally, so I left. Her husband was not at home, only that nitwit Birger. You're right, I am certainly not jealous, but she has completely forgotten that it was *she* who insulted *me*. Of course, it's a wise general who takes the war into the enemy's camp, isn't that how it goes? It hurts me a lot and I miss her badly, but I've gone on my knees several times now and have long since drawn a line through her insulting words. As Knud Rasmussen writes in his *Diary from Greenland*, only great souls can forgive. Obviously, she cannot forgive me for expressing my opinion on the triangle to Buller when he came to fetch tobacco from us and sat there pumping my daughter and me. After all, even though he is as dim as a brick, he still cares if we thought his wife slept with the other man or not. We said we didn't believe she did, but still felt that he, her husband, had been made a laughing stock. That is what she apparently finds insulting. I am very lonely, but I must be resigned, just as you must be. It is so sad we cannot patch up these troubles. By living abroad for many years, we've acquired different mentalities. People at home are so trivial and get offended at the least thing.

My darling, take care of yourself and God bless you – Your Glenda.

On October 26th, 1943, Li and Jas got married. She wrote to her father that, thanks to Gaus, the wedding had been splendid. He had arranged everything. Katze too, quite uncharacteristically, was thrilled with Gaus because he had bought the carpet for 8,000 kroner, paid Tobias' tax and refurbished Mama, Titta and Otto's apartments.

Jas was hardly even acknowledged, as if he was a slightly inconvenient adjunct to the wedding. Some might have thought that Li couldn't wait to get married because when the organ played "The Blessed Day", the eager bride joined in. Everyone in church looked at her in astonishment, and she grew quite red in the face when she realised it was only the prelude. "It was jolly embarrassing," Li wrote to her father. Afterwards they had lunch at Sundholmsvej. Katze's account said that it was all as she had imagined: tiny flat, the father awful, the mother better, the sister not too nice, her husband – a Nyborg – a higher class.

Thus Jas was allotted his place in the pecking order – and so was Liane's marriage. Despite the fact that they all lived together, Katze took absolutely no interest in her daughter's new status. "Now we're at home. Put your feet up. Like a drink?"

Tobias showed a bit more enthusiasm than his wife. "Dear little Mrs T., how do you like being married?" he asked on November 1st, 1943. "Do you find it a heavy and crushing responsibility to look after house and home, darn Jas' socks and be sweet, affectionate and cheerful when he returns after a strenuous day? Well, it will no doubt be fine, and the beginning won't be as difficult for you as for others for I understand you are staying with your mother. That will lighten the rent, housework and other tiresome duties.

Balder wished them luck as well and warned her not to be unfaithful for the first month.

Later on, Katze had trouble with her siblings, chiefly Musse, because they had not been invited to the wedding. Musse – fru Communist – harangued her on the telephone on topics ranging from Balder's conception by a Jew to Katze's enthusiasm for Hitler. Musse sank so low that, for once, instead of crying, Katze laughed.

13

DREAMS

Katze thought she was lucky not to have lived in the old days, back when the seams in the bridal sheet always had to be inspected. Katze protected herself behind the sacred peace of private life – the revolutionary discovery of the bourgeoisie. There she could speculate on whether Li was thriving in the state of holy matrimony; there she could have her drink alone when she returned from the office.

Li went to bed at eight o'clock every night. The blackouts suited her to a T. They were not so agreeable for her husband, who liked to sit in Tobias' chair until late at night. This habit irritated Katze indescribably. She had to stop herself from fussing and remind herself that the name Theisner on the front door protected Gammel Mønt 14.

Katze wasn't afraid of the Germans. "If they were all of a sudden standing here in the middle of the room," she would say, she'd give them such a piece of her mind, just as their mother would have done. How dare they soil her precious carpets with those filthy boots! Future generations all recounted this story of how Katze proposed to deal with the occupying forces.

Jas was studying for admission to the Niels Brock Business School and had decided to take the exam a year early to be able to provide for his wife. How honourable of him! The harmonica school he had been running only generated pocket money. Li had a new job with Gamborg, the barrister, where she earned 250 kroner. Which was good – 25 more than Jas earned.

Li promised to ask Gaus to help find Jas a job. Gaus, the sly little man, looked into Liane's yellow eyes, stretched out his hands to her shoulder-length amber-coloured hair and told her that Jas could look after a radio firm he had in Ryesgade. He pulled up the skirt of Li's tartan suit and, one day as he walked past the radio firm, took a 50 kroner note from his wallet and gave it to Jas.

It was none of Katze's business if Li always went to bed without Jas, though of course it wasn't easy to be the third party in a newlywed relationship. Katze's own marriage had also been a routine matter. There had been three – yes, three – happy days in Hareskoven. After that, there had been only shame, jealousy and disaster. Remembering the endless tears that Li had cried before her wedding, Katze couldn't cope with book-keeping and rising at 7.30 for work. It was no use involving oneself in women's troubles in hard times.

It was icy cold in the apartment because they had no heating. Li would have liked to listen to Jas playing. It cheered her up when he, like Teddy Wilson, ran up the scale in chromatic tenths. It set the blood flowing. But as soon as he sat down at the piano, the stockbroker from the floor below knocked angrily and threatened to complain about Jas living illegally at fru Løvin's.

On Christmas Eve of 1943, Katze considered – for a change – inviting KIS, who was always treating her to delicacies, real red wine and chicken with mushrooms. She gave up the idea at once, however, because she knew how furious Li would be. Liane – whom Katze believed to be gentle, modest and dutiful to the point of self-annihilation – would go berserk at the sight of KIS.

Tobias wrote: "Enjoy the goose with a bottle of burgundy, the apple cake with a vintage port 1906 and afterwards a real cognac. Then you'll be happy. Your devoted Henry."

Li missed her siblings and above all her father and promised that she would sit with her feet under the table only if they would come back. Gammel Mønt was so cold and lonely; particularly with Christmas coming. She dreamed of Tobias' table decorations: the Christmas before, he had spread a dark blue tablecloth like the gates of heaven. Tobias had sprinkled golden stars over the cloth and made an arrangement on it of apples with red ribbons. Now all they could look forward to was the company of Aunt Mudde – the one who embroidered for Magasin for 1.10 kroner an hour. She had recently come to see them with KIS, and Katze was speechless. Spinsters really were incorrigible: they never went home! They loved making other people wait on them hand and foot, as if life itself owed them something. Mudde sat there long past midnight, blind and deaf to the fact that the carriage had long since turned back into a pumpkin.

Li suggested that her mother invite Aunt Angelika, the Swedish countess with the see-through night-gown, the wide hats and the five divorces. Katze had always been scandalised and fascinated by her friend – she had once deserted her small child to spend six months with a lover with syphilis! Katze thought that deserting her children was the worst thing a woman could do, but it thrilled her to be in the presence of purely criminal behaviour. In her time, Katze had been drawn to Angelika and her famous night-gown. But now that Angelika had a rich new husband in tow, her sixth, Katze could do without her old friend.

The butcher adored Katze so much that he took the liberty of ringing her at the office and inviting her out for lobster. But there had to be limits! Katze wouldn't sacrifice herself on "the altar of the flesh" and preferred to go on surviving as a nun. Going to bed early was in her opinion both healthy and virtuous. Economical, too!

When one spends all leisure time in bed, sleeping problems are inevitable. Katze and Li both suffered from insomnia. They met one of Rebekka's student friends, a girl nicknamed the Mole – a daughter of the landed gentry with a moss-green, tailor-made suit and eyes like pebbles – in the faculty of medicine. She was madly in love with Jas. Katze though there was too much hanky-panky going on between them, but Li couldn't have cared less. As long as she had her pills. Sleeping pills at night, and the new ones in the morning, "Holiday tablets".

*

Gammel Mønt practically became a sepulchre during the war, but on the other side of the Sound, the refugees led a very different existence. Even though they lived in rooms with no access to a kitchen – only an electric ring – their mood was one of disciplined optimism. "You have to make the best of it," Georg Brandes, the critic, had once said, and Tobias agreed. Rebekka, who was never short of words when she wanted to describe the Løvins' special art of living, compared refugee life to a scene from *French without Tears*, in which Tobias alias Henry, and Titta alias Anna, and Otto alias Axel and Balder alias Peter and Rebekka alias Trille were queuing in their pyjamas for the one bathroom.

They comforted themselves with card games, little dinners – and not least the cinema. It was not by chance that Rebekka, who lay on the sofa dreaming, saw their communal life as scenes from a film. She was persuaded that a Løvin was self-reliant, capable of coping with any situation given a pile of newspapers, some chocolate and her feet up, preferably with a dog beside them. She had just had a cast taken off her arms and legs following a fall on the icy pavement as she walked from the cinema after seeing *The Awful Truth* for the fifth time.

Refugees always go to the cinema. In wartime, the cinema becomes a privileged space, the fascinating darkness in which fear and despair, hope and passionate yearning are assuaged in the imagination. But it is also a stimulus, a tension, or relaxation – in the body. "What else do you need in life besides the cinema?" Rebekka secretly wondered. She answered her own question: "A little dog!" She shared these two passions with her father. He also gave her a bottle of L'Heure bleue.

Tobias saw *Gone with the Wind* three times. He felt that it perfectly mirrored his own situation: it described a time when everything had been lost. He identified with Clark Gable and said with him: "What a pity we always loved at the wrong times."

Bekka proved to be the mainstay of the family group. She assured her mother that Tobias hadn't contacted either Madge, Mausie, Malene or Maj-Lis, and swore that the last was quite unattractive and boring. Katze wasn't at all mollified: why must Maj-Lis accompany him wherever he went? Must he always have someone by his side who adored him? Every night she dreamed terrible dramas of jealousy and Tobias thanked her for dreaming about him. He swore to her that he was not going to marry Madge, Mausie, Malene or Maj-Lis. He did admit to having an innocent flirtation with Maj-Lis, and thanked Katze for the ten razor blades she had enclosed in her envelope.

"You and your women! Be careful because it is a shame for her if (presumably) you aren't planning to marry her – KIS all over again. Just because you are lonely and needing female company doesn't make such behaviour fair. After all, she must think that the relationship is more serious than it really is – women always do," Katze wrote. She also wanted to know who Mausie fancied and asked Tobias to find out. He promised to investigate. "Like most women, she has no inhibitions about love," he added ironically, well aware that this was an insulting remark. Katze pounced several times to make Tobias report on what *really* went on. What about the divorced Eugenie?

Tobias replied that Katze needn't fear Eugenie; she was at least 36 or 37. She was sweet but definitely unattractive, and neither one of them had considered a relationship with the other. Just because they went to the cinema together did not mean that they slept together. Besides, hadn't Katze herself judged it perfectly respectable to go to parks, cafés, and even to the Hotel d'Angleterre when one's husband was abroad? "The company of widows, divorcees or spinsters cannot make me as happy as a letter from you. Yours and only yours – Henry."

Katze wrote to her youngest daughter: "One of the pictures of you is lovely – the one where you are standing . . ." To which Rebekka asked herself: Wasn't I lovely in the other pictures? Why am I lovely in one and not in the other? Does my beauty depend on the setting? Am I not lovely at all?

While Katze had transfused the magic she called sex appeal – without which life was worthless – into Li, she had not succeeded in teaching either daughter what it meant to be a woman: to embrace one's womanliness securely and strongly, and demand satisfaction from a man. Li had the makings of a seducer: one who delights others without understanding why. Rebekka, on the other hand, had a passion for books, films, dogs, and music. She also shared an enthusiasm for the anonymous captain whom Liane wrote about to her sister. The captain in question had just arrived at Marienlyst Hotel and said to the porter: "Can you get hold of a tall, blonde, slim young lady for me?" The porter replied: "Excuse me, sir, this is not a brothel but a hotel." After that, the captain announced that he needed 25 slices of rye bread, which must not be included in the bill, because they were for the birds. *He* was a personality.

Whenever Rebekka met a man, the first thing she did was get hold of his family tree. "They have a van Dyke," she wrote to her mother. It was code. "Sweet and cultivated" was another code;

that meant that the man in question was not one of the unspeakably ghastly people, people who didn't read books and knew nothing about music. Rebekka always referred to the cook in Riga and her recipe for *boeuf stroganoff*. She compared herself to the Russian aristocrats who drove taxis in Paris: "When you have once known 'the good life', you can live like a church mouse. It's worse for those who have never known it."

She was preoccupied with hairstyles and coats, but she alternated enthusiastically between fashions. There were "right" and "wrong" designs. In the summer, she plaited her hair into two little whips that made her look quite mad. As she got older, she opted for the "safe" styles: a "good" cardigan, a "decent" skirt.

All that goodness covered a state of painful confusion. Instead of focusing her desires on one concrete goal, she craved total knowledge. This had quite a wearing effect on others; people felt forever exhorted or corrected. The blind must learn to see, the deaf to hear and the lame to perform gymnastics. It was the messianic strain in Rebekka. She ordered Katze to read D.H. Lawrence's *Pansies* and Rosamond Lehmann's *Dusty Answer*. It wasn't enough for Bekka that Katze read them; she must like them as well. She also instructed Katze to take a new, fabulously beneficial medication called Samarin. Everything was either "immeasurably brilliant" or "excruciatingly awful". Only Tobias was able to counteract Rebekka's forceful opinions with his dry humour and make her feel secure enough to quieten down.

Katze was jealous. Everyone of importance had moved to the other side of the Sound. She admitted that she didn't have it in her to pack up the house and move; in any case, she was much better off than Tobias in his rented room with hot plates. Her quarters at Gammel Mønt were delightful, but she had no idea how to animate them.

And then the worst happened. Katze had been afraid of it for a long time: the house became infested by bugs. One night after midnight, Li came into her mother's room weeping and told her they had just killed two big bugs. So now all the windows had to be sealed and the whole apartment fumigated! That was a nice thing: to get bugs in Royal Copenhagen in 1944! Gammel Mønt was their refuge, where they rested after the toils of the day, and now they hardly dared go to bed!

Tobias felt sorry for the "poor little thing" who seemed to be pursued and attacked by bugs all over the world. He recalled a certain young lady who, when she lived in Riga, always said: "People in Copenhagen are lucky, where nothing of that sort is ever seen."

After her falling out with Glenda, Katze lost the last spark of life. At least it was warm in Glenda's apartment in Stockholmsgade during the Occupation. Of course it was – Glenda knew how to stoke up! She could survive the blackout by giving parties. That social parrot couldn't understand that Katze had to stay at the office until four o'clock. Her bird brain and weak character couldn't process the word "duty", the meaning of "in earnest" or the purpose of working for a cause. Having a good time – that was all fru Fonnesbeck understood. Her lover was furious that Katze had remarked how soft Buller was to let the two of them take turns to kiss his spouse. Still, Katze was sorry to have lost Glenda because she had at least been fun. Until she fell into her present state, that is. When the three of them sat glaring at each other, with Katze as chaperone, it didn't make for a good atmosphere. Katze would not let herself get involved in that triangle or be forced to think or speak ill. The world was bad enough at the moment, so you had to get rid of the evil in your own heart.

For Glenda's birthday, she was offended because Katze wore a short dress. But, considering her own attire – Glenda had dressed as the goddess of love and wore a new white gown representing the flower of purity – how *could* she be upset? By Katze's standards Glenda looked ridiculous. Even more irksome was the fact that Glenda had lost ten pounds – probably from running between two men. In Katze's eyes, Glenda was merely falling victim to an idiotic female game.

Katze felt that during the Occupation her old friends lived in the past. They talked of nothing but clothes and servants. As a self-supporting woman, Katze thought only of work, money, and sleep. Should she start selling pinecones because of the shortage of charcoal? When would the bank stop giving credit? Could she have another little drink, please? In her heart lurked the horrible consciousness that the world had no respect whatsoever for a single working woman, and that everyone just wanted to cheat her. Her male colleagues turned out to be undependable and lazy. They took baths or went to the dentist in working hours, borrowed money from the petty cash and paid no heed at all to Katze's reprimands. She could cope with the everyday business herself, but when the men were gone and she was obliged to ring Jutland to rush deliveries, nothing happened. Her voice had as little authority as a child's. Tobias had suggested that the male members of staff move into an adjoining room so that Katze could take over his office and sit in his chair. But that would not make any difference – especially since Glenda had told Gaus' wife that Katze hadn't the faintest idea how to run a business. That was what that vampire had said – she whose only talent was drinking liqueurs, lying on a sofa and winding her fat, silk-stockinged legs onto her lover's lap. Morals were pretty loose in the family at Stockholmsgade. But in spite of everything, Katze missed her.

From the other side of the Sound, Tobias tried to mediate without taking sides. It had to be said that Glenda was both amusing and hospitable. "So give her leave to be false, rude and amorous on the side." It wasn't necessary to be too critical of someone's behaviour just because they were a friend, albeit hard to understand how a woman married to such a delightful man could fall in love with anyone else and go off with them to the Schwarz, the Rome, the Adlon, or the Hotel d'Angleterre.

This was hardly courteous. Neither Tobias' mediation nor his attempt to comfort Katze succeeded. In Katze's eyes, every Dane was downright rotten. Danish men lacked courtesy; they didn't even bother walking a lady home after dinner. Katze was sick to death of living in a country without *gentlemen* – it was in fact the Germans, in spite of everything, who were the most polite – and of riding in a tram with her evening gown tucked up under her fur coat. Anxious about her morale, Tobias still tried to cheer up his old wife.

You must – and shall – tell me everything that upsets you. But you must also try to stop being upset and avoid getting bitter (sometimes it's hard). I talked to Trille about it for a long time recently. She knew a very fine word for it in Latin, which of course I have since forgotten. It was the opposite of *dementia praecox*, something like *melancholyitis* – meaning it could develop into a real nerve sickness, even insanity. If one has a tendency to melancholy and pessimism, one must do all one can to suppress it. Think of Aunt Olga.

Katze thought of her beloved cousin who had died of Spanish flu, and of her mother's Aunt Olga, who had given Katze money for her trousseau and then ended up in St John's Mental Hospital. Apart from her children, they were the only two people she had ever cared for.

Those who care for you, and I who love you, would hate to see you growing old, ill and bitter when you are still in your best years and have a long and happy life before you. Try to imagine that you are in love – maybe even with me! You know that makes you happy and beautiful. Don't say no five or eight times to Tom, Dick or Harry. Say yes. Go out and be merry. Be glad they want to see you – make them happy in return. You'll certainly regret it if, one day, you find yourself left with only Li and Jas, Vanessa and Marie. Invite some people, light the candles – stay up late! Uncork the bottles; let the burgundy flow and the smile – that vital smile – beam. My sweet darling, do you understand what I mean? I don't want to dismiss your criticisms, but do try to put them at the back of your mind, separate from your delight in the goodness that, despite everything, still exists in most people. I don't know anyone who can be so wonderfully sweet, charming, beautiful as you are – when you are happy and in love (even when it is with other people!). So get out your happy smile, then the "Danish" men, too – to use your own expression (which I actually can't bear) – will take you home. But above all: stop staying home every night with Li and Jas. As Trille said, it's bad for two pessimists to live together, especially with a man who irritates them both. (All my sympathy is with Jas, whom I greatly admire. Neither of you two girls are the light sort, by which I mean – now don't be cross – cheerful, happy, carefree.)

Go out – to the Royal Theatre – invite your friends. Put on the nice lingerie, a beautiful dress, have dry martini and a cosy little dinner with bridge or dancing. You will gradually come to enjoy life – until we meet again. As for the battle with the dragon Glenda: forget it. Don't get cross and don't bother to please me or the others – I'm solidly with you. If you don't want to be friends with her, then don't be. Full stop. I would absolutely NOT humble yourself by accosting her in the street. No-one is perfect, but even if you can be sharp you are worth a million Glendas, so just behave as if nothing has happened if you do meet her. Take it easy, my darling; life *is* good, after all. Now I must go, I must take the newspapers to Mama. She is so fond of you and asks after you often.

Kisses from your own Henry – and for my little Gazelle too.

Each time Tobias tried to cheer Katze up, she found some financial grounds for misery. Happiness was just not possible. Tobias was earning nothing, Katze was keeping the family finances going. She had initially worked only in the mornings, but her day gradually stretched to four o'clock, and now she often stayed at the office until far into the evenings. Tobias persistently urged her to take it easy or there would be nothing left of her when they next met. In his heart, he had a hunch that her inhibitions about love had turned into self-torture and punishment. She would beat herself with stinging nettles until she dropped, and afterwards she would demand rewards from God that no human could give her.

Then Tobias remembered some gold teeth in his desk drawer at Gammel Mønt. He told Katze to sell them and, with the proceeds, to buy tickets for the Hornbæk Cabaret so that she and the children could enjoy "an intellectual injection". Katze replied that she had already sold them to buy dishcloths. As if she alone commanded all the troops in Europe, she battled savagely with the columns of book-keeping. She needed 675 kroner to balance the accounts. Last month, when she discovered where the error was, Katze was beside herself with joy.

Tobias' attitude was: Who cares if the firm goes bankrupt? Then she could come and join him, and they could all have a good time! He didn't take into account how they would survive financially, of course.

Those who arrived in Sweden with Danish kroner fared well, whereas those who had brought sterling or dollars had to seek work at once because the banks refused to exchange their money. During the war, Sweden had bound its currency to the Deutschmark, and pounds sterling and dollars were worth virtually nothing. Without a trade, however, it was hard to find employment; there were openings only for skilled workers. Aunt Titta managed to secure a post as governess to a Hungarian diplomatic family; Uncle Otto found a job with a newspaper; and Balder joined a jazz record company. In spite of his aversion to bathing, Balder still managed four or five girlfriends in six months, proof of his irresistible charm.

Rebekka was employed at a laboratory – unfortunately, even wearing insoles, she could not manage a job that kept her on her feet all day – and was looking forward to studying medicine at Uppsala University. Rebekka had decided to study medicine because doctors were at the top of her list of human hierarchy. A doctor can say to the Pope, "You must have an operation next week." A doctor can say to a bishop, "You must stay in bed for a fortnight." A doctor can say to a general, "We won't operate until you are sober."

The only one who hadn't found work was Tobias himself. He considered producing harmonica cases that had long been obtainable, or selling everything from pencil boxes to sky-scrapers or manufacturing some new chemical product. "Could you think of living in Sweden after the war?" Katze did not reply.

On April 13th, 1944, he made one last attempt to be provocative. He wrote to Professor Stephan Hurvitz, chief of the refugee office in Stockholm, after the professor had promised to remember Tobias should he need to expand his staff. Tobias thanked him for the kind reception: "On the way home, an American proverb popped into my head: 'If there isn't any opportunity, make one yourself.' Then I wondered if you have what we would call in my old firm an 'assistant general manager'. I am – forgive me – so immodest as to recommend myself for that post, which as far as I know doesn't yet exist at the Refugee Office. From our conversation yesterday, I understood that parts of my career were familiar to you." Tobias described his career in an international organisation that had made him fully conversant with financial and administrative work, and how he had build up a profitable business in severely impoverished countries. He had visited New York, London, Paris, Hamburg, Moscow, etc. on business. "I am convinced that as your deputy, I could be extremely useful to you. If the plan appeals to you, could I come round one day to discuss it? Yours faithfully, Tobias Løvin." There was never an answer to his letter.

That was the last time Tobias applied for a job. Soon after that he got his fourth thrombosis. Then Rebekka's legs started to swell. She too had to tolerate loathsome massages and thick bandages on both legs from ankle to knee, then gauze bandages and finally five metres of elastic ones from toe to knee. She wore long trousers, but couldn't bear to think of how she would manage in the summer. No chance now of resembling Marlene Dietrich.

In addition to the bandages, Tobias had to put up with sharing a room with Ib, who had come to visit them. Ib was the bastard son of Aunt Titta. She had given birth to him while she was waiting for Otto to marry her. When he had finally caved in and their delightful life together became a reality, Ib reappeared.

He was a talented boy with velvet eyes, but when his father left for America there wasn't a soul to look after him. It was only natural for his mother to take him in – into her new marriage. Once he became part of the family, Ib upset the apple cart: there could only be one male in that household. Otto did all he could to drive Titta's son – Tittus, he called him – up the wall and make the boy's life a misery. Otto and Titta enjoyed society, and every evening they dragged Tittus to parties. He did his homework beneath a shower of bids in poker, bridge, seven and racing demon, and he slept on any old divan, breathing in cigar smoke and brandy fumes.

It was a real deliverance for Ib to be sent to boarding school at Sorø, where smoking was banned. In October 1943, when Aunt Titta grabbed the first place to cross the Sound, she forgot her son, obliging him to arrange his own escape from Denmark. The boy found safety with a kind family in Sweden. Now governess to a spoiled Hungarian diplomat's son, Titta was always terribly glad to see Ib – as long as he didn't get under Otto's feet. Aunt Titta wrote to Li that her husband didn't understand how Ib could have grown into such a sensible boy, but perhaps it was because he had had to fend for himself. He had won a prize for an essay about a skiing trip he had taken with his mother, and it had been read aloud in the school. A fortnight before, he had taken the Swedish Boy Scout's oath and declared that he hated the town and loved nature.

It was a somewhat strange experience for Tobias to have to share a room with a Boy Scout, particularly when he had to deal with 14 metres of tight bandage on both legs. Tobias had seen two doctors. When one told him to leave off his cigars, Tobias decided that he preferred the other one. He was convinced that if he stopped smoking he would become even sicker. Otherwise he did not make much fuss about his thrombosis because Katze fussed enough for both of them.

2/3-44. My dearest, was it the right or the left leg, and where did the thrombosis go? I had a presentiment that something was wrong with you. Oh, my darling, why did this have to happen? You *must* and *shall* get better – if you die I don't want to go on living. You must do exactly what the doctors say. I do understand how terrible it is for you not to smoke, but let's hope that you will be able to start again soon.

Here the all-important news – no, it really is exciting – is that Jas' wife is expecting a baby. I am sharing the young people's great joy and optimism. Everything is so difficult, I don't know where all they need will come from, but if only you get better, we'll manage. I do believe what Bunty says: "If a little child comes into a family, happiness will come with it."

14

THE CHILD

On a certain night Tobias fastened his pearl tiepin to the cloth on his bedside table as he always did. The next morning, the maid shook the cloth out of the window and the pearl was gone. Tobias laid siege to the lost property office, placed advertisements – nothing, nothing, nothing. It was terribly upsetting because Papa had given it to him. Instead of apologising or being sorry, the girl scolded him and said he should be glad it had not happened before. Tobias said, "You're quite right. Thank you so much for not throwing it out sooner."

March 30th, 1944, marked the silver wedding anniversary of Tobias and Katze. Tobias urged Katze to visit him in Stockholm to celebrate the occasion. He begged her to use her imagination as a businesswoman to convince the authorities to issue her a visa. Katze herself was more of an obstacle than the authorities, however, because she felt that it was impossible to leave the business unsupervised. Moreover, while she could obtain a visa for leaving the country, it was not at all certain that she would get permission to come back to Denmark again. Tobias, who had lived for several years without his wife, wondered if he still knew her. He certainly remembered her well enough to recall that Katze was as hard as stone. Once it became clear that she would not go to Stockholm, they continued their correspondence as if nothing had happened. There was one strange incident – Tobias ran into Dietlof von Sachensollen in a cinema. Just as the film started, he felt a vague unpleasantness in the air. He turned, and directly behind him sat . . . Katze had three guesses. There were ten vacant seats on Tobias' right, so it was a miracle that the monocled man and his wife had not sat themselves directly next to him. Now they reigned, alone, in the twentieth row. Other than the man's grunting to alert his wife to Tobias' presence, they did not say a word to each other during the entire film. After the performance, he and they left by opposite doors without acknowledging each other. The monocled man was clearly ravaged and miserable. That was probably not news to Katze. Didn't she see him regularly when he visited Copenhagen? If she was not too busy with the fur trapper?

For the silver wedding day, Tobias wrote:

How time flies, and how faithful I have been in fact! I think it was the Lubitsch that I saw, *Heaven Can Wait*, the movie that convinced me what an angel I am. Have I told you the plot?

A man dies and automatically goes to Hell. He is not expected and thus has to recount his life story. He thinks he can do his best by describing the women he has known , from the nanny, to young beauties, to his wife, to the nurse on his deathbed. In spite of frequent minor flings, he has always loved his wife and has never made any of these women unhappy. When the elevator comes to fetch him, His Excellency says: "Going up! Such a delightful person must of course go to Heaven!"

It is a really enchanting film that you would appreciate as well. Men in particular like it because they all think that it is a picture of their own life. They all feel – as I do – that we are angels! But alas, it is only a film. Reality is quite different. There we are, egoistic beasts and you are the sweet little angels! I must say I admire you for putting up with me for so long. Has Nimb closed or does Wivex still exist over there? If I were at home, I should certainly enjoy a quiet little dinner, sip a glass of Mumm (if it is still to be found), and thank you for many happy years and your unmatchable devotion to the whole family. How enchanting you were when we sat there in 1920: sweet, brilliant, happy. So much has changed since then. The world, human beings and ourselves with them.

The day will come again – soon I trust – when peace reigns, and then we shall meet and I shall tell you everything I can now only write. I shall kiss your sweet warm lips and your charming young girl's body that, despite children and illness and age, is as youthful, supple and beguiling as ever. Ask some close friends to share a bottle or two of burgundy in celebration of us and our three children. Your ever-loving Henry.

What an old ass he was to keep rambling on about the monocle and the fur trapper! If von Sachensollen had looked miserable, it was probably because he was with his wife and not his current sweetheart. For one thing was certain: he went from one woman to another in an endless cavalcade. The male sex were all alike.

But Tobias' words went to Katze's heart, and in reply she thanked him for all the rich and lovely years they had shared.

I wait only for you, my old and eternally beloved. May the day very soon come when we can drink that bottle together. Our melody has always been there, in my heart at least. I think a little noise now and then is inevitable in a long life. Only in people who never show any development can life play the same melody, and that would be monotonous. We have truly had a wonderful time together. You are right – we'll manage even if we're forced to live in one room. Wherever you are is festive. I enclose ten razor blades and do hope the censor will let them through. PS. The elastic you sent must have been lost, unless that harridan G. has pinched it. Ever, your Glenda.

It was not always Glenda who made off with the elastic, however. Sometimes the Swedish authorities felt it necessary to hold back any mail that might compromise whoever it was sent to in occupied Denmark. Around this time, Katze busied herself unravelling old blankets to knit nappies for Li's baby. How tightly the old great-grandmothers knitted! If the world had been like our great-grandmothers' knitting, no stitch would ever have been dropped. Tobias offered to send baby clothes from Sweden, if he could get a permit, and he asked for a list of all they needed at Gammel Mønt.

Katze found a yellowing photograph of Tobias as a small boy in Chicago, leaning against his mother, and put it on Li's bedside table. She should look at it long and hard during her pregnancy, Katze said, for they would all love a little boy with a sweet face like that.

Li hadn't yet felt the baby move, but every night before going to sleep she looked at the photograph of her beloved father and decided to call her little boy Michael. Rebekka, who told her sister to take plenty of cod liver oil, told Li that the name of *her* son – if she ever had one – was also to be Michael.

By a strange coincidence, Gaus' blind wife became pregnant at the same time. Aud gave birth just before Li, and it was a girl. Katze crowed about this to Tobias: "Oh, yes, I can hear you say, that's the best they can manage!" Every time Tobias heard about the birth of a girl, he would say that having daughters must be infectious.

Jas, for his part, was wild with delight over Li's condition – whatever the outcome. He loved everything small and cute – puppies, kittens or chickens – but in addition to his emotional side, Jas was also vain and socially ambitious. Now that he had produced "the heir", Jas felt that he had officially married into the Løvin family, whether he passed his Niels Brock business examination or not. He felt secure in his position now, confident that someone would certainly help him out in a tight situation, as Gaus had done.

During the summer of 1944, the fortunes of war turned. The Germans had suffered defeat on the Eastern Front and the Allies had landed in Normandy. Since 1938, the British had systematically ignored the warnings of the German resistance movement against Hitler. The Allies were not content to end the war; they had to crush the enemy. Between the summer of 1944 and the German surrender more than 4.8 million Germans lost their lives, and the massacres in the camps continued. In Denmark, a general strike was called in July. While the child grew in Li, the first concentration camps were liberated and the world fell into a state of shock. Li was "enormously inconvenienced by this child". When her legs swelled up, Katze predicted, "She will have trouble with them for the rest of her life." She was decidedly not a brood mare; she was like her father, a racehorse, impossible to order around.

Considering how difficult it was to get food, they managed well enough during the strike. Marie, the dear thing, offered them five newly fried pork chops. When she heard that Li craved strawberries, suddenly a basket of strawberries appeared on her bedside table. KIS was also sweet, trekking all the way to Gammel Mønt with her comically thin walking stick, carrying new potatoes. Li found her dreadfully irritating, but KIS had a good heart. During the strike, Katze completed all of her sewing projects. For Li, who could no longer fit into her own clothes, she made a skirt out of Aunt Mudde's old tablecloth.

As for the comical walking stick, Katze got to know it better when she agreed to go for a walk with KIS during the fine summer weather. KIS tottered at full stretch through the woods of Skodsborg, and Katze had difficulty keeping up and threw envious glances at the people sunning themselves on the grass along their way. Everyone in Denmark was relaxing in the sunshine, but Katze returned home like a corpse, ashen from over-exertion, sore in every limb.

That was no surprise to Tobias. How like his wife to go to the bitter end instead of giving up halfway and going home refreshed. Tobias told Katze that KIS was now in Sweden and that he saw her once a week. He did not say why she had travelled to Sweden.

*

The lover had apparently departed the scene, and Glenda's hair was turning grey. Marie, who also waited at table in Stockholmsgade when there were big dinner parties, passed on gossip about the Fonnesbeck family. Marie was convinced that fru Fonnesbeck missed Madam very much because the corners of fru Fonnesbeck's mouth trembled when she was talking about Madam. Though Madam was busy with her work, fru Fonnesbeck had nothing to occupy her since a certain person's disappearance. Madam must not say or do anything about it, however, for it was mere gossip. It was obvious that Glenda still hankered after Buller and invited him to dinner, but he had had enough of her and refused.

*

Another thrombosis plagued Tobias. He did not rule out the possibility that his condition was partly due to worry. Worry and cigars. Since he wouldn't abandon his cigars, he would have to eliminate as many other anxieties as possible. Glenda wrote to him suggesting that the family had managed for so long without Katze not because they didn't have time to see her, but because they didn't want to see her. It annoyed him that Glenda would call his wife beastly. Katze, with her searing candour, could be irritating, true, but she was never *beastly*.

When it finally came time to reconcile the harridans, Tobias suggested that Katze invite Glenda to her birthday party, to prove that Glenda was in need of forgiveness. This way, Katze could be the strong one, full of generosity. She had better hurry, Tobias told her, before Glenda hit upon the same idea. Imagine Glenda telling everyone: "I rang her because I felt sorry for her." Tobias told Katze that they were silly old fools, the pair of them, and Katze agreed.

In the end Marie became the mediator. She always carried greetings from Stockholmsgade to Gammel Mønt and probably added more to the messages than Glenda intended. But her loyalty was clear; Madam was not to humiliate herself, fru Fonnesbeck would soften soon enough. In October, Katze received a large birthday bouquet signed "Your old Glenda". It was not long before the arch enemies, both 44, called a truce and waltzed along Strøget arm in arm, giggling. Glenda tried to convince Katze that her lover wouldn't take no for an answer, and even though Katze didn't believe a word of it, she felt as if she could breathe again. In Glenda's company she could laugh.

One evening when only Katze and Li were at home, the doorbell rang. They weren't expecting anyone. Then there was a loud knocking and a voice barked commands in German. It took some time for Katze to realise who it was. In these times, it was a dreadful and tasteless joke. But since the Fonnesbeck family had been to a good dinner and were in high spirits, Katze couldn't be upset. Even though Katze was in her night-gown, she gave them something to drink, and they had a jolly time.

The previous day, she had been to the cinema with Glenda at four o'clock. Glenda had begged her to go, so Katze went home from the office to fetch her spectacles. They saw Selma Lagerlöf's *The Emperor of Portugal*, and Katze wept so much that her scarf was damp. Since she only went to the cinema once every 18 months, and then only to cheer herself up, there was not much point in dragging her to anything tragic. Afterwards they fooled around, as one did with Glenda. She wanted to take two lobsters home to perk up their modest dinner, but she couldn't find any, so instead they had two open sandwiches with salmon at the King Frederik, roast duck and a thin absinthe each. It cost Glenda 33 kroner – a bit more than they could afford. Then they made their way back to the cinema where Glenda had dropped a parcel containing her best stockings. She couldn't find a taxi, but finally they managed to catch a tram. They had just stepped inside Glenda's front door when the air-raid siren sounded.

*

One Wednesday afternoon in November, Li gave birth to her little boy, who turned out to be a girl. The previous evening, Katze, Jas, Vanessa and Li had walked to the clinic in Bredgade and arrived when there were ten minutes between the pains. Li was delighted, as if she was going to a ball. Katze, who had started to have pains herself and a fever, thought, "Poor little thing, she doesn't know what she's in for." Katze was right; the birth took almost a day. Li was given laughing gas and vomited the whole time. When the child was finally born, it was asleep and required no help from the nurses. Li was relieved, for in giving birth – albeit to a daughter – she hoped that she was getting a substitute for her husband, someone who would stand by her in sickness and in health.

On November 21st, 1944, Li wrote to her father:

Dear Henry, Well, now there's a little basket at the foot of my bed with a sweet, ugly little mug inside, weighing 6lbs. Jas is ringing friends and acquaintances to tell them he has a daughter with long thick curls, big blue eyes with black eyelashes and a Greek profile. Unfortunately I must contradict those claims. She has three hairs on her head, and little slits in a little broad nose. But she has her grandfather's delicate, oval arched nails. I am very proud of them. She holds her hand just as her grandfather holds his cigar. Of course she is an unusually lively and intelligent child and understands everything going on around her. She had her first smack yesterday because she wouldn't suck nicely. We had our photographs taken yesterday too, I don't know when you will get the pictures, but don't you dare say she is ugly when I'm there to defend her – remember, she is only three days old. I hear from Mother that you have bought baby clothes. That's wonderful. Many thousands of kisses from Ester and Li.

Li was in the lift, going up to the third floor in Gammel Mønt. She was about to faint and had to hand over the child to Katze. Katze held the baby and told Li to breathe in, breathe out, so that she wouldn't fall. In her haste, Katze put the baby on the dining room table while she got Li into bed. It was the start of a long bed-stay with severe haemorrhaging. Li hated to be in bed, and Katze had to take charge and rush about. At this time, too, she was cross with Jas for spending too much on himself, but Li was so sensitive that she couldn't bear to hear Jas criticised. She only cheered up whenever Katze said: "Isn't it funny, I really think she's getting to look like her grandfather!"

The child was named Ester because that was what Tobias had been called as an infant. Ester soon became Zeste, purely and simply, ignorant and innocent, born in Tobias' place, like an old roué with a cigar. Katze and Li, who had grafted the picture of Tobias into the growing womb, now busied themselves finding proofs that Tobias had been reborn and they had him back in a newborn form. The proof was in the baby's eyes. Would they remain blue – like Katze's almost dead fish eyes, or would they turn brown like Tobias' – sparkling with the joy of life? Inexplicably, Li felt that if the child had blue eyes, it would be so alien from her, so unlike herself and Tobias that she would have no idea what to do with it. How would it then survive?

They spent days rummaging in old cardboard boxes at Gammel Mønt trying to find a picture of Tobias at one month, looking as if he was bidding five no trumps. The days passed making sure the eyes would behave according to their wishes. The child's eyes would be brown. It would live.

15

THE LIBERATION

"I sincerely hope the New Year will bring an end to this terrible time, although we lucky ones, of course, have no right to complain because there are millions much worse off," Tobias wrote in a New Year's letter to his wife.

Katze spent almost the entire war searching for 23 kroner in the monthly accounts. She had become like her father, whom she used to criticise for going on and on searching for a ten-øre piece in the household ledger.

When Tobias was not playing cards or at the cinema, he spent his time reading his newspapers and polishing his shoes. He had – apart from cleaning – managed quite well without domestic help. After six pairs of shoes, with a lighted cigar in his mouth and a big glass of beer on the table, he enjoyed chatting to his old lover in his regular Sunday letter. As Katze turned into an active business-woman, Tobias gradually retreated into the domestic sphere.

As a neutral capital, Stockholm became a place where people from every country passed through (so why couldn't Katze come?). Tobias heard all sorts of rumours about the fate of some. A number of them had "disappeared", as the euphemism had it.

Katze had neither pepper nor spices throughout the war. Tobias assured her that Titta had masses of pepper and Katze should take what she needed from Titta's apartment, including jars of preserves that would soon go bad. But Gaus had, of course, rented out Titta's apartment, and they wondered if they would ever get it back. Tobias wrote that for Aunt Titta's birthday they ate lobster salad and *boeuf stroganoff*. The most important element of the celebration was when Mama's relatives had "come back" and were all right. "Come back" meant from Theresienstadt.

Meanwhile, at Gammel Mønt 14, the newborn baby was christened, thanks to Gaus who acted both as godfather and benefactor. He paid for the luncheon, including taxis for the guests to and from church. Despite being christened Ester, the little one was still only called Zeste. Mama sent 100 kroner for the baby's bank account – her "trousseau", as Tobias put it. He didn't think it necessary for the baby to resemble him when she had such a charming mother and grandmother.

Katze was still suffering from pains in her abdomen and a temperature. She was unsure whether her symptoms were due to the menopause, the immoderate engagement with her daughter's pregnancy, confinement and lying-in, or from living for almost five years in an icy cold apartment.

Rumours spread to Sweden about her ill health, and Tobias besought her to go to the doctor immediately, stop working and visit him in Stockholm. But Katze, still an inflexible martyr, had no wish to be cured. She had a new excuse for being unable to go to Sweden: she couldn't leave little Zeste. Zeste was not *her* child, Tobias reminded her, so she didn't need to jump to her every squeak. In addition, he argued, Li must be allowed to enjoy her child in peace for a little while. Besides, Tobias needed looking after much more than the child. He was so old that he had to buy a special stand for his playing cards because his hands were getting shaky. But why should Katze go to Stockholm? She lived at Gammel Mønt and was tired of being ordered about.

Yet perhaps Tobias had a more serious concern than the need for love. Perhaps he was worried that, after all these years, he might not know his wife? He threatened to stop writing altogether if she didn't go to the doctor.

*

In the 1930s a new beauty philosophy had emerged: married women were urged to do their utmost to look young by using powder, rouge and lipstick – a beauty routine that had previously been reserved for courtesans. When *Marie-Claire* launched this new ideal for married women in 1937, it was met with a shower of protest letters. Women didn't want to undertake the extra burden of *having* to look young when in reality they were both old and worn out. Nevertheless the ideal triumphed. So in 1945 – when Katze was 45 – there was no excuse for the yellow circles under her eyes. As well as taking care of the office, the house, the dog, her children and grandchild, she had also to be attractive.

Katze was glad to be assured that Tobias was not doing anything crazy:

> That is certainly good, because I had such a frightful dream about you last night and wept as usual. It would be so sad if, at the last minute, you went and fell for someone, but I fervently hope that our love will weather this storm. It is much harder for a man to be faithful than for a woman – and especially me, old-fashioned about fidelity as I am. Stay well, darling, and watch out for Dora, Maj-Lis, Mausie and Madge, for I do so much want to meet you on the same wavelength once more.

Tobias turned 50 in what he hoped would be the year of the Liberation. In the last days of April and the beginning of May, he stayed glued to the radio all day long. While they waited for the Liberation, Titta and Dot had an argument. Dot was one of Uncle Hugo's countless wives, around number five. We must remember that it was no crime to get married six times and that all the wives were peroxide blondes. One of them, Vips, lay down on the balcony in her party dress and jewels and died of an overdose. Dot was a Lotte, a volunteer in the Danish Women's Army Corps. On the afternoon before the Liberation, she said to Titta: "God, you look like a washerwoman with that new hairstyle!"

That comment generated a rumpus. After dinner Dot wept, and Titta had to comfort her. Dot was upset: "Yes, I know I'm too honest. You say the same things behind people's backs."

Titta: "Explain, please!"

Dot: "You say Ib is fed up with Otto, and that Tobias doesn't want to share a room with Ib. You also said something about Katze and Tobias that I can't bring myself to repeat."

Titta: "That's a lie!"

Dot: "Are you accusing me of lying? That's it then, I'm off."

Titta: "I know quite well you are jealous of me because everyone likes me and they don't like you."

Uncle Otto had to console Aunt Dot and arrange a reconciliation. This did not much improve Aunt Titta's standing in the household.

On May 5th, 1945, they no longer had to care about the censor and could use their own names in peace.

> My own darling, This is certainly a great day, and I imagine the town is in a whirl. The only sad thing is that we haven't been able to enjoy it together. But, God willing, it can't be too long before we meet. Mama guesses 10 to 30 days, so it may be around the first of June. It will be wonderful to see you and the children and Zeste – my spitting image! A moment ago, Bekka rang, and she was equally thrilled, of course. Balder is probably already in Copenhagen with the Brigade. You've no doubt gathered from my hints that he is a volunteer in the Police Corps, who were sent home today at noon – he may already have been in contact with you. Thousands of kisses of peace to you all, your TOBIAS, no more Henry.

When on April 9th, 1940, Denmark was occupied, no-one believed that five years would pass before it ended. But now that the reign of terror was over, the champagne was put on ice and all the Danes in exile embraced for joy. The next morning, Titta woke Tobias early so that together they could hear the king's speech – and the church bells.

The refugees, preparing to come home, assumed they could move back into their apartments and reclaim their possessions. Gaus had given them such generous help when they had departed, so they assumed that they would receive similar support on their homecoming. They had left all their bankbooks and property in his care.

But something very strange had happened to Gaus. As recently as November, *Politiken* had reported an ill-starred case that involved him. Although Tobias said that the article was not so much an attack on Gaus as on the law, Katze had decided that Gaus was not one of God's little angels.

Tobias had encouraged Katze to fawn on Gaus, but he was a prima donna and required attention. Before the war, Katze had needed his help to run her business, so she treated him well so that he would help her afterwards too. But it wasn't in Katze's nature to kow-tow to anyone, least of all Gaus. Ever since October '43, when he had literally pulled her carpet out from under her feet, she had felt uneasy with him. He had given her 8,000 kroner and although Tobias said that was a good price she could have made 14,000 six months later. No, she had nothing good to say about human beings.

Tobias didn't understand the loss of all the apartments. Rumour had it that Gaus had gone underground. That was true – he was on his knees in the cellar of his villa in Ordrup, playing with his toy trains. Tobias was alarmed. Why had Gaus suddenly become so strange? Had the radio business failed? He had thought that, with Jas as his colleague, all was going so well! It would be awful if something was wrong with Gaus. How could everything suddenly be so dire? And how could Mama's new apartment in Kastelsvej disappear into thin air? Had it been let or sold outright?

Gaus was up to his ears in trouble. Li waded into it as well when, in his office, she lay on a fine featherbed of black market money. They romped together in worthless shares, with braces and trousers at their ankles, feeling cheerfully amoral in such a moralistic time. As long as Li was sleeping on his bed of paper, the Løvins had nothing to fear. For Gaus did everything she asked of him, and Li's only desire was that he should help her father and family.

On May 20th, 1945, Tobias sent a letter to the family members in Sweden, encouraging them to contribute to a gift for Editor Dedichen of *Politiken*. Thanks to him, they had got away to Sweden in time to escape the horrors. Instead of giving him a silver salver or a porcelain figurine, Tobias suggested surprising him with a parcel of the rationed goods that they had enjoyed for such a long time. Coffee, tea, tobacco, wine, sardines, chocolate. They could make themselves responsible for 20 kilos each.

This gesture was typical of Tobias: he was the only one who remembered all the important details. On the other hand, his comprehensive view sometimes failed him. He didn't, for example, acknowledge that he had used up both his own and his brother's inheritances during the war. He hadn't just failed to earn money, he had amassed debts. This discovery would horrify

Katze. It was no consolation that he was always on the brink of winning individual bridge tournaments in Stockholm, but for some idiot forever letting him down at the last moment.

Oftentimes, the unconscious, pent-up, frustrated feelings accumulated over the course of war may be translated into the currency of money, both symbolic and actual. The family didn't understand that it takes three generations to recover from a war. The question became: who owes what to whom? When the enemy had been conquered, everyone owed some distant contact a slap in the face. But as a refugee, Otto felt solidarity with his big brother. He was in Helsingborg helping Mama pack. Because she was so nervous, Mama wanted to talk about money the whole time and Otto could not avoid the subject. Was it true that Tobias had been living on her money throughout the war?

"Yes, I believe so," Otto replied.

"He should have told me," Mama said.

"He did write about it, you know. Besides, you should have expected it in advance!"

"I thought he was more or less joking," Mama said.

"It wasn't a joke."

"I thought I had been saving up."

"There's no need to worry. You can live just as you did before."

"How can I, when Tobias has spent all my money?"

*

If Tobias thought Katze was ready to share her hard-earned savings with her destitute mother-in-law, he would have to think again. The reunion between Katze and Tobias was a shock. For 19 months, Tobias had tried to persuade her to look after herself. He wanted there to be something left of his sweet little darling when they met again. But there wasn't. The sweet little darling had died. In her place was a large, angry, self-supporting woman whose bitterness was impossible to assuage when she realised that Tobias had lazed away the war, playing cards and flirting. Her disgust and resentment became an unquenchable hellfire that tortured and plagued her for eternity. Even though she talked all the time of dying, heaven would have to wait. She realised that there was no recompense in life from people for the order and honesty one invested in them. Discipline and industriousness were prized no higher than chaos and destruction. The world, it seemed, had no morals. From that point on, Katze resolved to disintegrate. The camels she had to swallow were best washed down with schnapps.

Li eventually came to see that alcohol erodes a person's character. When you had money, however, it worked in subtler ways. For Katze did not sit in a bar. She didn't give up washing. She drank alone and still led a respectable life. She drank to cope with an unreliable male world that refused to take her seriously. "I just have a drink beforehand, then I give those gentlemen on the board my opinion." She had given up sleeping late, getting manicures, playing bridge and having her hand kissed. These pleasures had been exchanged for an insecure balance of payments and the condescension of her inferiors.

It was not until Li saw her mother positively drunk late one night that she recognised something was very wrong, but she still thought Katze would be all right once the others returned from Sweden. But it wasn't. Katze was convinced she would die of joy when they arrived. Balder and Bekka had written such lovely silver-wedding letters to her. Trille, who wrote so sweetly about Katze's "abundant good qualities" as the absolutely perfect wife and mother, thanked her for the two hand-knitted bathing suits Katze had made her. She would so much like to have had a mother like her, Trille wrote for the censor's benefit. Balder had complimented her on her youthfulness and self-sacrifice and for his happy childhood. He would never forget the night Katze came into his bedroom and kissed him and asked for his forgiveness. *His* forgiveness of *her*! She who was nothing but goodness and unselfishness. She who always put others first. She who, for all her life, had toiled and slaved for others.

The first few days were indeed festive. The others arrived at the liberated Copenhagen port laden with gifts and supplies, almonds, coffee, marzipan and chocolate that had not been seen for five years. Tobias brought a complete trousseau for Li with sheets and towels, and beautiful baby clothes for Zeste.

It wasn't long before the bitter feelings surfaced. But because they had so much to be thankful for – being alive, for instance – they had no idea how to express their anger. Both Katze and Tobias felt let down. She had neglected to take care of herself. She had not gone to him in Stockholm when he needed her. He had run away "with his tail between his legs".

16

LONDON

In December 1945 Tobias flew to London in a freezing cold aeroplane with an open cockpit. Even after padding out all his clothes and wrapping a travelling rug around his legs, he still felt as if he was on a polar expedition. The badly damaged city he came to was beset by shortages and restrictions. At the Cumberland Hotel near Marble Arch, Tobias was served a mysterious cutlet that tasted like chewed rye bread. The hotel had no heating, but he was lucky to have found a hotel at all.

Tobias wandered the snow- and ice-covered streets for saleable merchandise. "Goods – not money – are what's important today," he wrote to Katze. He had come to look for whatever could be sold, and also to get away from his wife. He thought that if he could find something for them to live on, she could be relieved from either the office work or running the household, and then she might become her old gentle self again. That was why he bought 50,000 kroner's worth of pipes for the Vulkan Company: perhaps they could live off them. Peat was no good any more now that petrol had come back.

The horrors of the war, and the price it had exacted from so many, slowly dawned on Tobias when he heard what had happened to his Jewish bridge partners from Riga. To start with, he used the euphemism "killed by the Germans", but the scale of the exterminations soon became clear – whole families had been wiped out, children and old people; 16,000 civilians were shot on one day in Lithuania. Tobias didn't need to hear any more.

He travelled by train out of London to unearth factories and buy goods wholesale. He sent Katze samples of bath sponges, babies' rubber sheets, nappy pants, bibs, ladies' aprons, waterproof capes, footballs and pot cleaners. He considered tweed jackets, powder pots, children's beds, and nuts, and one day, to her astonishment, she received a large empty sack. It was Tobias' new initiative, his sample of what they would live on in future: jute bags for sand and cement, charcoal and onions. In the meantime, he made his living playing cards.

He didn't hide his gambling from Katze, but explained how the game was played in England. Players did not introduce themselves to one another but merely took a card: "How do you play, partner? Two clubs? Blackwood?" "Strong No Trumps." When the rubber was finished, you paid. "Table up." Take a card again. The two lowest dropped out, and the comedy was repeated. There was hardly anywhere you could play with a regular partner, which broadened the scope for the game's sake. But Tobias did not play for the sake of the game; he played to survive. The most elegant club he played at was the famous Crockford's. It was a whole house, with a bar, a restaurant, reading rooms, guest rooms – in one you played for only 2s 6d, in another five shillings, and ten shillings in a third. Half the players in the ten-shilling room were ladies! With gold cigarette cases and jewelled gold lighters, mink and sable, they put £70 to £200 on a single rubber. At two in the morning, Tobias began a rubber with two women aged at least 70! He understood how this nation won the war – they never gave up! The food was appalling, but no-one complained.

Tobias knew perfectly well that whatever he wrote about entertainments, however pleasurable, Katze's comment would be, "Waste of time". He told her more about what he had seen – trucks, motorcycles, electric cars. Should he import them? He was most amazed at the brand-new material: tinfoil. It could be used for cheese, chocolate, beer, milk bottle tops. He bought vast amounts of parachute silk that he hoped Katze, Li and Rebekka could use. He also bought a kind of "liquid rubber", which he thought was the thing of the future. It was called "plastic".

To Tobias' dismay, the Danish Ministry of Supply refused a

licence to import plastic and cycles, and Katze had had no success finding buyers for rain capes or powder pots. She could sell most things in a trice; there was such a need after the war for goods of all kinds. But Katze had her own discipline and perseverance with work; the daily grind was her strong suit. She had never had much impetus and was no longer motivated. Tobias had obviously turned into a cross between a huckster and a magician: "I have a multi-coloured pencil which cannot break and must not be sharpened, it looks like a slate pencil!"

Tobias also tried to become an agent for Elizabeth Arden, the beauty salon, but it was no good just walking in off the street. He tried everyone he knew, but no-one had any connections with the firm except Madge, the red-haired *femme fatale* from Riga, who patronised the place. For some reason, this didn't help. "No, that didn't help," Katze sneered. She knew why that bloody idiot had gone to London: to run after that slattern.

Bunty was so overjoyed when she heard that Tobias was in town that she immediately rang Madge to tell her. Madge was very busy, but she did have time – between a lunch and then a concert and dinner – to see him for tea at the Dorchester. She looked – objectively – lovely. Five years of war and the loss of her son seemed not to have affected her. She said she had been very troubled by the war and had been ill for a year after her son's death, but she asked him not to talk about that. During the war, she had worked in a kitchen, peeling potatoes and washing up, which was better than working in a factory. Everyone from 17 to 50 had to work. After divorcing her husband, Madge bought her own house – close to Park Lane – with ten rooms. It was bombed. Luckily, she had been prudent enough to send all the contents into the country when the bombing started, so she lost only the house. After the war, the government restored it for the Polish Embassy, and she lived in a two-room furnished flat with a little kitchen, electric stove and fridge.

Madge invited Tobias and a couple of friends to her home. She roasted two birds that her brother had sent her from the country. She also served bacon, braised celery and boiled potatoes in a sauce thinner than water. Nothing to drink. The pudding was bread and butter pudding. Zeste would have loved it.

Unfortunately Madge did not have any business contacts – most of her friends were officers and rich people who had never worked. Madge's day began at eleven o'clock in the morning. She sold lace at the Dorchester, then played a few games of bridge and finished her day with dinner at the Savoy. That was how a society lady spent her day, Tobias explained in his letter. Incidentally, Madge was very glad to see Tobias again. Apparently she had been quite sure he was dead.

If only he was! What did Katze care how a society lady in London lived? She couldn't care less about the ruins of Europe when Tobias had left her own life in ruins. When she heard that Tobias couldn't resolve their future in four days as planned, she was no more amiable. Also, his "connections" in London informed him that he would have to stay there for at least six months. He didn't even come home for Christmas. It was the third Christmas he had been away from the family, and this time it was of his own free will. Katze was bitter. He didn't even telephone!

Rebekka decided to join her father because of course she sided with him. She stayed with the children of Uncle Sophus and Aunt Fanny. It was a good thing Katze had relatives in London because Uncle Arthur – one of "the leading sons of Denmark" – had died. Bekka wrote tentatively to her mother about a new suit that her mother would be sure to like – green and brown check, with a pleated skirt.

Rebekka maintained that she had kept a sharp look-out for any evidence of a relationship between Madge and Tobias, and she swore that she spotted nothing. Madge was, as Katze had said, pleasant enough when she liked someone, and she liked Rebekka. Bekka assured her mother that Madge wasn't slim – much fatter, in fact, than Katze – and that Madge had thin short hair and was rather scruffy. Otherwise she was sweet and funny and far more deserving of Katze's jealousy than the homely Glenda. Still, there was no cause for jealousy.

But Katze's fury was as old as the earth's, especially when Tobias was cheeky enough to give her a *watch* for Christmas. It was a good watch, but Katze was nevertheless upset. That watch was a great disappointment, she wrote to Tobias, who had asked Gaus to buy it for her. Gaus had taken the opportunity to buy two – one for Katze and one for his wife. The watches were identical, but Katze was convinced that Gaus had changed the watches round and given her the less good one. Katze was so irritated about that watch that Tobias had to beg her to forgive him. He swore that when he grew rich he would give her a watch made of platinum, set with diamonds, but Katze was not easily consoled. When she finally wrote to London again, the letter began, "Dear Sir, . . . "

Tobias replied PRIVATE and NOT FOR READING ALOUD:

My dearest one, a letter from you at last. Thank you so much. As you know, I am always very interested in what you all are doing – both in the family and the business. But I am disappointed and tired of your coldness. I know very well that, after 25 years of marriage, it's ridiculous to harbour warm feelings for one's wife (or husband). Nonetheless, I am the exception. "My feelings are the same as they have been for 22 years," you write. But when you have been married for 25 years, you can't hide the death of those loving feelings. For you, it was three years after we were married. Strange to sit in an agonisingly icy room in London in 1945 and discover that one's marriage ended in 1923. My whole day is ruined when I receive a letter that starts with "Dear Sir" or "Dear Tobias", which in your eyes is one and the same thing. Why? Madge? Bridge? Money? Extended stay? Real or feigned indifference? Let me try to deal with these consecutively, and then give me an answer.

Tobias explained for the umpteenth time that, yes, Madge was chic, cheeky and cheerful, but she had never been more than a flirtation. He only played bridge – except over the weekend – two or three times a week. This brought him a nice little surplus that he used to buy seven Marlene Dietrich records. Incidentally, she should not worry about money because he spent very little on his own living expenses. The National Bank calculated six pounds a day, and he spent only about four.

Perhaps Katze's indifference was at the heart of the matter. Or was it merely play-acting? He hoped so. But one thing worried him: what did she really mean when she said that "they couldn't really cope with that move to Sweden either". What did the "either" mean? Did she think they hadn't coped with it? It must be Katze who had not coped. For his feelings were the same as before he moved to Sweden, while he was there, and when he came home again.

Now I realise that in your last letter you asked if I might find something over here. Tell me, did you mean that I should stay here alone? You must be mad. Of course there is no question of that. We are together here or there – if you wish it. If I am to understand that you are really tired of me and want to be rid of me, then come straight out with it. Do you want to go to Stockholm and share love and money with me? Or are you tired of your old husband and in need of a little variety? I could understand that. I hope and believe I shall get some results from this trip, and then I can promise you it will be the last year you have to work. I would like us to go away to Stockholm together for Easter. I think it would be charming to go off with you again – even if it were just into the country for a weekend, but only if you want to do so. Do you?

MYREN'S BOOK

1

THE LITTLE RED DOLL'S PRAM

Although they had moved, Li and Jas still celebrated Christmas Eve of 1947 at Gammel Mønt 14. For Christmas Eve at Gammel Mønt was bound to be something special with Tobias presiding over the feast. The keyhole was covered with a sheet so that the children couldn't see their grandfather decorating the tree that towered up to the ceiling. Who could say whether the white sheet covering all the glory was more exciting than what it hid? Mountains of ashes and mass graves.

Tobias drove around all day with Christmas boxes for relatives and friends. The most wearisome visit had been to St John's, the psychiatric hospital. Aunt Bekka accompanied him – she was studying medicine and was almost half a doctor already – and later described the ghastly experience. Katze just wanted another drink. But on Christmas Eve they drank only wine at Gammel Mønt, out of respect for the festival; the hard stuff they reserved for New Year's Eve.

What they didn't know, during the Occupation, was that KIS – Kirsten Inger Svendsen, the woman with the protruding Bette Davis eyes – had been an energetic member of the Resistance! That smirking hussy whom Li hated so much, who adored the Director and was always ready with some moralistic verses by Stuckenberg – the self-same KIS had become a Resistance fighter! Imagine: they had been so close to the battle, and they had never known it! Truth to be told, KIS was the only freedom fighter they had known at all. Glenda's son, who had exchanged a bicycle lamp for a Resistance armband, was of course beneath Katze's contempt. They finally understood why KIS had been so sweet to them during the war, giving them treats of chickens and new potatoes. Gammel Mønt was close to Damehotellet, a cover address, just as the maternity clinic in Christian X Street was a safe house for the Resistance. And so it was that they had been party to the Resistance without even realising it!

Nor did they notice how schizophrenia had taken over KIS, though of course Li wasn't at all surprised when the diagnosis was finally confirmed. Now she understood her aversion to KIS, why she had once dug her nails into KIS for her hypocrisy: a nobody, and not the sage she tried to pass for. Li understood that all her pretentious letters to the family about ladybirds and the pine forest in her window box indicating something "greater" were just crazy.

KIS may not have been a sage, but she turned out not to be a nobody. She was unmarried and as a Resistance fighter she had risked her life – at least her sanity – out of love for Tobias. During the Occupation KIS had hidden Geisler, a Resistance man, in a wardrobe. Her insanity was a result of her war work – or menopause, or both. For a long time after the Occupation, she was convinced that she was being stalked. To rectify this madness, she in turn pursued some hapless wine merchant, making a misery of his life, sending him passionate letters and insisting that he loved her.

During the war KIS had complained about the quality of available spirits. The spirits or "spirit" in the shops was so weak that you couldn't feel you were on a gliding cloud. Spirits or no, it must be said that fru KIS glided all by herself and the universe had to look on patiently.

In the 1940s, back before psychopharmacology, St John's was anything but dull. It consisted of extensive wards of screaming and howling creatures. In the midst of the din, KIS sat beaming. She had a special connection. But of course she recognised Rebekka, Katze and – not least – the guiding star of her life, Tobias, who had been so faithful to her. But KIS asked them to wait a moment: she was about to receive a cosmic message. Tobias said, "Of course we'll wait."

When the secret message had been received, they carried on chatting as best they could over the screaming, as if nothing out of the ordinary had happened.

Soon enough, symptom-suppressing medication came on the market and KIS was discharged. Tobias found her a secretarial job in the fuel firm where he himself had been taken on as a sales director. He had landed the job through a bridge partner at the club when nothing else he had tried after the war had worked out. He had failed as a powder-box dealer and as a parachute-silk ladies' tailor. His London venture was over. When, after all that, in a grandiose final gesture, he invested the entire surplus Katze had amassed during the war on the Stock Exchange, and lost the lot, he had to take whatever he could get.

KIS had been hired on the condition that she took her medication. But she didn't: why on earth should a healthy and normal person take pills? And besides, how would the Director explain the invisible connections in the universe?

"I wouldn't bring that up at all," Tobias said.

"Can you explain the wireless radio or radio waves?"

"No, I can't," said Tobias, "I don't understand everything. But you don't understand bridge, and I can't begin to explain it to you. So just keep your knowledge to yourself, or you may lose your job."

In the long run he could not protect KIS from the cosmic messages or prevent the manager from firing her. She started to put five-øre pieces in the centre of the floor and issued ominous warnings to her fellow workers not to approach the coins because they emitted deadly rays.

*

The Christmas tree still sparkled with the same brilliance that evening at Gammel Mønt 14. The same Russian Santa Clauses of glowing blue wax with silver tinsel reappeared, just like the candlesticks shaped as little red wooden-soled boots on the Christmas table. But each year Tobias bought some new decorations; this year it was a golden merry-go-round with angels powered by the heat of the lighted candles. Li's eyes shone with amphetamines, which Zeste and Myren – the Ant – had taken with their mother's milk. Thanks to Gaus, who had found them a two-room flat in Hedemannsgade, a new block down by the Lakes, Jas and Li had their own home. Jas still worked at Gaus' radio business in Ryesgade. Occasionally he got the urge to try out something new, but Tobias said he must never risk losing his precious contact with Gaus.

Although Tobias took trouble over all the decorations, he was still a frightening grandfather. One thing was his Mephistophelian appearance – his big nose, his fancy red silk dress cloak. No fancy dress, however, could disguise Tobias' Jewishness. No matter how "unthinkable" a Løvin in prison uniform was or how certain it was that a Løvin would "kill himself after first having shot a German" – or so the Løvin sisters dutifully repeated – the children weren't convinced. Tobias belonged to a horrifying world. When he finished eating, he sat down in his armchair and yelled with the full force of his lungs: "Coffee!" The children took this yell for rage; they grew quiet and frightened and pitied Marie, who was always at the ready when the cry resounded through the apartment and came running on her little short legs with the coffee tray. They wondered how she could take it so naturally. Tobias added irony to his brusque manner. Li rebuked him: "Stop that, Father, children don't understand irony." When the children passed each other a piece of bread with their fingers instead of on the silver salver, Tobias would perplex them by rolling peas along the tablecloth with his long manicured fingers. "I'm not saying anything," was all he said, and that was the worst thing.

He always carved the best meat for Li, and took her children to the circus. In the stalls. And when they grew bigger, he impressed the following tenet on them: "Be costly!" When he saw his first grandchild after the war, he exclaimed: "Have I got such a lovely grandchild!" – for once without irony. But Zeste wasn't lovely. Myren was lovely. But nobody cared about her, because she had arrived so inconveniently a year later, by mistake, when Li was still run down. And then she had blue eyes. Myren was called the Ant – Jas' pet name for her – because she was so tiny when she was born she slept in a drawer. They couldn't afford a cot. When Li and Jas were moving to a larger flat down the street, they sat down with all the packing cases around them and said, "Have we forgotten anything?" They discovered they had forgotten Myren.

While the fairies queued up around Zeste's cot to ensure she developed Tobias' outstanding qualities and KIS predicted that the child could inherit Tobias' talents and his sound judgment, they left Myren in peace. When Zeste was born, Li decided she was a special child, and so must not be educated. She must not be intellectually warped. For the World War had shown that people were insane. "A person must rise uncorrupted by the madness of earlier times. Such liberation couldn't be just a day-long festival; it had to be embodied; a liberation from the subjugation to authority, from harsh discipline and slavery, from worry and duty: it would be only pleasure and play."

Since children are little geniuses, adults must keep their hands off them: Rousseau for the new era. The paradoxical result was that Zeste was housetrained after only nine months and that Li considered every other child who did not develop similarly to be backward. Li interpreted everything Zeste said as pure Shakespeare. Each time Zeste pronounced on life and death Li made sure that it appeared in the newspaper. Balder had taken a job at *Berlingske Tidende*. He had no business ambitions, so he was not expected to follow in his grandfather's footsteps, but still he didn't object to writing little paragraphs that could throw lustre on himself and his family.

In spite of her theories about freedom, Li had extremely well-behaved children. She had eyes that could kill, and neither child wanted to see the yellow in them vanish into white. So there was never any noise from Li's children, only rhyming melodies and sweet music.

To protect Zeste from the influence of giggling children who couldn't behave naturally towards sexuality, her parents waited until Zeste was two before letting her play in the street. One day, Li set Zeste free and she walked into a chaotic din reminiscent of apes. Obviously, amidst that brawling anarchy Zeste was helpless, and Li was proud to see her standing by herself reciting nursery rhymes.

Li's friend Sunne, who admired her brilliant pedagogic talents, did what she could to explain that Myren was not necessarily retarded because she didn't react to stimuli exactly as her big sister did. Li was not convinced. She wanted a personality.

A mother can really only teach her daughters one thing: what a man is good for. But Li couldn't do that because she herself didn't know. She had read that Scott and Zelda Fitzgerald dangled pearls before their daughter in her cot so that she would appreciate wealth and be sure to marry rich. But Li found that idea cheap. She read Sigmund Freud and A. S. Neill, the founder of Summerhill, an alternative to school as it had hitherto been known. She learned about the new type of human being capable of ensuring the project's success. In a tram one day, she even met S.H., who later became the renowned sexologist. His ideal for a brand-new liberal school was one with ten children to a class, which they attended only every other day; a syllabus with no cramming, where the kids danced to music they had composed themselves. It was just what Li wanted.

There was plenty of food for thought, but not a lot of regular food. Li's time at St Mary's had indeed been pretty expensive. The only thing she could cook was something she had invented herself, called "sausage dish". It consisted of boiled potatoes and frankfurters – cut into small pieces. Jas was nice about it. He hadn't married her for accomplishments in the kitchen.

Li couldn't whip cream without turning it into butter or breaking the bowl. If she had to clean up the mess herself, she would forget to rinse the cloth; the stale smell spread through the house. Li couldn't do anything practical, and when you are bad at something you grow to despise it. The children were brought up on Vitaminol, "bottled sunshine", a mixture of cod liver oil and carrots, which ensured that they survived. But Jas couldn't live on Vitaminol, and so, every once in a while, when Gaus had given him a bonus and hunger raged, he exchanged a pair of hand-made shoes for the services of a fru Jensen, who cooked a roast on Friday. They ate it cold on Saturday and served it as hash for the rest of the week.

Myren was two on Christmas Eve. While Zeste at three had dull straight mousy hair, Myren's was very fair and curly. When Zeste's interest wasn't kindled by something the grown-ups were discussing, and her eyes burned, she became charmless and invisible, while Myren was sweet, happy and extroverted. Li remained unimpressed because the child had blue eyes. Although she could not really touch her mother's heart, which beat to Phenobarbital and amphetamines, Myren could always seduce her father and make him run up and down the stairs – what wouldn't he do for his little Myren? Jas was a loving father, who read Hans Christian Andersen every evening, having fun in many voices.

The real personalities of the children were of no importance, as they had been determined beforehand. Because Zeste had been born into the euphoria of the Liberation, it was inevitably anticlimactic when her little sibling arrived, and Li, who had had to put up with all the fuss made of Rebekka, resolved that Zeste should not suffer the same fate. Zeste was not to be allowed to feel demoted by any new and exciting person in the household, nor would she be punished for aggressive responses to her sister. When Zeste asked one day if she could cut Myren up into pieces, Li nodded and smiled.

On Christmas Eve, after singing carols and dancing around the tree, the children unwrapped their presents. They got hand-knitted jumpers from Katze and – uh-oh! – a doll's house to share. Everything that is to be shared is a source of socialisation – and of course of rivalry. Zeste liked organising more than playing, while Myren preferred playing and making a mess. That year, Tobias gave Zeste a shiny little red doll's pram of varnished wood to take on walks by the Lakes.

One day the pram disappeared. Li went searching for it in all the entrances and basements; she even dared to go inside the Ryesgade courtyards, the haunt of flashers, who were feared by the children in the street, save Zeste who to her mother's satisfaction found them all perfectly natural. Li went into one of Ryesgade's back yards. Never in her life had she imagined such dank poverty; it was straight out of Dickens. What on earth was that stench? Was it old excrement, boiled cabbage or rotten wood? She had never confronted such destitution, such inconsolable human misery. Rats scurried among the dustbins; and there, in the innermost courtyard, stood the little red doll's pram shining in all the greyness. Li simply didn't have the heart to take it home. Certain that the children who lived in this filth had seen nothing so glorious in their lives, she pictured the joy such a toy must have brought them. Zeste agreed that Li couldn't take that from them.

When Li sang a song about a little girl who is dying, Zeste wept. "Mother dear, please be near, / Watch me while I'm sleeping, / You will never leave me, / I'll sleep with you beside me." She didn't know whether she herself or her mother was going to die: they were, after all, the same person. But in the picture there was a red jumper like a pool of blood that would never dry as if a spirit had entered Zeste and spoken with strange authority. There was only one thing in the world scarier than the illustrations in Grimm's *Fairy Tales*: the little girl in the delicatessen who always scowled at her. Zeste knew she had stolen her pram, and refused to cross the threshold into the shop. Finally, Li asked the girl why she stared so fiercely at Zeste, and the scowling child replied, "Because she thinks she's *something*."

*

For four years Li had walked the children through Østre Anlæg and Kongens Have, sometimes all the way to Frederiksberg. She pushed them in an eccentric, avant-garde pram that resembled the aeroplane that Tobias had imported from London and been unable to sell.

Li and her friend Sunne both walked with their prams along Langelinie beside the harbour. Sunne was married to Nølle, who always said: "I think you're gorgeous, what do you think about me?" Nølle and Jas often played jazz together in the evening to earn some pocket money, which Jas could certainly use. One day he was caught "borrowing" from the till in the radio shop, and that was the end of that job. "But, Good Lord," Jas protested, "it was only a loan, wasn't it, of course I would have paid it back!"

"He says it's mad to pay back money you've been lucky enough to borrow!" Sunne said.

"But he didn't mean it like that. Besides, he *has* repaid it."

"You can't really rely on him, can you?"

"No, not where money's concerned."

"Oh well, money isn't everything," said Sunne, whose rich parents forked out for her nannies.

"There's his health as well," Li said.

"What do you mean by that? Jas is always in high spirits – there can't be anything wrong with him!"

"He's always asking me to massage one of his shoulders, because he says he gets pins and needles down his right arm and it feels as if his hand is going dead so he can't play."

"Hey, when he asks you to massage him, don't you think he needs something else?" said Sunne, winking.

Li was unusually confidential that day; she seldom talked so intimately. But she had begun to worry about the future. A living or dead hand. She was insecure because she was married to a dandy who spent their money on silk shirts and tailor-made suits. Li felt she herself ought to take a job to straighten up the finances, but Jas wouldn't hear of it. He believed that women shouldn't work unless they were artists or mannequins. Even in his childhood home in Sundholmsvej, where they had been hard up, Mother had never worked. A woman who worked outside the home was a threat to her marriage. Jas dared not think what would happen if he sent his racehorse, his silken doll, out to work. And certainly not to work at night, which she suggested on account of the children.

Li had all her dresses made out on Amager Island and so was always fashionable, but Zeste and Myren wore English hand-me-downs sent from a family in London on Tobias' initiative. The berets and be-ribboned hats made other children laugh at them, but Zeste and Myren didn't mind. They knew they were well dressed, in matching hats and coats and embroidered frocks. Tobias had equipped their apartment with British inventions, children's beds made of metal, and a gramophone as tall as a man, which one day was painted dark red, and which played Beethoven's violin concerto and Ella Fitzgerald.

*

Yes, the war was certainly over, and people were happy. At the cinema, if nothing else was on, the Ry Kino showed *Annie Get Your Gun*, supposedly a painless way to put a stop to the independence women had gained during the war. But regardless of which film they saw, Jas' voice could be heard ringing through the auditorium: "Up in the hay with her!" And Li was proud. She loved to shock, particularly when she didn't have to pay.

As for the children, Li, like many young mothers, didn't worry much. When she and Jas went to the cinema at night, they left the children alone without a qualm. They were told that if they happened to wake up, they could ring the neighbour's doorbell. Late one night, when Li and Jas came home, the children were sitting wide awake in the neighbour's apartment, each holding an orange. It was time to find a proper babysitter.

Li chose Mogens Lorentzen's son, who, it was true, had been institutionalised. But Li didn't think psychiatric patients should be discriminated against. Li, who often visited Jacob in hospital with Zeste, thought the most important thing was that he liked children. She knew this arrangement was provocative, and she enjoyed it when Katze protested.

"I don't like that man," Katze said.

"Why not?"

"There's something not right about him."

"Jacob is very fond of small children."

"That's just the trouble."

Soon after that conversation, when Jacob was babysitting two other little girls, he shot them – to spare them this frightful world, he left a scribbled note to say. Then he shot himself, leaving Li without a babysitter.

There were parties at Hedemannsgade at least twice a week, with loud jazz until dawn. The children slept like little logs, but through their sleep they grasped an important life lesson: only ignoramuses sit down after the dance, when they think "In the Mood" has finished. The right people know there is still one more chorus. The wrong ones clapped in time to the beat, the right ones to the after-beat.

Sunne tacked some black material on herself, and that was an evening dress. When she went to bed, she – or Nølle, if he was at all *compos mentis* – unpicked the tacking stitches. There were strict norms at those wild raves. The American films that had intoxicated them during the Occupation had liberated the kiss, so they felt it was permissible to kiss anyone you liked – but nothing more. And so they kissed, and they danced, and they kissed, and they hugged. All the spouses kept their eyes on their other half, who in good faith was kissing a second or a third person while the spouses themselves, their eyes on stalks, kissed a fourth or a fifth. Secret tabs were kept on partners, and now and again someone went off the rails. Even though it was usually the men who couldn't stay within the prescribed limits, it was the women who got the beatings.

Early one morning, on the pavement going home to Østerbro, Nølle beat his wife black and blue because she had kissed a man too fervently. At the end of the day, they couldn't stick to the rules of American petting: the American film kiss was far too complicated for real life. And hypocritical: the Danes couldn't swallow the double standard in getting worked up for nothing. Scandinavians were at once too pragmatic and too pagan. After a generation or two, they definitely couldn't accept the double standard that blamed immorality on women alone. Women no longer wanted to be pillars of virtue, although that was probably not such a boring role as it seemed. A leader in disguise – even if unpaid in kroner and øre.

It was the end of fruit wines and Black Velvet, champagne and

Guinness, hay and chaff. Now they smoked Virginia tobacco, Players and Camels and drank real gin and Scotch whisky. And many of them drank plentifully. For there were bad nerves after the war. Some drank to forget their traumas in Resistance work, others out of shame that they had not participated. They drank because they had not turned up at a certain place to liquidate that traitor and one of their colleagues had been killed as a result. They drank out of sheer intoxication with life. Many people had broken down, and if there had been other substances on the market they would have taken them, too.

*

Spirits were easier to obtain once several young men who had started a student travel agency, STA, began turning up at the Hedemannsgade gatherings. After being caged for so long, people were frantic to go travelling, and a few bright young souls had seen their chance to turn a profit. All three pioneers – Skalle, Nagel and Rejn – worshipped Li. Skalle, a little round bald-headed parson's son with a moustache was, owing to his origins, both shabby and strikingly gifted. If he hadn't married a great deal of money, he would have anyway earned it himself. He ended up a prosperous businessman with a hunting lodge. Nagel was one of the few German refugees granted asylum by Denmark during the war. He ended up a prosperous executive in London in a Jewish family firm of coffee importers. Last but not least, Rejn Møller was a down-at-heel orphanage boy who looked a little like James Dean. He had worked on railway sabotage in Jutland until he went underground, became a student in Sweden and returned home with the Brigade. This trio made a great impression on Zeste and Myren. One of them had accidentally shot off one of his hands after the Liberation, and wore a wooden hand inside a black leather glove. Another was liberal with swinging trips and walked home across the ice at Dosseringen when he was drunk.

Rejn got Li a night job. And Jas' intuition proved correct, for soon afterward Li announced that she was leaving him for Rejn, who had courted her passionately, as a letter from London, written on both sides of a BBC Symphony Orchestra ticket, indicates.

> My own beloved girl, I believe that you love me – that we can
> be happy. I also know you are not happy now because

divorcing Jas will be a dreadful business. It must be done, for you to keep your children, and you are loath to hurt him too much. I realise how wearing this business is, and I don't know how to help you. I'm thinking about it a lot, but I haven't had any ideas yet. It is also unbearable that we can be together only so rarely and so briefly that our desires occupy all our time. I know that we were born to live together. Do you agree? I hope you never doubt us at weak moments, and I'd like to be certain you believe the same, wholly, and that I am not leading you into a situation you'll regret. I can't take the decision on divorce for you. You must do that yourself. But I promise to do what I can so you will not regret it. Until Friday afternoon.

The letter was unsigned, for the lover never needs to identify himself.

As luck would have it, when Li finally plucked up the courage to ask for a divorce, Jas told her he wanted to marry a raven-haired English mannequin called Gwendoline, who had spent the war with the Red Cross picking up bodies in the ruins of London.

"Let's take a stroll," Li said to Zeste. As they walked towards the Lakes, Li asked her daughter if divorcing Jas would be a good idea. Zeste agreed that it would be.

So it fell out that Jas was the first to admit that he had met someone else he wanted to marry. He flew into a violent rage when Li replied: "That's good – so have I."

"What do you mean? Are you out of your mind?"

"Rejn has been my lover for two years, didn't you know?"

No, Jas didn't know. This was a serious test of Jas' high spirits, and he was furious. "But you have been married to me! I can't have *my* wife . . . "

"But you have been married to me, I can't have *my* husband . . ."

"That's quite different, can't you see that?"

"No, I can't see that."

"You're the mother of my children."

"You're the father of my children."

"I play cards and chess with Skalle, Nagel and Rejn. They all knew about it and I didn't?"

"We didn't want to hurt you."

"I feel ridiculous."

Jas couldn't keep up the role of deceived husband for long. Soon enough, the comedian and the smile revived. "I can't help smiling," he said.

"What's so funny?"

"That you've chosen the wrong man!"

"What do you mean?"

"You had three worshippers, three talented worshippers, and you chose the most boring one."

"Rejn isn't boring."

"He's totally devoid of humour!"

"Is that what you think?"

"He's nothing but a ridiculous Boy Scout."

"There's no need to say anything more," Li said. She didn't want to wound Jas by telling him that she felt a passion for Rejn that she had never known with Jas.

"If you'd asked me for advice, I would've told you to take Skalle, for there's money in him, I can smell it."

"It never crossed my mind to ask for your advice."

"That's a pity, because I really think the Silken Doll needs to be looked after a bit after these miserable years in Hedemannsgade."

They didn't go into the question of why their marriage had fallen apart, for it had never been together in the first place.

*

Li's marriage to Rejn was a reaction against both her first *pro forma* wedding and Katze's shotgun one. This time Li married for *lust*. Li and Rejn were – openly now – in a constant embrace, kissing in front of everyone and hanging countless "Do not disturb" notices on locked doors. Hitherto, Zeste had been married to her mother, but now a new man had come and taken Li away. Zeste couldn't deal with this betrayal: she felt both abandoned and numbed.

Li hardly knew the man she had married. She felt proud that she had landed an academic. The family didn't have many of those, after all. When Li married Rejn she didn't just marry a person, she thought she had married into an intellectual world, one commanding respect, even if Li had never understood Rejn's speciality, numbers and statistics. She did sense however, that he lacked some of the more humanistic qualities. His student friend

Marsken was possessed of all the qualities Rejn lacked, and was "one of Denmark's leading sons", and a guarantor for Rejn. *He* was a personality.

Rejn had a good brain, but he was a poor student who brought no more to Li's impoverished household than a pair of rusty nail scissors and a *tupilak*, a small voodoo figure from Greenland. Otherwise he had nothing, just like his drunken father, a reserve postman who kept chickens in Ørslev when he wasn't staggering around with a bottle in his hand and sleeping in stairways. He had once had a job as a telegraphist at Store Nordiske Telegraph Company, but when he took his Swedish wife to Vladivostok, he deposited the two-year-old Rejn and his brother at an orphanage, where they lived miserably off lukewarm gruel and spurious Christianity.

It was for this reason that Rejn nourished a hatred of all that Jesus stood for. The very idea that a person called the Messiah should have existed, been killed and risen from the dead struck him as petit bourgeois rubbish. It was ridiculous to wash a traitor's feet; the so-called "God's way" was a foolish way. Man was the centre of all decisions. Behaving properly did not require a Christian foundation; it was mere logic. Rejn's two prime bugbears were pathos and the metaphysical gift of tongues. Apart from this he had not developed any significant emotional life.

Perhaps Li recognised her own inner poverty in Rejn. They were two inadequate souls who, for almost 20 years, would cling together in passion and desperation. In the beginning, they romped with a heedless sensuality that shut out the world. The children could drown in the bath and the neighbours' houses burn to the ground, why should they care? In the world of lust they were immune to everyday trivialities. Finally Li was happy.

One day, when her parents were dropping her off in Hedemannsgade, Li asked them to come inside and meet her new husband.

"No, thank you," said Katze, who had only just finished in the office, "I'm too tired." She was not amused at the idea of meeting a "Møller". Li felt again the stab of desertion she had always sensed in the faithful Katze. But Tobias, the unfaithful, said in a firm, authoritative voice: "Yes, thanks, we should love to meet your new husband."

2

THE FALL

They weren't called Mother and Father, nor Li and Rejn. They were the Cat and the Dog. In all the notes they left each other, they signed themselves with drawings of cats and dogs, or simply the signs for the sexes, as if they were no longer persons, merely male and female in the ancient game of love and war.

To inaugurate their new life, they moved from Hedemannsgade into a new terrace house with a kitchen-diner, a garden and a veranda, surrounded by a field in Sorgløse. They acquired a pale green VW Beetle and Li bought a pink sack dress. Now they were modern. They both had full-time work in the centre of Copenhagen, the Cat as a medical secretary for Dr V. in the psychiatric department of the National Hospital; the Dog still at STA, making expeditions around the world to expand travel opportunities for students, and those he did expand, using all of Scandinavia as his base. Moreover he had taken his master's degree in economics, he was very clever.

Nevertheless, Li had a breakdown at the onset of her marriage to the love of her life. It was partly to be blamed on modern living, which Li could not stand up to. In the '50s there were so many gadgets that gradually the role of housewife became redundant. Everything was bought on the instalment system. The so-called standard of living rose sky high while Li milked herself dry at work instead of breast-feeding. They had the car, with instalments to pay on it. Her inborn sense of duty combined with physical debility quickly brought about a collapse.

To begin with they were full of hope. When the Cat and the Dog were happy they ignored everything around them. Late at night the Cat could suddenly feel starved of fudge and marzipan, and the Dog was sent off to search for it near and far. When he was extra sweet he might be permitted to sit at the foot of the Cat's sofa and stroke her legs, in the right way miaow, otherwise he was kicked away. Woof.

So began the impenetrable game to which they were both sacrificed and which they could not escape because Li hadn't the strength to say that in reality he irritated her. Not on account of anything definite. He just irritated her. And then she took an overdose. All her life she had felt the need to be lifted up, but now she felt only that she was sinking. The whole thing was nothing but getting up in the morning, driving to work, coming home exhausted and going to bed. They hardly had time to be in love. Was there nothing more to life than this? What had happened to the wonder of it?

Some time after the Liberation, Katze and Tobias had given Li the classic Danish novel *Fru Marie Grubbe* for Christmas: "To our beloved little Li with best wishes for everything good." Li could see herself as Marie Grubbe, the eighteenth-century Lady Chatterley, but Rejn was no Søren Ladefoged. He may have had his brutality, but not his sweetness. The Dog's letters home – he was forever abroad – were direct. He always looked forward to feeling her hand "on my cock". All his letters mentioned "your cunt" and his longing to "crush you to me". He couldn't wait to get home so they could lock the bedroom door and "fornicate". Rejn wrote so freely to his wife because that was part of being modern. He was used to student circles where it was *de rigueur* to be sexually explicit. All that solemn sentimentality belonged to the past, over and done with. All the same, even if Li thought her mother ridiculous for reciting Heine, Goethe and Schiller while only half understanding the words, she was beginning to suspect that the academic environment, for which she had felt so much respect, was more loud undergraduate-speak than wonderful. She and Rejn had had such fun at the bawdy student parties with Skalle and Nagel in Jutland. She had loved the abandon. But when she was alone with Rejn she missed something. He lectured her about looking ahead and being on the side of progress, and she had to struggle for a response. Rejn was so articulate.

Maybe smuttiness and pornography were signs of progress. Li was no prude, but it was as if Rejn didn't know who she was. Perhaps he hadn't enough imagination to see it. He laughed at her when she listened to *The Messiah*, and when she read *Ulysses* – a book so dense that you could never be finished with it – he was bewildered by her perseverance. Rejn read books backwards, invariably starting at the end. He thought that if an author couldn't get across what he wanted to say in fewer than 200 pages, he was no good. Rejn was the consumer of the future.

But was he also a modern Søren Ladefoged? Li doubted that, just as she had doubts about herself, like Marie. Perhaps she herself didn't possess enough sensuality to do without all the embellishments. Yes, she felt it for two months, then two years. But would it last a lifetime? At the back of her mind she heard Jas' frequent complaints about her frigidity. But that was only with him. With Rejn she couldn't get enough. It was never enough, and so she overdosed. She had the strange idea that in the long run perhaps aestheticism meant more to her than eroticism. And that goodness might mean more than desire. And she felt ashamed, fearing that she had made the wrong choice. But, like so many women, she shunned second thoughts. She knew what she had, but not what she would have if she made a change.

She felt herself sinking deeper every day. Each time she saw Rejn come into the living room and put a milk bottle straight onto the table without using a jug, like a student, the aesthete in her winced. She didn't need to say anything, she just gave the milk bottle *the look*, and it seemed to splinter into a thousand pieces. The Dog said "Pearly" and "Woof woof", but the Cat did not miaow back. And the yellow of her eyes turned white. She had ended up in a scout camp, forced to live with a boy who contributed nothing to the household except a rusty pair of nail scissors and a cock. Day in, day out she had to live alongside this boy-like manner, no elegance, no humour, no style. And so, just as as a child she had punished the world by locking herself into herself and refusing to speak, now she locked herself in with narcotics. Alyprobymal and Phenobarbital were the secret, whispered code words, while the pill bottles were hidden beneath the underclothes with Rejn's love letters: "My greatest wish is to be a good husband to you, so that you can be happy, content and at ease."

Jas had called Rejn a boy scout without a sense of humour. There was something incurably *petit bourgeois* about him: imagine suggesting that they buy a piece of oilcloth for their table.

"You can't mean that!"

"But, Pearly, it's just so easy!"

"I expect you had oilcloth on the table where you come from!"

"I didn't know you liked washing and ironing tablecloths!"

The Dog's remark fell on deaf ears. The Cat reacted only with her eyes. She thought she might die.

The Dog rushed around, hoovering and dusting, shopping and cooking. He cut more and more recipes out of newspapers and stuck them in the cookbook that Li had when she took Home Economics classes. Under André Gide's *The Immoralist*, the Dog inserted a recipe for "Bachelor's Apple Pie". And yet, no matter what delicious dish the Dog prepared, the Cat wouldn't eat it. She lay in bed and Myren crept cautiously up with one tray after another. Li rejected everything, and was on the verge of looking like a camp survivor. The girls grew used to seeing their mother being carried away on a stretcher – either white as a corpse or unrecognisably blue and bloated. "Is Mother going to die?" they asked each time. Miaow. All the Dog asked was when he could fornicate with her again. Woof.

For a while Rejn took on a young girl from Jutland as a domestic help. The Cat would like her *fricassee de veau*. But when he noticed that Marta wore a cross on her necklace Rejn couldn't bear it. Nor could he ask her to take it off. One day Rejn found a note left by Marta: "A kingdom divided against itself cannot endure. And if a home is divided against itself, that home cannot endure." He thought it might not have been meant for him and let it pass. But when on another day he found a piece of paper on the kitchen table with "How can Satan drive out Satan?" scrawled on it, he threw her out.

Rejn had invested his passion in the belief that everything in the world could be explained logically, in figures and formulae, graphs and logarithms. Faith in common sense had saved him throughout his neglected childhood. Rejn, who felt comfortable with his sexuality but not with his emotions, depended on Li's attacks, on his reticence, and what she called his emotional obtuseness. He felt a strange satisfaction at seeing her on the point of death, then being able at the last moment to rescue her. It gave him a sorrowful hero's status which sustained him. Li's habit of playing with her own life allowed Rejn to replay the separation which he had endured as a two-year-old when his mother left him at death's door, in an orphanage. Now it was Li's turn.

Still, he was unable to calculate the cost of his performance, and it worried him not to settle every account in cash. Through the magic of numbers he had always ordered everything in his life, and so he would order his household too – without Marta. He sent for ready-cooked food from Virum's Dinners, which stood on the doormat in enamelled army containers when Zeste and Myren came home from school. Li wouldn't touch the lumpy boiled potatoes that Virum's delivered, and if she was sick or off work, she would not even carry the food into the house.

In sober moments, Li thought it was strange that Rejn put up with this. Gaus would never have stood for it, even if he too was from a lower class. So it was not so much a class question as . . . well, what? She had never been in love with Gaus as she was with Rejn.

During Li's illness, Gaus was arrested and sent to prison. It was a huge case, involving black market smuggling, Mafia and foreclosed banks. Bent policemen and corruption, a spider's web drawn through the whole community, from top to bottom, in all directions. Certain persons, Palle Gaustrup among them, had corruptly exploited the shortages during the Occupation and pulled many others down with them. Li didn't understand the ramifications of it, but Gaus was on the front page of the newspaper all the time and she was proud to have known him. The Løvin family continued to speak up for Gaus' help during the war: he was not a criminal, only perhaps just too clever. And he had made use of a gap in the law. Tobias didn't think you could blame a man for doing that.

At Easter 1952, the Cat lay in bed screaming. She wept and she cried out to the girls to find Jas, because her present marriage was a total misunderstanding. The girls had no idea what to do, for their mother had just had a new baby and, besides, Jas had already married that lovely English mannequin.

Jas' new wife, known to everyone as Velvet Arse, was creative and had a column in the *Politiken* magazine, in which she sketched and gave advice to women who wanted to transform lace curtains into an evening stole. Once, Jas and Gwendoline turned a whole row of terrace houses in Ørholm, where they lived, into an Italian village with a church tower. Bald Jas sat on top, moustachioed and wearing the cloak of a Benedictine monk, ringing a bell with one hand and waving a bottle of Chianti in the other. The newspaper had described the party in detail, except for the end, when Velvet Arse climbed into a tree and Jas stood below her calling: "Velvet Arse, Velvet Arse, do come down." But Velvet Arse refused to come down until he promised her a leopard-skin coat.

He was happy to promise her that, for they had just heard Jas was suffering from a deadly disease. Now he could understand why he had played the wrong note when he was playing the Polonaise in A flat for his final exam at the Conservatoire, and why one of his shoulders felt so strange when he was living with Li. And it was also why his right hand grew withered and all the nerves in it died. No longer able to play the piano, he sold it rather than have to see it standing there, reminding him of everything he could no longer do. He was 36. He had to keep the hand warm by wearing a suede glove all the year round and especially in winter, not because he was cold but because he couldn't feel if he was. He was diagnosed with a spinal disease called amiotrophic lateral sclerosis (ALS), incurable and congenital: the doctor called it a devil whom Jas had better try to come to terms with. So when the devil laughed, Jas laughed back, turned a whole street into an Italian village, and promised Velvet Arse a leopard-skin coat.

The Cat screamed for Jas and vomited because she had taken too many pills. And the girls cleaned up, mostly Myren, who was so good. The Cat begged Zeste to pass her the razor blades so she could cut her wrists again, so that everyone could see how sad she was. But Zeste's only reaction was to try passing the newborn child to its mother, without success. Rejn asked if she wanted to see its cock.

Li was afraid of her new baby. When she was in the Volkswagen on the way to Gentofte, her waters had broken and Li barely managed to climb the stone steps before giving birth to the boy through ice and snow. Her first son. She took one look at him and said: "He will be an alcoholic." He was the image of his father. And when the others tried to reassure her that everything would be fine, she ignored them. She had *seen* the child, who looked like Rejn's father, the sottish reserve postman who slept on staircases, bottle in hand; she had *seen* how the newborn boy resembled the whole of Rejn's family. There wasn't a scrap of Løvin in him.

Through her various whole- and half-hearted attempts at suicide, Li relinquished the last thread connecting her to what we understand as humanity and ventured into a no-man's-land. Out there she obtained absolute power and instead of being a human she became an element, like water or rock. Sailing in her skeleton sea was like paddling between Scylla and Charybdis. She had borne a son, given him the look that turned everything white, and then called him Orm, worm. The boy was always crying, because there was a limit to how much Zeste and Myren could make up for their mother's shortcomings. For one thing, they could not breast-feed him. On Palm Sunday Li crawled into the bathroom. When she ignored their knocks, and pale red water oozed into the corridor, Rejn kicked the door down. They found her in a blood bath. She could not manage her little child, but had not had the strength to lead it into the forest.

Six-year-old Myren struggled with the domestic tasks, but lanky Zeste with her bristly hair thought only of glamour. And compensation. On behalf of the family. Something wonderful must happen to offset their misfortunes and send them all off into the world, restored to happiness. Zeste promised herself that one day she would stand on a stage and declaim that no-one had the right to ill-treat a child just because it did not live up to its parents' fantasies. Zeste was too young to see that Li was tortured with shame at being such a monstrous mother and would rather kill herself than her child. She had married Rejn to break the straight line to her own mother, who had always been lying down with a damp cloth on her forehead moaning, just as Katze's mother before her had. But no matter how much Li squirmed on the hook, she could never free herself. Sexual passion had drawn her into a pit, and she did not have the emotional stamina to survive such a fall.

Zeste understood, young as she was, that she would have to assume responsibility for Myren and herself, and also for Li.

At that time there was no official supervision of children, no system for enforced removal. If there had been, the whole family would have been taken away. There was, officially, no such thing as post-natal psychosis or post-partum depression. There was stark staring madness and punishable ill-treatment of children, but never in a nice house with a piano or a happy family with spouses who were crazy about each other. There were long periods when the Dog and the Cat lay in a locked bedroom, and then the Cat had red cheeks, and she probably ate something that day, and the children would be happy. But when she was happy the children felt ignored, because then she no longer needed them. She only really needed them when she was cheating over prescriptions at the chemist's.

When the Cat was well, they all pretended that nothing had ever been wrong. Even when she came home from a psychiatric hospital, they had to behave as if she had never been gone. Li took pride in knowing everything about psychiatric diagnoses, which she had learned by heart when she was a secretary in a psychiatric department. It was unthinkable that so much as one phrase of a diagnosis could apply to her. It had become the private sport of the Dog and the Cat to trick the daft psychiatrists so they could have their little game of life in peace. To fornicate and to die.

Li didn't need a diagnosis. What in truth she needed was to review her life and draw some conclusions, but she didn't dare. So life drew the conclusions for her. Because it was impossible for Li to have any problem that the Dog couldn't fix – with fucking – the couple placed themselves outside any universal reality. This unreality was far worse than death by drowning or poisoning, worse than blood and vomit and even the crying child Orm. Thus it was that Zeste always fantasised about the theatre as the most real of worlds.

*

At Aunt Bekka's, for example, everything was more real. Aunt Bekka was beautiful, with her classic profile, olive skin, gleaming black hair, lovely letter-box red mouth and fine teeth. She wore full black skirts with a wide patent-leather belt round her narrow waist and carried a raffia basket over her shoulder. Though often courted, Bekka was indifferent and self-sufficient. No man could hold a candle to her father.

In 1950 Bekka had worked with the doctors, who prepared the *Jutlandia*, a hospital ship, for Korea, and more recently she had travelled to Hungary with the Red Cross. Above her bed hung a crucifix and she stashed a green pistachio cake with chocolate icing in the larder. She had moved from Gammel Mønt into the first floor of an apartment building near Myren and Zeste when she could no longer stand the explosive atmosphere between her parents. It was like sitting on an atom bomb that had been primed, then the mission aborted. Her pride would not let her suffer more humiliation.

Because she had failed the preliminary examinations, Aunt Bekka had not become a doctor. Perhaps it was because the exam was on a Wednesday, and everyone said that on Wednesdays the Evil One was watching you, so you might as well kiss that exam goodbye. Or perhaps it was because, instead of studying, she had spent hours in bed with a sexologist who later became notorious and had too many time-consuming problems for Bekka to get her work done, although they had intended to study together.

What pained Bekka most was having to beg her father for money to buy a textbook and hearing him always say, "Is that really necessary?" She would rather do without an education than see her father behave so pitiably.

So it was Bekka's fate to be half a doctor, half a Jew, half a writer. Like her sister, she worked as a doctor's secretary, and it was not long before Balder was publishing medical material in *Berlingske Tidende*.

*

When the Gammel Mønt bomb did not explode, but rather implode, Bekka sought comfort with the sisters at Farum, a Roman Catholic convent. Catholicism attracted her, but Judaism restrained her. "I feel torn," she always said.

Zeste sought comfort with Bekka, who gave her the sort of motherly warnings found in medical novels for sale in railway stations, the ones that always recommended the wearing of clean underwear. For Zeste wore a roll of foam rubber round her waist that she had sewn onto an electric lead with clumsy gigantic twine stitches. It was Zeste's attempt to fashion a stiff petticoat, which made her feel like a queen – albeit a scruffy one.

"But suppose you got run over!" Aunt Bekka said.

"Well?"

"But suppose you met the man of your life!"

"What man?"

"The consultant! Imagine, if you had to have an operation, and he saw your underwear!" Zeste pictured herself on an operating table, without arms and legs, and didn't understand how her underclothes would cause problems. Still, she appreciated Aunt Bekka's solicitude.

She and Myren appreciated Katze's solicitude as well. Whenever they spent the night at Gammel Mønt, Katze would praise her wonderful grandchildren. Tobias would search feverishly – under the table, behind the lamp, under the dish of potatoes – before announcing, "I can't see any wonderful grand-children anywhere."

What the girls liked best was sitting out in the kitchen while Marie made them little sandwiches. They joined in, baking Madeira cake and preparing stuffed cabbage with nutmeg, just as the Director (he was still called that) had liked it during the Riga period. The whole time, Marie chatted away about this and that, and life for the time being seemed real.

Katze was tired when she came home from the office and had her drink with her feet up, but she always put clean white rustling bed-linen on the big mahogany beds, and she let the girls beat eggs with sugar. Together they recited bedtime stories and prayers. With sweet-sour breath and big tears rolling down her cheeks, Katze wept because her children and grandchildren were the only ones who mattered to her in the whole world. When she was alone with her God she acknowledged that her children hadn't received the love they deserved, but she blamed it all on Tobias for being so full of deceit. He had robbed her of her strength, all the concentration she should have afforded to her children. But because Katze felt her failure as a mother so keenly, she was determined to be a good grandmother. And so, when her little grandchildren would ride the rickety lift past the mezzanine, she always called after them: "Watch out for needles and trams!" Afterwards, they would run to the corner, even if they weren't going that way, because Grandmother was at the window waving until they couldn't see her any more. Tobias mattered to her too, of course, especially when he was no longer there. One Whitsunday morning he quite simply was not there, not because he had died but because he had left.

Katze and Tobias were not divorced in the '20s when they realised that their union was an unhappy misalliance. Katze and Tobias were not divorced in the '30s, when abundant – and tempting – alternative offers in wanton Riga strained their endurance. They were not divorced in the '40s when flight and separation drained their patience. And when they were divorced in the '50s, it was not on account of any particular provocation.

Tobias moved into the architect-designed, modernist block where Aunt Bekka had been living, taking with him his heavy mahogany furniture from Riga and Rosenvænget. Katze wept, having no idea what had happened, thinking it was all a plot against her. It was the weak Balder, the crazed Li and little Miss Know-It-All who had conspired to rescue their idolised father from her vale of tears. She lost her will to live, and couldn't find a Biblical passage to inspire her to pull herself together.

Li got better. Tobias was the only one who could get her to leave her bed and brush her hair. He invited her out on a car trip through Jutland where they stayed at inns and he made sure that she ate. When Tobias asked a waiter for fresh prawns, Li felt as though she was hovering on a little pink cloud. When the waiter brought camouflaged canned prawns, Tobias would have none of it. The waiters bowed, sensing that they were dealing with an authentic gentleman. It might not be a sign of the highest intellect to be able to tell the difference between canned food and fresh, but Tobias had taken a stand against the no-harm-trying attitude that was gaining popularity. Because there *was* harm in trying.

So Li recovered and her world fell back into place. She knew that she made great demands on life that life could not fulfil. When everything was "sub-standard", she just wanted to end it all. Indeed, her sincere opinion was that her nearest and dearest would be better off without her. Only Tobias had lifted her spirits again.

On their tour of Jutland she realised that most of the world's misery had glanced off Tobias. He never bothered to regret all that he had lost in the Baltic. The fate of the Jews had not impaired his love of life. As for his flight and his own life, he was a fearless gambler. Only one thing wounded him deeply: his daughter's unhappiness. He had coped with the evacuation of the Danes from Riga when the Russians came. He had coped with the family escape to Sweden when the Germans came. But, faced with Li's misery, he was powerless.

Balder meanwhile followed in his father's footsteps and cleverly and conscientiously rescued a Danish couple who had landed up in Riga after the war. Engineer Leopold Freydberg and his wife had been unable to get out, however often they applied to the authorities in Moscow. Balder passed off their rescue as a complete coincidence.

> I was walking along the main street in Riga when a woman I did not know, seeing the Danish flag pin in my lapel, stopped and asked if I was Danish. She told me that a Danish-born lady, who would be worth my visiting, lived at Vielandes Iela 10. I went to see Mr and Mrs Freydberg twice during my stay in Riga, they lived in two rooms of their originally six-roomed apartment. Seven Russians lived in the other rooms.

*

It was quite an achievement for Balder to travel from Denmark to the USSR as a tourist, especially since he had married a very sharp woman who had never allowed her husband much latitude. She was nicknamed Sharpy because she couldn't pronounce the word "sharpy" as a child. At their wedding, the bride's father toasted Balder with tears in his eyes, "I am sorry for Balder, who is marrying my daughter. But I, her father, rejoice – I am finally rid of her."

The bride's mother sat smiling, as if it was pure honeyed oratory, but all the guests were dumbfounded. Some were shocked that a father could speak of his own daughter in those terms, saying that if the daughter was sharp there were obviously reasons for that. She would be different when she was married to Balder and had her own children. Others thought it interesting that a woman so apparently wicked could exist outside fairy tales. Especially when the wickedness was caparisoned in dark blue bourgeois dresses with white collars and cuffs, pearls, coquettish fringe and court shoes. Sharpy was a trained pharmacist and Li visualised her as a poisoner with the fringe transformed into snakes and the collar and cuffs into semen and mucus. A veritable Medusa!

It turned out that while many women of her generation were rejecting the role of mother and housewife to pursue their own careers, Sharpy resigned her post at the chemist's to devote herself to her husband's well-being. She spoke only of food and ruled the house with an iron fist. Much later, her children said of their mother: "She never showed love, but whenever she was particularly awful and threatened to kill us, she always made pancakes afterwards."

Sharpy didn't let the children or Balder out of her sight. Because she even controlled what the children and Balder thought, they didn't dare to think anything that would annoy or irritate her. She counted the minutes Balder took to walk from Dronningens Tværgade to his job in Pilestræde, and she telephoned to check that he had gone straight there.

Sharpy had enrolled both herself and her husband in the Conservative Party. A fierce anti-Communist, she was ready to fight any Social-Democrat attempt to stage a revolution in Denmark. She had agreed to let Balder take the trip to the Baltic only so that he could bring back accurate information for the Danes on how the people of the USSR lived behind the bars of their Communist prison. Balder was relieved to be for once allowed out.

After reaching home, Balder applied to H.C. Hansen, the prime minister, who subsequently appealed to Bulganin and Krushchev, who at last granted permission for the Danish Freydberg family to return to Denmark, "after sixteen hard years".

*

When Li was once more able to carry out her work as the conscientious and highly praised secretary she had always been, they had to find someone to look after Orm. Rejn found a family who took care of the boy, and Li discovered only one snag: it was a proletarian family, and the mother wiped Orm's face with a dishcloth. Li watched her son and detected him developing proletarian manners and pronouncing certain syllables unsuitably. She would correct him until he was on the point of crying. And when he cried, she hit him; when he cried still more, she threatened to throw him from their moving car.

When Orm was two, Li contemplated sending him to a psychiatrist, for she considered him alarmingly uncreative. "He is happiest just sitting and playing in mud!" She was also critical of his drawings, which were shapeless scribbles on white paper –

none of the glowing camels and burning desert suns that Zeste had turned out at Orm's age. Worse, when Li asked what the scribbles meant, he said "rain". Yes, he was sure to be an alcoholic.

Because Zeste, as the firstborn, was charged with restoring her family's honour, Myren carried the practical burdens on her shoulders. She was only nine and no-one ever thought about her, and her only survival mechanism was her big sister, who, by the fact of her older years alone, proved that it was possible to go on living. Zeste acted as a buffer and protected Myren from their mother's lethal gaze. All the same, her motherlessness produced alarming symptoms in her – the very symptoms Anna Freud discerned in London children orphaned during the Blitz. That autistic rocking backwards and forwards that nothing on earth could arrest. Nothing except Li, and she was never there. Myren sat on her bed for hours rocking back and forth with rigid, expressionless eyes. Zeste dared not look at her then for she would burst out crying, and she had vowed never to cry.

If Myren shouldered the task of serving the family, it wasn't altogether a Cinderella situation. She had been allowed to go riding with an English lady in Gammel Holte. On one winter's day, however, Myren fell from the horse. No-one had told her how dangerous it was to ride in snow boots. When she fell off, one boot stuck fast in the stirrup, and she was dragged along for four kilometres before anyone noticed. Her whole back was skinned until it was one bloody wound, only the patches of snow had saved her life.

Myren bore the accident stoically. She took the near-fatal fall – the fall that Li feared for herself – in her stride. At long last, something real had happened to her. The whole family gathered around her hospital bed, where Myren spent a month on her stomach. Finally she had the attention she had for so long deserved, even if she had nearly lost her life to get it. The family stood around, looking intensely at the wound. They contemplated it with horror and sorrow, but also with relief. Here, for the first time, there was evidence of the entire family's fall.

Except for Rejn, who had never fallen anywhere. He clung to Li because she was beautiful and came from Gammel Mønt. Parting from her even for a few days sickened him. He lost his inner balance, described his loneliness as empty and cold. Though Li was nothing but a bag of bones, to Rejn she was a great beauty, the light of his life.

> I think of you asleep, so warm and soft. I am so delighted with you that it's like a new present each time. I don't think many people have what we have together. Other men, forced to leave their wives, enjoy the change, but I just want to get home to you as fast as possible. I love you completely – you are the loveliest thing in the world. Oh, how good it will be to get home again. We should really make love on Sunday, for it has been so long.

Was Tobias as dependent on Katze, in his own way? For Tobias only lived by himself in the modern terrace for three months, relieved to be away from Katze and Gammel Mønt with its hidden bottles and bitter remarks. He didn't want to go on hearing that he had deceived her and squandered her hard-earned money. He was tired of listening. But then Katze fell on her knees and prayed to her God for Tobias to return. Her life was worth nothing without him. She prayed and implored him and promised to turn over a new leaf. In the end, unable to resist these symptoms of remorse, Tobias moved back. He reasoned that, although they had long been separated in spirit and had only one interest in common – American films – they did have a shared life that was worth more than their separate individual lives together. No-one could live in the past, of course, but they were more than 60 and couldn't live in the future either. So Tobias resigned himself and endured the streams of tenderness and bitterness that flowed from Katze. Perhaps it was just love.

Li dared not think of leaving Rejn, she leaned on him as if he were the pillar that supported the whole house. Divorce was growing fashionable – half the parents in Zeste's progressive school were divorced. Instead Li insisted that Orm be baptised. Rejn was opposed to any such hocus-pocus, but Li had stayed with the sisters at Farumgård several times in rehabilitation, and amidst the gentle maternal atmosphere, she had unburdened herself in an unguarded moment and asked if perhaps Orm's unhappiness stemmed from his unchristened state? All the nuns had nodded in unison.

And so, when he was two, Orm was baptised in Farum Church.

He was given the names Aske Johannes, but continued to be called Orm. He walked to the font himself with a sulky expression, carrying a red fire engine.

Rejn kept his head below the parapet. He didn't mind the Christian shit – as long as the finances held up. But if Li resigned from her job, they never would. During her last convalescence, Rejn had written her a letter with calculations showing the advantage of her keeping her full-time job, how no-one would benefit if she stopped.

Money wasn't everything, he wrote, but Li could put two and two together. If she stopped contributing to the family's survival, she was a worse traitor than before. Li felt that Rejn gave her no choice, even though the double shifts had been responsible for her collapse. It was true that, on the face of it, Rejn managed most of the practical tasks. And yet, when she was in hospital or convalescing, everyone noticed what was missing at home, all the details that saved it from becoming a Boy Scout camp. She was an aesthetic principle; she was their common memory, the one who remembered for them all – what she wanted to remember. Li was the one who transformed the ordinary into *life* – even if she died. She maintained standards – even when she lay in a pool of vomit. It was the Løvin in her, in spite of everything.

Rejn sometimes wondered if he had taken on too hefty a load in marrying a divorced woman with two children, but he never considered leaving her. He had been lucky with the children, who were well brought up and they were always overjoyed when he returned home with presents for them: jolly hats from Montenegro, jeans from America.

Breasts were emerging under the jade green angora jumper he had bought for Zeste in Italy. Li might refuse or be unable to play her part as the lady of the house, but luckily there were the two girls, Myren looking after the housework and mothering; Zeste always keeping Rejn entertained. The pair of them ensured the survival of the family.

Zeste was actually well-suited to fulfil the role of a grown-up woman. She never played and was always keen to listen to adults' conversation. When that bored her, she would fetch a botany book and go into the woods to count the flowers and memorise their names. Or she would disappear into the basement, or even – to Rejn's astonishment – into the church.

The role of lady of the house was a delicate matter when a child assumed it. The only time Rejn had ever smacked Zeste was when she had tried to throw him and the Cat out, just as if they were a couple of children interfering with Zeste and her playmate.

One afternoon during the Suez crisis, Rejn's friend Marsken turned up unannounced with his family. Zeste insisted that they stay for dinner. The yellow vanished from Li's eyes; she didn't like guests, certainly not for several hours, and now the child had invited the whole hunch-backed Marsken tribe to dinner! Afterwards both Rejn and Li scolded Zeste severely: what was she, a *child*, thinking of to take the initiative in the family! She must learn who the grown-ups in the family were, and who made the decisions.

Well, yes, she'd be glad to know that, and that, by the way, was the very reason that she had asked the Marskens for dinner: they were a real family. A family where you could tell the difference between the grown-ups and the children. She wanted Marsken and his family to witness the shame her pride prevented her from revealing, and she wanted his help. She regarded Marsken and his family as a light that illuminated the way ahead. For one thing, he had a job at the UN and might be sent to the Far East. He volunteered to try getting Rejn a job like that. It was well paid and concerned with helping the poor. Zeste believed that if Rejn had such work, he might help Li escape her feeling of perpetually sinking into a morass.

He applied – and had good references – but it was far from certain that Rejn would get the job. If he did, however, he would have to adopt Zeste and Myren, for the UN paid for the children's travelling expenses and education, and that would relieve the strain on the family budget. Rejn couldn't stand unnecessary expense, and Jas was hopeless at supporting his children.

Jas had always found it convenient to forget what he owed others, so when he was asked if Rejn could adopt his children, Jas readily assented. He was fed up with having the police at his heels ever since Rejn had reported him for missing child support payments.

Li was shaken when she saw that the man she had married was without mercy. A gentleman's agreement should have been enough to resolve the situation, and of course the moment the police stepped onto the scene, the family plummeted into the working classes.

Li was sent to a mental hospital, not an ordinary psychiatric ward, but a real asylum for hopeless causes. They said she could only get proper treatment in a proper hospital. There would be no more visits to the emergency room and stomach pumpings now. They would take her situation seriously, and she would receive all the necessary care. That is, so long as Rejn got the job. After all, it wouldn't do for a wealthy lady to be in a worse position than the poor and sick her husband was employed to help. Li was proud not to be in St John's, where KIS had been. She conceived during visiting hours, and some months later a strange lady with black hair and a baby in her stomach came home again. She maintained the hair colour was natural. The reddish gold from wartime had been scrubbed out.

Zeste looked at the new woman and prayed that she would become the lady of the house.

3

THE ISLAND OF PARADISE

On August 26th, 1958, Li wrote to her parents after Tobias had suffered another thrombosis.

> Dear Father and Mother, Many thanks for Mother's letter with the pocket money. What a shame that you're having such miserable weather, but I hope it's nice indoors at Hornbæk House. I hope Mama isn't too troublesome. Tell her I was very pleased with the Aarestrup poems, and yes, I have thanked her.
>
> All goes on as usual here – as I write, a little fellow with inquisitive brown eyes is trying to get at the typewriter. He can say "Mummy" now and take a few steps.
>
> On the last day of Rejn's holiday, we went up the coast to Louisiana, it was very beautiful – you really must see it if Father can drive that far; and we have had lots of visitors, so many people wanted to celebrate Rejn's new post – I only wish they wouldn't stay so long.
>
> Zeste has started her Academic Course, she came home with several tons of books, every day she has to get through 16 pages in four or five subjects, but she is thrilled and reads until late at night. Myren leaves on Thursday for Bornholm with her class and is away for ten days. We'll miss her, she is so good and helpful.

Rejn is working on the adoption of the girls, Jas has agreed to it, so we can take them abroad. Love and kisses, and a good recovery for Father, from Li.

*

In the New Year, Li embarked with her two boys, Orm and Tor, on a steamer bound for the Far East. Myren accompanied them as nanny. Rejn had flown out earlier to start his job with the UN in Colombo and to find a place for the family to live. Zeste stayed in Denmark to take her entrance exam for middle school. The Dog had worried about the Cat's ability to cope with the long sea voyage alone with two small children, but Li did have Myren and besides, she could summon incredible strength when necessary.

Rejn hoped for a fresh future for them both, after the beginning in Sorgløse had been so hard. At least in their new life the Cat would not be stressed. He could offer the highlife and servants galore. What more could she want?

Rejn wrote to Li from head office in Delhi.

Ah, my sweet little beloved, what shall I write but that I miss you more and more each day. I'm so lonely and have no human contact. I haven't been with any other girls, in case you're wondering. I'm even lonelier when I look at them, as for instance last night, when Dr H. and I went "out" to a place where there was a band and a "floor show" with two fifth-rate English girls.

As I sit here looking at pictures of you and the children, I am filled with longing. You may be sure all will go well. I think that you and the children will like the Orient when you get used to it – I see so much that would appeal to you. Zeste will be thrilled to paint all the women, though you must explain to Myren that people are not kind to their animals here. If she's not prepared, she'll be shocked. But they do treat their children well.

Tomorrow, hopefully, we go to Colombo to start on the job, and I can begin to organise a nest for my Mother of Pearl and our lovely children. I can't wait to see you again and kiss and hug you. Take good care of yourself now, and don't let the voyage wear you out. Love to all the children, be good and write, so that "Paradise on earth" will move from the palace in the red fort – remember the film? – down to my humble dwelling.

From your lonely and devoted . . .

Tobias accompanied Li to the Central Station, and she felt she had her father's blessing as the train set off for Genoa. There a ship waited to take them into their unknown future. Li was in good spirits. She had done her homework and was well informed on Ceylonese culture. She would get used to having several pounds of amethysts and star sapphires slide through her fingers like sugar and flour. She was going to live on an island in the Indian Ocean, which Sinbad the Sailor had long ago dubbed the Island of Paradise. Many had visited since Sinbad's time – Portuguese, Dutch, British – but none had disagreed with him. She would encounter a dual population of Singhalese and Tamils, pitted against each other by the British in the classical pattern: divide and rule. Tamils mostly originated from South India, they had been imported by the British to work their great tea and rubber plantations because they were a cheaper and more willing workforce than the native population. The Tamils had their own language and darker skin. At that time the Tamils seemed very "far away" to the Danes, and no-one would then have believed that the question of how the Tamils should be treated would ever generate a state trial in Denmark, or that the Island of Paradise would become a blood bath.

For the first time in her life, Li would see hollow trees with roots in the air, water buffalo, colobus monkeys and wild elephants. Cicadas, palmeira palms and malaria mosquitoes. She would be given live baby swallows, eat fresh flower heads and lotus seeds for dessert. She would watch the Indian Ocean's waves, as high as houses, crashing on the beach, grow accustomed to the rainy season at the end of April and look forward to the monsoon winds. She would think in yards, pounds, gallons, Fahrenheit; she would drive on the left hand side of the road.

The journey and the whole situation reminded her of her family's move to Riga 30 years earlier. She felt as if she was sailing, not only towards a fairy tale but also to a more dignified, safer life, a life in which she could find her parents. It was as though she was being carried back to her childhood on a wave. The ship moved both up and down, but she still felt she was rising. She was sure that however foreign the island was, Ceylon would recognise her.

In Port Said, an Arab guided Li, who could buy all the leather poufs and copper dishes she wished. She could always "pay later". Only three years before, in 1956, the town had been bombed by the British and French in response to Nasser's nationalisation of the Suez Canal. The solution lay for the time being with the UN's "blue berets".

At first they had to lie at anchor for several hours, waiting for a convoy. Then, because the canal was too narrow for ships to overtake one another, thirteen ships sailed in a line astern. On both sides you could see the desert, palms, small villages, and incredibly dirty Arabs.

She grew acclimatised to the heat on the three-week-long voyage and, on arrival in Colombo, was ready to strip off her stockings and crocodile shoes.

Throughout the voyage, Myren had to feed the baby vanilla ice because he refused to eat anything else. This idiosyncratic behaviour reminded Li of her beloved father, so she respected the little one's stubbornness. When Orm refused to eat, however, Li dismissed him as fussy. You couldn't of course bring up every child along the same lines, because children vary.

Everyone agreed that Tor, nicknamed Little Smallest, was quite special. Not only was he conceived in the waiting room of a psychiatric ward, he was so small that now and then his family wondered at his very existence. Even in the last month of her pregnancy, Li wasn't showing: she remained as thin as the starving masses that the UN were working to save. But now, thanks to Rejn's job, things were finally improving. Best of all, Little Smallest was a survivor, for he was born with brown eyes, like Li's father.

The United Nations, set up after the Second World War in 1949, turned out to be an aid organisation not only for the poor, but for the rich as well. The ruling class, which was threatened or obsolete in many wealthy countries, now had a fresh chance to rule the so-called underdeveloped nations under the guise of helping them.

While colonialism had left most subjugated cultures intact – even adding plantations, boulevards, railways and buildings – the U-Land Aid was indispensable in promoting the growth of a market economy, levelling wealth everywhere, and wiping out cultural variations. Thereafter, exoticism functioned only as a feature in a spreading global industry: tourism.

At the time when the Dog and the Cat arrived in Ceylon, the country was newly independent and still marked by old colonial ways. Everywhere placards advertised, "Your skin can get the attractive white colour with . . . "

On February 18th, 1959, Li wrote home to Gammel Mønt.

> We are finally here and it's splendid. We're staying at the Sea-View Club for a day or two, all the windows and doors are open, and I'm writing beside an electric fan. Black servants in snow-white clothes creep around tidying the room. You don't notice them at all, except when you need something, then they come up without a sound. Very friendly and efficient, nothing like Indians. The best part of all is that I have a nanny. A fine one, too! At first we had no-one, but Rejn put the word out that we needed one, and yesterday dozens came. They all had good references, but the one we chose has the best. She does everything for the children: she washes and sews and prepares food for Little Smallest.
>
> Soon we're moving into an elegant apartment in Galle Face Court, on the sea. I can't imagine the Waldorf-Astoria being better. The drawing room is so big you almost need a telescope to see one another. Deep, soft chairs and sofas in pale pastel colours, carpets on the floors, a birdcage with quiet little coral-coloured birds. Our bedroom is the size of Gammel Mønt's drawing room, dining room and bedroom put together, and every bedroom has its own bathroom. We are taking on the owner's servants as part of the tenancy. The owners, third-generation Harrovians, were sensible enough

to offer them a bonus if we are satisfied with them, ensuring that they don't slack off while they are away. We have a cook and first boy to clean the rooms and second boy to do floors and bathrooms, he cleans the taps and the lavatories every day and we have a daily *dhobi*, laundryman. It isn't as difficult as I expected to give orders – the blacks have enormous respect for Lady, Master and even the Little Masters. They stand quite still waiting for orders, and then you do what is expected of you. I think it can be quite hard to find out what one must touch and the other not. Our new nanny is a Singhalese and a Buddhist. The other servants are Tamil (Hindu), so I hope there won't be any trouble.

Now we're going over to the European Swimming Club, where two members must recommend the family before you can join. There are mixed swimming pools too, and many of the UNICEF people say UN people should be members there too, but we think the European one is more fun. The club is incredibly over-British. It feels like being on an English estate, with vast lawns, gigantic club premises, a library, bar, and restaurant. When I went yesterday, I was introduced to a handful of ladies, who were knitting and talking about "going home" the whole time. Very friendly and helpful. Strangely enough, the Scandinavians are always met with goodwill, for the British don't like the Americans and vice versa, the Singhalese don't like the British and no-one likes the Germans. Later in the afternoon, the women and children go home and the men come in and sit like statues, reading the paper and yelling "boy" at intervals.

Water, grass, sky, sand are so marvellous you think you're dreaming, it's the first time since Riga I have enjoyed bathing.

*

At Gammel Mønt, no-one questioned who could interpret Li's letters best. For, when it came to correspondence from the Far East, Katze knew more than Tobias, something she didn't hesitate to remind him of. Had *he* ever read the letters of Uncle Sophus, the Consul from Yokohama?

"No," Tobias said without taking the cigar out of his mouth.

"You should read them, my love, they would give you an excellent sense of the East."

"Li is in Ceylon, not Japan."

"But there is something I don't quite like . . . "

"Hm."

"She doesn't write about her reunion with Rejn."

"You get a good impression of their quarters."

"I'm afraid that she writes what she thinks we want to hear."

"It's a very well-written letter."

"I don't think her marriage to Rejn is happy."

"You're imagining things, as usual."

"You must admit there's a deafening silence about the joy of their reunion."

"Must we invent sorrows?"

"Well, I'm worried."

"There'd have to be something wrong if you weren't."

Tobias was in a bad mood. Although he didn't care much about Aunt Titta's son Ib, he was peeved. We recall that Uncle Otto made the boy's life a misery and how he and Titta even left him to fend for himself when they fled Denmark. And yet, despite it all, the boy had studied hard and was now a lawyer. He had even gone to Israel and married an Orthodox girl from the Mahler family. What infuriated Tobias, however, was Ib's plan to change his name to Løvin. The Løvins, his father and his uncles, had struggled to cleanse their name of the rubbish of swaying prayer shawls and earlocks. Løvin had become a good assimilated Danish name, free from religious overtones, and along comes young Ibby, purloining the name and having an Orthodox wedding! You might as well ship the Løvins back to the Polish ghetto!

Worse still, Ib had no right to the name, as it was only his mother Titta's married name, a name she had taken only after Ib had been born. Tobias thought of taking Ib to court via one of his bridge partners, who would help for a bottle of brandy, but Ib had specialised, not only in Danish law but also in Mosaic law. What a swindle! Tobias was forced to grit his teeth and suffer the humiliation of having a pious Jew called Løvin in the family. The family agreed that it would be better that the name die out altogether.

As for Ib, he was upset by the family's defeatism, at how ready they were to be annihilated by assimilation. Hadn't the war proven that assimilation was the coward's way? Why should a German Jew fight for his German fatherland in the First World

War if he was destined for the camps? No. Now they must fight for their new fatherland, the land of the Bible, so that the past should never be repeated. It surprised Ib that Tobias never used the word Jew, certainly not about himself. They had both fled when the persecution of the Jews began and yet still Tobias had never uttered the word Jew in all the time they had shared a room in Stockholm. Perhaps it was that very silence which had turned Ib into a Zionist.

No question that a kind of myth was associated with the name, even Sharpy had started to use it with pride, which seemed odd, for Løvin wasn't exactly Rothschild or Metro Goldwyn Mayer. Yet it was a name one had to live *up* to, although Sharpy did not realise that. She washed and polished, she scrubbed and scoured; she cooked and roasted, cleaned and ironed. The children were as well-scrubbed as the kitchen table, and nothing but Persil-washed politeness issued from their mouths. All the while, Katze and Tobias looked on with indifference. However hard Sharpy tried, she could never impress them. Plainly, it took more to become a personality, and she wondered what it could be . . .

Her watch over her husband remained ferocious: he couldn't relieve himself or play his drum without her watching him. And so, although Balder had played the drums, he had given them up when Sharpy declared this hobby infantile. The last straw came when he was no longer permitted to play his jazz records in his own house. When Sharpy insisted that the volume be turned low, for propriety's sake, Balder just gave up: what was the point of listening to Basie, Benny Goodman and Ellington as background music? He thought of the fun he'd had before the war when he and Jas had made music together.

It may seem strange that a man like Balder should knuckle under so willingly. But there is a particular road open to a man who, for whatever reasons, seeks protection in this life. If it is a domineering father he is fleeing, he might permit a mother to devour him. He can choose between the bad and the good mother only if he can tell the difference. But in both cases, she must be paid off. The price is the same, and Balder willingly pays it in exchange for the freedom to develop his creative talents.

He wanted to make his mark in journalism, and he wrote at a time when there was something worth writing about. All the new medical discoveries from America, which Balder gobbled up in the popular science pages of the glossy magazines, would heal the world. He passed on the news to Danish readers, who cherished their eternal life. With the war and the discovery of penicillin, we entered a new scientific epoch, and medical science could now cure almost any ill. To a man like Balder, who flung himself with a child's enthusiasm into every technological advance, eternal life was nothing less than a human right.

One day in Kronprinsessegade, Sharpy, having just finished the housework, sat on her flowery chintz sofa. Everything was scrupulously clean and tidy, and not a crumb disgraced the kitchen table. Sharpy was leafing through the directory when she caught sight of one too many Løvins in the columns, an unknown Løvin. And not even a married woman. A social worker, too! A Løvin who was a social worker!

"Balder!" Sharpy screamed.

"Yes, my dear." Balder slouched into the room.

"Balder, there's a new Løvin in the phone book!"

"Oh?"

"A social worker!"

"Oh!"

"She's not married. It must definitely be someone who has stolen the name."

"There might be a story in that. About stealing names . . . "

"First we must find out if she has the legal right to use it. We must ask for an explanation."

"Yes, that's obvious. We must demand an explanation."

"I'll call her at once. What are we waiting for?"

"Yes, what are we waiting for?"

And indeed, when Sharpy heard a woman's voice at the other end of the line with a somewhat proletarian intonation, she couldn't hold back. She yelled into the phone: since when was it the custom to steal other people's lawful possession? Sharpy roared until the mystified social worker slammed down the receiver. The woman – a plump, single mother with a pâté-coloured perm – had never heard that tone of voice before, and she was used to a lot.

"That was the height of insolence! She hung up on me!"

" Indeed, how insolent!"

"We'll go and find her at her address!!"

"And ask for an explanation!"

"Your tie is crooked, Balder."

"She's not going to get away with it," Balder said, straightening his tie.

It was a frightful side street off Vesterbro where Sharpy and Balder had never before set foot.

"A Løvin can't live out here!" Sharpy said, who had driven and found a parking space, although she was reluctant to leave the car in such a ghetto.

After walking up a smelly staircase, they saw it clear as day: the name "Løvin" on the nameplate.

"Bold as brass!" said Sharpy, finger on the doorbell.

"Not for much longer," Balder thought.

Else opened the door, and when she realised it was the mad lady who had telephoned, she asked them inside. As one used to working on legal cases, she believed in nipping a problem in the bud before it festered.

She did not ask them to sit down, and while Sharpy gazed in horror at potty and toys scattered about the floor and huge standing vases with bulrushes and unhygienic reed mace, she listened with half an ear to Else's story about taking the name Løvin from her mother, who took it from her grandmother, who had been "sent into the country" to give birth to her child. Fixing her eyes on the mess around her, Sharpy half-listened to a rambling story about an educational trip to Bremen, a fatal romantic attachment and flight to South America. Soon after Else's grandmother was born in Buenos Aires, her great-grandmother died of yellow fever. The father returned to Europe with his heavy sorrow and the little child. But, once in Marseille, the father was summoned by the health authorities on account of the yellow fever epidemic. When he got back to the harbour, the ship had sailed – with his little child. Else's grandmother grew up in Denmark and earned her keep playing the organ. She married the youngest of a poor farmer's twelve sons. "A marriage of love, damn it," Else said, "and here I am, Else Løvin, after my mother. And I live with my boy Tobias."

Sharpy and Balder rushed down the stinking stairs. When they were out again in the street in the – relatively – fresh air, Sharpy said: "It's all a pack of lies."

"Yes," said Balder, "a pack of lies."

*

On March 9th, 1959, Li writes to Gammel Mønt.

On Wednesday we drove to Ratnapura, which was quite an experience. Outwardly, Colombo seems a rather clean and modern town. You seldom go into the slum districts, and if you do you hurry out again; but on this trip, we couldn't avoid seeing how miserably the ordinary Singhalese live. Weird little dirty banana-palm huts – open to the street. Old people lay like skeletons on the earth floor, dirty children crawled around, and we saw many young teenagers with infants. Very few work. The men squat by the huts chewing betel and spitting it with a gigantic rattle. Women work under the baking sun beating clothes over a muddy pool. The coolies lie under their rickshaws for shade, an ox cart plods along with 100 gallons of Caltex – then I think of you and everything seems so unreal.

There is an enormous contrast between the wretched villages and the big tea and rubber plantations run by the English.

We arrived at the English Resthouse in the evening. It was quite high up a mountain that had a view of Adam's Peak (Sri Pada in Singhalese, which means "the divine footprint"). The Buddhists say that the mountain is holy because the footprint is Buddha's, but the Hindus claim it is Shiva's, and the Muslims think it is Adam's, the first man in the world, who escaped the catastrophe of the Flood because the mountain rose so high in the sky. Rejn says it's all nonsense, and that the "footprint" is nothing but geological deposits.

Nearby we saw the place where they recently made the film about the Japanese treatment of the Allied prisoners of war, *The Bridge on the River Kwai*, with Alec Guinness. It's true that the historic place where the prisoners built the famous bridge is in Thailand, but the film was made here.

After she describes accompanying Rejn and his team to a school to vaccinate 300 children, she writes that they arrived home to find "everything in order: happy children, clean house, dinner prepared, the suitcases unpacked as a matter of course", and that what was so nice was "they like to serve us and make life comfortable for Master and Lady".

Li and Rejn had given up speaking Danish with the boys. Orm spoke a mishmash of Danish and English, and Little Smallest didn't speak a word of Danish. In fact, when he arrived in Ceylon at 18 months, exposed to a mixture of Danish, English, Singhalese and Tamil, he stopped talking altogether. Only when the family decided to use English consistently did Tor consent to express himself. And then only to Nanny, for the most part. He cut himself off altogether from his mother, whom he called Pua. Nanny alone could persuade Little Birdie to eat, eggs, porridge, fish, fruit and meat.

Nanny had a special smell. The Møller family did too. They smelled of pig, she said. Nanny smelled of coconut oil, which she rubbed into her hair. She had red teeth when she chewed betel, and, under her cotton sari, she had an enormous soft rice stomach, which the children were allowed to punch. But Orm wasn't the type to enjoy hitting someone's stomach. He left all the play and tenderness to Little Birdie. Orm scowled and sulked except during Bible lessons at school. He loved Jesus alone.

*

Now that the Dog and the Cat had servants, they no longer needed Myren, so they decided to send her to boarding school. As the Cat wrote to Gammel Mønt, almost all the Europeans sent their children away. The few European children left in Colombo were ruined by adoring servants who cleared up after them, and whom they bullied. The children did nothing but hang about, pestering everyone and making trouble; you never saw a younger child playing or an older child usefully occupied. Myren had found a friend called Primela, but because Primela was coloured, she was not allowed into the swimming club. There was nowhere else for them to go, so the family decided that Myren would be happier at boarding school in the mountains.

Strangely enough, since Li thought American children the most spoiled in the world, she chose an American boarding school for Myren. When Myren complained in her letters to Gammel Mønt, Li insisted that her tales of woe shouldn't be taken too seriously. For Myren wrote only when she was homesick, dissatisfied or out of sorts, never when things went well. Her only chance of learning to write was in English, because Li said she would never catch up on her Danish. And even though Zeste would soon be coming to Colombo, Myren – a child unable to occupy herself, Li believed – shouldn't spend all her time with her sister.

*

Zeste would be travelling first class, as all UN people did then. But more wonderful than that, it sounded as though the Cat had recovered her appetite and was well. She had even written to Marie asking for her recipes for *boeuf stroganoff* and apple cake (the ones from Riga) so that the cook, who loved learning new tricks, could try them out. Li wrote that the cook had determined to fatten up Lady before she left (or however he put it), and the Cat had started to eat toast with crab salad, even for lunch. She was living a life, she wrote – as the tea trolley was rolled in before her and the newly ironed children came to see her after school and shower – you would have thought existed only in a film.

Zeste, who had lived for six months with her teacher in Ballerup, was amazed by the Cat's descriptions of Colombo with its mixture of all the world's nationalities. She wasn't surprised that her mother enjoyed it, because her responsibilities consisted only of telling the servants how many would be coming to dinner. Li always encouraged the Scandinavians to shake up the Singhalese, who were horrified at having to go to parties and always sat along the wall, never touching a drop of alcohol, only fruit juice. Still, Li succeeded, for the Singhalese seemed to enjoy her parties.

It was incredible that the Cat wasn't ill. Zeste herself was feverish for the whole six months she was separated from the Cat and got poor marks for her middle school examination as a result. Forget the exam, the Cat wrote, focus on remembering to bring rye bread, salami and schnapps with you to Ceylon. The Cat was obviously thriving . . . She wrote proudly to Gammel Mønt that she already weighed 38 kilos and didn't take any medicines except iron and vitamin K – her wrinkles had even disappeared! They were waiting for the monsoon winds, and even drawing breath was hard work. She was grateful that at least the children hadn't contracted "prickly heat", the terrible heat rash.

Apart from a violent attack of dysentery that had assailed both the Cat and the Dog during a field trip, Li seemed healthy, even if the tropics were not an ideal place to gain weight. Perhaps it was because Li had started to work twice a week: in the long run, she couldn't bear to live in luxury and be surrounded by so much suffering. She worked at an ambulant orthopaedic polyclinic, serving tea with two other ladies. It was hard physical work, up and down stairs with sweat pouring off her. The hardest thing of all was seeing so many poor, miserable and crippled people, who came in hundreds, always whole families. And there were only three doctors.

Reading the Cat's bulletins – in addition to working, her mother was taking driving lessons! – Zeste felt certain that the Lady, who was so active, was also the lady of the house. But when she arrived in Colombo, Rejn, who now looked more like Alec Guinness than James Dean, met her at the airport and told her that the Cat was ill. It was some mysterious tropical disease no-one could recognise or treat, he said, adding that she had liver inflammation as well. It had all developed quite suddenly. Zeste found her mother in hospital, deathly pale and skeletal. She lay hallucinating in half-darkness.

Zeste had always been mother-sick, but when a mother is always sick then love falls ill too. Beside the bed there was a table covered with a vast array of medicaments prescribed by a German doctor.

Tobias wrote to say that she must really come home *now*, to get proper treatment, a stomach ulcer was no laughing matter. If she couldn't afford the journey, she should just wire to "Løvin Vulkan" and he would send her ticket immediately. She should go to London, where he would meet her so that they could travel to Denmark together.

When Li received the letter, she wrote that there was nothing wrong with her. Her father was the one person she didn't want to frighten or disappoint.

24/7-59
Dear Father, A thousand thanks for your sweet letter, which must have been sent before you had Rejn's telegram. I'm really fine, and I'm not the only one who thinks so, my doctor, nurses, visitors all agree. I've been given big doses of bacteria-killing medicine and the infection has reacted very well. The strict diet is also putting my liver to rights and the doctor says I'm a miracle.

The Consul's wife came recently, quite alarmed, on your initiative. She was very sweet and helpful and took Zeste home with her to lunch. As expected, Zeste has been a big sensation in the town, but she herself does not realise how big.

Now my tea with dry toast has arrived, and I think life is enormously rich. A week ago I couldn't keep down a glass of water with rice flour. Thousands of kisses, Li.

But despite the Cat's objections, the family decided to send her back to Denmark to save her life. Though the disease seemed quite unprovoked – an unknown tropical infection – there was actually something else wrong.

When we consider how hard tropical life was for the European used to temperate environments, we can better understand the colonials' need for luxury, particularly outside the towns. So, even though Li was hardly hacking a trail through jungle every day, it wasn't safe for her to live in the tropics and weigh only 35 kilos. At that time, terms like anorexia or the immune system were not commonly known, but it was obvious that all sorts of diseases were making a beeline for her.

At last the Dog began to suspect there was something wrong with the Cat that fornication could not cure. If that were the case, he would surely lose his footing in the world. There was certainly something wrong that servants, luxury and leisure could not cure. He couldn't understand how anyone, carried though she was in a palanquin of whipped cream and goose feathers, could still have so many problems.

Admittedly, there was one black cloud on the horizon. Indonesia. They had heard that they couldn't stay in Ceylon, and the Europeans agreed that Indonesia was the worst place in all Asia. The thought of having to order all her goods in Singapore, from toothpaste to matches, sounded to Li like a life-threatening Boy Scout camp. She would encounter Communist propaganda and anti-European sentiment everywhere. She also heard that you couldn't cross the street without being accosted, and you couldn't leave the towns because robber bands were swarming over the countryside, and they didn't stop to look at your UN pass. Li dreaded the change. In particular she couldn't bear to be parted from Nanny, who – although she had long ago been forced to leave her own daughter in a convent school to take care of white children – now prayed to Buddha daily that she be allowed to stay with Little Birdie.

Rejn, who had been separated himself from his mother as an infant and sent to a children's home, regarded these separations as pretty normal, especially for a UN man whose job involved constant changes. Such rootlessness suited his temperament, and how else but for the UN could you earn $10,000 a month tax-free plus an education grant?

Li, hallucinating and saying things too frightful to repeat, needed help. She thought that everything was in order, and that it was treacherous of Rejn to send her to Denmark straight into the arms of the shrinks. Having diagnosed an extremely virulent typhus at the National Hospital, doctors had, she thought, successfully tackled her amoeba infection and liver and bladder problems.

It was bad enough to be a psychiatric patient in anonymous Denmark. But in a little town like Colombo, where word travels fast through the foreign colony, it was like being ill in a village. Everyone knew everything. The Dog couldn't keep her illness secret for financial reasons: the illness needed a name if he was to apply for travel expenses and insurance. Li was ashamed at the idea of having to go back. She had made an impossible promise to Dog: to get her weight up to 55 kilos, so he had something to hold on to and wouldn't have to listen to her bones rattling.

After Li left, Rejn wrote to assure her that he would not gossip about her illnesses. Zeste was left behind in Colombo as "the lady of the house". She felt she ought to see to everything, and at the same time she was aware of being watched. She initially thought it was her lovely new dresses that excited all the attention: the lilac one with princess sleeves and waist, and the pink one with tight sleeves to the elbows, the turquoise one with a tie belt. Rejn had suddenly grown very generous about giving her new dresses, because he said it was so cheap to have them made. But it wasn't the dresses that made all the people stare, because they also stared when she had taken off the dresses. She crept around the house, followed by eyes. There was nowhere to hide. Rejn followed her approvingly with his eyes, all too approvingly, and the servants slithered around her when she bathed. She didn't know what to do with herself and felt the tropical heat on her skin like a sticky damp mass inside her chest that stopped her breath.

Zeste hated being the object of this endless gaze from morning until night. But she also felt a certain pride: if only she was onstage, then perhaps the staring wouldn't bother her so much.

One morning she woke up to see Rejn sitting on the edge of her bed. She saw him stretch his arms under her mosquito net. She had nothing but a sheet over her and he could clearly see the silhouette of her hips. With a brief movement he placed his hands on her waist and brought them down along the sides of her thighs. "Just like a vase," he said, and left. Well, now I'm not a virgin any more, Zeste thought, unable to breathe.

4

PASSION

There are certain institutions a Thai respects . . . Religion, the king and his parents. If you tell a Thai that politicians are corrupt, he will kiss you on both cheeks. If you tell him he is a scoundrel, he will not be offended. If you say his wife is a bitch, he will entirely agree with you. But where the three institutions are concerned, I advise you to be careful, for according to police records in this country the number of premeditated murders is very low. So said the prime minister and author Kukrit in a speech to a group of foreigners, among them Li and Rejn, who had just arrived.

Thailand – *muang thai* – means "the land of the free", and you could feel that when you came from what was once a colony. Apart from the Japanese occupation during the Second World War, which stimulated a return to old habits such as secret betel chewing, Thailand had never been colonised.

Traces of the old habit were still to be seen in the gaping fiery red mouths in some old women's faces. The life of these old crones went right back to the turn of the century and they all kept to the same fashion, if you can speak of fashion among the elderly. Zeste stared fascinated at the old women with their white crew cuts, red teeth and sarongs tied like trousers. "Who are they?" she kept on asking. But the Cat and the Dog said they were nobody special, just old women. But they *were* something special.

They were concubines from the legendary court of King Chulalongkorn. When he died in 1910 he had had 77 children by 52 wives. The royal form of polygamy set the standard in Thailand. If you wanted to get on in life it was a good thing to have a little royal blood in your veins, and it wasn't so hard to come by. The entire upper class of Thailand were more or less of royal birth. And the old crew cut concubines with their red, toothless betel mouths were a reminder of the time when there were thousands of lovers at court. Since then there had undeniably been a decline.

The Thais lived their own quiet life beneath the temple roofs, by the klongs in houses on stilts. They washed themselves several times a day in water from dragon jars, with scoops of chased silver. Bangkok was called the Venice of the East and people were friendly and smiling – and brutal, as could be seen in the national sport of Thai boxing, in political murder and other commercial transactions. Of course they bowed and kneeled with their palms together and their heads to the ground – in reverence to their traditional superiors. And the Thais rose respectfully in the cinema when the king's countenance appeared on the screen and the national anthem was played – before the advertisements. And yet, despite the hierarchy, they were not a people set on earth to serve others. Nor to loose face. True, the wealthy Thais had several wives, *mia jaj* and *mia noj* – first and second wife – plus all the casual labour and numerous servants, but it was hard to say who was the "great one" in the relationship. When, as a foreigner – *farang* – you were served by a Thai, you could feel very small. And clumsy! Compared with the grace of the Thai women in particular. *Mai pen rai*, no problem, was the Thai motto, a mixture of the indifference to every problem shown by those who love life and Buddhist detachment. Leisured inactivity was life's great privilege. They lived only for the moment and for *sanuk mag* – good fun. Their favourite occupations were food and children. They left money and business to the local Chinese, who worked day and night. Interest in money and materialism did not surface until the Americans arrived to help in the war in Vietnam. And then the Thais began to go to the temple to beg Buddha for a Mercedes Benz.

In 1959 there weren't many westerners in Bangkok and Rejn writes to Gammel Mønt:

The children are attractive, the girls because they are tall and lovely, and the boys because they are blond and intrigued with everything. The girls will have to get used to the Thai children stopping them in the market to touch them, saying *soaj mag* which means "very pretty". The Thais are as fond of children as the Italians – and they have a lot of them. The smallest, up to two or three, are stark naked or only wear clothes down to their hips. But as soon as they are toilet-trained they are nicely turned out in clean, well-ironed clothes, in contrast to Ceylon, where the poor are all in rags.

Nanny had gone with them to Bangkok. Before they left, Rejn had sent her on an intensive course with "individual attention" to learn to read and write, and her brothers and fellow nannies laughed at her that winter. She couldn't take Birdie for a walk in the Buddhist monastery park without all the other nannies, who certainly weren't very literate themselves, giggling and pointing at her. But Nanny held firm, and Orm was proud of her. Because Master had said that if she wanted to go to Bangkok where no-one spoke English she would risk being lonely unless she could write and read letters and so keep in touch with her relatives in Ceylon. And she sat with her tongue in the corner of her red betel mouth chuckling when she had written one word correctly on a piece of paper.

On New Road she found a Singhalese jeweller and sometimes had a chat with him. The bizarre thing was that from the moment she set foot on Thai soil she spoke to the Thais in fluent Singhalese. She loved going round the market talking to the Thais in her mother tongue, and they nodded and smiled, although they couldn't understand a word of what she said. And when Zeste said: "But, Nanny, the Thais don't understand Singhalese at all", she looked blank, as if Zeste were the slow-witted one.

To see Nanny speaking her own language in a foreign land amazed Zeste. She herself had to grow used to having to adapt her language and habits to new conditions and customs. At the age of 14 she had already lived two lives. One in Denmark and one in Ceylon. Now she had to start on a third, totally new life. In Colombo she had gone to an English school wearing a white uniform, where you learned Shakespeare and Coleridge in a

Tamil accent. Now she and Myren attended an international school, in which were more Americans by the day as the war in Vietnam escalated. She had to learn to live in a military milieu.

One day when Li was again in bed in the house on Thanom Paholyotin with some mysterious illness, in the only room which had the new fashion of air conditioning, and Zeste kept away from her in a blend of sorrow and anger at her mother's absence, Nanny said to Zeste: "You are the only one who can make Lady well again."

"Me, what do you mean?"

"Yes, you are the one she loves."

"But she has her husband, that's enough, surely."

"It is not the same, only you can do it."

"Yes, but what shall I *do*?"

"Go and say something nice to her."

"I've done that so often. It doesn't help."

"Go and *talk* to her."

"What shall I say?"

"You are the one your mother needs. Go now."

Zeste's stomach turned over, she was allergic to sickrooms and all that was unexpressed in them. You always had to guess what was wrong because there were no words for it. Maybe the Cat was ill because she still couldn't speak Thai and the whole town seemed so overwhelming. Their first abode after the hotel was a dark, dank box of a place, so ramshackle and full of mosquitoes and other sinister creatures that no-one slept a wink. They moved again the very next morning, into a bungalow furnished by Americans. Maybe she was ill because it was even hotter than in Ceylon. And Li just couldn't bear the native districts – like the nearby Chinese quarter, where all the food smelled rotten in the heat. Maybe she was ill because she couldn't control her servants. One of the cooks was able to make toast only after four months with them – *kanom pang ping*. Another one was on opium and served snake ragout, and the third organised break-ins with bands of thieves in league with a whole industry of receivers of stolen goods – you could often buy back your own things at the Thieves' Market – and the fourth secretly set up a dressmaking business with the family's money. *Kamoi*, which means "thief", was the first Thai word they learned and had need of.

It took some stamina to keep the servants in order. The moment you relaxed and took your eyes off them, they took over and started to rule you. The washerwoman drank a whole bottle of the family's whisky and a whole bottle of gin in two days and had to be pumped out in hospital. Maybe Li lay thinking that if only they could afford a gas stove and a washing machine they would be free of the servants. One or more thick black heads were looking at you all the time, but vanished as soon as you needed them. And they always had numerous relations staying. Li was no longer the woman of the house. She hadn't really ever been, but now she had quite given up. Maybe she was ill because she missed rye bread. Maybe she was ill because of something to do with the Dog that couldn't be uttered. Bow-wow.

"I love you," said Zeste sincerely, now that she had an important part to play. And Lady sat up in bed, and recovered.

They soon realised that Zeste possessed special powers, whatever those might be, and on the day of her fifteenth birthday she said that she was not going to the American military school any more like all the other foreign children. She had nothing in common, she said, with the infantile American teenagers boasting about their ready-for-action fathers.

Zeste thought she might have a chance of being selected for Buddhist temple service, a school that took specially selected girls. She had met a French poet-diplomat, Serge de Clerval, and fallen for him on the spot because she supposed that he had connections with Parisian theatre. He had been to the school during a theme week and with his encouragement she had made a speech at the United Nations auditorium in support of the new young states seeking admission to the world community. The speech, which was simultaneously interpreted into five world languages, had been a great success. And when Zeste felt applause come streaming towards her she didn't associate it with herself, rather with everything she could learn from Serge de Clerval. The event was noted by the Bangkok press and Li, who had been the most enthusiastic listener in the front row, sent the cuttings to Balder so that he could write about the phenomenon of Zeste in the Danish papers.

There was no doubt that Serge de Clerval had excellent contacts in Bangkok, including some with the Buddhist temple service – dangerous connections, as he said himself, with a mysterious glint in his eye – and he had promised to see whether Zeste had a chance there.

"A chance of what?" asked Rejn.

"Chances of everything," said Li.

Rejn put out feelers around the town, but they were denied access to the stage Zeste intended to appear on. But he only needed to mention the name of the so-called Buddhist temple to people at the Sports Club, of which they were now members, to encounter raised eyebrows. It was whispered to him that the Buddist temple was in reality a superior brothel, run by a notorious Thai lady, what was her name, Khun Nui, or was it Khun Nam? They said she had been educated in France. It was apparently an advantage that she had translated a number of French books into Thai, they couldn't remember the titles. Anyway, she was close to the royal family, no doubt about that, and her girls performed as mannequins before the queen. They learned to sing the king's compositions and were well-read in classical literature, it was demanded of them. They learned to speak in public and make a good impression and play an instrument. Nevertheless the lady of the temple was a procuress. She had established this special school in a temple after the custom of Buddhist nunneries. But instead of educating the girls in the usual way she taught them all manner of other things.

"White slave trade," decided Rejn. And that was the end of that. He thought. That kind of school was out of the question. Zeste had a good brain and if only she could summon her energy and get those foolish dreams of the theatre out of her head she could be an academic like himself and get a worthwhile job. Zeste wasn't going to any "Buddhist temple service" if Rejn had anything to do with it. But he was not to have. Li held the trump card – and Li had taken after her father and become quite an expert bridge player.

When she discovered that the Thais were among the five best teams in the world to enter the Olympics and had beaten the British, the French and the Italians, she started to play in earnest. She wrote to her father: "Bridge is no longer my hobby, it is my passion."

*

Li was 40 now and better than she had ever been, Rejn wrote to Gammel Mønt. She slept like a log, without any pills. She saw to all the household chores and was as blithe as a lark from morning to night.

It was not simply playing cards or the ace's glittering prizes that had improved her health. The people who had made it at all possible for Li to throw herself into her new passion were In and Pim Pao, a married couple from the mountains in the north who had come to seek service in Bangkok. From the day they knocked on her door, Li's life changed. She had acquired a mother and a father.

In and Pim Pao were loyal, intelligent and independent. She never got In to make Danish rice porridge on Christmas Eve. Every year it went wrong, for he refused to believe you could boil rice in milk. Rice was his department. Every year he put on his I-won't-have-anything-to-do-with-it face and Li had to resign herself and say that he could just cook the rice in his own way and put whipped cream in it afterwards. The poor man had to work hard to hide his disgust. On the other hand, Li had to control *her* expression sometimes, when the family had been away, for example, and left the staff to take charge of the move to a new house. The joy of reunion was always lively, but the horror was likewise great when she saw how – very carefully – they had arranged the furniture. It looked like a shop, a sideboard had been placed just by the entrance as if a shop counter. On it was their entire collection of silver, all their vases and knick-knacks, and the pictures were hung in the most absurd places. In other ways Li could rely on them for everything, and they were given *carte blanche* to run the house.

Furnishing was a pleasure to her. If only she had had more money. No matter how much Rejn earned, they were always poor. Li took numerous part-time jobs: working at the *Agence France Presse*, a job which Serge de Clerval had found her, for an intolerable chatterer of a Chinese lady, where she learned not to mention any exciting news, only the boring kind, otherwise there was trouble – they lived under a dictatorship. She worked at an institute for the blind, learned to translate books into Braille. She riskily manoeuvred the little Austin, which Rejn had put at her disposal, through the chaos of the Bangkok traffic, practising Thai verbs as she waited in long queues in the heat.

She learned to speak and write Thai (88 letters or signs) and she played bridge with upper-class Thais, normally inaccessible to foreigners. That was the difference between a former colony and a free country. In the old colonies there was always a secret or open link between the overlords of the colony and the local upper class. Not so in Thailand.

Zeste was Li's trump card, indeed her only ace, which she had in mind to play boldly. What did she care what "people" said. Envious little people, who had never had an exciting life themselves and were reduced to gossiping about other people's. Li had no intention of subjecting herself to that sort of mediocrity. Besides, Zeste was *her* daughter. And what were Rejn's motives in sabotaging Zeste's future? Rejn said the whole thing was decadent. All right then, decadent it would be, and surely that was better than American militarism!

Li planned to confer with her father and put him into the picture, as they were due for home leave. They intended to spend part of the holiday at Baden Baden to play bridge and take part in an important world tour, with Li as cheerleader of the Thais. The Cat and the Dog got on fairly well when the Dog played properly. They communicated solely through the various bids and moves: 22 points, four diamonds, two minutes' silence, a resounding double. Miaow. Bow-wow. But if the Dog played a wrong card the Cat retired to bed and wouldn't speak to him for a week.

They couldn't really afford to stay at Baden Baden, particularly not after another burglary.

Katze and Tobias were upset about the primitive, barbaric conditions Li had to endure. Not in their wildest imagination did they dream of the statistic – one break-in a year – which every Dane would have to live with 35 years later.

After that story it was crazy to go to Baden Baden and live in luxury, Tobias wrote. But the cards called and the Cat was deaf to advice, even from her father.

Tobias struggled on with the pains in his leg, hoping to avoid an operation. That meant eventual amputation, but he wouldn't hear mention of that word.

*

Uncle Max's son Henry had been invited to speak at Rebild, in

Jutland, where the annual Danish-American celebrations are held. Tobias had arranged a welcome dinner for him at the Langelinie pavilion in Copenhagen. Ten thousand people were invited to Rebild, but the Løvin family were not invited. Tobias claimed that the Rebild committee didn't like Jews. It was the only time he uttered the word Jew. He and Rebekka watched the Rebild Festival on television. But what was this they saw? Why was Henry speaking so strangely? "This is the happiest day of my life . . ." He stood on the heath, the place above all others in the world that his father loved. Ten thousand Danish-Americans had gathered here. It was his father's life's work. But suddenly his speech seemed so slurred. Bekka and Tobias couldn't recognise the Henry from the evening before. Now he sits down in his place of honour beside the bishop's wife, who whispers "That was a beautiful speech". After which Henry drops dead. As if on cue from his father Maximilianus. A grandchild of Uncle Max, a crew cut woman in military uniform, speaks into the microphone: "It would be in the spirit of my grandfather that we go on with the festival."

It fell to Tobias to arrange the practical matters. He drove with Rebekka to Aalborg. Bekka took her dog because she couldn't get it looked after at such short notice.

"You haven't brought the *dog*?" the others snapped at her.

"Yes, we have brought the dog," Tobias replied for Rebekka. And she enjoyed the way her father took responsibility for her, how he protected the dearest of her possessions. Tobias had brought the car, which the others resented, because it cost extra. But Rebekka was delighted about that too. Her father's car, its mere existence, allowed her to lean back in life and be carried along. It was also Tobias who had the brilliant idea of wiring to America: "Was Henry a Christian?" Not until the reply came one way or the other could they arrange the clergyman and everything else.

A wreath from the king lay on the bier. Tobias rose, limped over to the coffin and said: "So, after all, the Løvin family came to Rebild. Although we had not anticipated that it would be in this guise." Afterwards Tobias had an audience with the king, to thank him. He wore his top hat and white silk scarf. Tobias was always dressed for the occasion. Beneath the finery, his legs were blue. He had not much longer to live.

He was looking forward to seeing the whole Bangkok gang in Copenhagen and he wrote to Soi Ruam Rudi, their new address:

> Well, one must admit you experience quite a lot, burglaries, new house, no house, journeys, no journeys, horses, dogs, cats and performances, etc. etc., but as long as you're all well and can cope with it all happily, we can only be glad. And now my dear girl, I'm looking forward enormously to seeing you again, and luckily it won't be long now. Take care not to lose a child on the way. We know there'll be a passport, a ticket, a handbag left in the various towns you stop in, but it would be nice if all six of you could get to Kastrup together! Au revoir!
>
> My best love to you all. Your old father.

Li would like to have stayed at Gammel Mønt with her father that summer, but Tobias did not dare ask the family to move in. Marie had cycled into a car and fallen over her handlebars. She had suffered serious concussion and lost her sense of taste. Katze was still working like a demon at the office at 61, didn't get home before 5.30 p.m., and then insisted on doing everything in the kitchen. That was Katze's tyrannical martyrdom. And her big act. Whenever it was time to wash up, Katze barricaded herself behind the kitchen door, which she defensively locked behind her. That gave her two advantages. She could drink in peace and then complain that she had to do everything in the house herself, with no help.

*

Li wanted to discuss Zeste's future with her father tête-à-tête, so he had arranged to meet her at à Porta, an art nouveau café on Kongens Nytorv, which was still cosy with its red velvet and gilded cupids. Li was in a brand-new silk outfit, slightly creased after the journey, now she didn't have Pim Pao to iron. She had had her hair done up in the bouffant French back-combed style she wore at bridge tournaments and Tobias said: "I don't want a daughter with hair like that!" And Li rejoiced. On the question of Ib's rape of the name of Løvin, she was entirely on Tobias' side. And really shocked to hear that Ib had chosen an Old Testament Jewish name for his firstborn, a girl. That was a clear anti-Danish manifestation. The next thing would probably be that his sons, if he had any, would be called Abraham and Moses Løvin.

She had so much looked forward to seeing him again, but was a little bit disappointed that he hadn't swooned over her success at bridge. Since the last home leave she had read all kinds of bridge books for three or four hours a day, although she knew he despised books. But as she had discovered the most exciting thing in the whole universe so late in life, and after all was no genius, there was no other way: "Father, play with me. You must promise to play with me when I come."

But he hadn't played with her. For six months she had posted her bids to Tobias and reported how she had played her tricks, to get his response, but he had merely replied: "As long as you are happy, my dear." As if he didn't quite believe in her prowess, despite her assurance that she didn't play "ladies' bridge". She had won various silver cups, but that was the least of it, for she had gone to Manila and Hong Kong with the Thai national team and they had won! They would probably win at the Olympics too. And now she wanted to discuss Zeste's future with him in confidence. She sat there with her ace, they had tea at à Porta, where the waiter – in honour of Li's sense of security – bowed low to Tobias.

Li began play: "Zeste has been accepted into very exciting circles."

"A child shouldn't be in exciting circles, a child should mind her lessons."

"Zeste isn't a child, she is sixteen."

"A girl of sixteen is a child."

"But you know Zeste, she's something special."

"All the more important for her to do well at school, so she can have a good education."

"Yes, exactly. This will be a very special education."

"How special?"

And Li told him about the relationship with the French poet-diplomat, who was, it was true, married, but who managed to be nice to his family and to Zeste, about his wide reading and connections and about the temple service with Khun Nui. And she told him about the king and queen, and the Thai upper class. And it was all very exciting.

Tobias just stared at her and asked if she had gone mad.

"So you won't give it your blessing?"

"Blessing. It's lunacy!"

Li left the meeting strangely numbed. Oddly enough she wasn't in despair over the outcome. For Tobias couldn't know everything. He didn't know the Far East. To him Thailand and the entire Orient was an uncivilised jungle, full of monkeys. He didn't know any better. Li had to remember that Tobias didn't have a monopoly on knowledge. She intended to do something that in her father's eyes was madness. She wanted to stake a great deal. He ought to have understood, but Tobias was not widely read. She would have to acknowledge that he had limitations. This was the first time Li had rebelled against her father. And it felt quite good. She was a free woman. Tobias, for his part, had begun for the first time to fear for her sanity.

Zeste had become quite impossible, she put on such airs. Li wrote to Gammel Mønt on December 6th, 1960:

> Zeste's social life makes great demands on us. Last Saturday when she was going to be fetched to go out, she insisted that we should all be dressed up, the sitting room tidy, the little ones shut in. We were given instructions on how we should introduce ourselves, offer him a drink, after which she would swan down the stairs.

When Zeste became too unbearable Li had to warn her: beauty and learning are not enough in themselves. If beauty was not worn with modesty it had a repellent effect. You only needed to see the difference in the way the American and the Thai women conducted themselves. The former stumped along, the latter walked softly. Be happy that you look nice, it is a gift, but think no more of it than that.

Zeste certainly didn't feel *nice*. Deep inside she felt poor, clumsy and frightened. But the Cat and the Dog obviously held shares in their daughters' appearance. They were quite simply absolutely nonplussed at having produced two such tall, sensational ladies and they got a special kick out of showing them off everywhere they went and harvesting the enthusiastic compliments. Myren took it relatively easily because she had invested her energy in animal welfare, but for Zeste it signified something else. By making use of herself in the way they wished, she could save the family from the ever-present threat of bankruptcy.

All the same, she would no longer take advice from her mother. She had been disappointed far too often. "My mother is well because she has started to educate me." She had so often told herself that. But the attempts to educate or give advice lasted only a week, then the Cat would fall ill again and resign from the world. But as far as can be gathered from the notes, Li attempted suicide only once while In and Pim Pao were in her service. And that was when they rented a weekend cottage on Ko si Chang Island, and all of them were looking forward to it. At the last moment Li decided not to go, she said she couldn't stand all that sand and water. Or else it was because Rejn had forgotten to buy her rye bread. Nevertheless, he had driven off with the children for the long-awaited trip. Later that day a messenger arrived on the island from Bangkok: "Lady dead." Li had succeeded in getting her way yet again by means of an overdose, and they returned, petrified, from the beach believing that she was dead.

Zeste's new life in the service of the temple had placed an effective barrier between herself and the Møller family. And that was the idea. She took an immediate liking to Khun Nui, who according to tradition had her coal-black hair put up in a knot on her head with the irregular hair of temples and forehead removed to make her hairline harmonious and perfect. (She belonged to the generation who had had all their hair cut off at puberty for the ritual baths.) Her skin was cool and pale as ivory and she treated her beautiful lips with beeswax, which she kept in a sapphire-studded jar on a silver tray. On her finger she wore a gold ring in the shape of a serpent. And she had a black mirror and a silver pond with a carp in it, which was 200 years old.

Khun Nui set the girls to read Montaigne, Rousseau and Voltaire, but it was Racine and Molière who made Zeste's cheeks glow. She learned long passages by heart and they took her straight on to the stage, where she saw herself pelted with flowers like Sarah Bernhardt.

They were allowed to read the philosophers of the Enlightenment and the encyclopaedists as much as they liked, because the rational interpretation of the world was in agreement with Buddhist pragmatism. But Catholic, metaphysical works Madame Nui shunned like the plague. Lightness and clarity, *s'il vous plait.* Therefore the libertine writers of the eighteenth century also won her affection. You could learn a lot from them: namely, to take love not too seriously, but easily, without committal. It was all samsara, after all, much ado about nothing in the world of illusions.

Unfortunately Zeste had developed a preference for Monsieur de Clerval, but Madame Nui would not tolerate that kind of fancy. Love, and in particular its actions, should be carried out with empathy and sympathy, and reflect the universally human. Rather Mr Anyone than Mr Special. What had this one man Serge de Clerval achieved to deserve Zeste's love at the expense of other people in the world? But Serge contrived secret meetings with Zeste, and he put a hand under her elbow and led her out on romantic trips to the edges of the jungle near the klong. And one day they came on a so-called Bo tree, a fertility tree from an old, animistic cult, hung with carved phallic symbols. At its roots a row of them was arranged, one was painted with a red head, and Serge stole it and gave it to her, and she hid it in her skirts, crimson in the face.

But Khun Nui came down on secret meetings with a heavy hand. And gradually Zeste learned to understand that this new ancient doctrine of love, which was impressed on her at the convent, was an effective weapon against the so-called love and romance she had grown up with, which the Cat and the Dog practised under the prevalent definition of "passion". And which the unhappy Katze, Zeste's grandmother, had practised before her. The only difference was that they did not know they "practised" anything at all, they experienced it as incarnate nature. This intoxicated predilection for one's own emotions was one of the worst pitfalls of the illusion. Khun Nui demanded kindness and condemned passion.

Zeste was not slow to learn. With all her heart she wanted to be the woman for anyone at all, wherever it might be, and with open eyes only to avoid being "the woman of the house" with closed ones. And out of all the girls, she would become the most devoted and uncompromising in her calling. She had become a complete stranger to Myren and although they still shared a room at weekends in the garage they now lived in with the Cat and the Dog and the whole crack-brained family, Zeste was unrecognisable.

"I've licked the arses of many men – it's called *'feuilles de rose'* in French."

"Ugh, how disgusting," said Myren as if on command, looking at the strange unconcerned Zeste in turquoise silk, who cited Colette to herself: "Many a chaste woman has sought corruption, but only a few are chosen."

Myren didn't know whether to feel envy or sympathy. Zeste was admitted to a Nursing Home with a mysterious rash all over her body, and Serge de Clerval brought flowers and French perfume.

Marsken had been to dinner on his way from the head office in Delhi to the residence in Hanoi. Tobias remembered Marsken as the big guy who turned up at Li and Rejn's wedding – without a tie. Although Marsken was officially stationed in Saigon now, he tried to spend most of his time in Hanoi. For what interested him was the Vietnamese struggle for independence, and the Communists in the north were the only ones who had any control over things. The Vietcong hadn't a chance without them. Rejn didn't share Marsken's passion for Communism.

"Obviously, the Americans have made a right cock-up in recent years, both militarily and also by allowing the situation to develop without any safeguards for so many years."

"But that doesn't alter the fact that North Laos is now a fully liberated – or integrated, if you like – Communist area. And it's impossible to turn back the clock of history," Marsken said.

Zeste looked at him. He was a paterfamilias gone native, with a dark brown face. He drank whisky all through his meal and resembled Marlon Brandon in the role of Kurtz in the film of Joseph Conrad's *Heart of Darkness*.

"A war intended to win back the area from the Communists, even one waged with American aid, would be incredibly hard to win," Rejn had to admit.

"The Americans will have to give up Laos," said Marsken with the older Brando's hoarse voice, knocking back yet another double.

"I don't think the Americans should give up the rest of Laos, but it's bloody well time for them to change tactics and go to war in the same way as in Vietnam. The aim shouldn't be to present the leaders with Coca-Cola and Cadillacs, but to raise standards and potentials for the people. Ordinary people have not benefited from progress, that's why they have taken the fight into their own hands."

"The Americans have no business in South Asia."

Li agreed with Marsken, but said nothing.

"Progress hasn't done the population any good, that's why they have taken the fight into their own hands."

That was Marsken's last word before they left the table, decorated so beautifully with jasmine and lotus by Pim Pao.

Marsken's great bulk filled out the basket chair as he sat waiting for coffee and brandy. Zeste sensed the vapour of comforting masculinity. A paterfamilias. Myren looked at Zeste uncertainly and recalled uneasily everything Zeste was learning in the so-called school she had been selected or condemned to attend. But Zeste looked at Marsken with joy and relief. At last, she thought, here is a man I don't need to seduce. It was a slightly forbidden feeling. And she knew that Khun Nui would call her selfish and lazy, unkind and self-absorbed. But Zeste held the feeling of freedom inside her like a great passionate secret.

At Loy Kratong, the full moon's festival of the twelfth month, Zeste, with the rest of the townspeople, launched her own banana leaf of a ship on the water with candle and incense to pay homage to the river Chao Phraya.

5

THE JADE CAT

In November 1963 John Kennedy was shot and later on everyone remembered exactly what he or she had been doing at that moment. Li and Rejn were playing a late night game of bridge with Dr A. and his American wife. It was she who heard the news from a servant who crept into the room and told her. Li insisted they go to the embassy to seek shelter with Ambassador Ebbe Munck, perhaps out of old habit. At the back of her mind lay the memory of how Tobias had evacuated all the Danes from the Baltic. Would Munck evacuate all the Danes now from Thailand in the event of a world war? It was largely due to the ambassador that Li had found her feet in Thailand. Not that she cared much for embassy parties or Danes. On the contrary. But there was something special about Munck. He wasn't any old ambassador, he was a *personality*. A one-time freedom fighter, polar explorer and journalist. And from the very first day when they reported their arrival at the embassy, he had kept an eye on Li, in that he knew who she was. She was a Løvin. And he never forgot that as a young man he was employed at *Berlingske Tidende* and Papa had promoted him over the heads of others with greater seniority. And it was Ebbe Munck who was sent down to Berlin after the outbreak of war to meet Katze and the girls at the station when they were returning from Riga to Denmark.

So at this moment when they might be faced with a new world

war it was natural to report to the Danish embassy. On the other hand: was the Møller family still Danish?

*

Myren spent all her time at her Thai riding school, where she had stabled her own white horse, Bucephalus, known to Rejn as Phallus. Lacking in any real sense a mother and a father, Zeste was the person Myren felt closest to, but it was a painful dependence. Myren wanted Zeste to herself and flew into hysterical rages because Zeste had involved herself in a life that excluded her. Myren didn't begrudge Zeste all the sophisticated and artificial French business, because Zeste was much too good for it, in Myren's opinion. And Myren meditated revenge as she devoted herself to animals and children, who didn't put on all those airs, for God's sake. Meanwhile Zeste hung on Khun Nui's every word in the temple, where she was being made into a Thai woman with French ambitions.

After In and Pim Pao had taken over the house and more or less the administration for the Møller family as far as emotions went, and Nanny had gone back to Ceylon, Orm and Birdie, who had changed his name to Kwanki Wanki (because he was such a funny little thing), slipped into a vacuum, from where they couldn't be reached – from a European view. The boys went to a Thai school, didn't speak a word of Danish and only a little pidgin English, like other Thais. They played almost entirely with Thai children and mostly with the servants' Bulød and little Aju Pa. They seldom ate with their parents and their favourite dish was *kuay teo*, scalding noodle soup which they bought for twopence when the street seller came by with his bell and the food on a bamboo stick over his shoulder. The boys almost lived in the servants' quarters, and if Li had not placed the Thais so high in her inner hierarchy, she would have regarded her sons' lifestyle as a shipwreck into the sea of the proletariat. Orm and Tor did not identify with their parents, they didn't see themselves as Danes, even as Europeans. Rejn was astonished one day when he gave Orm money for a taxi and the boy bowed and said: "Thank you, Sir." Rejn and Li looked at each other in amazement, for neither of them had taught their children to speak like that. But that was how Thai children addressed their parents, with respect.

Orm could write only mediocre English, but Tor couldn't write either language, so it was hard to see what the Cat and the Dog had in mind for the boys' schooling. Rejn was very worried about Orm's reports, which he thought atrocious. Every time it was "poor considering his intelligence", "can if he wants to, but is flippant and inattentive", Rejn threatened and beat him, which only resulted in Orm shutting off completely and making himself invisible down in the servants' quarters, where he lay all day on a mat listening to his transistor. "The silly clot!" said Rejn and reflected that he had been just as lazy at school himself, and that one day it would pass . . . Li shook her head. Her other children had never had school problems and it hadn't been necessary to beat them. But Orm had turned out badly. While Tor was her blessed little one (with brown eyes!) and had excellent reports, full of stars, a credit to the family, Orm had always been alien to her. Orm had no interests. He didn't care about the world around him, as if he didn't expect anything from it.

If you asked Orm: "How goes it? How's life?" he invariably answered: "Life is life" – as if he had a share in some secret religious tradition. Orm knew the family is sacred even if it doesn't have that "yellow on the head", as he said. And although he had become a Thai and respected Buddha, he did so only because he believed in many kinds of Jesus. Orm was so locked up in himself that Li was genuinely frightened of him. She valued happy playful children who could bring her the spontaneous inner life she lacked, but she had no idea at all of how much she herself frightened the children, who crept around in the shrubbery among the snakes and whispered softly for fear the yellow in her eyes should grow white.

Later Li would say that she had always had a foreboding about Orm, and that all her efforts to give him a happy childhood and proper upbringing had been in vain. For the time being she trusted that precisely his disillusioned view of life for a human being on earth, coupled with a sincere religious sense of another dimension, would enable Orm to cope with the harsh realities of existence. And although it was impossible for him to speak to his father of such things, as Rejn couldn't bear to hear the word Jesus or other woolly chatter, Orm had in fact inherited from his father a certain knack with figures and money, which one day might prove of use to him. He didn't collect stamps like other children for their unusual designs, exciting countries or attractive pictures, but solely for the digit down in the corner. He knew exactly how many dollars, cents, kroner and øre he had spent on stamps. Otherwise Li didn't see much of her children, who swam around in the klongs with fishes and eels along with other Thai children, *sanuk mag* – running wild. And wordplay resounded through the garden – *Dee dor pa do gai chai.*

One day, when Li had taken the boys with her to the Sports Club and was playing bridge in "the Thai Room", Orm jumped into the swimming pool, which was not full enough and hit his head. He knocked out all his new front teeth and fainted. Li was called and took a nerve pill. Orm was accident-prone. It didn't matter whether you took him to out to ride or play tennis, he didn't want to do anything. And if he did, of course he met with an accident. Like the day when he was playing with the servants' children and shot little Aju Pa's eye out with a snake gun.

Pim Pao lit candles and burned incense, which she sacrificed on the house altar in the back garden behind the servants' quarters, to placate the evil spirits – *pi* – and stop them making further mayhem, just as she had lit candles and incense to pacify the same *pi* when her daughter Aju Pa was born.

For Rejn it was primarily a matter of insurance. At that time he was working up-country on an integrated development project and his letter of comfort to Orm ran: "Tell In and Pim Pao I'm so glad they are looking after Mummy so well."

You might think that in this situation others needed help more – the girl who had lost her eye, for instance, or the boy responsible for it – but Rejn was so accustomed to the fact that the object of need at all times was Li. That was how it had always been. Without realising it, Li had captured the place of child in the house and thenceforth she devoured all Rejn's strength. He never came to terms with the fact that he had other children. He simply couldn't cope with Orm and Tor. He sent the Cat kisses, pats and a nudge with his nose. For the boys a smack or two. That was Rejn's way of showing the fatherly love he had never known. There were only two things that could make Rejn's wheels turn merrily: money and sex. And the boys didn't fit either scenario.

But this didn't mean he was not interested in his work, on the contrary. Besides, the interests could very well be combined. At the moment he worked in the north, not so far from the River

Kwai, where the prisoners of war who were forced to build the bridge famously blew it up in a final act of sabotage.

*

War had broken out again. Said to be Communist infiltration from the northeast, and the prime minister said that the unrest in the area was due to poverty, linked to the timber concessions given to the Danes early in the century. The rooted belief that Thailand would never "fall" from the established kingdom it was might be mistaken. Not all kings had been as intelligent as the present Bhumipol, and not all queens so beloved as Sirikit. All the same, people no longer felt secure. Thailand was surrounded by regions ravaged by terror and Communist propaganda. The peasants in the northeast corner were poor and survived by cultivating opium. You couldn't expect them to acknowledge a ruler they hardly knew in a town far to the south. It was easy to tempt and threaten these poor unstable souls, but now there was hope of aid from the capital. At any moment Rejn expected a Hawker Hunter squadron, the forerunners had already arrived in the form of a couple of transport aircraft and two Canberras. But they were required to set up ground-control radar before they sent the fighters from Bangkok. Or they could easily overshoot their targets in this cloud cover – they were only five or ten minutes' flying time from China.

Meanwhile Rejn visited the jungle villages, taking people's temperatures. He instructed the Thais, weighed and measured; the aim was education and health, but he always had a "counterpart", a native Thai who could map out the ground for Rejn to see whether it would be useful to introduce foreign ideas.

It can be said that Rejn, with his computer model of welfare was before his time in the '60s. At that time a computer took up as much space as a house and no-one believed that a computer could have any influence whatsoever on the way of the world. While the older generation, both in Delhi and Geneva, were sceptical about Rejn's model – "not everything can be solved by numbers" – a very few realised that he had thought out the most revolutionary invention in science and that the future would acknowledge him to be right. This confirmed his self-evaluation as "the superior intelligence, planner and working power".

The doctors were Rejn's No. 1 enemy. They were trained to

think in *people*, the individual's symptoms and possible cure. Rejn couldn't care less about the individual. He thought in "trends", curves, parameters, statistics, anonymous movement patterns, which made it possible for him to encode health, water supplies, education, family patterns and forms of work into a dynamic whole. This "merging" of factors was a gigantic irritation to Rejn's team-leader in Nakorn Sawan. Ian Mclean, a Scot, was quite unable to get on with Rejn's computer model, and he got on Rejn's nerves with his individual journals and careful emphasising to a patient "that he *must* remember to take his medicine". Rejn tried to explain to McLean that the word "must" did not exist in Thai. There is nothing one absolutely must do as an inevitable necessity. The Scot would have nothing to do with people who had no notion of the word "must". He spoke of the Thais as "the bastards" and said "leave them to the Communists".

The aim of the project was of course that one day the Thais should take over the work and carry it on themselves. But how could the team leave effective guide-lines when that village idiot McLean hadn't the least concept of treatment administration, control methods and teamwork, and knew practically nothing of Thailand, and played too much golf, and besides was a bad doctor. Rejn lived in Thai style without home comforts, ate Thai food (which, unlike Li, suited him) and slept in wretched hotels without air conditioning, butter or rye bread. If he had the faintest hope that the Cat would ever come and visit him she would have to bring ant powder, mosquito smoke tablets and a cool box for her butter.

When you consider that their whole marriage was based on fucking, you wondered how the urge could transform itself with one blow and without problems into a passion for an electric train and bridge. In fact it could not. It played its own game with them and practised various ways of crushing them with the aid of quarrels and fights the children named "world war". And that was what people still expected with armament in East and West – and the conflicts in neighbouring countries, for instance in Vietnam. Li maintained that the "world wars" were less likely to break out when she and Rejn were alone. But as soon as the girls were there the Dog and the Cat were obviously so busy making themselves popular with them and attracting their attention that the result was power struggles and jealousy. Normally it is the children who fight for their parents' attention, but the opposite was true for this family. Moreover they were always waiting for the newly invented hydrogen bomb to explode.

Rejn wrote from Nakorn Sawan:

> Dearest Mother of Pearl, I've tried to write several times and given up. I have thought so much about you and about us without getting any the wiser. I can't find out what goes wrong all the time, we just quarrel and quarrel and quarrel, but I do wish it would stop before we get too worn out. Maybe we lack tolerance, and spend the time reminding each other of what "you said last and said again". I love you and I miss you when I'm away from you, and it's absurd that we can't live together without tearing each other to pieces. When I come back, or you come up here, we'll try again, won't we?

He also wrote that he was bored to bloody death up there. So he longed like a whole pack of puppies to be let loose and go down to Bangkok and his beloved cat. He had been on top of the world during their sexual weekend orgies, as he wrote to start with. But gradually he grew dissatisfied with her. Now he reproached her for not being keen enough, and Li wept, for how could he demand more of her when he himself wasn't anything to write home about. And he admitted to being no longer the fiery passionate lover Li read about in books. He was less demanding, more considerate, and Li had a suspicion. And not just one. What did he really get up to up north? Had he gone astray and was he living in masculine luxury while she was slaving away running the whole menage at home? She was in fact quite glad to be without him, life was much easier then, but that attitude didn't help to give Rejn feelings of guilt. Time after time he rejected her accusations. He assured her he hadn't had anything to do with "the little girls" and promised and repeated that he would try to keep clear of them. But what did he mean by "try to keep clear"? Who did he think he was? And then he asked for his golf clubs to be sent up as a guard against the perils of sexual life.

Rejn lived at close quarters with the lovely Thai girls, who always offered their charms willingly and 25 years later would become a whole industry on the global market. Li had an answer for this. One weekend when the Dog was in Bangkok, the Cat ran out to the car in her nightdress, started up and raced through the dark night streets to end in the river. The Dog tore after her in a taxi with a police escort and once more saved her life. For a while all went well again, as it always does when death has come close. But strong measures were needed to keep passion going, and moreover Rejn had begun to be worried about his electric train, which was getting rusty in the tropical climate. And he grew more and more desperate up north in the impossible collaboration with that hopeless Scottish nincompoop.

Li played with the idea of going back to Denmark to be near her father. Rejn was never at home and the boys could probably look after themselves. Now the girls were away studying the house was so empty, and she had given up working in the hospital. She did miss Myren's care of the boys, which had meant that Li at least got a glimpse of them in the living room when they were doing something with Myren. She didn't know how they would have got through the business with Orm's teeth – he now had new teeth made of tin – and Aju Pa's eye she had a glass one – without Myren, although Li could have done without her hysteria. And most of all she missed Zeste, who could be guaranteed to keep spirits up in a household that threatened to sink into a depressive, suicidal state. Zeste could always find sketches she acted brilliantly, frightful satires on the Cat and the Dog on a sinking ship with a drowning man on the horizon. The Dog swam (doggy paddle) on his way to rescue the drowning man. The Cat, in silk with a bouffant back-combed hairstyle and long lacquered nails, and her hand full of playing cards and jewels: "All is well, dear, he doubled my four of spades."

Li envied her daughters their Christmas at Gammel Mønt, but was glad Zeste had had a black lace blouse from Rebekka and black lace stockings from Tobias and Katze: "But blouses and stockings can't be enough, you must find something more to wear," Tobias had said and Li enjoyed herself on behalf of Zeste, who had been accepted for the drama school in Paris, where Serge had introduced her. The same school where Sarah Bernhardt had been. And it surpassed all Zeste's expectations, if not Li's. She had always known it.

It seemed to be much harder to get Myren placed. Rejn didn't feel it was any use starting her on higher education. After the separation from Zeste there were rumours that she took pills and threatened to die. Li suggested nursing, because she was always so good and helpful – and so practical. When Myren said it sounded boring Li reminded her that nurses were needed all over the world and were paid as well as doctors in America. She didn't say that she herself had always had need of a nurse. But Myren had begun to be contrary. To begin with she had given way to her mother for fear of seeing the yellow in her eyes disappear, but now she began to resist her. Only a little. Myren questioned whether the Cat had been as good a mother as she herself imagined. This wasn't the kind of correspondence Li cared for and she soon shut her daughter up by calling her hard, critical and intolerant. And what did it mean, anyway, to be a good mother? Myren would never be one, Li was convinced of that, from the way Myren had always crawled after the children and given way to their slightest whim. Myren would be one of those mothers who used their children as compensation for the deprivation she herself had suffered.

Myren had tried to talk it over in a letter to her mother in the belief or hope that at least she could be honest:

"Why do you say I should be tolerant?" Myren asked her mother. Myren thought she was the most tolerant of the whole family. She complained about the special contact Li and Zeste had had and which she had never shared. She had always been afraid her clumsiness would irritate Li. The more she failed in her attempts at contact the more she tried, and the clumsier she felt. Myren also complained that Li and Zeste had teased her for being dirty-minded. She felt she was the least dirty-minded of the whole family. She had never understood what Li and Zeste were laughing at when they claimed Myren's eyes shone suggestively.

Li put down the airmail letter from Gammel Mønt with a feeling of irritation. How could you love your children equally when one wrote ironic, witty, entertaining letters that cheered you up, and the other wrote sorrowful, reproachful, clutching ones that just made you sick and tired. Li ruled her family with the aid of judgment and projections. Zeste was the pure and innocent. Even if you threw her into a latrine she would emerge smelling of violets. Myren had the role of the grubby Florence Nightingale, and she couldn't run away from that even if she tried to seek shelter with her father.

Jas had just got divorced from the shopping-mad Gwendoline,

known as Velvet Arse, who bought two vacuum cleaners in one day simply to annoy Jas. She had steak with her children, but gave Jas only porridge because she didn't get enough housekeeping, she said. But that was it, Jas said. He took his hand-made clothes and hand-sewn shoes and bowler hat and pewter tankard from Amager and left home. Myren greatly enjoyed this new chapter in the story, but Li didn't want to hear Myren's reports of Jas' doings. She read how Jas had met a new woman in pale blue stretch trousers and pale blue sweater, who had a friend in pale blue stretch trousers and pale blue sweater, and they both had a white poodle. It looked as if Jas was on the wrong track, so Li in Bangkok went around wondering whether after all Jas hadn't been the right man for her, and whether she ought to get him back. He was at least amusing, which someone else was not. So Li didn't care for it in the least when Myren wrote how she went waltzing around with her father at the Bellevue Beach Hotel, had hash at d'Angleterre and went to concerts at Montmartre. Li thought Myren's attachment to her father was intolerable and that it was sick to use her father as a substitute boyfriend. She reprimanded Myren strongly for her passion and jealousy where Jas was concerned.

*

As time went on Rejn grew more and more unbearable. Li had asked if she might not as well go home, then he and the boys could come on later. After all, they would be changing post soon, India had been mentioned, but Li had determined that ten wild horses couldn't drag her there. Never again would she live in an ex-colony full of enslaved souls, to live like colonials, a lifestyle she despised and loathed, in contrast to Rejn who thrived on club life, whisky and golf. The Indians were humble and self-assertive where the Thais were gentle, friendly, dignified, tactful and proud. If she really had to live in a poor country, it would have to be a place where all followed "the teachings of Lord Buddha" and where that insight pervaded the whole of society. Not only the religious rituals, but the popular festivals and the daily custom. Li was not going to exchange this for the servile Indians, she would rather go home to Denmark. But she didn't declare that aloud, she played her cards in silence. Tobias had advised her most firmly to go to India with her husband and make her home there.

He drew a parallel with Katze who had complained about going to Riga, but who gradually accustomed herself and came to love it – despite her endless complaining and grousing – and afterwards spoke of the years in Riga as the most wonderful of her life. But Li didn't appreciate being compared with her mother. There was obviously something Tobias hadn't understood, or that she hadn't expressed clearly enough.

Rejn said no to all her suggestions for travelling. It was his money, he said, he had earned it. Their exhausting discussions circled almost entirely around money. Time after time he had put her in the painful situation of not being able to pay the rent. Usually the Chinese landlady sent her messenger with a threat to put Li and Co. out on the street when the money failed to arrive on account from Switzerland, or when the mail was delayed and Rejn was out in that bloody jungle up north. Li felt she was on dangerous ground and had no-one to ask advice of, for when it came right down to it they had only acquaintances, no real friends. She missed Marsken, his relaxed, sunburned authority and hoarse voice. He hadn't appeared for ages. She felt she was sinking deeper and deeper into poverty, which meant wretchedness and pain.

There was never enough money, and now they had Rejn's close-fisted engineer brother staying, which had loaded the fragile budget even more. The brother was a children's home child like Rejn, and they had always stuck together. They had this in common, that it was a physical pain for them to spend money on anything they could get free. Yet no matter how mean they were they never had any money. There are some people to whom money flows, and others it flees from. Rejn and his brother were the latter sort. Jas and Tobias were a bit like that too, but at least they had enjoyed themselves when the money came along. Rejn's brother couldn't be called amusing. He had proposed to stay two days, but now he had found free bed and board there was a risk he might extend his visit. The house wasn't large, so Rejn had moved into Li's bedroom, where he slept on a mattress and snored loud enough to wake the dead. Everything was scattered in the wrong places and with Rejn on the mattress her room seemed as crowded as a railway terminus. "Cannot be done," Li wrote to her father, while admitting that she was difficult herself.

One day Tobias replied to an SOS from Li:

My dear little girl, Your letters of January 3rd and 4th both came this morning before Mother went to the office – and before I got up, so she knew at once that something was wrong, and called home to hear what had happened, so I had to tell her "something". Although I can understand that one was written in deep despair and the other was meant to partly cancel out the first, I can see clearly that things aren't going well with you and Rejn. It's not a complete surprise after your last letters, and the prospect of improvement seems dim.

All the books tell us that Europeans find it hard to cope in the Far East without drinking. Whoever is to blame – and maybe you have a share in it – we see that nerves give way. The heat, the rain, the people, family problems and so on, are all part of the trouble and it's hard to be here in Gammel Mønt giving advice – even good advice. But let me try to sum it up like this: Wouldn't it be an idea to try to get a job at the Danish embassy? There can't be many people who know Danish, English and Thai, like you. Perhaps you could get a part-time job, and Ebbe Munck, who of course was at *Berlingske Tidende* and knew Papa, will surely help you. I think you should try him – also because he could be of use if it all goes wrong and you have to come home.

The best thing of all, in my opinion, would be if you could all move to another country with more civilised conditions. That is known to work wonders for people who couldn't stand the special atmosphere of the East. If that's impossible, I think you must make the best of it until you come home on leave in the summer. If you can't get a move, I think the marriage will be hard to haul ashore and then you might as well, in all friendliness, get divorced. As a Danish citizen you are liable to Danish law which means that Rejn is obliged to support you and the children, but if you suddenly run off it would be hopeless, as you'd have to provide witnesses to support your claims, and think how impossible that will be when you are here and Rejn and the witnesses are in Thailand. If you *must* get divorced, let it be by mutual agreement, whether there or here. There may be something that Rejn is upset about as well, so he would be glad to accept a peaceful and sensible solution. There are masses of work opportunities for you here. Every day there are advertisements for doctors' secretaries, both full and part-time, and many other situations. Rebekka hopes to get a job abroad, so you might be able to have her apartment.

I have tried to tell you what might be done, but of course I should be glad if everything could be sorted out happily. Surely it might be possible for you to talk to Rejn and get him to cut down or stop drinking altogether. It can be a considerable burden, and perhaps it might deter him. I have thought of writing to him myself, but I won't do that without your permission. I'm afraid we have little to offer you. As you know, I am completely retired now, so when I have paid tax, rent, telephone, insurance etc. we have only 15,000 kroner a year to live on, but naturally there's always a bed for you here. And for the boys, but now Rejn has adopted the two girls it isn't certain that he would let go of both boys, and if you leave it might be best if you had just one to look after, if you are working as well.

I'd like to get a job too, but it's a bit complicated. Only by *not* earning anything can I get a tax reduction of 20–25,000 kroner. And I'm not too well. The leg is under control with various medicaments, but my right arm and hand are bad too (presumably calcification, for nothing seems to help). That's why my writing is so bad, but I hope you can decipher my crow's feet! Write again soon, my dear girl. You know that if I can do anything for you, I will, and if you want to make sure your letter gets to me alone, send it c/o Glenda in Stockholmsgade.

Well, my love, that's enough for now. Keep your pecker up and don't do anything stupid, and if you're worried, write or come home to your old father.

*

But just between the two letters Li had sent her father, her grounds for divorce vanished like dew before the sun. Not because Rejn had stopped drinking, or his brother had left, but because he got a new team-leader. It was a Japanese *doctor*, and Li wrote about him to her father in enthusiastic terms. Dr Y. was wise, clever and highly cultivated, civilised and interested in the same things as she was, for instance, Asian culture. He taught her to see the grace in a Tang camel dating from 600 AD; the imperial treasure of Ju, baked from fine white clay with traces of copper dioxide, that in the baking took on a faint yellowish tinge, which according to Chinese experts was called "boiled lambs' liver". He showed her drawings so she could decipher the emperor's poems and verses inscribed in the glaze, he taught her the difference between sky-blue, pale blue and eggshell blue and she never grew tired of listening to him.

Through Dr Yoshi, Li found room for yet another passion in her life: Sung porcelain. The Chinese porcelain from the Sung period of the thirteenth century was what was needed to reclaim the potsherds of her marriage. Li was not content with studying the books and pictures and becoming expert in the various glazes, she grew proficient, with Dr Yoshi as guide, at finding the treasures buried in small, dirty antique shops and coming home exhausted from their successful expeditions.

The very first time they were out together, she tripped over a rare find: The Jade Cat. It was curled up, milkily green, with every sign of well-being on top of a little bed of Chinese rosewood, cut to the exact size. Li sensed that it was purring comfortably. And it had lain there ever since 1217. She recognised herself in it. The Dog had always said the Cat was so good at drawing cats when she signed her letters, but here was a genuine Sung cat with its whiskers quite unruffled by the passing of centuries. It had remained itself. Rivers could burst their banks and kingdoms fall but the cat always crept away to a cosy spot in the sun. Li immediately fell in love with it and was surprised to be able to buy it for a song. Obviously the shop owner didn't realise what he was selling. You could often come across that sort of miracle, said Dr Yoshi cryptically.

So Li became a collector. And as it brought about a transformation that arose from the current of sexuality itself, the Dog went along with the Light of his Life in her passion and willingly forked out for all kinds of antics. He even sold his electric train. And if they were apart they exchanged the caresses of their Tang and Sung and Ming and Ting Yao. When the Dog wrote a love letter to the Cat it was no longer clear whether the kisses were for the flesh and blood Cat or the jade one. Now and again he could be "quite sick with longing to feel the latest Temuko pot in his hands". At other times, when out in the jungle, he thirsted for their ceramics books.

"Why didn't you send more details of the celadon Sung frog, which I'm mad to see?"

*

She developed her aesthetic feeling for interior decoration to accord with Japanese tradition: never too many pictures on the wall, never too many ornaments. But, "come, let us expose our eyes to beauty", and she opened a silk box and picked up a silk cover, and there the animal was revealed: a jade green Sung frog in celadon glaze from the imperial kiln. It was her favourite from the thirteenth century. And her dictum, for all the important affairs of life, was: if your pot risks lacking the necessary oxygen for the glaze to succeed and you have no more wood for fuelling, then, like the imperial potter, you must throw yourself into the kiln. Amen. Li could very well say that, she who was notoriously ready to quit life every time it looked like sinking and losing its lustre.

But at the moment she had a different joy to uplift herself and her life. While Rejn was up north and Zeste had gone to drama school in Paris, Serge de Clerval was paying regular afternoon visits. They had one thing in common: how much they missed Zeste. They sat together, listening to tapes of her reciting long monologues, and Serge looked long and hard at Li's elegant thighs beneath her silk dress. She felt a special pleasure at having given the best thing she owned to this learned man. They sat together praising Zeste's attributes. And at the same time the pleasure was not lessened by his desire for Li. He wrote to Zeste in Paris that Li was so gracious and fragile, so refined and ladylike and her soft thighs so delicate. As the libertine he desired to be, he particularly enjoyed the lust in this somewhat coquettish combination: mother and daughter. But, regardless of what Zeste felt, she had long since decided that she could always make use on the stage of whatever feelings she experienced.

That afternoon Serge had come to beg Li for a piquant service. No, not what she thought, she could stay quietly in her chair. And no, it wasn't a tape of Zeste's he wanted to hear. He wanted to ask Li to write to her daughter about a particular matter.

"I thought you two carried on a lively correspondence!" said Li.

"Yes, but this is something I can't very well write myself," said Serge a little anxiously.

"I thought you felt free to say anything to each other?"

"Zeste has fallen in love," said Serge, smoothing his moustache.

"Good Lord, she's been in love constantly for the last three or four years with all kinds of people, besides you."

"This is something different, it's a mess."

"What d'you mean, mess, she isn't pregnant, is she?"

"Well, yes, she is, but I've taken care of that, you needn't worry."

"That's a great help . . ." Li was confused. "But nothing has happened to her?"

"I want you to write to her and insist she breaks off the relationship."

"You mustn't ask me to do that, I have never interfered in her sentimental life, ever."

Li could say that with a good conscience, for once when Zeste had come and reported she had had a charming offer, which was only to lift up her dress for a Chinese merchant who was prepared to pay her the price of a Ting Yao, precisely the pot from the imperial workshop which Li so passionately desired, she had of course encouraged Zeste to accept the offer. Say yes! Say yes to life! But for some bashful reason or other Zeste had refused, so Li could say with a good conscience that she had never interfered in her daughter's intimate affairs.

"The whole world was against me when I allowed her to continue her relationship with you. You have me to thank for getting the two of you together!" she said.

Serge ignored her resistance, he didn't like being reminded that there could be the slightest obstacle either in initiating or continuing his relationship with Zeste.

"It is a totally foolish affair, which compromises Zeste and ruins her possibilities. Her behaviour shows a lack of reason – in short, a lack of style."

"Where love is concerned it's not easy to talk of 'reason' or 'style'," said Li with a subtle smile.

"No, dear lady, it is precisely in love affairs that one must insist on reason and style."

"Well, I don't understand that kind of French love. I have always agreed with Hemingway that where sex is concerned we're down on the animal level, and there we can't decide for ourselves."

"I have never heard a worse misconception. There was no sign of Hemingway when French literature produced a de Laclos or the Marquis de Sade," said Serge de Clerval and took his leave, leaving a couple of periodicals on the glass table. He was incredibly irritated with Zeste for being ready to ruin everything they had built together. He had his wife and he had Zeste, and he had arranged things so that everything went smoothly. But when Zeste's feelings ran away with her she became a different person. And he was afraid of losing her. He had just sent her a parcel of Greek classics, Aeschylus, Euripides and Sophocles – containing roles for her, of course – and he believed in her talent. But you had to watch your step to keep the whole thing in balance.

"I hope you will think it over. After all, it concerns your daughter's future," he said and left.

But Li soon had something else to think about.

*

Tobias spent his days vacuum cleaning and emptying ashtrays. He might perhaps console himself with the fact that they were not the ashes his six million fellow Jews had been reduced to during the war. But in fact he didn't think of them as his fellows. He didn't think about them at all. Neither did he complain over the humiliation to which Katze subjected him. Not that he had anything against housework, which he carried out with grace and dignity when Marie could no longer come on her bicycle, but he did have to bear with Katze's revenge. It is always the old women who hold the winning cards. And Katze did not fail to let him feel who was the strong one, who earned the money, the one who wore the trousers at Gammel Mønt 14. All the same she was in no way proud of the situation, for the reason why she had to "go to the office", that damned prison, was that she had a nitwit of a good-for-nothing husband. No, soon she wouldn't be able to put up with everything that weighed on her. And now Tobias was ill again! He kept on! He had dropped his hat and stick on the floor, and Katze glowered. But Li feared that Tobias had had another heart attack and on June 17th, 1965 she wrote to her mother:

I pray to God things are going a little better. If only there were something I could do from here, I feel restless and frightened and think of leaving for home at once. Tor said spontaneously, when he heard Father was ill: "Dear Lord Buddha, don't let Grandfather die." Dearest Mother, keep your spirits up and be cheerful, I know how awful it must be for you to be at the office all day seeing to other people's affairs and inwardly being so worried and tired. And if it can help a little, remember I love you. All my love, Li.

PS. Dearest Father, you *must* get well.

In the middle of the night, when Rebekka helped her father get to hospital with the final thrombosis in his heart, after packing his weekend case, Katze stood in the doorway and said: "Is this necessary?" It was. For now Tobias was dying. And he wanted his cigar and his newspaper to take to hospital, thank you. And remember the cigar for the ambulance man. Goodbye, my dears.

Katze wasn't in her right mind and sent a letter to herself, Katze Løvin, Gammel Mønt 14, reporting Tobias' death. The letter was really meant for Li in Bangkok, but as in this family they had the habit of mixing up who was who and found it hard – ever since the war – to separate the various identities, Katze addressed the death notice to herself, and Li never received a letter.

Tobias died on Christmas Eve, and Li decided to take Orm with her to church and hear *The Messiah*. True, he didn't understand much English, but when they sang: "He was rejected. Rejected of men" – he felt the meaning plainly. Not long afterwards, he was playing tennis in the garden and the ball flew straight into the house and smashed the imperial Temuko. He wished for nothing but a magic wand with which he could conjure the pot together again. But according to Li the catastrophe was no more than you could expect.

6

INSHALLAH

Tobias was buried at the Jewish Cemetery, in which the Nazis had once written that the Løvins were poisoning the Danish ground water. Mama, who was well into her nineties when Tobias died, was said to have declared that now her son was dead she wouldn't have to find birthday presents for him any more. But we rather doubt this, as she was so particular about giving birthday presents and often sent Zeste and Myren pocket editions of Danish classics, Herman Bang or essays by Knud Sønderby.

Glenda, with the copper-rinsed, permed hair and cheeky freckled skin, behaved as if it were her own husband who had died. Who did she think she was, that tart? But Glenda, unruffled, kept on telling Katze what Tobias was *really* like and what was *actually* needed to keep him happy. Henceforward there could indeed be doubt about which of the two women *in reality* had been married to Tobias. Every evening Katze worked out of choice at the office, to bolster her independent pride and to find nourishment for her deep lamentation.

With the death of Tobias in 1965 an epoch came to an end. With him went the differences between deep and flat, high and low, which for a brief interval were replaced by explosive revolutionary differences between right and left. But those too would one day vanish. Of course, no-one noticed that Tobias' passing coincided with the start of a new era. Merely that a well-known, unifying structure had fallen out of existence. The entire prerequisite for becoming "high" – without drugs. As Li later wrote to her mother at Gammel Mønt on her birthday, wishing her joy, consolation and contentment in daily life: "But happiness without Father is – impossible."

Orm had been dropped off in Denmark and sent to boarding school. For Rejn and Li now thought it was time the boy turned over a new leaf and started to prepare for an education. Zeste and Myren went along when they delivered him in a residential part of a Danish village. There stood little Orm, forsaken, as the English has it – a word unknown in Danish. He had been stuffed into a blazer and given a straight parting. But inside the blazer was a small, terrified Thai boy, and the saying *"dee dor pa do gai chai"* kept going round in his head. And the question of how he would manage if they couldn't make *kuay teo* in Sorø. What would he live on then? The Cat had made him go and see his grandfather in the chapel where Tobias had been on ice for a long time waiting for Li and the family to come home from Bangkok. Tobias' small blue-white face with the big black eagle nose poking up into the icy cold air of the chapel was reminiscent of an awe-inspiring underworld full of ghosts, devils, and skeletons in the cupboard. Orm didn't know any hymns or prayers that could help with that sight. He barely knew the word consolation, but he did feel how one of his hands, the one he tried to wave with, grew paralysed when his parents and siblings drove away and left him in a strange village in Denmark. He was twelve years old. Zeste and Myren, who had grown quite apart from each other, spontaneously seized each other's hands as they watched Orm disappear over the horizon.

Later the Dog and the Cat would chorus that children have survived being sent to boarding school for centuries, so why shouldn't Orm manage too? Stop being hysterical!

*

Li returned to Bangkok to pack for their next posting. Rejn had gone ahead to attend to a leprosy project in south India, which happened to be supported by Denmark, and famed world-wide for its quality. Li wasn't keen on travelling alone and not at all happy to leave Bangkok.

Throughout her life there had been war in the world. But she had never experienced it at close quarters. It was not until she arrived at the airport in Delhi that she was exposed to an air attack and had to crouch down with Kwanki Wanki in her arms. They were bombed three times that night. The regular hostility between India and Pakistan had blazed up again in the battle for Kashmir. Crying, nagging and weary children surrounded Li. She didn't mind dying herself, now that her father was no more. But Kwanki-Wanki held on to her without a sound, and she wondered at having such a blessing of a child.

Rejn wrote to the Light of his Life that the region was one of the poorest in India and it hadn't helped that the monsoon had failed for the third year in a row. Most people lived on the ground under a scrap of thatched roof. What they ate and otherwise did he preferred not to think of, but apparently they survived year after year if they just came through the first five. It was a daily battle for life and death, all the little hills had been eroded to the rock – and most of it had happened during the time old men still remembered.

He wrote to Zeste:

> To think that you want to "study India" for another year, sometime, makes me smile. Nothing but layers and heaps of shit. Their "spiritualism" falls into three sections, bottomless ignorance, fear and hopelessness for the masses, pure escapism for the minority with open eyes and empty pockets, and the crudest, most revolting exploitation for the other minority that sits on the cash. That will go on as long as there are castes and temples and so forth. Of course, there's corruption and exploitation in Thailand as well, but nothing like so all-consuming and downright inhuman as here. "We, the people of the United Nations . . ." we set out with in 1945. But here in Andra Pradesh, Srikakulam District, what the hell shall we do, where shall we start?

The propaganda for an integrated development linking literacy with hygiene and irrigation was fed to the people through epic plays, moralising comedies that were intended to inspire the locals to adopt a more sensible lifestyle with better chances of survival, namely in the combating of leprosy. The schoolteacher with a hand organ was the music, three boys on a rug the drama.

The biggest one in the middle dressed as a great mogul, the two small ones in the wings as court jesters. First a prayer in music and the Mass. Then a simple performance emphasising the rule not to wash hands in the river. Very instructive and excellent, this play for the people. But the whole impression of the region was so appalling and the doubt over probable survival so all-embracing that the aid workers could only function by putting on blinkers and thinking solely of leprosy. At the market the Dog bought a little bronze lama from Tibet with a top hat and a magic sign on his long cloak. With its aid he conjured himself every day back to Bangkok in the Cat's sweet claws.

Li had decided that she didn't want to go to India. Because the Indians played bad bridge. But now, thank God, Rejn had got cold feet. So when he was offered a post in Afghanistan instead, he took it. It was so suitably far off the beaten track and so suitably magical that he might hope to get Cat to go too. Afghanistan, like Thailand, had never been a colony, he avowed! The British had tried three times to take over the country, each time without success. Afghanistan was a land of proud tribes no-one could suppress. But Li remained unconvinced. Did the Afghans play bridge? Did they collect Sung porcelain? Every time she heard the word Kabul or transfer, she ignored it and changed the subject.

After Tobias' death there was nothing to tempt her back to Denmark. A single mother in a cramped apartment with a secretarial job, no thanks. But to live in Asia without a husband, and perhaps one day without children, was hard, a frightful thought.

Li was convinced that Tobias had died of a thrombosis because Ib had stolen his name. Even though Ib only had daughters, – "But we are well off now with Michael," said Rebekka. Yes, clever Sharpy had borne a son – the only and final "genuine" Løvin. Take good care of him!

*

On Mayday Rebekka and her dog were in their cosy little apartment in Helsinki. They were too grand to mix with the numerous and incredibly drunk people in the street. Now Bekka had a touch of grey in her black hair, and now she looked to a bouquet of old lilac, "Glücksuchen", for happiness, just as they had done in Riga as children. Her father's death had coincided with the collapse of a long-lasting love affair. Things had gone badly between Rebekka and Dr Reichendorf for many years. They were forever quarrelling, and at last for the 27th time they were to be married on the 28th. But if the man had signed the papers, he hadn't posted them, because "he hadn't got a stamp". And so she broke with him, until it all started again. No wonder that Rebekka had often thought of taking a job in Bangkok, but Li had to disappoint her, saying there was no paid work to be had. That was why – once more a secretary – she was at a hospital in Finland. True, it was a humiliation to have to write diagnoses and treatment dictated by a doctor, when she knew she would have been a better doctor. But as her training had instilled in her respect for the hierarchy she had grown up with, rebellion was impossible.

Rebekka's universe was made up entirely of "over" and "under". Upstairs and downstairs. It was her fate to feel herself as "over", nevertheless to be employed as a subordinate in hospital. It would have been unthinkable for her to have fallen in love with an "under", i.e. an equal at the hospital. It was necessary for her – by the rules of her fiction – to fall in love with a Copenhagen chief physician, although he was so promiscuous that every attractive woman in town could praise his abilities in chorus. Normally the chief's behaviour would be beyond Rebekka's respectable limits. But in Dr Reichendorf's case his conduct seemed rather to be a "literary talent". And there was truth in Rebekka's view that some love affairs are suitable only for literature, whereas others are suitable only for life. Aage Dons, the Danish author, had hit the doctor's type right on the nail in *The Soldier's Well*, an invincible Don Juan, who relies exclusively on his red-haired Viking physique to conquer women.

Countless were the times when Rebekka and Dr Reichendorf had gone together to the Town Hall to get the famous papers. But for inscrutable reasons the doctor had never signed them, "because he didn't have a pencil". That was the justification Dr Reichendorf presented the 30th time, plus a charming smile. But Rebekka found that reason really too absurd. So shortly after Tobias' death she applied for a vacant post at a hospital in Helsinki, gathered up her dog and flew off with an author in her stomach.

At least she had a gigantic love story on the tip of her tongue.

And everything would be expressed so lightly and elegantly that no-one would discover how painful it was. A single sentence from her sharp tongue and that man would be wiped out. Her exemplar for this was Karen Blixen, recently dead, on whom Rebekka lectured to the Finnish students learning Danish. For she reckoned that surely Bror Blixen would feel like a beaten man if his ex-wife wrote that he couldn't spell Hemingway.

"Tooth and claw" was Rebekka's motto now, and in time her tongue grew as sharp as a razor blade. It made a straight cut and left all its victims bleeding to death without noticing how they had come to be wounded at all. For the most part she wrote readers' letters, although she tried to control herself. Otherwise she discussed everything from bull fighting and abuse of animals to anti-semitism. According to Rebekka the world was in need of instant cure, and she was the real doctor. But her father had once said that if she went on like this she wouldn't be able to use the name of Løvin much longer and would have to sign herself "The Grumbler".

Balder too was very much opposed to Rebekka's stream of readers' letters. At that time he had not begun to write them himself. He wanted to cure the world as well, but was still married to Sharpy and dared not kick over the traces with his personal opinions in print. Besides, Balder was convinced that if Rebekka had to choose between Dr Reichendorf and the dog she would choose the dog. Li, on the other hand, had quite another suspicion about the affair between Rebekka and Dr Reichendorf. The man wasn't in the least bit in love with Rebekka. He was in love with Tobias! At that time the doctors had fought over Tobias' blue legs. The surgeons held their knives at the ready. As long as Tobias was alive Dr Reichendorf saved him from amputation, but the moment Tobias had died the doctor too vanished from Rebekka's life.

*

This introduces a new chapter in the history of women. Rebekka would no longer prepare herself for life as a spinster, like Aunt Mudde and KIS. She realised, of course, that her own mother looked down on her as such. She belonged to the previous generation and so she saw it as a failure to be unable to get married. Rebekka, however, knew that she was perfectly capable of living alone. She wasn't going to be a maiden aunt – she would be *single*. And that was something quite different. A new culture. When people looked at her, they might well think she had a mysterious past, that perhaps she might have been de Gaulle's mistress.

Bekka read feisty books about the new status that was emerging. You could read columns of advice encouraging the self-employed, usually by Americans who gave hints on love, work, clothes and accommodation. "Now, here at last you've got the apartment. You want to make it nice, you have no money, how is it to be done? Very simple – it can't be done." Bekka is cheered by the festive tone of the book. The writer opines on hopeless men and vindictiveness: "Leave it out, it isn't necessary. You'll probably come across the hated one without teeth and hair, or in court for child molestation – Fate will see to that." "One of my friends is going to feel guilty for the rest of her life about two big air crashes, involving some of her hated former friends."

Instead of moping over the discarded Reichendorf, Bekka tried to make use of her Finnish-Russian contacts to secure compensation for Tobias for what he had lost in Riga. True, he was no longer among the living, but he rose again so much the more vividly in her imagination. She no longer needed any future, as long as she had her parents' past. Everywhere she went, she enthusiastically searched out people who might have known her parents in Riga. The smallness of the world made her feel great.

*

Zeste had passed her final examination with flying colours in a performance in which she appeared as Medea in a homemade sack dress. Li wrote to congratulate her:

> My dearest Zeste, congratulations, congratulations, oh, how I wish you a good life so you can learn to make use of your great talent and intelligence and don't let anything get you down. You can't fail to have discovered that you are one in a hundred thousand or more, and it's your duty (forgive the word "duty") to make use of and cultivate your gifts for the joy of humanity. It sounds very pompous, but it's how I feel and I haven't the ability or talent to write easily, flowingly

and humorously. But let me cite my beloved Scott Fitzgerald: "An artist who manages to look a little more deeply into his own soul or the soul of others, finding there, through his gift, things that no other man has ever seen or dared to say, has increased the range of human life."

On May 8th, 1969, Zeste finished her course at drama school in Paris, where they called her Zezie – and *Z'est zi bon* as a nickname. And she had finished with yet another idiotic infatuation. This one had humiliated and enervated her. These attacks of passion meant dependence, subjection and illusion and were completely inconsistent with everything she had learned from Khun Nui about the generosity of love. Zeste's love affairs were full of hate. And she couldn't understand why she always fell into the trap and landed in situations that flew in the face of reason. Like the latest, when she had waited feverishly for two months for a reply from some shit of a lad who would rather play at bandits and soldiers out in the jungle than get involved with a woman. But that attack was over now and she spent happy days, mostly at the cinema, with daily inspiration from Bunuel, Bergman, Godard, Truffaut, Ray, Kurosawa, Orson Welles, Antonioni. Samuel Beckett had made her aware of the theatre in earnest. He had anticipated the true note behind the collapse of civilisation they were experiencing now, out in the street. Zeste wasn't gregarious, and people shouted and screamed for "participation" and democracy, the power of imagination and the dream made real.

South East Asia was still too close for her to swallow the current slogans raw. But it wasn't popular to be ambivalent in 1970, so Zeste kept quiet, though she corresponded with Rejn, who replied in his usual ironic manner:

Of course there's no elegant, convincing "solution" to the Vietnam situation. For no-one is doing anything "wrong" that can be condemned and punished, although the whole thing is tragic and in its way meaningless. These power conflicts seldom lead anywhere, merely onwards through time, and then they are succeeded by other flash points.

It wasn't long before Zeste happened across Marsken. Typical of him. She found him carrying a placard in a Vietnam demonstration. He had been to a meeting at the Elysée Palace. After Algeria, his last revolutionary post, he had been promoted and was now the highest placed Dane in the UN hierarchy in New York. He had begun to resemble Willy Brandt and had his suits made in Savile Row – he was too large for ready-to-wear clothes – and he bought his shirts at Brooks Brothers. Nevertheless he ran around among the young people with a placard, typical! They had Pernod at a café to settle affairs of the world as they had done so often with the family.

Marsken chain-smoked: "I can't see where we're going."

"Try!" said Zeste, thrilled to hear the hoarse voice again.

"If we take ancient Mediterranean culture from the start, the western world doubled its knowledge the first time in 1780, again in 1860, once more in 1905, in 1930, in 1950 and in 1960."

"I can't keep up!"

Strangely enough, Marsken's pocket-philosophy aphorisms, as he called them, didn't depress Zeste. The worst-case scenario was always exhilarating.

It had made quite an impression on her that before they parted he asked what she was doing in Paris and why she wasn't in Denmark. But every time she thought about Denmark, she thought of who would take care of Jas, who wouldn't be able to look after himself much longer, and her responsibility for Orm, where the question was whether he would ever learn to. And she thought, not least, of her responsibility for Myren.

On top of the actual responsibility for father and brother and sister came the long weekly lists of things Rejn demanded should be done for him. Like paying Orm's school fees with money from Rejn's account, which was constantly in debit. Going to talk to the bookseller who was about to stop Rejn's credit. Talking to the accounts office at Magasin, where the account was overdrawn with shopping for Orm, for which Rejn might well not want to pay. Rejn loaded Zeste and Myren with responsibilities. He pushed everything onto his furthest contacts, as his nearest ones were no use. Li and the poor had always devoured all his strength. But Zeste did not dare be in Denmark for fear of his taking advantage of her. She felt that her first duty was to herself and her own life, and had let Rejn know this when he tried to force her into getting a proper education at Copenhagen

University. That was education on *his* premises. In which case, he would be glad to allow her 100 kroner a month. But if she intended to go on with her theatrical fantasies, she must face the fact that all help from him was irrevocably at an end. And he concluded his letter with a "Cheerio, my tall, depraved, naïve, immature . . ." Zeste threw the letter into the wastepaper basket.

Marsken no doubt had a sentimental relationship with Denmark because he had been out of the country all his adult life. But after their talk in Paris, Zeste started to ask herself whether after all she ought to go back and act in her own tongue. Serge only came to Paris now and then, and there was really nothing that tied her to the city. She did feel that she ought to be available to him and his expectations, since he had paid for her training. (He had four other children to support.) But now that she did not feel herself bound to sit about waiting for her man of destiny from the jungle, she tried to decide for herself if she really loved him.

If she were to be level-headed, she had to admit to being unable to distinguish between her feelings for him and the feelings she had for her own future. It was the same uncompromising, ruthless feeling. If she used him for her personal ends, this corresponded precisely to his use of her, a maiden of fifteen summers, as she had been when they met. Would he have loved her if she had been "an ugly little man with spectacles", though the soul was the same? He loved her merely for her naked breasts and for being a flattering realisation of his dreams. He loved her for the pride he felt at having formed her. Pygmalion. She ought to play that part every single day. If her mere thoughts departed an iota from his beaten libertine road, he was furious. He could not bear the powers of darkness, hated Beckett and metaphysics. He didn't wait for Godot, he took hold of the good things of life *now*. He made fun of her Scandinavian addiction to impeding introspection and always responded with a new seduction, a new meal, and the rational light of the Gauls. But when Zeste was most uncertain about what she felt for Serge, she could invariably get confirmation from Li:

> I can't say how happy I am to see that you have come to your senses about Serge. Because he *is* something special, a lively, intellectual person with the capacity of being enthusiastic and disgusted and with taste, whether it is women, books,

music, food, clothes, and art on the very highest level. He has taught you everything you know about that kind of thing, and when that fool of a jungle man turned up you were irritated that Serge loved you too much. To start with we wondered at Serge's wife, who put up with so much, and we thought she had no pride, but I've begun to understand her. Better to have a little of Serge than nothing at all. He is one of those rare people who make you feel, when he enters the room: "Here comes life," and when he goes "There went life," but you feel like a flower-bed which has been watered and fed for a good while. I'm not in love with him, but I love that type of person, they are *so* rare, we've probably talked about this before, you have something of it yourself, little Smallest has it, Marsken has it, to mention just a few. Grandfather had it before Grandmother broke it down. Remember not to leave my letters about so Grandmother can see them if you're at Gammel Mønt.

*

Actually she no longer had any ambition to stand on the gilded boards. Zeste had started to see the theatre as a dead end affair and several times during her training had to ask herself if this was what she really wanted. There was no longer any use for art, artifice, structure, when life itself was theatre. Everyone was an actor, everyone played his or her part unceasingly, all of it was theatre. And you could take your stand anywhere – you didn't even need costume – and draw attention to the situation. "Hey, ladies and gentlemen." Zeste had started to make herself up in the street. She sat on the pavement, while people crowded in a big ring, and the drama began.

It turned out that she was not the only one who thought along those lines, for soon a group had formed, who refused to work on a stage. Instead they acted where there was need for inspiration and encouragement, in prisons, hospitals and factories. For the incarcerated, the sick and the suppressed. In short, for all the victims of the system. Zeste and Co. played "Medea" and *The Lark,* Anouilh's "Jeanne d'Arc", and every night as Nora she left the little doll's house where the walls were too narrow and the husband a pathetic little boy. When you had to write the history of victims, you couldn't be in doubt for long that women held first place. Soon Zeste began to feel herself as a victim in a straight line from Katze through Li. Love had betrayed them. There seemed to have been only two possibilities: to avoid it like Katze – or go under like Li. Either some old knowledge had got lost somewhere, or women were only now starting to collect their thoughts and recover themselves.

All her life she had played the comedian to keep her family together, but never before had she questioned the role. She had gone on, quite unconsciously, playing it. Now she had collected many more people to hold up and inspire. Precisely the same role. She had to make several hundred people weep, shudder or laugh. She had hoped she would forget herself, that this would happen when she came to stand on a stage. The moment, when she was liberated, delivered. But she was the same as she had always been, and it didn't surprise her that a certain patient had been about to commit suicide when she had cancelled a performance. She was conscious that she must not fail, while asking herself why she had chosen to uplift others, that is, to hold a hand beneath them. Could she herself keep going in the long run?

It helped when a member of the group in the Rue de Cluny gave her some cocaine. Hash did nothing for her, only made her sleepy, and Katze had monopolised alcohol, it had no aura. Cocaine could do all Zeste couldn't do by herself: keep her spirits up. The little white strip brought a rush of breath from infinity's workshop. A thousand thanks.

One evening in that same group of friends Zeste caught sight of a young girl she thought she recognised. It turned out to be her first cousin Merete – daughter of Balder and Sharpy, who was now grown up! Zeste hadn't seen her since she was a little girl at Zahle's College in a pleated skirt and dark blue lamb's wool sweater with a V-neck and white blouse. Now here was Merete in an Indian embroidered shift with her long fair hair parted in the middle and her attractive dark eyes and a rolled dollar bill pushed up her nose.

"Hi, you two!" grinned Zeste, beginning to introduce herself, but Merete interrupted:

"You always know someone older in a school or a family," she said, looking round for her new man to introduce him. He had shoulder-length hair and was famous for being far out, because he was not content to smoke or sniff. Isaiah was known as a real junkie in his circle – and he knew his worth. There was something tough, professional about the stringy man. He was ready to run a risk and was the object of reverence among all of those who despite the hashish pipe had secured their existence with belt and reins. Isaiah had grown up in the Paris ghetto and run away from the rabbinical school to see the world. God couldn't object to that. Besides, there was nothing in the Bible about narcotics. Merete was proud.

"What else do you do?" asked Zeste, suddenly seized by familial solicitude, long since relinquished by history.

"My parents wanted me to read medicine, but I didn't want to."

"What do you want to do?"

"I want to be a druggy."

"No, seriously, Merete."

"I mean it, seriously. Ever since I was small, I've read my father's medical reference books. By the way, they're getting a divorce!"

"Balder and Sharpy?"

"I'd never have believed it myself. Even if she threatened him with a kitchen knife, he just bent his head. It was only when he joined the television company and she made fun of his acting, that he left her."

"You don't mean it!"

"See you!" called Merete and slouched happily away.

"Well, but give my love to Uncle Balder and Aunt Sharpy!"

"I don't see them any more. We're going to India soon!"

*

Zeste hadn't thought she could be shocked. All the same, there was something about Merete's risky rebellion that jerked at a family tie she had supposed herself free of, but which tricked her with incalculable reappearances. One thing was that she herself could nourish the dream of going to the dogs, but the image of the young woman who had totally rejected herself before life had properly begun, that was impossible to escape from.

Zeste went to find Merete again to see if she could help. Didn't she need to contact her parents to settle accounts with them? But she hated Sharpy, who was a member of parliament for the Conservative People's Party, so bitterly, that reconciliation was out of the question. She had lost all faith in her father, because he had allowed himself to be wiped out by his wife and had always taken her part against the children, although in his heart he was with them.

One day when Zeste was on a visit to Copenhagen, she went rushing up to Gammel Mønt. Katze met her in tears.

"Oh, what a gift you have for coming just when you're most needed, my dearest child. And little Elle, who said in Riga: 'What does an attractive woman like you sit waiting for?' And now here I am waiting for Hass from the dairy and Geismar, the laundry firm. You can't rely on anyone any more."

It was rather a burden to be Grandmother's "dearest child", for it meant that in addition to the love, you had to accept all Katze's bitterness and sorrow and help her to bear them. And you had to hold her hand as she pulled you out to the guest lavatory, where Tobias lay on the shelf, reincarnated as a white pigeon from the Rådhuspladsen.

"Hush," said Katze. "He's asleep."

At long last she had him to herself. Now he wouldn't be going over to Glenda's to play cards.

Drink and feet up. On the footstools lay stacks of tabloids and weeklies. Zeste couldn't understand how Grandmother could take in all that women's lib stuff about wearing bras outside overcoats which covered the front pages. But perhaps Grandmother could learn something from the revolution.

"When you were young . . ."

"Yes, my dear . . ."

"Were you sexually repressed?"

"No, we weren't," said Katze.

"That was good, then."

"But all these women now and their carry-on, women's liberty, ha! From now on all the men will be homosexual, mark my word! Women in parliament, God help us! They need a good thrashing, silly idiots!"

"Some of them may well be bright."

"Bright? Women? Of course they aren't."

"Aren't there any clever women in the world, Grandmother?"

"Yes, *you*, my love. As the nuns always said: You will go on the stage. You are the only one who may. You and Bodil Ipsen. All the others may just as well pack up and go home. A woman is no good when she falls in love. Remember that: fall in love, and you lose your platform. The whole stage will collapse."

Zeste couldn't help feeling this was quite a declaration of confidence, no matter how unjust – that she was the only one who might. Might what? Live, she supposed. Katze started to look through the stacks of newspapers to find one with Zeste's photograph.

"You don't need a picture, surely, I'm here!"

"Glenda has taken it," Katze seethed, sitting up in her armchair.

"Merete has gone over."

Katze scowled: "To convert to Catholicism, you can understand that. But to Islam or Judaism which is nothing but hot air! And then to have a child! No good can come of that."

"A lot of non-Jews come to no good either!"

"No, but there the misfortune isn't so bad. I'm no Hitler, but I believe in his theories of race. And Titta, born Monies, which means 'money', as you know. They have to go to dinner here and a party there. They think they can just go out and have fun and think of themselves. They don't know it will all come back on them."

The phone rang and Katze said: "It was excellent, my darling. Splendid. Grand."

It was Balder, calling to be applauded for a television programme.

*

Balder had got a divorce from Sharpy. One day he had just picked himself up and left, hidden himself at a hotel for fear she would follow him and order him home. Katze, who had hated Sharpy for 20 years, now took her part 100 percent. She mourned that Sharpy had not had "reserves" of men up her sleeve, as a woman always should, and when it was Sharpy's birthday, Katze called the poor woman to wish her many happy returns. Rebekka thought that was really too much, and said Sharpy had "thin lips". Katze replied that Tobias had those too, and Mama's lips were even narrower. At which Bekka didn't speak to her mother for a week.

Zeste got the better of herself and called Aunt Sharpy to tell her she had met Merete in Paris, but without offering more details. Sharpy only said: "Why can't these students attend their lectures instead of running around having revolutions at the state's expense?" and put down the receiver.

Zeste decided to look up Uncle Balder. Now that he was a free man he might find the energy to think of his daughter's future and save her from her erring ways. True, it was a couple of years since she had last seen him, but she had a shock at the sight of him! She remembered him for his pinstriped suits and fine ties, tied by Sharp to throttling point. But lo and behold! Now he had grown a full beard and long hair and wore a red sweater. It went well with his having left *Berlingske Tidende* in favour of television. And maybe what rumour said was true, that he had met a woman who belonged to SF, the Socialist Party.

"I bumped into Merete in Paris . . ."

"Did you now?"

"I saw her taking drugs, unfortunately. I'm no angel, but Merete is young and it might help if you took a hand."

"Yes, I'm just about to make a whole series for television on drug misuse in the young. I'm to make ten programmes."

"I was thinking of Merete . . . "

"Oh, well, cool enough."

"I thought that if you took some leave and went travelling with her for six months you might get her interested in other things and give her the will to go on living."

It was stupid of Zeste to interfere. Balder had become a free man at last, escaped from the witch's claws. It wasn't the moment to bind him to the past. Zeste left the meeting with a strange feeling. When she met the family she always felt unfulfilled longings. Perhaps it was this accumulation of karma, this karma constipation that made "the bosom of the family" so killing and yet so invigorating. For it was precisely here, at the heart of the family, that all the myths and the stories, all the lies and repressions – the whole of memory – lay hidden. This bosom was the treasure, which you couldn't touch without being poisoned.

Myren didn't want to be a nurse after all. She had become quite a competent bridge player, but you couldn't live on it. She tried her hand at being a potter, and this Rejn supported as he had no faith in her literacy. Finally she chose to study Japanese calligraphy.

In the meantime the newspapers were filled with still more scandals relating to Zeste's stubborn determination to break down every imaginable moral and social norm. The latest shock was her interpretation of Antigone and her intimate acquaintance with the dead. For Zeste it was decisive to show Antigone's eagerness to secure a decent burial for her brothers, and she did this by literally dragging two corpses on to the stage and by actually burying them in a huge mound of earth which she dug her way physically through. In reality and not symbolically, she risked her life. She considered faithfulness to the gods a higher duty than obedience to the dictates of the king; there must be a higher law in the universe than that which issues from the state, and in this way Antigone – and Zeste – bound herself to Fate.

With prophetic clear-sightedness – for up to now only Tobias had died – Zeste declared to the press on the occasion of the première: "I devour all my relations." As to her dealings with corpses, she was accused of cannibalism, but Zeste retorted: "I am not the one who slew them! It's like the peasant who finds the body of his dead mother in the field. He pulverises her and uses her as manure, and he feeds his children with corn from the field. When the children discover the truth they refuse to eat, but he forces them: 'I was not the one who killed her. Nor did I lay her on the ground, I only found her there. I merely did what I had to do.'" The press concluded that it must be a curse to have an artist in the family. "But don't they understand that I am trying to *lift* the curse?" cried Zeste into the mirror.

*

While Zeste was beaten black and blue in a French prison, where she was playing Antigone naked, and the prisoners ran amok, Myren got married.

At the university she had met a shy Maoist who reminded her of the animals and little brothers she had looked after all her life. At the news of Myren's wedding, where Jas with his big moustache and long unsteady legs had towed the bride down the aisle to the safety of her intended Pierre's arms, a stone lifted from the hearts of everyone – both in Paris and Afghanistan.

It was a small miracle that Jas could stand upright at all. His new wife, a millionairess, had sent him to hospital for an operation in the hope of getting back a new man. By dint of careful research into the work of various scientists he had well-grounded hope of a new diagnosis, a perfectly ordinary prolapsed disc, from which they would be sure to free him. But when they opened Jas up, all they found was his old spinal disorder. The operation had drained Jas' strength and made him look twenty years older. He was still under fifty.

Myren, however, was "disposed of", no longer a worrying psychological burden on the family. By her marriage to Pierre she had become part of an enormous tribe that could carry her. Pierre, one of twelve siblings, looked like one of the defenceless beings one senses out in the forest, which hunters ruthlessly shoot, but whom Myren had determined to protect in the attempt to survive herself. From now on the two of them would guard each other against the world and the evils of life.

The happy couple set out on their honeymoon to Afghanistan, for a visit to Li and Rejn. There a great adventure and a whole new life awaited them. Li and Rejn both took immediately to Pierre – because they really believed he had the ability to manage Myren.

7

THE BOND

"Cat is sick, her liver swelling up because of fat she eaten last night for dinner. Dog is good, but sometimes barking at Cat and Koala," writes Tor to Gammel Mønt. He is eight years old and is known as Koala now like the little bear, but soon gets called Teddy, because he is sent to an American school and makes an American friend.

War has not yet broken out in Afghanistan, the coup is yet to come, the king is still on his throne. There are almost ten years to go before all that happens. But Li is sick with disgust over whatever she contracts when she can't satisfy her passions and doesn't eat anything.

However, she consented to come, because – after the unpleasant experience of being a tropical grass widow – she prefers after all to live in a desert with a dry stick. She is 45, still as beautiful as a lily, but with the years she finds it harder to adjust. They have been married, the Cat and the Dog, for 15 years now. And when they realised that they could no longer get their weekly bridge, they sank into an inner desert that corresponded to the one outside. They felt threadbare and dried up. The mountains were brown with dust like cocoa and the rivers dark brown with mud. And there was this particular thing about Kabul: now and then when you thought there was a smell suspiciously like shit where you put your feet in the street, it *was* shit.

Otherwise she had tried to be positive from the start and she wrote to Gammel Mønt that Kabul was a dream with camels and donkeys in the streets. The donkeys, shaggy little fellows with ears that wobbled as they walked, had enchanted Rejn. They were always laden with a gigantic double sack, held in place with a wide belt of "genuine carpet" under the rump. Sometimes a man sat on top of the load, sometimes he drove a dozen of them. Incredibly, they never rebelled despite the harsh treatment, and either stumped peacefully along or just stood for hours waiting. The camels were of a very different stamp, bad-tempered and cantankerous. You kept clear of them, and they weren't attractive, but big and scruffy. They, too, moved soundlessly.

As usual Rejn and Li had done their homework: the modern history of the country started less than 50 years before and before that it had been feudalism and dark Middle Ages, and outside Kabul it was still like that. The national sport was boushkahzi, a kind of polo, the mallet a newly slaughtered sheep's body and the ball the head, leaving a bloody track. A sacred sacrificial ritual combined with battle lust. The king often attended the contests, sitting under his baldachin, following the moves. No-one in the country had such sumptuous treatment as the horses, who enjoyed a diet of oats and egg yolks. Down in the bazaar sat the great storytellers recounting the old myths to a crowd of listeners, who came day after day living and breathing the old tales as if every single word was still a part of their own lifetime.

The living myth, however, defied the modern reality. Kabul's enlightened academic clique was microscopic, the apparatus of government and administration loosely connected and bureaucratic to the nth degree. It could take months, as it turned out, and more than 30 signatures, to get 1,000 copies of a form letter run off. Rejn's first task was to find out how many schools and hospitals existed. No-one had done this before. But even that seemed to be almost impossible, because in Kabul's offices it was considered, in Byzantine mode, to be a matter of honour to keep all information secret. There was pride and prestige in knowing anything and the risk of seeming ridiculous if you gave out information that revealed a limit to your knowledge. It was extremely trying for Rejn to confront a bureaucracy based on ideas of honour from the time of the *Iliad*.

To begin with the Cat had been a good sport and taken an

interest in carpets. That was certainly something the Afghans could do, weave carpets. She had also fallen for the charming custom they had of deliberately weaving a small error into the design, since only Allah may be perfect. She developed a mania for finding the fault, walking around the town with eyes on stalks. As was not the case in other Islamic countries, here a woman could walk safely alone, for she did not exist in the masculine context, which is a town.

One day as she was out walking she thought she glimpsed a familiar face. It looked like Balder's daughter, Merete. A young couple, dazed, sauntered down the street. She didn't know the man, but the woman was the image of Merete! She had Tobias' eyes, only dulled. It couldn't be. They had been together not so long ago at Tobias' funeral. Already she was scarcely recognisable.

Li was searching for a particularly exquisite carpet. The Dog had given her 10,000 Afs. Carpets were everywhere, on walls and on the ground, especially down by the river, as decoration and as protection covering cars and donkeys, a touch of aesthetic cheerfulness in the midst of a medieval society, which, as the days went by, grew more and more dismal. Once she had regarded Delhi as a hole in the ground, now it was an eldorado she longed for.

They had moved from the marble palace into a little mud hut for practical reasons of heating. And the Dog wrote that when the fire was crackling in the stove and the ice cubes clinking in the apéritif, the mud hut could serve quite well as a home. Li did not think so. She had no apéritif in her glass and couldn't look at life through the glamourising fogs of alcohol. She lay in bed weeping, in her Persian furs, raging over the wallahs in the house, who were not called In and Pim Pao. The plumber wallahs, who came to see to the taps, had fixed things so that cold water came out of the shower and hot water from the lavatory. Stupid, butter-fingered dimwits. Including that sly-boots of a tailor, who sat on the sitting room floor pretending to sew curtains when he couldn't even thread a needle. Although the population was made up of 60 different tribes each with their own language, she called them all "Arabs". And in her eyes they were people who did not wash, did not work and prayed four times a day to a god whose nature meant nothing to her. Apart from weaving carpets – women and children's work – they could do next to nothing. What the men could do, she invented a word for: "to afghane". High and stoned on hash they afghaned from morning till night. One day she would sack that caliph Razak, who just stood there, glowering under his big turban. The only thing he could do was roast mutton on a fire in the garden, while Li lay sick at the thought of all the fat on top of the amoeba and stomach worms that were devouring her from inside. She lay in bed in her furs, taking stock: rather leave here today than tomorrow. But Tobias was dead; there was nowhere for her to go; and she hadn't the strength to write to anyone. The words seemed to die when they came from this wilderness, where not even tears would get you anywhere.

Gaus would always help her, of course, but she had just read in a yellowing Danish newspaper that he was in prison again. He was simply too clever, that man. She loved cleverness. So they did in prison, too, apparently and when Gaus was to be released the first time the governor wouldn't let him go. He had made himself indispensable. He had rationalised and organised the prison finances and set up a fine library. Gaus was in fact a delightful fellow, popular with all, and several years later Gaus was still telling people how much of a favourite he had been in prison. Aunt Titta and Uncle Otto had helped Aud with money while her husband was inside, so she was able to stay in the house at Charlottenlund, for Gaus had long ago squandered her entire inherited fortune. Titta and Otto did say, as Tobias would have said, when they had to listen to the story of what a prize he had been for the prison administration: "You don't need to brag about it!" In spite of everything there was an unwritten law in the Løvin family: Do what you like where Eros is concerned, but don't break the law. Thus a code was handed down which suggested that Eros was a law-free area whereas in the world of money the law held sway.

As soon as Li thought of Gaus, Jas automatically came to mind and then she wept still more.

"Never thought my heart / could be so yearning / why did I decide to roam? / Gonna take a sentimental journey / Gonna take that journey home."

Strangely enough, it consoled her to think of Jas, of what fun they had actually had, and how beautifully he danced, little tiny steps he had taught her in the mambo. How right Hemingway was: "They say the seeds of what we will do are in all of us, but it always seemed to me that in those who make jokes in life the seeds are covered with better soil and with a higher grade of manure." Jas did make her laugh, and that's the hardest and the only thing a proper princess wants. Who gives a damn about the pea, if only you can laugh at it?

But now Zeste wrote that everything had gone wrong. It wasn't only Gaus, Jas too was being sent to gaol. But at the last moment they – Jas and his new wife Medde – had fled the country. How were they getting on, Li wondered? In a way she hoped badly, for she begrudged any other woman Jas. Save Gwendoline, perhaps. Of course, it had been wrong for years, it was nothing new. Gwendoline, alias Velvet Arse, had ruined him, and he simply couldn't earn enough for the standard of living she demanded. Even if her mother was a British millionairess, there was nothing doing there. "It's your prrroblem, Jas," said the millionairess with the blue rinse and the rolling r's. She pronounced Jas like music.

It had long been rumoured, indeed even in Bangkok, that when creditors turned up at Jas' office the accountant had instructions to shout "take cover" and all the staff hid under the tables. So you couldn't blame Jas for marrying a millionairess after getting rid of the affordable Gwendoline. Li had in fact kept a soft spot for the original Gwendoline, who always had new ideas for shopping and refurbished her house every day so Jas never knew what he was going home to after work. Gwendoline painted and papered, she re-covered furniture, she was certainly artistic. A *personality*. Whereas Medde, who had got her claws into Jas now, and who had run into Zeste and Serge together and pronounced that Zeste lived an *immoral* life – poor old Jas, to be involved with such a woman. Could nobody save him from this boring Medde's petit bourgeois views? When she and Jas first married, he had *loved* immorality and loathed all that suburban "feet on the ground", "right and proper" stuff with coffee table cloths and carnations, everything "nice" which his childhood home had stood for and for which he despised his sister. Now he had married into that self-same vein! Unbelievable. The truth was that Jas was just so weak; he ought to still have a mind of his own, but obviously there would always be a woman sitting on him. Who could save Jas from this one?

*

Zeste wrote saying that Father was beyond salvation, because it was Medde who had saved his business. She had put half a million into the firm so that Jas could be his own master and take over the company where he had been employed for years. But even so he had gone bankrupt – on account of the depression. And then Medde's mother had put her money into it. An old lady on Strandvejen whose dictum was "Fish must swim" whenever she gave a toast in white wine, and whose daily joy it was to gaze through all her rooms *en suite* right down to the Sound. But suddenly one day when Jas and Medde had used up all the old lady's money, she was sent to an old people's home and Jas got a prison sentence for overdrawing his account. But Medde, who had lost her house in Rungsted plus all the furniture for Jas' sake, wrung her hands: "We didn't mean to do anything wrong," while Jas made plans to flee. For who would want to stay in a country where every business went to the dogs, and you were sent to gaol! The ready-made clothes business in particular was in danger. Only what was state-supported succeeded in Denmark. Unfortunately the police had confiscated their passports, so it wasn't that easy to flee. But Medde went to the police in tears, to save Jas – and herself – if only they could get a chance in another country. She told them about Jas' inherited spinal disease, his recent unsuccessful operation, she had an invalid husband who wouldn't survive in prison. "Give us a chance," was her tearful refrain and that, incredibly, softened the hearts of the police.

In spite of Medde's efforts to save her husband, she got no sympathy from Li. If Medde had had her famous "feet on the ground", she would – according to Li – long since have lowered their standard of living and taken a job as a shop assistant.

*

As to her own husband, she discovered that she hadn't after all married a dog, let alone a dry stick, but a crocodile with white eyes. The crocodile had decided to write a doctoral thesis. The idea was that as Rejn now had plenty of time, with postal deliveries at camel pace and innumerable religious holidays, he

241

should do a Ph.D. on his leprosy experience in south India. It was now or never. It would, as it turned out, be never.

The snow lay thick, at night the temperature dropped well below freezing, but during the day the sun reached tropical levels. He still did not know how many hospitals or schools there were, for it was out of the question to get around the country to count them. First, you would have to do a road check. Next, you had to discover whether they were negotiable. He had just returned from a trial excursion in the provinces with his counterpart Sharif. The Cat had not wanted to go. She dreamed only of the Intercontinental Hotel in Peshawar, where there was good bridge even if it was a difficult journey, necessitating crossing the Khyber Pass, where only the highway itself and 50 paces on each side were under Pakistani rule. The rest of the country, as far as the eye could see, belonged to a warrior tribe, the Pathans, who were liable to rob or kill everyone who travelled through their land. Armed to the teeth, they would come running up to stop you, and make you sign in a little lined exercise book. Presumably it was a mutual non-aggression pact you were signing, but often they left you to swelter in the car under the merciless sun and a watchful guard, because they couldn't find the exercise book.

The morning Rejn started out in the jeep the cannon went off without warning to announce the start of the Id festival. It lasted for three days at the end of Ramadan, giving the Afghans an excuse to do even less than usual. Normally the cannon was fired daily at the high point of noon, but now the festivities were on – even if it hadn't been due to start before the next day. (The phase of the moon did not depend on the calendar, it was decided by a consortium of wise mullahs, because almanacs and suchlike were regarded as foreign devilry.) People in unusually bright clothes already thronged the streets, even the coolies had found clean rags.

On the outward journey Rejn and Sharif had helped four bruised and bleeding men out of a taxi that had slipped seven or eight metres down the mountainside and ended up on its roof. It had only just happened and it was a miracle that they were all alive. That day they passed a bus that had crashed into a cliff wall, not too badly, but a fire engine and a huge tanker were hosing down the bus, smoke still pouring from the back seats. Next, a motorcyclist lying naked and bleeding badly, surrounded by a crowd of spectators. And then a car that had crashed through the rail of a bridge, fallen fifteen metres and lay with its wheels sticking up out of the water in a torrential river. They assumed there was no-one left to rescue. They drove more slowly for the rest of the trip.

Ancient Buddhas had been carved out of the rock in mountain caves, with smiling Greek profiles inspired by Alexander the Great.

It hardly seemed worthwhile to go out counting schools, when all children learned was the Koran. Everything else was sin, said the mullah of the village. A school or a hospital was really no more than a mullah beneath a shadowy tree whom people could consult when they were ill or wanted advice, and there was only one answer to everything: Allah.

The Dog had met his match in Afghanistan. He deliberately walked over people's prayer mats when he entered shops to buy paraffin to keep the Cat warm. The caliph, who was in the middle of his prayers, gladly cheated himself of a larger sum, just as the waiters often did in restaurants. To go into a petrol station, to get hold of a mechanic was always sheer catastrophe. They had no notion of the European way of survival and died like flies in bicycle collisions. The traffic was a battlefield and they obviously didn't care how many survived, although they were safe enough on horseback. The back rooms of most shops were chock full of weapons, war was never far away.

He longed for letters from Zeste, that "sun in the house", that "sparkle in the eye". He missed her sorely and seldom were there letters. Zeste maintained that the postal service was to blame, but why were only Zeste's letters misdirected? He accused her of not putting enough stamps on. The caliphs who collected foreign stamps had to have something extra and he knew that they sometimes stole them and threw the letters away although they ran the risk of having their hands cut off. At heart Rejn felt the void caused by Zeste's absence had nothing to do with the mail. Instead of sending him the letters she wrote to him, she sent them to Serge. All the letters he should have had in Kabul went to Damascus, where Serge was now stationed. When Rejn complained about Zeste's crazy life and Li's eccentric way of bringing her up, Li wrote to her eldest daughter: "As long as you don't get married, everything you do is fine. The more people you get to know the more it will develop you and the richer will be your life. But I'm sure you have realised that."

*

Li's youngest son was eight and the blessing that kept her alive. But it was not least the thought of Zeste's success that made Li get up each morning. How sad for Myren, who had come all the way to Afghanistan with her new man, hoping to find a mother and an intimacy that was her due. If Li had been a normal mother, Myren would have gained the respect she needed. But Li wasn't a normal mother, she did not value marriage or maternity in the least. She respected only intellect and art, and in Li's eyes there was no art in marrying or having children. That was something which came as a matter of course. As Katze said: "Any fool can manage that." Moreover Li was bluntly of the view that Pierre had married Myren only because he had not met Zeste. That was how it had always been at Gammel Mønt: Rebekka had never dared invite her worshippers home as she could be sure that Li would run off with the prey. Not because Li – or Zeste – did anything special, just that they couldn't help it.

So, since she couldn't impress her mother by landing a husband, Myren would try art. Every Saturday evening she sang for the guests – free – at Kabul's only hotel. And very charming it was. But Myren's eagerness to assert herself made Li fear what might happen if Zeste should become famous, while Myren had merely got married. Li did not believe Myren capable of forgiveness, and that was the sad thing about her: the capacity to nurse a grievance for ever.

It also worried her that Zeste seemed to have one abortion after the other. As if she was divided in her desire for glamour. Each time she wrote to Li that she was pregnant Li had to impress on her not to reckon on excelling at anything at all in the world of art if she came to heel and followed the pattern of her foremothers. If she wanted to achieve distinction and take that seriously – become a *personality* – she would have to break it. The pattern. And what was the best way to break with the past: by refusing to give birth and thus avoid the cycle. Li happened to be there once when Zeste was pregnant. She took in her mother's "look" and immediately made an appointment for curettage. Li silently

244

willed her daughter into heroic renunciation, while at the same time fearing that Zeste might be too soft to nurse her talent and develop it. The problem was that she was unable to fall in love with anyone without immediately wanting to have their children. The only person she didn't want to have children with was Serge. So in Li's eyes Serge's was the best card to put her money on.

In a way, Zeste and Myren had been mixed up. Zeste was the ambitious one, on the surface, but really she was at the mercy of men's desire and unable to take care of herself. Myren was to all appearances the self-sacrificing Florence Nightingale, good with children and animals, but beneath the selfless goodness a hysterical prima donna held sway. Everything Myren did not want in the world was just not there.

*

As time went on the Cat – without lifting a finger, perhaps because she *didn't* lift a finger – drained all the Dog's strength. One day, without his realising it, there was nothing left of him. The Cat still couldn't help at all with any of the housekeeping chores. It was a dog's life, and he was lucky if there was so much as a bone for him if he went home for lunch. He had to carry out his work in a hopeless desert, look after the house and write his thesis, either for Cornell or for Prague University. But Li forbade him (with her eyes) to type in the evening, because the noise disturbed her when she wanted to listen in peace to Schumann. So he stacked away the thesis with all the baskets of leprosy data in a corner. But she still complained that he made a noise and woke her up in the morning when he got up in the next room and noisily snapped the elastic on his underpants.

Added to all this, family litigation didn't make it easier for them to live together. She could not grasp it and wanted nothing to do with it. It had something to do with an old note of hand from Tobias' time, which Katze had inherited by accepting the inheritance and the debt. Rejn wanted to ensure that they did not themselves get further into debt than they already were if Ib, heir to Titta and Otto, should one day demand that the debt be honoured and so insist that Li should repay what Tobias had squandered in Sweden during the war from his maternal inheritance. Katze was not proud of that bond, it reminded her of Tobias' easy going, *laissez faire* nature. She had always called him Mr Micawber when he took after the family from Stockholmsgade in the worst possible way. Now the Løvin family was in distress because Tobias had exposed his powerlessness and bequeathed the consequences to his children. But Uncle Otto had immediately made it clear to Katze that she needn't worry. Of course he would let her stay on in Gammel Mønt, in undivided possession and he renounced the portion of his inheritance that Tobias had owed him. Uncle Otto was no monster. She was not to give a thought to that note of hand. That was said in a friendly way, for it was part of the good faith they naturally had in each other, but Rejn poisoned the family atmosphere by insisting that the bond should be legally annulled:

> It must be absolutely clear that we will not be responsible for that IOU. If Otto should demand a corresponding sum in advance from Mama's home, so be it. But certainly not because we find it reasonable, only because we don't want to split up the family.

Rejn's letter caused resentment throughout the family. Even those who admitted he was right thought that he was wrong. You simply did not talk to each other like that, especially not in a family. Rejn's attitude was that if a family couldn't tolerate a spade being called a spade, it could go to hell. Katze remarked laconically: "Rejn is Rejn" – and that sounded anything but promising!

Li tossed and turned, weeping. She thought the Crocodile was both right and wrong. And when he finally settled the matter through his solicitor and eliminated the IOU, he met only ingratitude on every side. Even Li could not support him whole-heartedly, for he lacked something she had no word for. It had fallen out of the dictionary. Maybe it was *Polish*. But Rejn would gladly do without polish if polish cost him 50,000 kroner.

He had more pressing problems, with his sons, for instance. Tor (or Teddy) was still the only bright spot in the house, the little blessing that looked after the Cat. He had been conceived in a mental hospital and had thereby saved his mother's life. And when she looked into his shining brown eyes it was Tobias she saw there. Little Tor was also immensely popular at school, but his teacher was shaken at the boy's ignorance, how was it possible? Perhaps the effect of growing up in the servants' quarters was now surfacing. He had to repeat a year in class four, but that was no misfortune.

With Orm things were worse. He had altogether stopped writing home. "Pierrot wrote and wrote – but what about you?" Only sporadic messages reached them from Denmark. Such as, that one day he had been to the open-air art gallery, Louisiana, with Zeste and Serge. They had asked him out and Serge had given him some stamps. They walked through wind and rain, Orm showing every sign of displeasure. Obviously nature wasn't his element. But which *was* his element? The next day Zeste had taken him to the cinema. She had laughed and cried and shrieked with horror, but Orm remained unmoved. Another day they had seen "The War Game", about slow miserable death in atomic war. Afterwards Orm had declared: "I would just cut my wrists. I want to die properly." Zeste shuddered. Why was the boy so strange? Cat and Dog were very worried at her report, but one day they had a letter from Myren saying that she had met the boy by chance, and had invited him to à Porta for a beer. And that he had smiled! He had amused himself working out that if one Beatle earned 10,000 kroner a day, how much money did four Beatles earn in a year?

Rejn replied that it was great to hear that Orm could smile and there was some activity in his grey matter. Sometimes you wondered whether he had inherited his thin skin from both Cat and Dog, and that would certainly be a sad fate.

8

THE FIRE

"What does it look like when I walk?" Jas always asked. In truth, it looked terrible, but no-one wanted to upset him, especially now, when he needed all the strength he could muster.

Jas and Medde had fled to Portugal where – without a sou to their names – they were going to teach the Portuguese to manufacture trousers. So it was exciting to see how many pairs could materialise from the "expertise" the poor wretch Jas had brought with him.

According to Jas, the Portuguese could supply cheap labour, while he had the more important know-how. It was something quite new, and there was money in it. They had gone in with a Portuguese "ready-to-wear firm with plenty of capital behind it" and were now ready to start on their own. There were just one or two "unplayed moves" back in Denmark, such as Medde's furniture and Medde's mother's furniture, taken by the bailiffs though they had no right to them at all, Jas wrote to Zeste and Myren. Now he had a first-class suggestion for his daughters: a suggestion that could save Medde's furniture. And her mother's too.

Zeste and Myren and all their friends were to club together to buy Medde's furniture from the house in Ordrup. And Medde's mother's furniture from the apartment on Strandvejen. For the net sum of 5,000 kroner. Myren and Pierre refused point blank.

To them 5,000 kroner was a sum heard of only on the Stock Exchange. As a young couple they had tried to establish themselves simply and thriftily and were not disposed to embark on complicated transactions. Besides, Pierre wasn't keen on Jas' capitalist manipulations, for it was obvious that he and his like could survive only by systematically exploiting people in third world countries and at the same time causing unemployment among Danish dressmakers and workers. If Pierre had his way, the revolution couldn't come quickly enough, and would embrace the cause of the Portuguese textile workers. And when history came to its senses, what difference would it make whether Medde and her mother had got their rococo furniture back? Moreover Myren and Pierre had Orm staying with them to help him salvage a modest education out of some course or other after he had been thrown out of his public school at Sorø.

Zeste, who was acting in sheds and halls without a salary, in solidarity with the scum of the earth, reacted more angrily to Jas' castles in the air. It was as if she had reached a limit to how much childishness she could put up with from her parents.

First Li had got divorced from Jas. Then she had howled because she wanted him back. First she had been cold to the one she loved, and then she had had the hots for one she didn't care for. Jas had married Gwendoline and brought a lovely little girl into the world that he had abandoned, just as he had abandoned his first two daughters – in just the same light-hearted way you might take your leave of a picnic. "Bye, bye, I'm off," as Gauguin said when he left his entire family walking in the Deer Park, while he set out for Polynesia and never saw them again. Some thought that romantic, but Zeste did not.

Now Gwendoline and their lovely little Naja with her green eyes had come down in the world and were forced to live in a one-room apartment with cardboard divisions. "Homeless hutments are splendid!" roared Gwendoline – in her cups, it is true. And only if luck was with her, this once so beautiful mannequin, could she get a job at Ebberødgård Hospital, cleaning the arses of the half-witted, or if Dame Fortune should smile on her and she was taken on at the local supermarket could she afford riding lessons for Naja. She might as well cry for the moon as for any help from Jas, maintenance, child allowance and whatever else was her due in the way of legal paternal liabilities.

There's an old saw: you can't cut a bald man's hair. And Jas had grown bald in various ways. What with the inherited spinal disease, which had sapped his strength, and other knock-out blows dealt by life, the frivolous dandy had gradually become quite groggy.

He tried to mollify Zeste, he perfectly understood her point of view, he wrote, and promised that money should never come between them. When he suggested she and her friends should save Medde's furniture and Medde's mother's furniture, it had been a last desperate way out. If it had been his own furniture, of course he would never have worried her. But Medde, who had already lost so much, naturally would have liked to keep the last of her possessions, and as it was all entirely his fault he had to try everything to help her.

They had gone to Portugal with the idea that Jas should be the head and Medde the body – as the doctors had said. But the body was in such despair now that it was considering coming home to the children in Denmark, partly to see about the furniture, partly to be with her mother and earn her keep. But Zeste must agree that it would not be any help in the furniture case if Medde went home, and besides she couldn't live with her mother. They would tear each other to pieces and be even unhappier. Besides, he would have to give up his job in Portugal as he could hardly walk unaided, and he would have to come home and live on a disability allowance and porridge without the pat of butter, which would be no solution at all.

So Medde stayed with him because she knew he couldn't manage without her. Everyone would say it was Medde's duty to stay at home with her mother, but what would the consequences be, and would she make anyone happier? No, he had brilliantly made everything as dire as possible for as many people as possible. One small detail was his illness – that, at least, he couldn't help. But it had pretty effective consequences in the current situation. If you only took the present situation into account, however, you would have to agree that he had got a job where the expertise he had amassed over the past 20 years fulfilled a need in Portugal. He was paid enough for the two of them to exist on, with a little over for brandy with their coffee. Medde and he would get four free trips to Denmark a year, and there was also a chance down the road of earning a lot more money if everything turned out as expected. Besides, the bailiff had taken the dining table and eight chairs, Medde's gilt wall clock and Jas' grandfather clock, which he had no right to do as they were not on the original list. And so on and so on.

Zeste was caught between anger, sympathy and sorrow. Poor little Dad. When you had parents like this, you didn't need children. It was incomprehensible to her that a grown man could act so irresponsibly. And a father into the bargain. The very word father was one you linked with a higher order of existence, which should and could save you from the muddier snares always lying in wait down in the maternal ocean. But when Jas had been on the way to prison, suddenly the word *criminality* was imprinted on Zeste's consciousness like a mysterious reality that had once been distant and abstract. How could her sweet little father be a *criminal*? A cheat? She had heard the word *psychopath* used as well. And it reminded her again of all that people had said about Gaus. Her godfather, for heaven's sake, who had notoriously been to prison. Several times. Was the whole *family* criminal, then?

At Christmas time Jas and Medde lost all courage in Portugal, and Zeste feared Medde would have to go back to Denmark when her father was alone in the world and ill, and couldn't manage by himself. For Myren had her own affairs to see to. It was always more legitimate, when you were married, to care for your own stuff, while the unmarried had to look after the rest of the world. Zeste prayed that Medde would stick with Jas to the bitter end. But she conceded that this was an unreasonable expectation of a person who had been robbed of her last stitch.

Jas wrote just before Christmas – 1969, that is – that his right hand was now so bad that he could no longer hold a pencil, but Zeste could hear his voice beneath Medde's elegant handwriting. He apologised for not sending even a Christmas card, but everything had collapsed and they had been left with almost nothing. They had ended up at the Danish embassy in Lisbon, where the ambassador and his wife had taken them in and given them a Christmas in luxury. The letter ended: "We are about to be driven to Oporto with a private chauffeur in a Cadillac. With much love, and happy New Year, when we'll meet again. Your own Medde and Father."

It wasn't long before Jas was back in Copenhagen. Without

Medde. Without a body. She had left him at the municipal hospital, as his legs and bowels had given way and the contents found themselves in his cashmere trousers. They had spent their last sou in Hamburg getting their poodle Bubbi washed and clipped at the poodle parlour. But now all the money was spent – her own and her mother's – and as there was no prospect of his earning any more, Medde had come to the conclusion that it would be reckless to expend any more effort on Jas. They had had fun. Indeed, they had had so much fun that she could forgive him for squandering her whole fortune. But now she would get a teaching job and put a little order into her life. Chaos was festive and enjoyable, but it mustn't be allowed to go on. After all, Medde was renowned for having her feet on the ground, she couldn't get away from that.

The day when Jas staggered out of the front door in Ordrup with his last possessions and got into a taxi with 28 suits, 28 pairs of hand-sewn shoes, various hats including a bowler in a hatbox plus a pewter goblet from Amager and an erotic mirror he and Medde had been given as a wedding present, he met the neighbour, Dr Jensen, who looked extremely surprised.

"We're just off on our summer holidays."

"But what a lot of luggage you have!" said Dr Jensen, staring at the mirror, a pair of brass candlesticks and a box of books.

"Yes, nowadays you need a lot," Jas said. And he said to himself: "I'm walking very well now." But everyone looked at him. Not because he looked like an old man, for he was still not 50, but because he looked like someone marked down by death, but who nevertheless went on living and staggering along to found limited companies and make himself a millionaire.

*

Jas moved into a rented room whose hostess was delighted. He lay speculating over how he should organise the ultimate goal of his life: a U-shaped drive on Strandvejen, on the coast.

The first and definitive idea was to let the state pay. When he looked into the legislation, it was extraordinary what a citizen had the right to demand. But in spite of everything Jas belonged to the old school. He didn't mean to demand anything, he meant only to be charming, as he was when he went food shopping and the assistant said: "That'll be 7,75 kroner", and Jas would smile: "That sounds lovely, it's my favourite price, you know."

In short, he would exploit his charm.

So the first thing he said when he limped up to social services to get a Cadillac, was to ask whether the official in charge would like to hear the story of when he was buying socks in London. The official opened wide her eyes and with the help of his good hand Jas crossed his long, weak legs.

"Well, I wanted a pair of cashmere socks," Jas said, twirling the points of his moustache between two fingers. The official looked bemused.

"Then I ask how much these really lovely socks cost, you see?" The official nodded uncertainly.

"The shop assistant says 550 kroner. 'For a pair of socks? They'd only last a week,' I said. 'But what a week, sir!'"

He didn't talk down to the official – he assumed she understood English – he raised her up. And she swiftly understood how essential it was for him to have a car. She would manoeuvre it through the bureaucratic system so that he wouldn't have to wait six months. Because it would be wasting state funds to have him idle when he was ready to start in on any kind of work tomorrow. For a start he had seen an advertisement in the paper for brand-new one-room apartments beside the Lakes, and the official in charge quickly took it on board that this man must have a four-poster bed with curtains from Lysberg, Hansen & Therp, or he wouldn't get a wink of sleep. Jas always knew what he wanted, and it was always the most expensive. And social services at once apprehended that this man could not be satisfied with anything less.

He was settled into his new apartment in a trice, with four-poster and curtains around it and a brand-new car parked in the courtyard. He used his handicapped card only when he parked in town.

*

At last Jas, at 49, was ready to start on a new life. But first he must determine what had gone wrong in the old one. For if he was ever to attain his life's goal, the U-shaped drive on Strandvejen, he would have to grasp what kind of mysteries life held and what role he himself played in the puzzle. So he bought Aldous Huxley's *The Perennial Philosophy*, in two volumes, because he simply could not conceive why everything had gone so wrong, why life had so taken the mickey out of him. He had had wives, houses, cars and money and amusement galore. And now he was suddenly alone in a one-room apartment, without work, friends, anything. The Lord gave, the Lord hath taken away, the Lord is a guitar. Everyone he had once known and called his friends were, despite everything, possessed of a certain standard of living, and he was ashamed to present himself to them as one of life's losers.

For a long time his former business associates had warned him against showing his face in town, for there was no money in his sickly appearance. His faltering gait and paralysed arm did nothing to strengthen his credit. In commercial life it is necessary to hide your real cards and set up a façade that inspires confidence. Everything in the world of trade rested on this false confidence. That was why Jas threw himself into "the perennial philosophy". There must surely be other values than those he had previously subscribed to. He was persuaded that there must be a natural law, in the soul as well, which posited that after you had reached bottom you would be raised up again. There must be a balance. He read of good and evil, time and eternity, salvation and redemption, prayer, suffering and faith. Of charity and self-knowledge. Of mercy and free will.

But no matter how much he read, his life reminded him most of the story he had told his daughters so many times when they were small. The story of the little man and the tailor. Of how the little man takes a large roll of material to the tailor to have a suit made. Of course, sir, certainly. And the little man went to fetch his suit. But unfortunately there was not enough material for a suit. Well, but what could there be? Well, a jacket. Many thanks, said the little man. But there was not enough for a jacket, only for a waistcoat. And then only enough for a handkerchief. And finally there was not enough in the large roll of material for anything at all. Many thanks, said the little man. And now Jas himself had become the little man in the story he had told so many times, who had got precisely nothing out of his whole life.

He drew a line under Augustine's words: "One should rejoice in God alone; creatures one should not rejoice in, but use – use with love and sympathy and a thoughtful, detached appreciation, as a means of understanding what one may rejoice in." And that was precisely what he had done: he had used Medde and her money with love and sympathy and a thoughtful, detached appreciation! And he drew three lines beside the quote: "Love is unfailing; it has no fault, for faults are lack of love." He had loved and yet he fought for peace of mind. He read that no-one shall set up as a judge of anyone else, and yet he judged himself. He drew a thick line alongside a sutra about the art of restoring the original purity of the mind and becoming like a child again: "If you wish to calm your mind and restore its original purity, you must proceed as you would if you were to clean a bowl of dirty water. First leave it alone until the dregs sink to the bottom and the water is clear."

Nevertheless he worried over how he would ever be able to earn anything again when he had compromised himself in the whole clothing trade and had been close as a whisker to being banged up. *The Perennial Philosophy* had no advice on that. He tried, with the concept of "active resignation" to follow Chuan Tsu's counsel of allowing neither good nor ill to disturb his interior balance. And he nodded affirmatively to the observations of blessed Francis de Sales. For indeed it was so true that there was no point in getting upset over events that were not in our power to prevent. We did not even have any power over something called our psychophysical armament.

So as it seemed that we didn't, when it came down to it, have much influence over anything and as the "interior balance" was a bit boring in the long run because it was inclined to become addicted to self-reproach and self-pity, he decided to drag himself up by the last few hairs on his bald head and sheer willpower, and start up again as a man of business. Surely his Portuguese connections could still be of use. For even if things had gone wrong down there, it was an incontestable fact that the Portuguese could make trousers cheaper than could the Danes. Perhaps he had gone astray in Portugal because of exchange difficulties, but he knew the Danish market like the back of his hand, and he would build his future on that: selling Portuguese trousers in Denmark. And this time he presented himself to the Portuguese as "Professor of Economics from Copenhagen University", so they could respect him down there in the hot countries and realise it was not Mr Anyone they were dealing with.

*

It wasn't the best moment to start up a business. The strikes had just begun in Denmark. In these uncertain circumstances, the Danish men's clothiers were nervous of buying. And when they finally plucked up courage and gave an order for an extremely exotic consignment of trousers, they did it more for the sake of old friendship and to thank Jas for all the good stories he had told them over the years. Crome & Goldschmidt and Havemann's Magasin were not slow to recognise a man in need.

It was worse for Jas when he *did* get an order. For it was extremely doubtful whether he and the Portuguese were able to effect it. He many times had to wait in vain for a consignment. But as it was important to keep hold of his customers, however fictitious they were, he wired down to the Portuguese at their expense and said they must think of any old story in explanation for the non-appearance of the trousers. They must say the factory had burned down or been flooded, that the ship had sunk or a volcano erupted. Anything but the truth.

The sad truth was that the Portuguese were beginners at the art of satisfying a wealthier, northern clientele with such huge beer stomachs that the southern sewing machines and scissors could not cope with them. So rumours were rife in Denmark that the Portuguese stole all the trousers they made. And the Portuguese happily admitted that it was "quite possible that the trousers had been stolen".

Jas could only fight on, try to keep his clients calm. He wrote to one, assuring them that it was impossible the trousers had been stolen during packaging or in any way at the factory, for in Portugal conditions were different from Denmark where you can get a few months' holiday at the state's expense if you make free with other people's possessions. In Portugal you would get your head wrenched off and put through the mincer three times, and this had the wonderfully salutary effect that crimes in Portugal occurred only in big cases, of life and death. Jas was therefore convinced that all the trousers had left Portugal.

But it was still worse when the trousers actually arrived. "Full length." Although Jas had given instructions on style to the Portuguese they always arrived in Denmark as a heap of miserable-looking cloth. The Portuguese tailors were taught that the trousers would look quite good as long as they lay "flat on the table". But as soon as you held them up they turned out either to have legs of different lengths or to be impossible to fasten in front. "And that, dear friends and gentlemen, you will agree is unfortunate for your agent, who has to travel around selling these pathetic garments!" And Jas always ended his letter with a request for more money to keep the often-fictitious clientele going, and himself in particular.

*

Every day he parked in Købmagergade, because in order to eke out the meagre Portuguese revenues he had taken a job, which aimed at retraining home-bound housewives for business life. He gave them marks and one in particular always got full marks.

To Katze he said: "She has met me as I really am, without my past."

And Katze threw her arms around old Jas and embraced him. Then she pulled him out to the guest cloakroom so that he could see Tobias still on the windowsill, just as his coats still hung in the hall. In honour of Jas' coming to dinner (Glenda and Buller had invited themselves and were bringing the prawns), she had found one of her nicer dove-grey cardigans from Tobias' day which went well with her blue eyes, white hair and pearls. She was getting on for 70 and still working at the office.

"Oh, but Jas, the most infamous thing is that Her-from-the-Muddy-Ditch, as I call her at the office, calls *me* a little grey mouse! But shouldn't it be *me* who's the *cat*? I've been called Katze all my life! I, who had so many admirers – in every language – and could have married them all, especially the fur trapper, Dame Muddy Ditch dares to call *me* a grey mouse! And I wonder if she knew that I have a grandchild on the way to being a famous actress in Paris! That's how I shut her up!"

Jas never forgot the first time he saw Katze at Gammel Mønt, in a blazing red dress, with a diamond brooch and a drink in her hand, standing in the middle of the room on the great carpet before Gaus had it "stored". Like a play in which the curtain had closed on the first act and the *femme fatale* seduced the whole menagerie with every imaginable disaster resulting. The fiery red dress had been a savage warning. But now she and Jas had become bosom friends in their old age. He did notice that the apartment hadn't been cleaned since Tobias' time. Marie came only once a week, actually to take over Katze's weekly magazines, after she too had been widowed. Every other day Katze said "poor Marie" and that Marie was her only friend in the world. The other days she said "That fool Marie" because she had nothing else in her head but running after some widower down at Korsør she had to cook for. How daft women were, clinging to a man like that. At least she, Katze, had never done that! But Katze didn't give a hoot for housework. She even took a marked pleasure in seeing the place go to rack and ruin.

"Jas, sit in Tobias' chair, it was yours during the war, do you remember? What a cosy time we had."

Katze had quite forgotten how irritated she had once been at seeing Jas take Tobias' chair. Now she was glad. Something bound them together. Not just the past or their modest origins, but rather the fact that things had gone badly with them both. But when all the fiascos had been pared away they were left with a pang in the heart and a pleasure in seeing each other that might seem like love. He couldn't care less that Katze drank, which would be a shame to say of Rebekka, who went out into the kitchen and helped Marie taste things. And Katze couldn't care less that Jas had gone bankrupt and threw away a fortune that didn't belong to him and escaped prison by a hair's breadth. Katze invariably spoke ill of her nearest and dearest, but never of Jas. Perhaps that was because they both had their hearts in the right place, even though it was obviously not an especially smart one.

"Oh, Jas, how good to see you. Let's have a bit of a chat before the idiots from Stockholmsgade arrive. Why don't you move into Gammel Mønt just like old times?"

"Well, Grandmother, I've been divorced from a crowd of women, for to tell you the truth, all women are totally mad, but I'll never be divorced from you, we two will stick together and the whole crazy world can go up in flames or do whatever it will."

"All the world can go to hell, but Gammel Mønt stays fit and well!"

Katze didn't say "Skål", but nodded at Jas with tears in her eyes and took a slurp of her cocktail.

"Yes, and it's thanks to you, Grandmother, it's all due to *your* efforts. And d'you know what, Grandmother? I'm going to take you to Hotel d'Angleterre, to the bar, where they make the most delicious casseroles."

"Come on, Jas, you can't afford that."

"Of course I can afford it! I can afford anything! I'm a free man! And I've got the whole of life before me!"

"Oh, Jas, how lovely it is to hear you. If only we could be on our own without those nincompoops from Stockholmsgade. Hum, has Aunt Mudde come to a stop? You remember Aunt Mudde, don't you? I'd better wind her up, she's usually a bit fast." Katze rose and went over to the bureau with the silver clock she had inherited from Mudde as well as a few shares.

Rebekka, back from Helsinki, had a job as secretary to a Danish doctor in the USA and was temporarily staying at Gammel Mønt, where she got on her mother's nerves and vice versa. Katze sighed deeply.

"She does all she can to hurt me. You know, Jas, what a sharp tongue she has. We must talk quietly or she'll hear us. But do you know, Jas, she wants to go over to the Jewish faith, just to break my heart. She loves her father more than she does me."

"*I* love you, Grandmother!"

"She has pictures only of Tobias in her room."

"D'you know what, Grandmother, I'll have pictures of you on *all* my walls!"

"Now then, Jas, no more of your nonsense. You and Li stayed with me in Denmark, at Gammel Mønt 14."

"Yes, but I mean it!"

"And she's so proud, she is, she walks down the street as stiff as a board without so much as looking up and waving to me. And then I tell you – for you never know when Our Lord will call us to Him and then we'll be gone – that all my grandchildren have always waved, while she was away. Just like Aunt Mudde always waved to her mother in Fredericiegade. And even little Orm, who is so good and sweet, and who's such a worry to me, he waved to me, too, when I stood at the window and he was going somewhere far away. But she won't."

"I'll go out and talk to her."

"Don't tell her anything."

In fact Jas wasn't thrilled at the idea. For Rebekka was expert at giving other people a bad conscience. She had found the world at fault, and it had to dodge her fists. She had written to him several times demanding money on behalf of Zeste and Myren and had appealed to his paternal feelings, sense of responsibility, decency and so on. And he had replied that she was not to interfere in his affairs, and if he had as much as one krone at his disposal he would rather invest it in antelope coats for his daughters, rusty nails or old banana skins, according to the state of the market. But Bekka had turned into the Queen of Reprimands, still a classic beauty, still under 50, but with grey strands in her black hair which she wore in a bun at the neck. How beautiful she could be, thought Jas – she too had her heart in the right place. But that place didn't do her any good. After her setback over the Reichendorf affair, Rebekka had based her interpretation of life on the wrong position of her *arms*. They had been screwed onto her body in the wrong way. And since the opposite sex – quite rightly – was obsessed with physical details in women, and in particular with the way their arms were placed, you couldn't blame a proper man for chucking her over in favour of one whose arms were on the right way round. Rebekka was so sure of her view of arms that she always wore long sleeves, even in summer.

"Why won't you wave to your mother?" laughed Jas, giving Marie a hug, as Rebekka took her Craven A out of her mouth so he could kiss her, and pulled Jas into her room. Where the gift of the gab was concerned, she was like Madame de Staël. Rebekka's torrent of words was a real trap, an anaesthetic that sent the person addressed into a zombie-like state. If against all odds you actually managed to stammer out a couple of words or maybe a whole sentence on the way to the next one, you were savagely despatched. The torrent in Bekka was an urge that automatically sensed when the "opponent" was about to draw breath. In precisely that place, that weak place, in the middle of this nanosecond of silent emptiness, in the moment of this taking of breath, the torrent of words would pour out of Rebekka, who would go on talking, seductively, self-forgetfully, while the listener was already beaten, taken over and deprived of the use of language for a long time.

"I can't be bothered to humour her. She must look the truth in the face. All this self-pity comes from the illusion that she has been allotted the role of tragedienne *à la* Bodil Ipsen or Betty Nansen. If she wants to see anyone, and she does of course, for she doesn't want to go to the dogs, she must let go of that illusion."

Jas could barely stand upright on his bad legs and needed to move somehow, get away. But Rebekka held on to his sleeve:

"She must start to admit that she is only a perfectly ordinary person, an ordinary self-supporting woman like thousands of others – I can't be bothered with the rest. And even if she does offer to pay my bills, I shall go on hearing about it for the rest of my life, and I don't want that."

Jas looked at his watch: "Don't you think Glenda and Buller must be here at any moment?"

"No, they're always late. If I were to tell her everything Father said to me about her before he died, it would take that illusion from her. It was a good thing in a way that he died, because he really couldn't stand her in the end. And it was a good thing he asked *me* to phone for the ambulance, or she would have found him dead in bed next morning. You can't stir her once she has fallen into her drunken sleep. For all that she maintains she never closes an eye. No, you must be mad, I'd never dream of telling her what he said to me."

Jas was about to find a chair when Katze came staggering in and tried to rescue Jas with her tipsy consonants. Katze could not handle spirits any more. Two drinks and her speech was slurred.

"Sho, hazh she been talking about me? Rudle, rudle . . ." Katze came out with a Yiddish expression.

"Oh, now Grandmother, you know Rebekka."

"I'd only juszht offered to pay 300 kroner for her bills, because she hazh so many expenses now she'zh going to America. And then she comes out with such a palaver on hearing about it afterwards, and that'zh not nice, for you know very well, one thing izh zhure: I'll do *anything* for my children and grand-children."

Tobias would have appreciated the arrival of Glenda with her copper-toned, newly styled hair and bowl of peeled prawns and little bald Buller, who without introductory manoeuvres or other forms of sham politeness helped himself to a Martini, lit a good cigar and leaned back in his chair.

They all raised their glasses and Katze cried: "A woman of 40 is finished!"

"How can you possibly say that?" said Glenda and looked from Rebekka to Katze and back in confusion. But Buller saved the situation with his incontrovertible assertion:

"I'll just say that those who start to call themselves Communists are stark staring mad. In America, the land of freedom, the workers drink whisky and drive cars. In Russia they have bicycles and a bayonet at their backs."

Marie came in and nodded to Madame that dinner was ready.

The guests had probably thought that the gold-rimmed plates or the Russian glasses from Riga would have been brought out for fun, as Katze hadn't had anyone to dinner for several years. But they had to think again. She wouldn't give them the wine she had kept ever since the war. The wine was to remain part of her estate, like the Russian glasses, which had grown quite white with dust and whitewash that had tumbled from the ceiling because people tramped about above – the ones who had started a brothel. Right over her head.

*

Not long after that dinner Zeste was back in Copenhagen looking after Jas. He had pestered Myren so much of late that at last she had had to ask him to give her a break. As newlyweds they did have their own life to live and he must respect that. But he didn't respect it. "I'll go on coming round until you ban me!" So the day came when Myren forbade her father to turn up unannounced, and Zeste came home and moved into Gammel Mønt.

Every day Zeste had to trim either his nails or his moustache. Or he asked her to write for him, as he still couldn't get his trouser business going. "To begin with they must only just sniff at the trousers," wrote Zeste to the Portuguese about Jas' customers, "next they must like them and finally need them." Jas had actually sold 440 pairs of trousers in the six months he had been living by the Lakes. Next season he promised to sell 10–12,000 pairs and the next one again: 30,000 pairs – "if we all live that long," he added. Zeste looked up at her father from the typewriter, hoping in a way that he *wouldn't* live that long. He added a postscript saying that the day before he had been lying on the floor unable to move. "Everything is political," Zeste replied automatically with one of the slogans of the day. She didn't know what else to say. She couldn't imagine her father in a wheelchair at a home, he wasn't the type for nappy-changes. He was for women, champagne and dancing.

It was awful to see a father go to pieces before one's eyes. He was her little boy who had suddenly grown so terribly old, at nearly 50. It was with a lump in her throat that Zeste tied his shoelaces and his tie. He had begun to use the same shirt two days running. Many people might make a shirt last a whole week. But it seemed wrong to the swing-mad Jas if his patent shoes weren't chalked. When she arrived in the morning he would be sitting in his silk dressing gown in the kitchen playing roulette. On a little toy wheel. He had locked himself in now that he could scarcely walk. "I've just won on 17 and black, Zessie."

But when they were going out to hear Teddy Wilson at Timme's in Nørregade, he pulled himself together and booked a table.

"Just see how it looks when I walk?"

*

One evening they were having a whisky together. He had put on a cassette of Mozart's clarinet concerto. At the end of the second movement he dried his tears.

"Zessie, you've got a clever father. It takes great talent to pour away a million."

Zeste smiled at his everlasting ability to turn everything on its head. And all the birthdays he had forgotten. And when he did for once remember your birthday he had gone bankrupt and given the oddest presents. Once, when all her friends were getting silver forks and gold watches, Jas had turned up with a cake box full of – live ducklings. All that scrabbling around in the box, it was appalling. Zeste had only one idea, to get rid of the creatures as fast as possible, although she couldn't just chuck them in the dustbin or a nearby stream. She hadn't even given a thought to the chance of one of the ducklings turning into a swan some day. But lately the gift had come back to her again and again like a real live present you kept for always.

"When the day comes that I can't walk at all," said Jas, "I'll just get in the car and drive flat out into a tree."

"Dear old Dad, you haven't got the courage for that," Zeste thought, but reminded him instead of the U-shaped drive on Strandvejen.

In some ways his life had become like the story he had always told them about Nikolajsen when they were small. The Nikolajsen who was shown the door again and again and pushed into the lift, but who came back every time explaining that he had been chucked into the dustbin twelve times now, and that should be enough. But Jas loved life. For him it was never enough. And one day Zeste had to say stop, she felt herself persecuted by his weakness and devoured by his sufferings. He had turned into a child she could not drag along. She had to think of her own life as well, and Serge had arrived in Paris and was waiting for her, so she must go back.

"You mustn't marry him," said Jas, quite unexpectedly.

"?"

"Foreign escapades are all well and good, I've had them myself. But you mustn't marry them."

"Why not, in point of fact?"

"Because one day you'll recall a song by Osvald Helmuth or a joke by Storm P. and then you'll find it can't be translated. They won't have the slightest notion what you're talking about."

Suddenly Zeste said: "Why don't you marry Mother, then?" Like some impulse from the depths where children always want their father and mother to stay together. Zeste was almost 25.

Jas gave an intimate explanation.

Zeste didn't care for that confidence. Was there anything worse than being let into one's parents' bedroom?

*

In the evening of July 6th Rebekka rang to say goodnight to Jas and almost as soon as she had put down the receiver, Katze rang:

"So, she's hung up at last? How did it go?"

"You must go to bed, Granny, and try to sleep. Have you borrowed some good books?"

"Yes, one by that Muriel Spark. 'What kind of pornography is that?', asked fru Muddy Ditch at the office, she sees everything that's lying about, sticks her nose into everything. Yes, Bekka is unhappy, that fool Reichendorf must have married someone else, but it's no use hanging on to a man."

It was time to say goodnight to little Granny and thanks for everything.

"You know, Jas, Gammel Mønt is your home," was the last thing Katze said.

The next day, the police on Nørre Søgade telephoned Rebekka about a fire. Jas was dead, burned in his four-poster with all the synthetic curtains from Lysberg, Hansen & Therp. He hadn't been as charred as he might have been, most probably he had passed out with carbon monoxide poisoning. Only his moustache was burned. And the whole apartment. The autopsy showed the deceased had consumed both a sleeping tablet and whisky. After that he had lighted a cigarette.

9

THE WOMEN OF THE KASBAH

On July 12th, 1993, Laila Khasani went underground in and around Algiers. She never spent two nights running in the same house after she had been condemned to death by the Islamic organisation F.I.S.

Marsken was an old acquaintance of Laila's parents. He had taken over their house when he lived in Algiers. The Moudjahadin inscription VICTOIRE à FLN, LE PEUPLE LE SEUL HÉRO, was still in red lead paint on the façade, and it was this house he passed on to Rejn and Li in 1970 for them to live in for the next three years. Not a wonderful French medieval villa from colonial times or a tumble-down magnificent palace from the Turks' time, but a concrete bunker in the inner labyrinth of the Kasbah alleyways above the Place des Martyrs, where most of the bigger guerrilla battles had been fought out. Since then the Kasbah had deteriorated into almost a slum.

Normally Li would never have agreed to move to "yet another" Arab land, let alone settle in an Arab district, where as a white person you risked being stoned. Right back in Boumedienne's time there had been a high-level plan, a hidden one, to sow the seed of a fundamental revolution which was later to be directed at the so-called western civilisation which was destroying itself and the rest of the world, chiefly because of the uncontrolled rampaging of the women. As the youngest of the three monotheist religions, Islam was closest to its original, zealous obligation: to keep women down. All intrinsic civilisations rested on this. Boumedienne had studied at the fundamentalist university Al Azar in Cairo. The most intelligent of the fundamentalist leaders were indifferent to the "headscarf", but they knew the masses needed easily understood symbols in the fight against western decadence, and they had learned the lesson of history: if female insubordination was not kept under control it would develop into all-destructive chaos. Mothers would marry their sons and eat their daughters, there would be no end to their regressive power, in which the men would sink and be overthrown. Islamisation, sharia, was the only answer to the saving of man and therefore the world.

It was astonishing that Li could bring herself to live in such a country. But the sole reason for her accepting to do so was the fact that Marsken had lived there. As far back as she could remember, he had rescued the poor, the sick and the weak from imperialist exploitation and suppression. He was one of the few people, thought Li, who was actually worth anything. His unassailable moral strength spoke its own clear language and overcame Li's usual tendency to hysteria. She had taken no part in the Resistance during the war. Now, through Marsken and the house, she was a part of the history of the greater *résistance*. It was here that Li determined to take up arms against her husband and finally break him.

It could be argued that it is really a sign of weakness for a woman to have to destroy her husband, but Li had reached the point in her life where she no longer had any choice. What she hoped for, of course, was to destroy herself in the same action, a kind of death stroke that would disavow the life that had existed, and was no longer alive. And should never have happened. Li had made a terrible mess of her life, and now she could not now allow Rejn to run away at the last moment and leave her in the ruins. If she was to be deserted and go under, they should go under together.

The most obvious method would be to let life dissolve in spirits. She was, after all, a Løvin!

Rejn had never drunk much more than is customary to the norms of global nomadic life, drinks from sunset until bedtime. But Li, for many years, because of her disgust with drinking and guilt over her own misuse of medicines, had seen Rejn as an incurable third-degree alcoholic. Now she was going into battle. Partly by emptying his bottle into the sink, partly by starting to drink herself. She poured milk over his clothes and smashed his typewriter with a hammer. And everything around them seemed in harmony with all this – even Tor at 13, standing there paralysed.

The world itself was in the same mood. Algeria was full of savage Arabs glaring vengefully at every white person and throwing stones at Tor when he was going to school. They played appalling bridge and had no appreciation of Chinese porcelain. The Møller menage was sunk. After five years' trial in the deadly Afghan desert, which just lay waiting to be strewn with mines so that all the children who were sent out as diviners could have their arms and legs cleverly amputated, the Møller marriage was finished.

So that was Li's situation. She was almost at the menopause, Tobías and Jas were both dead with only a few years between them, and no-one called her "a lovely little girl" any longer. And the first thing she did when she sensed the risk of Rejn leaving her was to gather up all the Chinese porcelain she could find in the house, Sung and Ming, the frog in particular, and pack it in a cardboard box which she put under her bed. Then she sat on top of it like a refugee with her wig askew. Wigs were modern that year. There she stayed with the jade cat in her hand waiting for Zeste to come and rescue her.

But at that moment Zeste had other pressing business. For as no-one else was prepared to deal with the formalities of Jas' death – Myren was so busy in her newly married state – Zeste had to get out the funeral trowel and bury the charred remains.

Some were scandalised because she had arranged for Jas' old friends to come and play Chaplin's "Smile", but it was precisely that love of life which was important to keep alive, in spite of everything. Jas owed Nølle, the bass player, 50,000 kroner – he was the one who had once beaten his wife Sunne black and blue in the street because she had kissed the wrong man. Nølle had to wave goodbye to 50,000 flat: Smile! And among the congregation in the chapel sat a perfect stranger, an attractive woman smiling graciously. No-one had ever seen her before. But she must be the housewife from the school in Købmagergade who always got

"Excellent" and had known Jas, "just as he was".

Zeste was 25 and gave the eulogy:

> If you didn't manage to realise all your dreams, it owed more to the unkindness of fate than the touch of the gambler's nature that was you as well. Any feeling of responsibility, of deep seriousness, was remote from you. But apart from an affectionate, open mind you possessed a very rare gift – you possessed the grace of life. (Or just charm??) You didn't burden others with your troubles, you were a very brave man. Your radiance enriched not only those of us who knew you, everyone was brought enchanted into your sphere of charm and sincerity. But behind all that lurked the pains you bore so courageously and which slowly took you away from all the life you loved. And then came solitude – and that was not you. As you read to us when we were small, about "The bear who wasn't": when you can move no longer, then it's time to find a cave and go into hibernation. You grew up in the middle of a jazz age – you swung your way through life to your own special tune, which we loved and were happy to sing along with. And it is in that spirit we say farewell to you, beloved Father.

*

"Speak for yourself," was Myren's immediate reaction. She certainly didn't want to be included in any "we", for she could clearly see that both the Løvins and the Møllers with the ill-fated ø in the middle were sick, pernicious families with Zeste as the clearest proof. That Zeste should be capable at all of burying her father was nothing but narcissistic pleasure at having secured herself a sympathetic, captive audience and the dramatic self-satisfaction in the power which is to stand over one's father's coffin. She didn't give a fig for him. It was the visibility afforded her, as the daughter beside the coffin, and the admiration attached to that, which she collected with hypocritically heroic tears in her eyes. That was what she wanted. Indeed, afterwards she did admit to Myren that the speech hadn't been absolutely honest. It was a lie of course to say that Jas had never burdened them. She and Myren had felt helpless over their father's fate, regardless of which of them had borne more.

As soon as Jas died, the first incurable rift began to show. What had been latent as perpetual conflict between sisters and ordinary sibling jealousy now broke out into a fight over an old raincoat. Zeste had been down to apologise on Jas' behalf at the cigar kiosk, where he had left a five-figure debt they would never see one krone of. After that she had walked around the charred ruins of an apartment with a handkerchief to her mouth to clear up the last few things. Before she left, she distractedly picked up an old Burberry, which had escaped burning, and slammed the door behind her.

But now it transpired that it was *that* particular coat Myren *had* to have. You might well ask what she would want with such an old coat, she who had everything, husband, house and no doubt in time a lot of kids. She had succeeded beyond all expectations, so why would she need an old coat? And for her part Myren had to say: Zeste has everything. Everything with glamour, at least. She has power and honour, she has success and something like fame. She has won a place in the sun, she's on the front page of all the papers, so why does she want an old raincoat? But Zeste wouldn't give way. For wasn't she the one who always had to carry the load? Hadn't she come all the way from Paris to cut Jas' nails and trim his moustache and wash his socks while Myren justified her absence behind the private domain of marriage? Wasn't it reasonable for Zeste to feel that she had a claim to a "wage" and that she could take her due . . . with an old raincoat? No, wasn't it more natural that Myren, who had been ill treated all her life and had forever played second fiddle, in compensation for that unhappy place in the shade had a legitimate claim on this coat? The only one who could have brought the strife to, if not reconciliation, then at least to a *modus vivendi*, was Jas, and he was dead. After the deaths of Tobias and now Jas there was no man left in the family who could act as problem solver.

Now you might think that Myren's husband, the pedagogue you always thought would start the revolution – and who was thus one of the founders of the legendary Tvind schools – would also be able to mediate between his wife and sister-in-law. In speech and writing Pierre carried on a dogged battle against bourgeois ideology, and you might have expected him to use his fighting spirit in the service of family peace. But the Løvins were not his family, and besides he was beginning to find to his cost that beneath the delightfully practical façade, which was Myren's, there lurked madness. It was bound up with her family and especially with her sister. Every time she had been with Zeste there was trouble, upset and weeping.

The simplest thing would be to break off all relations. Moreover, Pierre himself felt extremely insecure about Zeste. The name alone! And those observant yellow eyes, as if she studied every movement, every spoken and unspoken word around her that she might make use of on the stage. Really, one didn't want to be a part of her world. She had that kind of radiance Chairman Mao would define as weeds. You were easily carried away by the lively interest she took in everything, but it was a trap, for no-one could talk without giving themselves away. You don't mind doing that with some people, but you were frightened of Zeste. It was as if with her big mouth she pulled each word out of you by imitating the word before it had been said, even thought. And most of all you felt uncertain about what she wanted of you. Besides, her outlandish clothes, her mauve velvet cloaks and black ostrich feathers were unmistakably of bourgeois origin. According to Mao that kind ought to be swept away with a hard hand. In the intimate sense Zeste had a corrupting effect that had to be erased.

Especially where children were concerned. The idea of leaving your children alone in the room with Zeste wasn't comfortable. You couldn't help wondering if she wouldn't devour them raw – if she hadn't already done so. Hadn't Zeste killed off with her yellow eyes any attempt at growth in Myren's womb? Myren's inability to get pregnant and having constantly to go for examinations and hormone treatment were undoubtedly caused by Zeste and her yellow eyes. At the moment they were con-sidering – and no-one at Tvind must know this – consulting a clever man who advertised in the newspaper. A special decoction had to be taken under a full moon. It was particularly important that Zeste should not know of it because she could thwart every-thing with her infectious barrenness. Myren was convinced she would lose the foetus at the mere sight of her sister.

No doubt a break with Zeste was in the offing. It was a question of waiting for an opportunity: given her scandalous behaviour, you wouldn't have to wait long. Zeste the shameless was secretly engaged to shame.

Rumours flew that she had seduced Marsken's son, to the point that he had completely neglected his schoolwork. He was only 15. She was all consuming. Baby, great-grandfather, never mind whom, she seduced them all, and we must make fast the shutters with strong nails. Myren and Pierre were laboriously building up a kind of re-education camp where life could begin from the beginning. It was a little paradise, a family idyll that built on the future, and cleansed the past.

Pierre, then, was not a man to be relied on as a mediator. Besides, he was only a boy. The prerequisite for a family not to disintegrate into pure oestrogen soup is for an older man or two to cut through all the jealousies created by women. A father or grandfather can say: you are all the chosen. And then the women can relax for a while until the uncertainty recurs. Only an older man has the power to issue a declaration of love that covers many women.

Jas' death set the devil loose. And the only remaining man in the family, Balder, was ashamed of being a man and hid himself in his red polo sweater and long hippie hair and beard behind his new wife, Plys. His daughter Merete had converted to Judaism and settled with her own hippie king in London, where she gave birth to a child with two heads, which lived only a very short time.

*

Some time earlier Zeste had come across Merete in Paris, they moved in the same circles. The artistic and the orgiastic over-lapped. Merete and her hippie king Elias invited Zeste to dinner. This time Merete had had a lovely little boy with withdrawal symptoms. When Zeste arrived Merete was stiff with dope. In her distress, or high, she had put two red splotches on her cheeks. She was no longer the daughter of Balder and Sharpy, but of Abraham and Sara, after she had sunk herself in a ritual bath in Amsterdam and changed her name to Bilha. Now she wore the Orthodox wig, crookedly, because she was so skew-whiff she couldn't put it on straight. When she wanted to walk through the room she had to support herself on the walls so as not to fall down. She served spaghetti onto the table *beside* the plates, knocked over a lamp and poured sauce onto the tablecloth. Elias excused her by saying she had drunk a whole bottle of white wine. They were out of their minds because the child's carer had just been arrested. They told some story about her friend having a car with Dutch number plates, but *narco* was written in invisible ink all over the apartment. When Zeste was on her way out Merete Bilha snatched the child up from its cradle so it started to cry. She put it brusquely down again, disappointed.

The following day Elias phoned and asked Zeste to talk to Bilha. What about? Well, Bilha had been picked up by the police on the Rue Saint-Denis with the baby screaming, so now they were afraid the authorities would take the child away. Could Zeste not help? But what was she to do? She had once gone to see Uncle Balder and Aunt Sharpy, albeit in vain, and Li had only said:

"Funny how history repeats itself."

"Yes, but what can we do for Bilha?" Zeste said. Li was supposed to be the expert in the family. And the expert replied: "No-one can do anything."

But Elias was not content to have a wife who had gone to pieces, and who went and pinched his methadone, so they had to hide the pills from each other all the time.

"Do you want to be like Aunt Liane? It's Li all over again!" he yelled.

Elias had believed he had found a nice girl, a student from Zahle's College on her way to university, who could help *him* up from the dung heap and on to a *straight* path, and had not in his wildest fantasies imagined that the nice girl was driven by a secret desire. As the daughter of Abraham she could distance herself from Balder and Sharpy. No sooner had Merete met Elias before Sharpy stated: "Don't count on me to serve kosher".

But hardly had Merete "gone over" before Sharpy set about following suit and fraternising with an Orthodox gentleman and then frequenting the synagogue and worming her way into the innermost religious circles. This meant that Bilha couldn't go to synagogue any more without being recognised: "Ugh, how like your mother you are." That was why she went to London. Only there did she keep the illusion intact of having escaped and was not being recognised.

Balder was hardly to blame. He couldn't help having been the only boy born to carry on the inheritance. Family historians maintain that the first son in a big family will be an inventor, the second consolidates, in the third generation the whole thing disintegrates. It takes three generations to make a gentleman.

Thus it wasn't so strange that Balder bore a secret grudge against Ib, who had stolen the name of Løvin and whose four daughters all throve on the Sabbath and black locks. With his kosher life Ib had removed numerous stains from the impious name. Balder couldn't bear to be the stain himself while the other shone like the fire in the thorn bush.

*

Zeste had dyed her hair black. She didn't want to be blonde any more. No-one respected blondes, or perhaps there were no gentlemen left. She really wanted to be a witch, Myren decided.

But he didn't see the colour of her hair. When Rejn fetched her from Algiers airport she suddenly noticed two terrible things. One was only a sober recognition that Rejn could not be counted as a *man* in any familial sense. Li had long since taken power over life and death and thereby reduced the Dog to a feminine principle with no drive. He would never be able to mediate between women. But the frightful thing Zeste found was that despite his rational nature, catastrophe had struck. His dulled fish eyes rested on her heavily, stickily, and imploringly. Take those eyes away! But he couldn't. He was so worn down that he could not fight any more.

"I have to count her pills all the time," he said, to change the subject.

"Perhaps it's just a question of adaptation. It took her quite a time to get used to Bangkok, too."

"She will never come to love Algeria," he said, looking at Zeste with those eyes.

The inevitable had to come. Now he would tell her what she feared: that they were going to be divorced. It was their anniversary today, into the bargain. But who would look after Li? Zeste would be forced to shoulder the burden. Although the marriage was damaging to them both, the Dog and the Cat, as to the rest of the family, it must be clung to with the devil's grip. Otherwise Zeste risked being married to her mother. And what would happen to little Tor? Could he sleep in her wardrobe while she was on the stage, and was that a sound education?

Zeste longed for her own child, to start on a completely new life. At night, in dreams, the milk ran from her breasts, her womb swelled, the waters broke and she gave birth . . . to guts, chicken intestines, kidneys and hearts. For how could she allow herself to have a child when she was up to her ears in the whole Møller family's adjourned game? But thank heavens, they were not getting divorced. Rejn went on in the usual old groove:

"Tor came in and woke me up at four o'clock this morning: 'Dog, Cat is on the floor, calling you.' Then he went back to bed and fell asleep again. The Cat had hit her head on the stove and had burned cheeks, nosebleed, blood in her hair and on her nightdress."

Why am I here? thought Zeste, then immediately came an overwhelming idea: Marsken must save me. Rejn drove down the Boulevard de la Victoire towards the old Turkish city wall. They passed the Ketchaoua mosque that had been alternately church and mosque. Above it in Moorish style lay Dar Aziza Bent el Buy, Princess Palace. Only Marsken could save her. She didn't know which country he was in now, she only felt sure that he and she had no other choice.

The last time they met, Marsken's wife Kidde had been so charming, and Zeste had been so charming. They had been on the terrace of a holiday house in Denmark, and the Cat had been good and not on any medicines. When she spoke, some of what she said was understandable. The rest could be lip-read. Marsken's authority gave her the discipline and backbone she generally lacked, and the Dog enjoyed that moment with its apparent lack of drama.

But it was a brief interlude. Li wept all the way home, her hand on the door handle as if she might leap out at any moment. The question was: would Rejn stop or run over her?

Marsken had sat heavily in his chair. It seemed to Zeste that not even Marsken was happy in his marriage, and she took it as a human duty to be happy. He had looked at Zeste as he clinked the ice cubes in his big American glass and said: "The bees sit down and the flowers go from bee to bee."

"The flowers come flying through the air," Zeste had said, giving herself to the inner vision that sometimes came over her and said clearly: "You must rescue me." She had been "rescued" once by Serge de Clerval and he still sent her red roses, but she always cried when she got them.

She hardened her eyes against Rejn's, and the stories he told her from behind the wheel as they turned into Boulevard Hada Abderrazak. Just to be free of his gaze. She sat practising how it must feel to be black haired from the roots of your hair to the ends.

*

Before Zeste arrived Li had planned to greet her in elegant style in her pure silk dress. Instead she was lying in the bathroom, weeping, with cheeks burned and dried blood in her hair.

"Well, Cat love, now I'm here everything will be fine," said Zeste with baleful eyes.

Li looked up at her imploringly: "No-one calls me lovely little girl any more. You've got black hair!"

"It's not too easy, Mum, with you lying there on the bathroom floor like a lump of meat."

"I am a bad mother," wept the Cat.

"Now, now." Zeste didn't know how to contradict her. Li gave Zeste a hug: "I love you. I live for you. You are the only one, wise and good. I'm going to pull myself together. I will." She whimpered and sobbed: "I will, I will!" But an hour later she was unconscious.

Zeste inwardly held her nose and sent Myren a pretty unfriendly thought. That's how it was to be the chosen one. Chosen to live in the stench. Zeste ended up giving the raincoat to Myren. For when all was said and done, Zeste didn't need it. She would really rather avoid it all. Everything. So when she had got the coat Myren wasn't satisfied either. If Zeste no longer cared about it, neither did Myren. She wanted to win a more momentous battle. If she couldn't be sure of being the chosen one, she wanted to be the good one. But it was not enough to be the good one. She wanted Zeste to be the evil one. That was the price she ought to pay for all the homage she was so obviously dependent on. And that was the price Myren had set!

The Cat stank of medicine and booze, as if she had begun to rot inside. And Zeste asked herself why she had come running just because the Møller menage had sent out alarm signals once again. A line from Euripides, which they had just performed, came to mind: "The boldest man becomes a slave, if in his soul he feels his parents' shame." She had been programmed to hold a marriage together. How long would she have?

Tor's life was at risk. When Li had decided to destroy Rejn and herself, it would not do to leave "the little blessing" alone in the world. True, she was not a good mother, but she was not so inconsiderate as to run away from that responsibility and leave him on his own. She would take his life too. She was not so chicken-livered in this Moudjahadin house, certainly she could kill when it was necessary and there was no other way out.

That day she ordered him to go to the pharmacy for more medicine, but her little blessing refused, to her speechless astonishment, because the Dog had forbidden him. Oh, he had, had he! The Cat couldn't believe her ears when Tor faced her and said No! So the blessing sided with Rejn! In the afternoon she sat at the kitchen table wearing her wig, with a bottle of Campari. Then she looked in the drawer for the knife. The Dog would find no good come of contradicting her orders. He would regret that. When Tor had gone. The right thing was to get rid of all life in the house. From now on there would be only silence. Peace.

But when she raised the knife to stab Tor, he bolted out of the house at top speed. When he got home from school he stayed at the parking place for the rest of the day, waiting for the Dog.

It was Tor who vouchsafed the whole story to Zeste: ". . . she says that Dog thinks she's crazy, but she's not crazy, she's just mentally, a bit . . . she must have damaged her brain with all those pills. The worst thing is when she cries in the street . . . then I run."

The mad, thought Zeste, ought to be shut up in a little wooden box and put in the attic.

They had gone for a drive into the Sahara, Tor had been promised the trip since his sister was visiting, and she didn't mind getting away from the grisly atmosphere in the FLN house. The idea had been that they should all go. And they talked about it for a long time. In this family no-one could put a kettle on to boil without discussion and planning. And it wasn't really strange, since the "head" of the family bore the title of "Family Planner". Any spontaneous suggestion was a threat to solidarity. The internal competition in the house went thus: who is most ill? Haven't I got a temperature of 38.2? Whoever had the highest temperature was the centre of attention, accordingly a temperature was the most sought-after situation you could have in the Møller household.

Although the trip into the desert had been on the schedule for several days, and the Cat had sat shaking her doped head, which would benefit from the desert air and the feeling of something greater and stronger than herself, at the last moment she changed her mind and took an overdose. For the first time, Rejn took a decision despite the Cat's being sick. They drove off and left her lying on the floor. They travelled down through the desert to the Ghardaïa oasis, where they arrived at sundown with the Cat's impending death in their spines. Just like the time they had once driven down to the island of Ko si Chang in the Gulf of Siam with her death in their luggage. But this time perhaps with the "higher" aim: to rescue Tor, all the time blinking to stop the tears pouring down.

*

When you were going into the Sahara, *le Grand Sud*, you had to observe a minimum of rules. You should always take provisions for two days, plus ten litres of water per person in addition to what you had planned for the journey itself. Zeste could feel Rejn was tempted to lose the way. For, as the guide said, the chance of being found was very small.

The Cat was the central character of their drama. They spoke of her through the desert, as they sat there with scarves over their faces and got sand everywhere, between the teeth, in the ears and between the buttocks. And they spoke of her at meals. A new word had begun to figure in the conversation. Not divorce, but "sectioning". And "psychiatric ward". At first Zeste didn't dare to utter the words, because she didn't want to talk behind the Cat's back. And she knew those words were the worst ones, the most feared and tabooed.

"There's nothing wrong with her," said the Dog.

"Would you call her behaviour normal?"

"She's tired."

"What is she tired of?"

"She hasn't the strength to adapt herself constantly to new countries."

"Then let her stay in a country she likes!"

"I can't decide for myself where I shall live. Next time it will probably be Africa, maybe Rwanda."

"Do they have Sung porcelain in Africa? Can they play bridge? In Rwanda, for example?"

Rejn didn't ask after Orm. And they talked most naturally and enthusiastically of intellectual subjects, such as Eldridge Cleaver's exile in Algeria and the probable role of the Black Panthers in the World Revolution. But however important the World Revolution might be, Zeste felt she would not deprive Rejn of the knowledge that his son had tried to commit suicide. She told him. But he did not react.

"There's no need to get hysterical," was all he said.

"I am not hysterical, but I am frightened all the time that Orm will fall out of the world, it wouldn't take anything at all to tip him over the edge. He has his own gospel, which reviles everything to do with material dependence."

"If he ever writes, it's only to ask for money!"

"But he is dependent on hash and LSD and I don't know what else. He calls them 'spiritual means of intoxication'. So if you try to warn him about dependence on drugs you get a long lecture telling you you're out of date because you haven't understood shit."

"When is he going to get an education?" Rejn said.

"He doesn't want to get educated! He *won't* be part of the *system*."

"So he spends all his time on girls and drugs!"

"No, not on girls! He talks of the love of nature. Spiritual love. He prefers psychic love to physical."

The desert heat burned through the skin. After that last sentence was uttered there was no more to be said. Nothing could be called by name. Rejn sat as if completely at a loss and drove the car through and around sand dunes, but he couldn't see where he was driving because the windscreen was covered with sand.

Really they ought to be grateful to the Cat for her threats of suicide and cries for help. She was the one who assigned herself the task of persistently drawing attention to the fact that something was wrong. Just as in the play Zeste was learning, about a family who were destroyed by the war. Not because the members of it were killed or lost, but because it always takes three generations to get over a war and its consequences. War puts a stop to all genuine desires and creates sheer perversion. But the only way she could escape from her family and lift the curse was, paradoxically, by playing it out evening after evening, *delivering* her family in all its helplessness in the hope that someone would intervene.

The desert bloomed in the Ghardaïa oasis. They booked in at *l'Hotel Mille et Une Nuits*, because it was the cheapest. Zeste went to look for the "blue men" of the Sahara, the tradesmen of the oasis, who wore blue tunics and strong glasses, because they all had bad eyes, and she amused herself with them to get Rejn definitely out of the picture. How could eyes be good – with sand in them? She had been prepared for the people to be hostile. After the whole of the traditional Sahara trade with salt, textiles and feathers from the Sudan had vanished in favour of imported goods, the last outposts of oasis and civilisation were threatened with annihilation. Zeste bought a sweet steel knife in a sheath of pink leather.

*

When they came back to Algiers a few days later, Li had had a bath and had her hair done. She emerged sober to greet them, apparently not doped, in a freshly ironed pale blue silk shirt. But it was not long before the old tub began to leak and anon capsize. It needed no more than an innocent remark from Zeste: "It was a pity you didn't come, Mother."

Li looked at Zeste in a way she had never seen her do before, perhaps because Zeste had called her Mother. Li didn't use language, she contented herself with *looking* at Zeste.

Zeste was obliged to explain: "You always think a desert is just grey sand. You seldom think of it as red and blue and mauve and orange. The desert blooms!"

"Have you got me some Campari?"

"Campari? In the Sahara?"

"You don't think of anyone but yourselves."

"But you didn't ask us to buy Campari, we didn't know . . ."

"No, and you couldn't even work out that I've only got two bottles for the whole weekend."

"Now, Cat, you be quiet," said Tor firmly. He had benefited from the trip.

Li went into the kitchen and in a moment had downed half a bottle of Campari. At the thought of Rejn leaving her, she suddenly saw Zeste in a new light, as a strange person. She had never had anything against the gossip that really the daughter and the stepfather were the couple in this family, she and Zeste had been the same person for so long. But just now anything could happen. Would Zeste go to Africa with Rejn? She woke up in a flash, she saw life was definitely about to slide away from her.

In the evening, when she had emptied the two bottles of Campari, she yelled at Zeste: "You have ruined my whole life!"

At first Zeste was upset. Then she smiled at herself under her black hair. It was the first time her mother had made herself distinct, a separate independent person. "You have ruined my whole life," she repeated quietly to herself in quite a different tone. She would one day use that remark on the stage.

"I love Rejn," wept Li.

"You are a wimp!"

"True."

"Why don't you kill yourself?"

"I haven't any pills."

"Surely you can find a way."

"I'm frightened."

"Wimp," said Zeste and stuffed the steel knife into its pink sheath.

After that Li lay in bed for several days, until it was decided to send her to Denmark for treatment.

Tor, her little blessing, bent over her and for the first time in his life called her Mother; with a child's innocence he pronounced the forbidden word: "Mother, you're getting the best doctor now, a psychiatrist!"

Li arrived at Kastrup airport in a wheelchair. She was 49. Tor ran ahead through Customs, as if he didn't know her.

10

THE CRIME

Zeste came back from the prison, where she had been acting, with the taste of sperm in her mouth. Katze opened the door: "Oh, my dearest girl, I've been so lonely watching utter rubbish on television. The Danes are hopeless. No, my dear, thank heavens you've got a head on your body. Titta and Glenda have phoned and asked me, it isn't that . . . certainly, I'm a lonely soul, on the other hand *not.* I'll have to listen to all that twaddle about her lymph cancer, well I've got liver cancer, but she always has to have more cancer than I have, she's always been a bossy-boots. I can't phone anyone any more, for no matter whom I call, I always get a woman called fru Larsen. On the other hand, she's very sweet, we've become real friends."

Tobias' coats hung in the hall. On the dining room table lay the old albums from Riga, opened at the pictures of the ones who had died, and the de Thuras' family tree. "Yes," said Grandmother – "this is where you lay when you were being born, on the dining table, while your mother breathed in and out so as not to faint. Breathe in and breathe out, dear, in and out, I said to her." Grandmother got on to the table with her legs spread wide, in her faded kitchen smock and old red plastic slippers and demonstrated: "'In and out.' And as I was having *her* and the waters had broken, I had to knock very gently at the study door where your grandfather was playing cards with that cow Baby Zornig. And how little Liane cried when she came into the world, so bitterly, with big tears. I know we mustn't speak ill of the Jews, but I can to you, my dear. Just a little. Come, we'll creep out and say hallo to him, he's so quiet out here on the windowsill," she whispered.

Katze didn't switch the light on, so as not to disturb him. It was a bit crazy, Katze knew quite well, but she enjoyed it, being a bit crazy – and besides, the little dove outside the window was the only really *living* thing left in her life. "Don't be frightened," she whispered to the dove.

Afterwards they had to go into Katze's bedroom to find her knickers.

"Where can I have put them? Your grandmother's such a muddle-head! You mustn't tell anyone, but I probably took them off because I was on my way to bed.

"Some Germans came to the office today. So your grandmother of 73 had to translate . . . Konradsen can't do anything. Any fool can speak Danish when they're born in Denmark, what's the big deal in that. 'You must give them champagne,' I said to Konradsen, 'after all, they are Germans.' But two of them were Jewish."

She can't find the card with the crown on it from the Czar's cousin. Instead she comes across a love letter addressed to Tobias: "Hello, boy!" it begins. Tobias was 65 when he flirted with the barrister Frederiksen's wife. She was a 50-year-old blonde who signed herself "Floosie". Normally Grandmother kept all the floosie's letters in her own bed. But now she's mad at her and the whole affair again and so the letters have been banished to the bureau.

The letters rake up the old unhappiness: "When I'm dead you'll find a letter saying your grandfather was too good for me, that I was only a barmaid. Take the letters, my dear, when I'm dead, they'd make a good play, there's a fine part there, remember that. My motto will be: 'You only regret what you haven't done.'"

Katze showed Zeste the pile of new nightdresses she would wear if she ever had to go to hospital. Tobias had given them to her. "I don't expect I'll get a single room. When I die you must look after my Bible. I really must write my will soon."

She has been talking about writing her will for the past eight years, but doesn't *want* to do it.

She opens another cupboard, where Elle's dresses are kept.

Elle – with the flower between her legs, who was married to a captain during the war. "Elle, the little tart, she slept in your mother's room."

"Did she?"

"I knew very well that Dietlof wanted to have two girls in bed at the same time. But I didn't want to!" Grandmother bangs on the chair and stamps her foot. "I didn't want to!"

"It sounds as if you despise Elle?"

"Yes." And Grandmother goes on, for the twenty-fifth time, with the refrain: "Wouldn't you like to go into the country to have your child, Miss Thura?" And her sisters who edged round her when they met her in the hall, as if she was a leper.

Katze was in her open-handed mood that day and took Zeste over to the chest with all her old dresses. Was she going to soften today and part with the cream-coloured gown that had belonged to the countess? The old transparent dream with fluttering wings and the erect nipples she kept deep in a special drawer. Was she going to give it away now? And could you dare ask? For even though Katze would never dream of wearing it again, she liked to be able to dream of having worn it.

Also in the chest were the countess's Pompeii-red pleated crêpe de Chine, Glenda's silver fox and Elle's dress of transparent flowered chiffon. "Street girl," mumbled Katze automatically, like touching the pearl in a rosary. Katze pulled splendours out of the chest. A mustard-coloured silk affair from the '20s she had worn that New Year's Eve in 1940 when Tobias smashed a whole pile of gramophone records, the idiot, and a sky-blue velvet cape, which they put aside for Myren. A long, bell-shaped taffeta skirt with wide purple stripes cut on the bias. A brown velvet dress with a bustle and bolero, and two white silk tennis frocks. One had belonged to Glenda. "I am so passionate," jeered Katze, and banged the lid of the chest shut. "Stuff and nonsense."

"And Angelika's nightdress . . . is that stuff and nonsense too?"

"Do you want it? Take it," said Katze suddenly. "I probably shan't use it." A door was ajar in her voice. Zeste took the cream-coloured dream with angel's wings from the depths of a drawer. She could take care of the nipples herself. She knew the nightdress had fallen into the right hands. She would know how to fill it out and show that the cream-coloured silk was still alive.

"Farewell, dear Dietlof," said Grandmother with theatrical

tenderness. "Would you like a yellow Chartreuse? The bottle has been here since before the war!" she offered, full of fun! She was in her magnanimous mood. Another day she would regret having given anything away and curse the world for it.

They had a drink and Katze put on the television.

"What do you think of that gangster Nixon? It looks like being a military dictatorship!" said Zeste.

"Yes, but think how clever Franco was. Spain is fine, dictatorship may be the only thing that works when people can't be bothered to do anything."

"Imagine, they have been on the moon already!" said Zeste, as the newscaster reported that the astronauts were not too fit after their return.

"But what do they want to go to the moon for? What good does it do when they come home and find their marriages ruined?"

A railway station appeared on the screen.

"Oh, God almighty, think of all the stations I have been on in my life! Remember when Ebbe Munck, the ambassador, came to meet me in Berlin. And my friend there took all the illegal papers over the border folded into his silk socks, oh God yes. He was a Norwegian who had a mink farm in Lithuania and a Greek profile. He was always around me. Have you been to bed with Rejn?" Katze asked suddenly and sent Zeste a keen blue glance. As if she really would like to be emancipated. Or was.

They sat in their respective armchairs at Gammel Mønt, each with their yellow Chartreuse, a pile of newspapers on each footstool and their feet up. Zeste couldn't believe her ears. How could Grandmother ask such a hurtful question? Was it the porno club on the floor above? Grandmother was convinced Rejn was planning to go off to Africa with a young woman, but which . . . that was the question.

Grandmother muddled Tobias and Rejn and all men as one big faithless pack of scumbags. They all had syphilis. In Grandmother's universe, a man was something that you had to conquer with toil and trouble and then sacrifice yourself for – "in order to keep hold of him". Why on earth you should have to do all that and suffer so much for such scum, the story didn't say. Katze just hoped that when Rejn, who like Tobias "had never stirred a finger in his life", beat it to Africa, he would take the longhaired Orm with him. Katze couldn't endure the sight of that boy. A child of ten had just been kidnapped, the television newscaster said, and a picture of the boy came up on the screen.

"He looks like a girl, he's been up to no good," Grandmother said, with every sign of disgust. Every time a boy with long hair was shown Grandmother, who sat close up to it, she put her hands over the screen to cover the hair, just as she covered up Jews' noses and ears: "You must see about getting them away from television, there are far too many of them."

"No!" Zeste cried out. "No," again.

But the question remained hanging in the air, where it had hung for many years.

*

As it had hung in the air recently in the holiday house Rejn rented, which they called "The Basket", for the Cat's sake, where Li went round slamming the doors. They didn't want to live at Gammel Mønt, anyway it was impossible with Orm and that hair. Orm had made himself comfortable in a cave, where he sat in thick fume-filled clouds of incense and hash, listening to beat music. On the walls he had written: "I get so mother-fucking mad there's nothing I can do." And "Hey you, what are you doing to the earth?"

"Hooligan! Creep! Provo!" Li screamed at him, and at night she vomited with guilt and shame. When she woke up in the morning, she took an extra dose of Restenil because she hadn't had a wink of sleep all night. All she wanted was for him to get an education! Surely that was a very normal wish to have for a son. But Zeste shook her head at her as if there was something she hadn't cottoned on to at all. That the die had been cast ages ago, and that there was nothing now left to save.

"Tell me honestly, *am* I mad?" she asked Zeste one day. And Zeste replied yes and went into Orm's cave and played with his hair – for comfort – and Orm fell into a happy snooze.

"This is more like it," he mumbled, "if only I could lie here like this until my final sleep."

It might not have been necessary for her to feel this urge to protect him, for it was as if the Cat's screams didn't get through to him, he was so enveloped in insulating clouds of hash. But as long as she felt that strong protectionism she was free of her despair and impotence over his situation, and there was still

286

hope. For Pete's sake, he was not 20 yet. As long as she had this feeling, she could more easily forget how much his mental dullness and egoistic idleness got on her nerves. His headlong escape into music. But each time she tried to discuss it with him she ended up on the verge of a generation gap row, which invariably ended in tears and recriminations. It can't be my responsibility to make a man of him, she thought, at the same time dreading that there was no-one else.

"I see you in dreams, not you but other women with your nature and your face," he whispered. Zeste was touched and felt ashamed, as she let her fingers run through his fair hair.

"It's the best thing in the world when Zeste does it," Orm said to Rejn, who suddenly appeared in the doorway. "Makes you feel like a cat."

"That may have something to do with the sexy way Zeste does it."

Orm sat up suddenly. "Incest! Can you get sent to prison for incest?"

"Father and daughter, mother and son aren't so good, but in any case I'll support you all the way," said Rejn and left with the sound of Orm's postscript: "'Let not your hearts be troubled. In my Father's house are many mansions. I go to prepare a place for you.'"

In the evening when Rejn and Zeste were watching television and discussing Nixon's China policy, Li came reeling by and switched off the TV and all the lights, because *she* was going to bed now. Next day Rejn phoned the doctor on duty and asked for her to be admitted for safekeeping. But first he must give his identity number, which he didn't know, so the doctor immediately questioned Rejn's mental equilibrium. It was no better when the doctor came and talked to Rejn and Zeste together. "Who is *she*?" asked the doctor, pointing at Zeste. Rejn didn't know what to say, which made the situation even more suspect. Zeste's mere appearance, with flowing black hair and yellow eyes, long-limbed body and full lips, warned of trouble in the family. Zeste could not find anywhere to hide herself. And it wouldn't even help if she stopped dyeing her hair. She had tried mouse-coloured, but that hadn't either helped or saved the family. Who was she? What should she reply when the doctor questioned her?

Then she said: "She is my mother." But that didn't mean Rejn was her father. So who was he? That question too hung in the air, while Rejn tried to explain to the doctor why he was obliged to have Li admitted, because she was a danger to herself and others.

But the doctor wasn't forced to do anything. Li had gathered all "the things" to prove she wasn't hallucinating. And although with enlarged pupils, nervous tics of the face and wringing of her hands she made up stories about a potato peeler baked into Aunt Mudde's china bowl, pills sewn into handkerchiefs and liquorice sweets woven into a basket chair, she kept insisting that she would *not* be admitted:

"You can't make me, I won't let you, I won't. Let me stay here, give me a chance, let me come with you to Rwanda!"

The doctor felt sorry for her. With such a disloyal husband and daughter it was no wonder the wife was in despair. And since Rejn still could not remember his identity number the doctor decided that Rejn was not in his right mind anyway. "Are you sure *you're* not the one who should be admitted?"

Fortunately or unfortunately grim reality came to his rescue. For what he had said turned out to be true: Li *was* a danger to herself. At four o'clock next morning Rejn knocked on Zeste's door.

"It's your mother."

"Is she dead?"

"She's in the bath, unconscious."

The duty doctor was strangely flippant. When Rejn said it was a pity he couldn't come sooner, even though Rejn had warned him earlier in the night, the night doctor replied: "Rubbish!" And of course you can't leave your post just to unravel old marital knots. It's no good shouting, "Wolf, wolf!" and relying on the night doctor to come and sort it out.

All the same, the need for something to be done must have been in the air, for the duty doctor started counter-attacking by pointing to the empty pill bottle: "Why have you left all those pills out?"

"That's a 20-year-old story," said Rejn.

"And who are *you* then?" The doctor looked accusingly at Zeste, who had got up again, her long black hair all rumpled.

"She's my mother," said Zeste again. At the hospital, the doctor came to the conclusion, which also became the explanation of the suicide attempt that he wrote up in the case history, that fru Liane Møller, born Løvin, had tried to take her life out of jealousy because her husband was in love with her daughter. That was the impression one had simply by looking at Zeste and Rejn, who seemed 20 years younger than he really was because his development had come to a halt. The doctor looked up at Zeste and asked if the explanation was correct.

And with a dramatic expression in her eyes and head proudly raised Zeste replied coldly: "I should not exclude that!"

"I can't go on any longer," she wrote all over her dialogue in the script. The play was called *Last One Out Switch off the Light*, and was partly inspired by Strindberg's *The Father,* which also makes it hard to place the madness in the marriage. One speech in the play runs: "It is my duty to destroy all marriages", and Zeste made it her duty too. It was her duty to bring evil to life, evil must be driven out by evil, and her hair flashed black. It was a remarkable solace to her that in her solemn undertaking she was not alone, and in this play had an ancient partner-in-crime, the devil himself. "I will be wicked", "Remember to be wicked", she wrote on little slips as part of the great task of demolition that was necessary in order to explain the crime. The evil bits were always the best bits.

*

For three days Li had lain unconscious in a respirator with the jade cat on the table beside her. The doctors warned that cerebral paralysis might have occurred.

The person who finally emerged from the respirator in some kind of living state was different, odd, and with aphasia. Once you were able to talk to her about everything. So it seemed. Now everything was one-syllable words and short sentences. But no sooner was Li able to stand than she was discharged and took a taxi around to all the places in Copenhagen where she had stored her Chinese porcelain in order to "see to" it. She took the Sung frog away from Gammel Mønt for fear the family might get hold of it and stored it with Adam's removals. From there she fetched a Sung bowl with green hare-fur glaze and an octagonal cream-coloured bowl with a lid and hid them under her bed at "The Basket", and she put a green bowl with celadon glaze and a little Sawangkalok jar at Gammel Mønt.

She got herself discharged without Rejn's knowledge, for she wanted nothing to do with all those "apes" and "thieves" – her words for psychiatrists. But only a few days passed before she was admitted again. She had her jade cat with her. She was discharged on Wednesday and re-admitted on Saturday, and discharged on Monday, blue and yellow all over because of a bad liver. And admitted again to be pumped out. Her jade cat was still with her. Now she had surpassed Zeste in theatrics. At that time, misuse of drugs was not so common as it is now, and ceremonial in hospitals more authoritative than later when they turned into helpless factories. The chief physician said her prognosis was nil.

All the same they insisted that Li agree to have "treatment" if she wanted to go to Africa with Rejn. She would be living in an obscure country where the only entertainment was provided by mass public executions and torture. White people were invariably set upon and robbed and then tied to a lamp-post. Rwanda was a hardship post, so if Li wanted to go she must also agree to sort herself out, as Rejn said. She was to be admitted to the municipal hospital in Nykøbing.

*

She stood by the window with her jade cat waiting for the family to visit. She watched them in the parking place getting out of the car. Zeste and Rejn and little Tor. Myren was busy with her own affairs. Orm hadn't come, thank God. He had sent her Laing's *Bird of Paradise* with the dedication: "Hope you can get something from this book. I myself have music, you know."

It was up to her whether all the people who made up a family would still be part of it in a month or two. She had agreed to what they called treatment. Detoxication. New medicine. She had made a small bag in therapy and was rather proud of it. She, who had never been able to hold a needle. Myren, who was so good with her hands, and Zeste, who was so dignified, had always been ashamed of the dolls' clothes she had made for them when they were little. "Don't bother, Mother." Now she could hear them on the stairs. She had decided to behave exemplarily. So as not to be rejected and deserted. The anxiety about losing status reminded her of being sent to a concentration camp. She didn't mind dying, but if she were to live, she wanted it to be in Africa. The last time Rejn had visited her in hospital was the time they had conceived

Tor together. Now Tor was 13 and they couldn't beget anything any more.

He still called her "Little Pearl", his eyelids were heavy and he laid his tired hand on her skeletal thigh. They drank Campari out of plastic cups. She had a single room. She gave him a sideways look, which said, "It *will* be all right." She deliberately overheard Tor's frightful, childish announcement: "My friend's mother has a home like this for old and mad people like Cat." At the moment the survival of the whole family hung on overhearing announcements. She tried to read the Dog's expression, because divorce was in the air. And she wanted to conjure away that black cloud with her old wiles. But she wasn't so wily any more.

He had come to tell her that when his holiday was finished he would have to leave, and that he would wait for her in Rwanda. Zeste automatically put her arm around Li to assure her she would never be abandonned.

When she was discharged, the whole of her family and all her things had been dispersed to the four winds. Some on their way back from Algeria, others stored at Adam's in Denmark, stacked up in "The Basket", or at Gammel Mønt, others again on their way to Kigali. When she realised that Rejn had already sent a carpet to Timbuktu, she screamed: Asshole! That was *her* carpet!

Li was in despair over that carpet. The estate was already divided up. And it was – as it so often is – an estate, which couldn't be divided. For Li owned the things because she had affection for them, cultivated and took care of them. She had taken the initiative of buying the beautiful Chinese lacquered cupboards and leather chests in order to feel surrounded by beauty. But Rejn owned the things because he had paid for them.

If at that point Li had decided to remain in Denmark, she could have moved into an apartment that she liked. Rejn would have given her anything.

Mama had just died, at over a hundred years old. And Susanne, the famous columnist in *Berlingske Tidende*, wrote that she had been an unusual centenarian, who had received congratulations throughout the day in the apartment in Kastelsvej. She was so hale and hearty that she went out for a walk every day with the lady who looked after her home, and refused to allow the weather to prevent her.

In her day Sara Løvin had married Louis Løvin, renowned administrator of *Berlingske Tidende* . . . Fru Løvin still remembers a lot of things from her childhood, the very old days when children were brought up strictly and taught to be modest. Fru Løvin kept that old-fashioned modesty, although she has been the lady of a large house with its sophisticated social circle.

"You must always remember to say thank you. And I have had and still have an immense amount to be thankful for."

She envied only two kinds of people: those with naturally wavy hair, and those who have someone to go home with after a lovely festive evening.

*

Li didn't go to the funeral. She was drunk. But she inherited. Not money, because Tobias had spent all of that during the war. But furniture and linen going right back to the happy childhood days in Rosenvængets Allé, when Papa had taken books down from his library shelves and initiated her into the world of treasures.

No cushions were ripped open or feathers divided into heaps, as usually happens with inherited goods and division of property. No-one said afterwards that they would never set foot in each other's house. Myren would represent Li, who was too ill to do anything. Myren surprised everyone with her skill, as if she hadn't done anything but attend to property division all her life! She discovered what everything was worth through the auction rooms, and she looked up the paintings in art catalogues. Myren had taken care to appropriate most things in Li's name that had disappeared, of which she was so fond. She only regretted a parsley chopper that had disappeared, because she liked it so much. But everyone wanted the portrait of Tobias, so it was decided to draw lots for it, with the ace low. Myren drew the king of spades!

Li had the children store the whole lot at Adam's. And one day, when she didn't have enough money to buy a bottle of Campari, she sold it. Silver candlelabra and sewing tables, and a whole specially designed dining room in birch with 24 chairs. Mahogany bookcases and books, glass, china and linen. Apart from the portrait of Tobias, which she clung to in her various rented rooms, she never gave another thought to the inheritance from Rosenvænget. All she thought about was the carpet Rejn had packed off to Africa without her consent.

Only one person still had any sense of family: Rebekka, whose noblest task in life was to keep Mama's name spotless and the flag in her spirit flying, which meant never complaining.

*

Rebekka, as the family person she was, had taken it into her head that Li should be normalised. She should do morning exercises, eat three meals a day, find a job and a place to live. After Rejn had flown to Africa leaving Li alone, Bekka felt that they were now on the same footing: two sisters, just as in their childhood. But Li was determined not to be normalised, she wanted to do what she liked, as she always had. She did not want to eat, and no-one was going to make her wear woollen over-trousers. And besides, was it quite normal for an elderly lady to take an interest in whether her 50-year-old sister wore over-trousers?

A family took Tor into care.

"What shall I say when they ask, what's the matter with my mother?"

He had started to speak a little Danish in the summer holidays. The social services were shocked to encounter a boy who had been so neglected. And he was a son of – wasn't it UNICEF? – the children's organisation. Lack of care, and abuse, they were accustomed to but Tor Møller hadn't learned the most elementary things. He could not read or add up, and he couldn't even speak! Just a little English! The little blessing was graded "anti-social, immature and passive".

It was not easy for a 13-year-old who had spent his early years abroad, under a regime of servants, with Thai as his mother tongue, to adapt to the Danish children's care service. He ran away several times "just to teach them a lesson". But Rejn warned Tor: if he groused over his quarters he would be sent to a children's home. Zeste wrote back complaining of Rejn's tone of voice, and besides, Tor needed a watch, so Rejn had better send the money. But Rejn wrote back that he had no plans to buy a watch, and if Tor wanted one, he must earn the money himself. From having been totally ignored, with no gift of speech, now it was demanded of him that he get a job and look after himself! Zeste was indignant. "I piss on your plans . . ." Rejn sent her a large parcel of pictures of herself, which he had taken with loving care through a long life and now torn out of all his family albums. She could burn them if she wished, he wrote.

Zeste was flabbergasted to have the photographs hurled at her, although it was something of a relief to see such an unequivocal admission of shame. To hell with it! But in the night she had the most revolting dream, in which Rejn pressed his abdomen hard against the back of her head. Katze and Tobias turned on their heels and left her, and Li pointed menacingly at her saying: "There, you see how repulsive you are." They had all left in disgust. The next morning she found his testicles like two gallstones and his severed sexual organ in her bed. He said it didn't matter.

*

Zeste's heart writhed when she played draughts with little Tor and fetched water for a hot bath at "The Basket", where he had fled and where she had entrenched herself in order to learn her part away from the family problems. She told herself that Providence had landed her with this ghastly family precisely because there were so many good roles in it.

But there were also hard facts to face up to. Tor had to be rescued from the catastrophic aftermath of the children's service private housing system. This was a teacher called Gyda whom Pierre and Myren had recommended. When one of the children couldn't find what they wanted in the fridge, Gyda said: "I can't bloody help that." Gyda complained that Tor's thinking revolved around violence and sex and drugs, and she certainly didn't like the stories he wrote. He had written a very wild essay about trees growing out of a father's head while his son drove into a roadside tree and died. That was really too macabre. He was a worrying boy to have among the other children. Perhaps you should be thankful he never wanted to be with others. But his lack of the need for human society was also alarming. Besides, he had far too much respect for adults. He was simply not ready for socialism.

Myren and Pierre sent a message to Zeste, saying she was not to meddle in this. Because of her lifestyle she could not possibly assess a child and she certainly had no right to do so. But there was simply no room for quarrels over trifles as long as Orm's life hung by a thread and Tor had to adapt to the social services. Li meanwhile drove to and from hospitals in ambulances, and Rejn got married down in Africa, and indicated that he had had enough of everything to do with Denmark, including his sons, who from now on would have to manage as best they could. In this painful situation Zeste, as the eldest, realised that this was no time for bickering. So she had gone on her knees to Myren – somewhat tongue in cheek – and said: "Shouldn't we agree not to fall out any more?"

"Certainly we can, and you, for a start, can stop stealing!"

But it wasn't long before Zeste's white bicycle had vanished from "The Basket" and then a silver bottle opener.

Considering the wicked role Myren had assigned to Zeste in life, it was odd that she asked her to be godmother to her firstborn daughter. Zeste was afraid of not doing it well enough. She came from Paris with Serge, half an hour late for the service. There had been a strike at Orly airport. Myren was breast-feeding angrily in the porch while the organist played the entry hymn for the fourteenth time. Serge apologised, it was his fault, while Zeste took the child in her arms and rushed down the aisle in a vodka frenzy. When she renounced the devil and all his works in a clear voice, many expected the candelabras would come crashing down.

*

Katze was now a great-grandmother. But as long as she had a grandchild in care, she could cope with no more. She couldn't even cope with Tor, and tried to forget him. She knew perfectly well what had become of him, but as she couldn't go on living in the knowledge, she only knew just a little, all somewhere far off. As soon as she felt pain, she said to herself and others:

"But how could I take on little Tor? I shall soon be 70 and I have to do my work at the office and manage Gammel Mønt. It wouldn't be any help if I burdened social services as well, would it?"

No, it wouldn't. And she always ended her monotonous litany of excuses with the famous words:

"Gammel Mønt is home to all of you."

The reason none of them took her at her word was that no-one could bear living with Katze, who kept endlessly driving through Germany, where they couldn't stop for the night because all hotels were closed to Jews. Instead they had to find private lodgings, and Li had had to be billeted in a brothel. It was there that she had been ruined. All the same, Katze couldn't understand how things had got so out of hand with Li. She must have taken leave of her senses! Surely she knew that in marriage it was essential to have a life of your own up your sleeve. Have your own intellectual and financial life. You had to know that you couldn't rely on other people. And how could a mother leave her children in the lurch?

Mercifully Katze lived in happy ignorance of Orm. She was told he was working in a plastics factory! Her own grandchild, in a plastics factory! She didn't tell anyone else, but was obviously relieved when she heard that he couldn't cope with the work. It was more humiliating still to hear that he had a job in a nursery! God be praised, that didn't last long either. No more than a couple of days. For there were a few things he had to find out for himself. He had to get hold of a Bible. He had to know whether he was condemned or saved. He started to talk about Jesus and about giving his life into the Lord's hands. But Myren said it was just to make himself interesting and Katze shouldn't listen to a word of all that rubbish.

"He phoned here the other day and said: 'I *sincerely* hope you are well, Grandmother.' Just think, Zessen, I can't pick up the phone any more in my own house! He'd better do something worthwhile pretty soon, he's nearly 20, and that long, girlish hair! He ought to be in the Navy, that's what I think."

Next the plan was that he should take a preparatory course for university entrance. He did attend it for a week, but when he discovered that even with his intelligence he couldn't beat any of those he reckoned to be considerably less talented than himself, he decided to become a "street guru" instead, in possession of higher wisdom than that granted the rest of humanity. Everyone who wore himself out for "the system", whether in schools, offices or factories, was a total idiot. He had left the rat-race, man.

One morning Police Commissioner Børge Madsen phoned Zeste and asked if she knew about Orm Møller's habits, because he had come running stark naked into the police station, screaming, with cramps. He yelled at the officers at the reception to shoot him, his testicles had moved right up into his chest, he said, and he was going to die, so they might just as well shoot him there and then. He was examined in hospital and found to have taken an overdose of LSD. The Police Commissioner read the report to Zeste over the telephone: "The patient is slightly psychotic," he told her.

Li had eaten nothing for ten days. She was so ill that Zeste and Myren shielded her from news of their brothers, but Rebekka found her, drugged, in a boarding house, took hold of her collar and was brutally frank.

"It's a wonder both your husbands didn't leave you long before they did. You've never lifted a finger. You hated Rejn for years, but you were too cowardly and too lazy to let go of that easy life, you just clung on. Coward! You sold your soul for money. You sold yourself for Chinese porcelain and Persian carpets. You're worth no more than any . . ." Rebekka didn't dare finish the sentence, for zealous as she was for truth, it could be too much of a good thing; she was to some extent a good Catholic too, and they do not judge.

Li said nothing. Rebekka was just jealous, and on her high horse, enjoying the fact that Li had no man. For the moment.

"Have you got my medicine? I haven't slept for a week," she mumbled.

"No, because you just lie here moping while your children's lives are wrecked."

That was obviously jealousy, because Bekka didn't have children herself. Other people's children are disasters. Li's children had always been sweet and easy, but now they were gone. And Rejn was gone. All of them gone. How would she manage without them? Without everything?

"When you were small and something went wrong for you, you sulked and hid inside yourself. Now you just hide inside a bottle with your pills. You haven't changed one whit."

Bekka hadn't changed either, Li thought. Always Miss Know-It-All, she has to poke her nose into other people's business, as if her own life was so wonderful and so successful that she had something to teach other people! Deep in her drugged ecstasy, Li accepted Rebekka's assault with the greatest equanimity. Morning exercises! And in a strange way Rebekka took it with the same equanimity that all her criticism and advice was nothing but water off a duck's back.

It was only when Katze fell off a stool when she was blotto and black blood gushed from her head, and she said to Zeste that you mustn't speak ill of the Jews, or only a *little* ill, that Rebekka decided to leave for America.

Katze stood at the window of Gammel Mønt 14, waving: "Watch out for trams and needles!"

11

TRIUMPH

Tobias was dead, Katze grown anti-semitic and Li was going to the dogs. Even Rebekka's strong family feeling couldn't hold her in Denmark a month longer. As soon as she heard of a Danish doctor who needed a secretary in New York, she was as good as gone. It couldn't be too soon when it was a matter of arriving at "the heart of the world". That was how Rebekka saw the metropolis, and she wrote an article for *Berlingske Tidende* about it. How when you arrive in New York you feel in some absurd way at home again, welcome. "Absurd, because every unreciprocated feeling must be laughable."

Although Rebekka had not come lugging bundles and sleeping bags and toddlers in her arms, worn out and bitter, hunted from land to land in sophisticated old Europe where there was no room for her on account of race or religion or politics, she found, like so many other victims, a sanctuary in New York. Emma Lazarus' words on the plinth of the Statue of Liberty was no empty phrase to her: "Give me your tired, your poor, your huddled masses yearning to breathe free."

When Tobias died Rebekka felt the worst had happened. From now on nothing could hurt her any more. She instinctively thought of Anna Freud who was interrogated by the Gestapo, cool as a cat. Threats of torture and execution glanced off her like pleasantries. After she had lost her father, all fear of death vanished.

Rebekka undertook the task of maintaining Mama's legacy, to keep her spirits up, as her father had done. She saved cuttings that would cheer her up and keep melancholy at bay. She made lists of uplifting ploys: entertaining books, warm showers and keeping occupied, these were useful. But the best cure was simply New York – that construct of concrete, steel and glass, which might perhaps after the end of the world remain like the pyramids to recall a fantastic civilisation, which had once existed, like the Inca kingdom. She walked about the town and absorbed it. In her shoulder bag she kept a cutting to allay her own anxieties:

> Never look too far into the future. Ask yourself: are you happy right now? Does it look as if you have a chance of being happy before this evening? Or next week? Or next month? Then why spoil the joy of this moment with the thought of a distant misfortune that may never happen, or which you may not experience. Each little fear casts twenty shadows, and most of them we have created ourselves.

At the very point, then, at which Rebekka was becoming an artist of living, history broke into her own life. A woman turned up on the media scene from a kibbutz in Israel, where she lived as a closet Buddhist. She had a manuscript under her arm entitled: *Hitler's Daughter.* There was only one snag: Hitler did not have a daughter. But this incipient celebrity of a Brünhilde soon changed that, and Rebekka pulled off the scoop of snatching the translation of these controversial memoirs from Yiddish to Danish from under the noses of all the professionals. It was the start of Rebekka's literary career, and she defended the "kibbutz outcast" with the sensible observation: that if Hitler *had* had a daughter you could not reproach her for seeming a tad cracked.

Naturally, Hitler's daughter was a Jew, as, according to certain obscure scholars, her father turned out to be – in his case only "half", but enough for him to know what he was talking about when he expressed his urge to exterminate them. In fact he had, at the bottom of his oceanic self-hatred, but a single desire: to exterminate himself for the scumbag he knew he was. The world likes to be deceived; he was enrolled in political power struggles, one speech led to another, the people demanded his protection and devotion and suddenly he, who had wanted to be an artist, had become "Der Führer". Then he gradually acquired a taste for it. All this astonishing stuff could be read in *Hitler's Daughter*.

It has to be admitted that Rebekka lived next door to the American agency who owned the rights to the book, and that through Tobias' Riga connections she had nourished great hopes of a new and important life in America. She felt like Karen Blixen when she lost her farm. Rebekka had burned all her bridges. She lived with her dog, on a modest secretarial wage, nothing to boast about. Nevertheless she felt she was treading in Uncle Max's footsteps. Every great personality sooner or later had to leave Denmark. The USA had always been the place where great personalities could come into their own. And one day the orange would, for better or for worse, quite simply fall into her turban: she netted the translation of *Hitler's Daughter*. Thanks to the fact that she every day walked her dog round the block of 76th and Lex, where an elderly gentleman also took *his* dog, and he happened to have a top job in Hitler's daughter's agency!

Moreover, Rebekka was asked to give a talk at a charity dinner at the Waldorf Astoria, at which Elie Wiesel was the main speaker. She told the story of Mama's flight to Sweden and those who were caught in the hayloft in Gilleleje. And just as Karen Blixen had told the natives about the king's healing letter, Rebekka drew a scrap of paper from her handbag, which was addressed to "fru Hansen", the pseudonym Mama had been given at Bispebjerg Hospital. The dinner was taking place beneath crystal chandeliers in Manhattan, and here stood Rebekka Løvin, Mama's grandchild. It was a far cry from lying huddled together in a fishing boat. Rebekka did not feel persecuted. On the contrary, she grew under the wing-beat of history and took revenge on behalf of her race.

She had entered a weird world. Just imagine being Hitler's daughter! How different from her own experience is that! Brünhilde painted her father in the most gruesome light, which you couldn't blame her for, but at the same time she loved him dearly. She had naturally suffered from his need to keep her existence secret. She had been born out of wedlock to one of the countless attachments of his youth, often with Jewish women, whom – not surprisingly – he tortured and sexually humiliated. An illegitimate daughter did not suit his political image. He had to be the father of his country. Not the father of an ordinary, flesh and blood – Jewish – daughter. Anybody could be that, but very few were chosen to be father to a whole nation. Brünhilde came to hate the nation.

Regardless of what Brünhilde felt for her father, Rebekka noticed at once that in some respects they were on the same wavelength. When Brünhilde arrived in the USA to promote the American edition of the book, she let it be known that what she wanted most in the world was . . . a dog. Several times Rebekka asked for a meeting with Brünhilde – she was her translator after all – so that they could discuss dogs, but always without success.

It transpired that there was a reason for Rebekka being prevented from meeting Hitler's daughter: she was a fraud! The thing was pure fabrication, a creation of hype by the media and the publishers of some wretched woman, a concentration camp survivor, who was immediately dropped by the publishers when it became evident that she was unable to handle the media frenzy and live up to the part of the dictator's daughter. She finished up as a bag lady in and around London's Underground stations.

The book, however, turned out to be a success. The piquant thing was that this non-existent woman was suddenly discovered – as a symbol, an idea and an image that would not go away. Unfortunately, the inexperienced Rebekka had allowed herself to be fobbed off with a lump sum for the translation and so failed to benefit from any percentage of the considerable royalties earned by the bestseller, which sold even more when a film was made. But the present that Hitler's daughter did give Rebekka was to have ignited her old, hidden dream of becoming a writer. She thought of the translation as simply a stepping-stone to the world she considered her own. "I'll go on to that at the first opportunity, if I can earn enough," Rebekka wrote to Gammel Mønt. And, "as Father would have done", she sent photographs of herself to the publishers, so they could see she could certainly be used for publicity.

Rebekka's arms weighed as much as Selma Lagerlöf's bad hips. They explained and they explained away. Rebekka's arms were heavy with import. But she had learned to keep herself in trim with the aid of morning exercises and excellent deportment, which ensured that her arms retreated into the background. If *she* could drag herself up by the hair, then Li too, who had been fashioned so felicitously by nature, could surely put a stop to her decline. It was just a question of willpower. Even though she felt the writing business was a tough one, and had worried over whether she could handle it, she thought, "as Father would have done", that what counted was to keep a really cool head. And she sent her mother, "as Father would have done", a cheque for new underclothes: "You feel better, even though you are the only one who knows!"

Rebekka had started secretly to write 20 chapters about life and people, here and there, although she found it hard to get down to it in New York. She wrote under the epigram: "*Dixi et salvari animam meam*" – I have spoken and eased my soul. It was difficult because she vacillated between what she really felt like writing and trying to create something fine. She would like to have written about Reichendorf, the one who had cheated and written: there was enough for a whole novel there. But she did not want to write vulgar confessional stuff like the new feminists. One should be sophisticated like Marlene Dietrich or Karen Blixen. The former wrote of Clark Gable only that he had false teeth. "You don't need more than that," Bekka said. And went on, because she needed more, that Karen Blixen needed only to state that Bror couldn't spell Hemingway. "You don't need more than that," repeated Bekka. "A single sentence is enough."

In case anyone should object that Dietrich and Blixen were hardly congruent, Bekka would make it clear that in the Løvin family you read both *Hudibras* and Søren Kierkegaard, "just like Father", ignoring the fact that Father didn't read Søren Kierkegaard.

Gradually Rebekka went over to writing a series of little epistles on dogs, for they were staple and would never go out of fashion.

*

She had settled herself nicely in a comfortable little apartment with her piano, her typewriter, her books and her dog, when she received a telegram announcing Zeste's imminent arrival. The *succès de scandale, Last One Out Switch off the Light,* which in English was simply *Lights Off,* was to tour America. Zeste's breakthrough to the world!

Zeste had been to kiss Grandmother goodbye. Now it was not

only a brothel which had moved in upstairs, it seemed to be a sort of squat. Once it had been a high-class residence, you read *Hudibras*, erotic cartoons, and Kierkegaard, but now, complained Katze, there were communes everywhere:

"And they don't move in with furniture, they arrive with bricks and planks."

And Clark Olufsson, the Swedish bank robber, he was there too, Katze was sure of it, she had seen him several times. And the caretaker, hr Hovedløs, the headless one, was going to murder Katze with his broomstick because she had complained about the porno club with the bank robber and about the whole underworld moving in upstairs. When she was in the lift, the caretaker tried to shoot her with his broomstick from the landing, she was sure of it.

Buller had just died, the little bald man in coal and coke, the one everyone laughed at because his wife Glenda deceived him right under his nose. He had been more interested in good cigars and coal prices on the Stock Exchange. It was beneath his dignity to worry about what his wife might be up to. Anyway, he didn't need to give a thought to it now, presumably you didn't have to worry about that when you were dead. But Katze moaned, "She has snatched *him* away too," implying that Glenda had made away with her husband to rob Katze of a possible pleasure.

"I shan't write, I'll phone and I'm not going to the funeral," she said. And she called Glenda "fru Fonnesbeck".

"She was crafty enough to get him into hospital before he died. She's always been cunning and underhand; it's nicer when they die in hospital, then you're free of the trouble. Bekka did help me when Grandfather died. She is my own child, of course, but Grandfather should have died in *my* house, at Gammel Mønt 14.

She has been so wicked to me, that street girl. I was a *lady*, darling. But *you*, you must be happy in America and not behave as foolishly as your grandmother. Be careful not to marry a Jew, for the children will be odd. I am *very* sorry Merete got together with that rabbi from Transylvania. They are not suited. They are pushing, and it's only an urge, not tenderness or love."

"What is love, then?"

"Love is sitting all night in an *izvostnik* and *talking* to someone without going to bed, that's love, but you know that very well, my dear. I have managed Gammel Mønt, but Li is completely useless.

Last time she phoned she said that a *jade cat* had been stolen from her room, she had had a man in her room. A man in your room! I said. Like any servant girl! Are you going to the dogs, Li? Next day she rang and said that the detectives had been there, and I said, my girl, you'll be thrown out of the boarding house, and that'll be the third or fourth time. But then she rang again and said in an icy tone: Yes, I do take men up to my room. And when I asked if she really was set on going to the dogs, she put the receiver down. I rang to say goodbye properly, and she started defending Glenda, so I banged down the receiver. Haven't heard from her since. Remember to take my Bible and all the letters when I'm gone."

Grandmother stood by the window and waved: "Watch out for trams and needles."

One day Zeste would play Grandmother in the star part of her life. Babushka's great dream of appearing monumentally. And Zeste, perversely, would add: how could you ever be a human being in this family?

In the hope of finding an answer, Zeste went to say goodbye to the most "normal" individuals in the family. Uncle Otto and Aunt Titta. The latter had once in Zeste's childhood, when she fell in love with Serge, taken her to the doctor and had her measured for a pessary, for Aunt Titta, with her little white collar, who had been painted by Fanny Falkner (Strindberg's last wife), *en miniature*, was always on the side of youth and very flirtatious. At her house you got good food and comfort. Roast veal and lemon soufflé. Wicked tongues maintained that she saved on the butter and cream. Gaus, Gammel Mønt's old friend of the family, who was often with them, had just been released from prison and had somehow built himself a huge villa on the Riviera with the tax inspector's money, which he had kept in an account in Switzerland. According to Uncle Otto that wasn't anything to boast about, but on the other hand you had to admit: Gaus *was* a *personality*.

Uncle Otto preferred to sit in his chair reading his newspaper. And if anyone invited him out to dinner with the formula: Would you like to etc., there came the prompt reply: If you ask would I *like* to, the answer is NO! Unlike his brother Tobias, Otto had never been able to rise to flamboyant heights. As we know, Uncle Otto stuck to light irony, spoke in brief advertising texts, and had a firm ritual for all gatherings. Point 1. Whisky or sherry, with or without ice? Point 2. Health? Point 3. Work? Point 4. Love? Point 5. General well-being? Those were the five questions he asked when you were visiting them, and suddenly life acquired structure when it was divided up into categories, just as on the stage where life is divided into acts. That was the bourgeois drawing room, a stage with well-planned roles. And comfortable dialogues. And when Uncle Otto had had enough, regardless of the weather, he went over to the window and said, like Uncle Emil: "Well, now it's stopped raining." And that was the signal for the guests to leave.

But he had never spoken like that to Zeste, because she reminded him of the head of the Metropolitan Opera who went to the Adlon alone on his wedding night. Uncle Otto went on talking to Zeste ("any other business" on the agenda) and then it was not boring. How was Katze? Well, she was sozzled and mad as a hatter. How was Balder? Well, he appeared on television being funny about alternative medicine while his daughter was wasting away on drugs in London. I see, how was Li? Well, she had just been divorced and was in and out of mental hospital like a pendulum. I see, but how was it going with Myren? Well, she was all right, except that she won't have anything to do with the rest of the family because she's afraid of being infected by their wickedness. That was understandable. Moreover she had had another child and was breast-feeding both of them at night in spite of the fact that one of them was two years old. Ah, well, how was Orm, then? Well, he seemed to be living in a hostel as an acidhead or an alcoholic or both, if he was not in the psychiatric ward. I see, and how was little Tor? Tor? Well, he was in care.

It was clear that Uncle Otto viewed these isolated fates as individual chance misfortunes. He didn't see the *pattern*, the wreck of the family. And when you asked him if in his opinion the Løvins were "something special", he said, "Stuff and nonsense, it's a perfectly ordinary family."

*

Aunt Bekka was more than willing to help and put herself at the disposal of features departments of newspapers and theatrical agents to tell them about her niece. It's true that Rebekka regretted the dramatisation Zeste had created of a family curse based on Ovid's motto: *Video meliora, proque, deteriora sequor*. For that was Zeste's answer to Aunt Bekka: "The better course I see and approve, the worse one I follow." But in Aunt Bekka's opinion, that was disloyal. For, after all, the family was the only thing left to us. Without it we were nothing. Therefore we should honour and support rather than do it down. All the same, despite refuting the message of the play, her family feeling ordered her to help Zeste. It was the *Jewishness* in her, she claimed.

Rebekka went around, in her good suit and sensible shoes, talking at length about her niece, saying she was not at all the horrific *femme fatale* they wrote about in the papers, but an unfortunate girl who had had a difficult childhood, but who came from a good family; and now she was to charm America in the same way as Max Løvin, the famous Max Løvin, who . . .

"Max who?"

All the same, it gave Rebekka a peculiar satisfaction to launch her niece. For Tobias had admired beautiful, sensual women. Not intellectual ones.

"People think that just because you're single, you're gay, that's so Protestant. But there are people who are downright ugly. And they know that if they propose to anyone they'll be turned down."

"So what?" Zeste played it cool as usual.

"There are people whose lives would be crushed. Ugliness is insoluble!" Aunt Bekka said. And she always said it with the same suffering in her voice, as she recalled a hopeless ball gown with an artificial rose! "There was the artificial rose," whether the world liked it or not, and although the world loved artificial roses it was soon rescued from its delusion when Rebekka's tongue was loosened and Aunt Titta had said, thank God: "We'll find a way out . . ."

The fact was that Rebekka was not at all unattractive. In fact Zeste was struck again and again by how beautiful she was. She had simply taken on herself the role of the plain one, she saw herself through her mother's anxious and her father's critical gaze. The shame of being unable to attract a husband. So it was rather a relief to promote Zeste, she who could apparently choose and discard all the husbands she liked, but just didn't want any one of them. Maybe that was silly, but it was brilliant! Zeste turned every woman's shame into victory!

When Zeste landed at Kennedy airport after Labor Day, she landed like the orphaned dreaming child in Karen Blixen's story, who recognises everything in advance. The taxis were yellow as in films, the bridges rusty lace and Chryslers in art deco ripe to embrace. And where was the tour, Zeste Løvin's American tour? For when the tour had been requested after the European success, there had been a radical wave in America, but that had been quietly drowned out by a romantic wave. So suddenly there was no interest in *Lights Off*. It had been cancelled. Despite Aunt Rebekka's efforts.

Zeste put all her energies into switching them on again. She hadn't come to the USA to languish in a hotel room, and with Sarah Bernhardt's motto *"Quand même"* in mind she flung a nougat-coloured feather boa around her neck over a see-through parrot blouse, took with her a little leopard cub she was baby-sitting for a friend, and thus equipped arrived at a dinner party at Le Carousel and made her entry with the famous words: "I have just swallowed three goldfish." So Miss Løvin wasn't hungry, but contented herself with ordering one serving of fillet steak for the leopard, "medium rare, miaow".

The agent was speechless, but he was very quickly persuaded to reinstate the tour, for Zeste swore the show would easily fill houses, for that had happened in Paris, Holland and Italy. She explained that the right actor seldom found the right play at the right moment, but she had been lucky because she had found someone, her "right hand", who had written the play specially for her. And *Lights Off* was the preliminary culmination of a blossoming career. Instead of elaborating on the sad plot and the wrecked family and the whole of the Nordic self-torturing tradition pioneered by Ibsen and Strindberg, Zeste took care to point out that it was in reality a comedy, and that at the climax of the play she wore a see-through dress with angel's wings which she had had copied from one belonging to a Swedish countess – the Americans were snobs about European nobility – and she would quite definitely be a success.

Zeste knew that you couldn't risk a chutzpah like that in Denmark, where boasting is not allowed, but the agent was charmed by her self-confidence and kept repeating: "She wants all America to love her." True, he wasn't absolutely convinced about the show, but Miss Løvin herself – by the way, now you should say Ms – in her there was mileage. And the more Zeste boasted, the more she felt ability and strength grow within her. And she flung off her feather boa and waved her arms in the air: "I am ready to seduce a whole scout camp." By which she meant the whole of puritan America, while the agent hugged himself at the thought of all the little scouts creeping into all the orifices and darknesses of Miss Løvin when the lights were off.

Aunt Bekka was nervous, for although Zeste was grown up there were so many temptations for her to be aware of, and did Zeste have proper information? Time after time Bekka returned to her favourite subject: venereal disease. Even when they were in Zeste's dressing room after a rehearsal she couldn't refrain from pointing out – she was, after all, a semi-doctor – that venereal disease could lead to cerebral paralysis, scaly skin, loss of hair, boils, rheumatism, open wounds and leprosy. "People just don't know about it!" she said, at intervals, interrupting herself to say: "Yes, she is my niece," to whoever might be listening: People crowding into the dressing room for drinks, people going in and out while Zeste took off her make-up.

"Have you read *The Blessed Birgitta* and *Hildegard von Bingen*?" Aunt Bekka interrogated Zeste, caring nothing for theatrical circles where you had to talk of leopard-spotted dildos if you wanted to be *comme-il-faut*.

"Can't it wait till another time?"

But Aunt Bekka wouldn't be brushed aside, and she went on with her monologue, unconcerned even when the people standing around gaped or turned a deaf ear to her. People streamed in and out of the dressing room – a wild confusion of drinks, snacks, smokes and slander – but Aunt Bekka in her tweed suit loudly persevered undaunted:

"Did you ever hear of the two women travellers, two theology students? They went to a church in northern Greece. One went inside and never came out again. She hasn't been seen since. It's a mystery. Was there a back door, and a young man with a scooter and a trip into the mountains? Was it so simple? Or what did happen inside that church?"

No reply.

Zeste hung the copy of the Swedish countess's transparent angel dress on a hanger and put on a Chinese Cheong Sam, Suzy Wong in ox-blood batik with long slits up the thigh.

"It's a good thing to be a bit self-critical when you're past 30," Rebekka remarked.

"Why don't you become a nun?"

Aunt Rebekka took the question seriously. "Firstly, one would have to be Catholic – and that would mean betraying Judaism."

*

When Zeste was in a train on her way to upstate New York to visit Marsken and his family and relax at their country idyll after the rehearsals, she felt relieved and happy.

She thought about Sarah Bernhardt's memoirs, *My Double Life,* in the context of her own secret love of generous ordinariness – or dare one say healthy normality – that characterised Marsken and his family. Li would be glad too to hear about the visit, no doubt about that.

After the announcement of the New World première in New York of *Lights Off,* Pierre had sent a telegram, stating that from now on they were severing all communication with Zeste, as they totally condemned her open treachery and cruel betrayal of the most intimate family secrets. That was what it said: "Traitor, we don't wish to know you any more." Before the play was first performed in Copenhagen, Zeste had talked to Myren about a possible candidate for the second leading female role, and Myren had suggested herself! And was deeply offended at being rejected. She couldn't understand that to work on the stage you needed experience. But Pierre was more than happy that Myren was not to be part of that decadent world.

In one scene the two sisters competed for the young men. And because the two girls were so alike they were sometimes, with luck, able to substitute themselves for each other's lovers without at first being discovered. In *Canterbury Tales* style they tried to snatch lovers from each other. But that was more than Pierre's morals could take. He realised that by marrying Myren he had inadvertently become part of a life-threatening, incestuous family. When nothing is sacred no-one is off-limits in a family, and where there is no protection sexuality rules. And in dreams he was seized with the horror of all horrors: not to be able to distinguish between the women.

Zeste saw the future of the family as a series of incurable ruptures unless an older man with authority, Marsken, for example, could enter the arena and lift the curse. With a wise word he would be able to detoxify the poisoned and the envious and give them back their ability to forgive, and their natural boundaries and their dignity. Even though Marsken didn't belong to the world of fairy tale, she would at least do all she could to persuade him to soften Rejn's heart towards Li and the children.

As far as they knew Orm was wandering the Sahara, searching for his father. He had celebrated his twentieth birthday alone in the desert. It was no lie when Rebekka said: "I believe that Orm is the loneliest boy on earth." But there was nothing Li could do about that, she had enough to do finding out whether she herself could or wanted to survive. Rejn must be brought to realise that he couldn't just leave her with a minimum of support. Rejn respected Marsken, he was perhaps the only person he had real respect for, and the same applied to Li. Zeste felt, as she sat in the train, that with the welcome break from the theatre and the enforced relaxation in the golden-red autumn landscape she was passing through, she had embarked on an important mission.

It was a pleasantly intact family to visit. They had always sung the Internationale on Christmas Eve. Zeste played Frisbee with the children, who were too big for that sort of thing, but in honour of the occasion they were all children and Marsken joined in the fun. And they ate masses of raspberry ice cream. Kidde with her delightful violet eyes was domesticated – but not oppressively so – she was also at university. All in all it was an edifying proof that the family as such wasn't a condemned, hypocritical or hollow undertaking. He showed her the garden with the dangerous marsh behind it. Zeste developed red cheeks, which matched the red of the maple trees. Marsken was going to drive her to the station the next day.

Suddenly, by a little driveway into the woods, he stopped the car. And he took her hand, in a most decisive way, with a desperate sigh, which seemed to contain 30 years of unspoken words. Not necessarily words minted on her. But words from a man who had never spoken. True, he had spoken at meetings and conferences, he had given political speeches in which everything was ingeniously concealed and indicated by a pause, but the man had never spoken from his own heart. His hand lay in hers for a long time and she saw it as a foreign body, which had always been part of her life. Just as the snail must find its house of calcite and mother of pearl. When Marsken placed his hand on her lap it was like a bomb. But it was the old familiar one. To be chosen by the king. As queen one had a share in the beginning of all things, the rising of the sun in the east. Now nothing bad could happen any more, the world had arranged itself in its finest spring attire for a pure new beginning. Zeste dared not breathe, and there were no words. For it was also a sentence of death, the slide down into a pleasant, warm and damp swamp, but paralysing as quicksilver, in which one completely lost the contours of one's own person and energies. It was like being referred to an ancient Shinto ritual, with hundreds of naked men pounding a 500-metre-long pole into a giant oval wooden gateway to ensure the crops grew well. The feeling was that it had to be like this, it could not be otherwise.

But when had she discovered the marsh in Marsken, the perilous places in his soul and dreams? Was it when he held the big whisky glass in Algiers, or in upstate New York? Time would tell whether it had bottomless regions or how far out one could paddle. For the time being nothing must darken the triumph and joy it was to be chosen. And it was a particular liberation when she thought of Rejn and Li. Zeste had completed her mission.

She wrote to the Cat care of Gammel Mønt that she had visited Marsken and Kidde, that Marsken was truly magnificent and had promised to talk Rejn into more human ways, but that she mustn't nourish too high hopes. With love, love.

After that all took its predictable course in conformity with the old laws for older men and younger courtesans. With the slight difference that in her meeting with Marsken Zeste was richer by a lover, but poorer in her faith in a husband. The only family left in the world she had imagined to be a safe and inspiring place existed no more.

Next day they met for lunch in the dim Chinese restaurant Thirteen Grades of the Imperial Treasure, where other illicit meetings took place between highly placed big shots in public office. The guests were waited on very discreetly. At another table in the darkness Henry Kissinger sat with Liv Ullmann. Zeste felt she was moving from triumph to triumph. At this moment, as long as Marsken clung to her hand, success or fiasco in America meant nothing. Zeste had been trained to step into any gap where there was need for her and to create happiness. But she had discovered many times that other people's needs were destructive. She was certain Marsken's were not. In reality she was tired of walking in Sarah Bernhardt's footsteps, seeking one unhappy relationship after another only to balance all the success she had on the stage.

She stroked the hand he clung to her with, and said: "It's quite uncomplicated." Although he was happy now, he was also in despair. Nothing in his life was uncomplicated. It was one gigantic muddle, which he had allowed to grow for 30 years, while he used up all his energy saving the world.

In a way it was uncomplicated for Zeste. For since the French diplomat Serge de Clerval in the morning of time had conquered "the man's place" in her heart, she couldn't be conquered by anyone else. Serge held the key to her psychic chastity belt. Physically she could do whatever she liked, but the lover always came to a frontier beyond which he could not reach her, and then he would burst into tears.

She felt safe with Marsken, whose strength and integrity she had known all her life. He had a strong head, she was sure of that. He would never make a fuss, or be difficult, he wanted only to live *for pleasure*.

"You have a right to be happy," said Zeste, pressing his hand. "What thanks do you get for being sad and doing your duty?" It was unreasonable that he should spend the rest of his life and all his strength helping others, with no any happiness of his own.

The best thing would be if she could help him to talk things through with Kidde and go back to his marriage with renewed strength. But that was not sheer saintliness, for in the meantime Zeste enjoyed being the object of such great admiration.

He sat there in the dark in his Brooks Brothers suit, and with his Marlon Brando voice said, "I will give you the whole world." But it was a dubious world. He had come to the point where he couldn't save it any more. He knew the world was fucked up, that the smooth, the mediocre, the stupid, would rule. His love was buried with one of his friends, a revolutionary hero, who had staked his life on a better world. In Indo-China and Algeria. Now he felt he had been given the last chance to – if nothing else – save the last scrap of humanity in himself.

12

TAKE THE WHIP WITH YOU

On holiday in the Caribbean Rebekka had met an Irish solicitor and fallen for him hook, line and sinker. And vice versa. He had blue eyes and a crew cut. She was a real lady and he was a real man, who swept her off her feet. Bekka wrote home at once to Katze that the new man in her life was used to people jumping and hopping at his command, but that was not so strange since he was an officer in the reserve and always full of smiles and charm, and everyone jumped for Father as well, and this patriarchal system with a man who knows what he wants wasn't so bad after all.

To be sure, Rebekka had checked him out with a lawyer to make sure that his divorce was indeed under way. She wasn't so dumb that she rushed into a holiday affair without a second thought. In any case, the idea of hurting another woman was more than her conscience could bear. Nor was she so impressed by his Cadillac, which moved seats up and windows down at the touch of a button, or by the fact that he owned the whole of his office building, plus masses of other property on Manhattan and Long Island. She wasn't going to be taken in because she knew languages, which he didn't; she could tell the difference between Brahms and Beethoven, which he couldn't.

In any case, she was going back to Denmark to celebrate her mother's 75th birthday.

The day before the birthday Li had had to face a serious dilemma. She too had planned to visit Katze on her birthday. Not least in the hope of seeing her children, who had quite deserted her. Perhaps she could catch them at Gammel Mønt. She particularly longed for Tor, her little blessing, who was still a part of her body. But it was a tortured body, and she couldn't let herself be seen anywhere in the state she was now in. It was true she wasn't so thin any more, or rather, her stomach had developed a little bulge from all the liquid nourishment she consumed. The new Indian dress she had bought for the occasion had to be given away at the last moment with a sigh of self-realisation – she was too old for it. "If you wear that, you'll have to go and sit by the Hippie Fountain," said her drinking chums. But the worst of it was not what to wear but being black and blue in the face. Some man or other must have beaten her up, but she couldn't remember which one. Another time – or perhaps the same one – she had been raped as well, in her room. The only reason she reported it to the police was because the man had run off with one of her bottles. But now she was black and blue and dared not go to Gammel Mønt for the family would think she had hurt herself when drunk. But she *hadn't*. Though they wouldn't believe that. In any case it hadn't been the Baron, whom she had taken to bed because he was "a hell of a guy, cultivated and arrogant". He had come over to her table and said they should go to her place to look at her Chinese porcelain. She thought of Zeste when he sat there in her nightdress, looking not in the least ludicrous. A real aristocrat. Next morning they had gone to see some of the Baron's friends, he had a lot of estates and everything you could imagine. Li had never had such fun in her life . . . But she couldn't go to Gammel Mønt because she couldn't stand the thought of her mother's disapproving looks or Rebekka's Miss Know-It-All attitude. How she had got the bruises or who had done it, what did she care!

She loved those hard, arrogant, insensitive men. He had just come over to her table: "We'll go back to your place." And he had bought two bottles of wine and three *glasses*. "One of them might get broken," he said. It was that third glass she fell for.

Zeste called from New York from one of Marsken's offices to tell her she had had huge successes in Atlanta, Nashville, Memphis, Louisville, Colombus, Dayton, Indianapolis, St Joseph,

Leavenworth, Quincy, Springfield, Milwaukee, Detroit, Cleveland, Pittsburg, Toronto, Buffalo, Rochester, Utica, Albany, Boston, Providence, Newark, Washington and Baltimore. She avoided mentioning that Marsken had cried at the première and sobbed over her success and asked if she wouldn't like to have a child. When it was two, he would look after it, he'd love to be a single father!

Li's speech problem didn't allow her to say much on the telephone. But Zeste felt her unspoken pride over the line and the indefinable way she had saved Li through her success.

"And do you know, in Chicago . . ."

"Uncle Max," whispered Li.

"No, in Chicago they had put me up by pure chance in Sarah Bernhardt's old hotel. At Palmer House, in her old suite, super Pharaoh sofas, lamps with bronze sphinxes, clocks on marble pyramids and pictures of lazy days on the Nile."

"Uncle Max," Li whispered again.

"No, Sarah Bernhardt. And d'you know what, the best thing of all is that the press say I ought to be banished from the USA because I'm ruining American morals, and they wrote that about Sarah Bernhardt too. They say I challenge their values, family values, you know."

Li complained about her black and blue face which stopped her from going to Katze's birthday party and meeting Rebekka and all the others.

"But, Mother, you must go. You must stand by your own life. We must stand by our lives. I just don't understand why Rejn hates me so much, I've never done anything to hurt him."

"Neither have I. When I met him he was just nothing. I had to teach him to eat with a knife and fork."

Suddenly Zeste found herself with words pouring from her which she hadn't intended to utter: "Marsken and I ran into each other by chance in Geneva at the weekend. I was just about to run into Rejn there. And his new wife. A stumpy little nurse, you know. They went to see Marsken at his hotel suite. Thank God I wasn't there. But there was a programme on the table with a picture of me. In an icy voice Rejn asked Marsken to 'remove that object'. And when his new wife saw the picture, she screamed and fainted!"

Li lapped up this story as if she had written it herself. She couldn't have done it better. Something in Zeste's account hinted that Marsken and Zeste were of the same mind about Rejn. It couldn't be better. Zeste's story was delivered as ordered.

"Now, Mother, I must run, maybe I'll pop home for Grandmother's birthday."

She didn't say that Marsken was standing right behind her with his hands round her neck. But she hoped that Li would feel it. By telling her about the weekend in Geneva she must have implied that the relationship had been consummated, as Li in her heart of hearts had wished.

They had had their first squabble in Geneva. Or rather: the first worm in the apple crawled out of the apple there.

"You and Rejn didn't have a relationship, did you?" asked Marsken, as if it was the most natural thing in the world to ask.

"No," said Zeste abruptly, but inside it felt as if the world had run amok, to find it so natural for a stepfather to have a relationship with his stepdaughter.

"Everyone thought you did. That it was the reason for his marrying Li."

"Oh, did everyone think that," Zeste said.

"Not everyone in the world, but the people at UNICEF and their circles and so on."

"Oh, and so on."

"It wasn't condemned, you mustn't think that."

"Why did no-one help?"

"Help? What with?"

"Isn't the UN an aid organisation?"

*

As Li rode up to the third floor of Gammel Mønt 14 in the ramshackle lift, past the mezzanine, in the hope of catching Tor, she couldn't help thinking of Katze during the war. When Katze always said: "Just let them come", about the Gestapo, it certainly wasn't courage she was showing. Because she *wanted* them to come, all those German officers, the real gentlemen, the Baltic Germans she had danced with in Riga. If only the Germans would come, Katze could again be the fêted *femme fatale*, the ideal she had always longed for. If the Gestapo had rung the doorbell to arrest Tobias, Katze would have said, "Come in", and put on her ball gown.

Li dreaded that Katze might be drunk. She couldn't stand drunken people. If only Tor were there. She might have lost Rejn, a good riddance anyway, but she didn't want to lose her little blessing. And Rejn would come to a bad end, for it was his fault she had wasted her life. She had taken an extra dose of medicine so as not to notice if people stared. But when she met Tor, little blessing, he had become a Christian! And so had Orm! And they had both got new – Christian – names! Orm was Luke and Tor was Peter.

Orm had been picked up by a Christian missionary in the sauna of an inn, and from there he had been sent to a Christian commune in Jutland, where he spent all their cash and then made off with all the fittings, which he traded for alcohol one weekend. He ran up a Christian debt of more than 100,000 kroner and then was excluded from the Christian fellowship, which was as close as you could get to terminal in Denmark.

Things had gone differently for Little Blessing. He hadn't been picked up by a missionary, but he had got a job on a farm. He needed to be somewhere where his lack of elementary knowledge would not be noticed. One day when he was driving a tractor in a field he saw a strange sight, an unknown light phenomenon, so he had to stop and get off. He had a strange sense of a figure, a very strange presence, and yes it was he, it *was* the Saviour who told Tor to follow him. Tor said yes. But not only that, he felt happier than he had ever been in his life. He wept with joy and rolled on the ground like a newborn babe who hadn't yet learned to walk. He would not join the army and learn to kill, nor would he even be a pacifist, he would only serve God's natural world.

He had joined a free church and had been to their office to talk to the Christian leader about an important subject, marriage. Tor had been in love with the Faroese girl Sullima, for a year and had come to the realisation that it was more than sentiment, it was the way he wanted to go. Before he wrote to her, it was important to consult the Christian leader in order to have his case backed up by the congregation. Sullima's mother had already sent him a big parcel containing a hand-knitted Icelandic sweater, toothpaste etc., "just like a real mother", as he said. Sullima was 27, so ten years older than he was, and he was rather frightened of what people would say about the age difference. But he had grown a beard and his eyes shone with conversion and love. He had been standing between two cliffs for over a year, and God had given him so many signs telling him he would succeed in getting ashore on the opposite cliff. And perhaps Tor was right, that God was with him in the matter. Surely he was. But the girl wasn't.

Tor's conversion wasn't clear to Li in all its dimensions, as she had installed a protective chemical filter between herself and reality. But she wanted to talk to him to establish contact: "Can you forgive Hitler?"

Tor nodded earnestly, with starry eyes.

"But if you can forgive everything, everything is permissible, so nothing matters," said Li.

Tor just sat there shining.

"Can you forgive Hitler?" Li asked again to make sure she had heard aright.

"Yes," said Tor, "I have forgiven you too!"

When Tor was leaving Li tried to follow him. She asked him: "Are you going north?"

"No, the opposite way."

Li tried to touch Little Blessing. He was only 17. But about to sink into the ground at her touch. And then he ran.

*

In New York Zeste pushed Marsken's hands away from her neck. He had got into the habit of taking time off from work to accompany her, as often as he could, on tour, because he could scarcely exist for a moment without her. In Louisiana she had bought a baby alligator called Calypso. It stayed in her dressing room in the evenings waiting for her, and shared her bed at night to indicate that Marsken must adopt a more discreet position and keep an appropriate distance. Zeste Løvin was not to be engulfed. But it's only love, said Marsken, at which Zeste burst into tears.

She fed Calypso on strawberry yoghurt and champagne, until one day she found her dying in the bed. Zeste bent down and gave her artificial respiration and mouth to mouth, she slept with the dying Calypso, pressing her to her breast to give her life. But naught availed. Calypso was buried in Milwaukee, embalmed in a little coffin lined with mauve velvet. Marsken exploited Zeste's sorrow to be with her the more; on her part she was too weak to reject him. When the tour was over and she had resisted the usual persuasive attempts to get her to appear as a calendar girl in *Playboy* and whatever other kinds of fame the media had on offer, Zeste found herself in an artistic limbo without a scrap of energy.

She was tired of acting in sadistic plays in which the audience had to be spanked the whole time for their thinking way of life. And she didn't want to act in the ones portraying the revolution just round the corner as the solution to all problems. It became evident that all the audience wanted from theatre was a thrashing. A psychiatrist had written in the *New York Times* that there were far too many masochists and not nearly enough sadists to cover their needs. Zeste complained to Li, who replied:

"You could try whipping them, just a little."

Li felt sorry for the needy. That was why she had always encouraged Zeste to say yes to people on the street asking for a kiss. You shouldn't be mean. But Zeste couldn't use a whip, she could never hit anything at all. And she had no laurels to fall back on, because after all the tour had hardly been a success at all. Only a scandal in the press. Zeste Løvin was a "chokeroo", as they wrote, a *femme fatale*. But the play had not drawn full houses and the fiasco was not only caused by the tragedy in 20 scenes in a country demanding comedy, comedy and again comedy. In addition to spanking, by all means. Not an easy recipe.

Another fiasco was that something had happened to Zeste's voice. Sometimes it seemed about to break in two, between the two registers, into two different characters which were impossible to hold together. In that situation the audience witnessed something close to breakdown in an actor who certainly wasn't supposed to be breaking down. And if anything is fatal for the art of acting it is *real* pain. At other times the voice vanished completely. That was when Zeste tried to keep the situation under control and avoid breaking down. Then her voice disappeared for long spells. It would eventually return, but there were limits to how long her fellow actors could wait, and in Milwaukee they had had to cancel the performance and give the audience their money back. So much for the "serious European culture" that had been so widely advertised.

Marsken always sat in the wings, often drunk, to "support" her. No-one else could see him, but Zeste had a phobia for intoxicated or drugged states and could smell a whiff of spirits a mile off. He said he was ill and had a temperature and it was psychosomatic. Zeste said: "You just drink too much." She had her cocaine, of course. So they had nothing to say to each other, although he tried to pour more whisky into her the whole time for the sake of companionship.

In fact he stayed there because the theatre was his real passion, and his secret, deeply buried dream was to stand on the stage where you can shout your despair and your enthusiasm, your fear of death and your desire. He had always wanted to be an actor, but he had never had a chance to satisfy his passion. And he transformed it into the desire for power and called that *work*, as he condemned the narcissism and exhibitionism underlying his deepest wish.

He showed Zeste several times how she ought to play a certain scene. He tore the script out of her hands and she merely glared at him. But he wanted to help. Help her to realise she had suffered a defeat and was not quite as outstanding as she thought.

In reply, Zeste made her eyes go white.

*

Marsken always arrived two or four hours early when he visited her. She enjoyed the time she had to herself in peace and was furious when he called from the airport: "I'm here already! I caught an earlier plane!"

He started a long declaration of love: "I don't want to boast, but I'm not a cynic." He was often "like that" when he came. Like Tobias being afraid of seeing Katze again and like Li and Orm and . . . Marsken had brought caviar and pale green silk scarves. It was at the Mark Hopkins Hotel in San Francisco, and he had just flown in from China. But Zeste interrupted him.

"I don't want to boast, but I *am* a cynic."

Marsken was in love with her uncompromising attitude, which he set out to break down. He wanted to influence her, to think in her way, marry her, to be her. And completely remake her. But Zeste thought: It's strange, no sooner do you get a sugar daddy than you fall in love with more or less every street boy you would never have glanced at before. And she embraced Jimi Hendrix or someone who pretended to be him. Marsken put up with the pain, and when his work took him away from her he sent her big bouquets of long-stemmed red roses every day from wherever he was in the world, and she had herself photographed in bed covered with roses so that it looked like something between a grave and a childbed.

Marsken plainly suffered from the illusion that he was going to marry Zeste. For when she issued in print what he would later come to call her 47th Street Declaration, that it would never come to pass in her lifetime, he went into shock. For her part, she couldn't understand how he could have imagined she would ever be able to be his wife!

The only symbol of their shared secret life was a plastic orange squeezer which he had bought in London and faithfully carried around from state to state, from inn to suite, and every morning squeezed five oranges, because she had once said she liked that. Oranges. He loved the squeezer, and he used it everywhere. He squeezed himself and his blood into it, and she hated that squeezer. When he laid his hand on her stomach she screamed. The bomb in her womb had imploded and her body had become radio-active like poisoned lace curtains.

*

She crept into the opposite corner of the bed and held a little corner of the duvet up to her chin like a shield. He shouted angrily:

"You sit there like a tiger defending her young."

"I'm protecting the last vestige of my dignity."

"To hell with dignity. I don't drink for the sake of the whisky, I drink to get unconscious."

For 25 years he had been unconscious because of the loss of the mother who died while he was an infant and whom he must therefore have killed, and he spent his childhood in the churchyard. Without feelings. In the world's eyes he was a hero, but he knew himself that he was a coward who never turned up that day on the corner by the grocer's shop in Søllerød where the informer was to be executed and his friend was shot instead of him in the scuffle. That was why later in life he had stayed married. He could not bear to be the one who betrayed.

In Zeste he had met his mirror image. And now it was his turn. For once. Now *he* wanted to be saved. And he wanted to be saved by her. And they melted together in a tender and hostile combination without contours which both of them came to hope would break apart, but which they were equally powerless to effect because of their guilt. Zeste couldn't say no to him out of consideration for Li.

In her letters she tried to make the relationship as entertaining as possible so as not to disappoint her mother. On August 14th she wrote from New York that Marsken had rented a little apartment for her beside the UN building, close to his office.

Dearest Mother, Well, the fantastic truth does indeed surpass reality. I've moved into an *Algerian* apartment with little nylon insects in various colours stuck on the fridge. The lamp (which I've put away in a cupboard) in the bedroom was a little man with a top hat holding balloons in various colours. There isn't a white lamp in the whole place, all the bulbs are red or turquoise. All over the walls there are Muslim cuttings from coloured magazines. The cot beside me is in Mickey Mouse design. The curtains in my bedroom are pale yellow plastic (the shower curtain), so I can wipe them with a damp cloth when I wake up, very practical. I have had a great clean up, the first thing I did was to buy cleaning materials. I may not be fastidious, but there are still masses of curly black hairs in the bathroom, and I seem to find toe nail clippings all over the sitting room. Marsken brought a vacuum cleaner last night. The loo is quite interesting too – in turquoise plush, even the cistern is covered with it. Marsken has paid for the whole month and it wasn't cheap, for it's in a very nice, safe district. And he wanted me only a millimetre away. He's not in his right mind.

When I arrived there were 25 bottles of whisky. Apart from everything being awful, nothing is lacking. A bit too much of a good thing, though. He has completely lost himself and weeps and sobs. He says he will have to tell Kidde about me: he can't live in this schizophrenic state. I dread he will fall apart. (Why do all the men who get to know me sob all night?) "You must remember," says Marsken, "that no-one gets to know you without cost, you leave deep marks on those you meet." It sounds flattering. I'm good at making them break down, too. But strangely enough I'm not interested in sticking the pieces together again. Much love from Zeste.

Zeste had tried in this letter to appeal to Li's *aesthetic* sense in order to get her blessing on breaking up the relationship. Zeste didn't suppose his falling apart would affect her mother, though. But the lack of so much as a Sung cat or a Ming frog within reach was a situation which could well be listed under the heading of SOS, *force majeure*.

At the Ritz in Paris he lay wailing that he wanted to leave his family. He woke up at night and cried out because he dreamed he was dying. And he talked of his marshes and the dangerous places in his soul and his dreams and asked Zeste to hold his hand, or he dared not . . . He also cried because he couldn't bear to fall asleep and so be separated from her for seven hours. He wanted to give up his marriage and his work, none of it meant anything.

"Stop it!"

Next morning he bought two snake skeletons for her in an African shop to wind round her neck.

She lay with them in her bath in Vienna, made up her eyes and drank chocolate while he was at a meeting of the Atomic Commission.

*

On the ship across the Atlantic for which he had booked tickets to please Kidde and pay off his bad conscience, he had hidden himself in a cabin and locked the door. Awake and sober. But it ended with Kidde and the children finding him sobbing. When they arrived he smashed his Chevrolet to bits and pieces with a hammer, because the boot had jammed. He said he felt shut in, like the pilot who flies all around the world confined to his cockpit.

Zeste saw the last exemplary family in the world broken up before her eyes.

"Well, now the king has fallen off his horse, now you can't keep me out any more," he said and asked leave to be just a quite ordinary person. He asked if Zeste could be satisfied with being a human being as well, but she started to yawn.

Zeste developed a rash on her face, so she could not go out. Marsken had stolen her script. Not until the day he returned it did the fiery red blotches disappear.

Zeste was in Denmark at Easter time when she had a letter

from Marsken, telling her he was on a slimming course and the kilos were streaming off him. He liked his new self. He had ordered new suits from Brooks Brothers. But Zeste sent a telegram: "Cancel the tailor, I love you as you are." She didn't want to lose the man she had attached her loving feelings to since childhood. He mustn't change. He mustn't go away from himself. Above all he mustn't get divorced. "I will only see you if you are married," she said. That was her Copenhagen Declaration. But Marsken couldn't go on with a double life, he couldn't treat his good comrade of a wife like that and look into her reproachful violet eyes. He made mistakes all the time, mixed up telephone numbers, addresses and names. He called Kidde in America from Abu Dhabi, cancelled the call because it took too long to get through, called Zeste in Europe. When he heard the receiver picked up, he said: "Zeste? Beloved." But it was Kidde, who screamed:

"Have you gone mad?"

But he said nothing, ignored it. He had the idea of writing a book, but the most important thing was to keep it secret from Kidde. She mustn't know anything. That was the most important thing. Nevertheless in his vague way he contrived to get the bill from a luxury hotel in Switzerland, where he had stayed with Zeste for a fortnight, sent home to Kidde. "Well, are you paying her for that too?" said Kidde.

But actually Zeste's contribution couldn't be paid for in money. To have to watch another person one is fond of disintegrate. After the slimming course he looked a shadow of himself. They were to celebrate with dancing in the Rainbow Room. The dress he gave Zeste for the occasion consisted of three small flesh-coloured silk scarves from Saks Fifth Avenue. The dance of the three scarves ruined the atmosphere at all the tables, where none of the men could manage to keep up a conversation with their ladies. The result was that Zeste and Marsken were thrown out. The manager regretted . . . But Marsken was delighted to have caused a scandal, and Tommy Dorsey jumped down from the stage and said they were the loveliest couple the orchestra had ever played for, and Marsken embraced one of Tommy's cousins with joy and lifted him high in the air like a baby.

No-one knew it was the dance of death they had set out on, with the exception, perhaps, of the audience, who had been so painfully moved. Marsken went on talking of getting divorced, and Zeste kept on forbidding him to do so. But he had to say something. And as he was not allowed to say it in so many words, his body began to talk. It tried to drive itself to death at night on the motorway in a drunken state. It attempted to set fire to itself. And it tried to drown itself at the hotel room in Rome, when he was so drunk he had allowed the bath to run over all night. He knelt on the floor and slept with his head on Zeste's feet. From time to time she kicked him in the face when she turned round, but he couldn't think of a better place. At half past six he woke her up. The room was under water.

"All that water," he said, pointing at it, "is my tears."

"How corny can you get! Ring reception."

Zeste saw that Jonah's journey into the whale's stomach was at an end. That no birth was likely to come from the efforts, rather death by drinking. And everything that should have been symbolic, had become reality.

The maid found him walking around the room unconscious, wrapped in a sheet like a fallen Roman senator with a glass of whisky in his hand with water up to his knees. She screamed: "Madonna, Madonna!"

Three weeks later he tried to drown himself at Niagara Falls, and you would think that was easy. But he failed there as well. Zeste took no part in it, she was not of a mind to hold his head under the cascades of water as he had begged her.

Zeste said: "I don't want to see you again," but she took pity on him and added "before you have seen a psychologist," and that was her Paris Declaration, May 4th, 1977. But was it Zeste who was driving him mad?

It is true that Zeste suffered as an actress from a spurious image of herself, which her press helped to magnify – and sometimes demolish – which contributed to her exaggerated idea of her own destructive powers. It is true that in time she grew more and more convinced that if a man fell into her arms he would die. Sooner or later. And she might have been right about that, in so far as her embrace was not a haven of immortality. But here she might have overlooked the fact that there are people who deliberately, wilfully do their utmost to bring about catastrophe. There are people who have worked all their life for the community and been engaged in connecting, weaving and joining together. In organising and creating cohesion. Dionysus stands in wait for these people with the temptation of: total wreckage. For a long time this industrious, dutiful person has courted powerlessness and dreamed of the final demolition of everything. But it takes courage to destroy everything, stake everything on one throw and go under. Most people are not granted the catastrophe. They have to resort to infidelity, where the maximum damage can take place, unless one wants to kill one's children.

*

Marsken sat picking at his food at the Belle Terasse in Copenhagen's Tivoli and spilling bits on the cloth. From having been an exceptionally well-organised person – which his family no doubt relied on – now he was the one who missed a plane, forgot his luggage and couldn't order a meal at a restaurant.

He agreed to talk to a psychologist, not only for Zeste's sake, but also because two of his children had refused to go to school. Finally Kidde objected, although she had tried to get him to seek help for years. Now she said: "Why can't you talk to *me*?" while everything collapsed around her because all nine children broke their bounds at once and wanted to live in their respective countries. "All of your children have totally lost respect for you," she said. And Marsken moved to London and would not take any of them with him. Thus the family was broken up at one stroke, one snap of the fingers, even though they had sung the Internationale on Christmas Eve.

Marsken got on really well with Dr Nordenlicht, who said it would be best if Zeste came too. "You can both go to hell," she said. *He* was the one who couldn't cope with life. She herself was fine, if only she was left in peace. When they first went to the Thirteen Grades Zeste had emphasised that it was *not* compli- cated, but now he said, "I knew it would be complicated, because I knew I would commit suicide if you didn't marry me."

One day Kidde called her husband while he was in an important meeting and announced that she wanted a divorce. She would rather pay $20,000 a month in tax to the state than allow Marsken to spend the money on diamonds for Zeste. Moreover, he might like to know that a newspaper had reported that Zeste had danced naked with Mr Universe, and she would be delighted to send him the pictures.

Beside himself, Marsken consulted his eldest son as to whether his relationship with Zeste had anything to recommend it. His son must know, since rumour had it that he too had enjoyed her favours. But his son did not recommend anything. He merely said that according to statistics that kind of relationship was seldom long lasting. Either Kidde could not manage it, or Marsken couldn't. The son had evidently enjoyed an affair that was precisely as uncomplicated as Marsken had hoped for and which Zeste had assured him of.

But now she was feeling strangely out of sorts. With nausea. Not a headache, but the other thing. She took a long look. Had Jimi Hendrix left a souvenir? This time there was no doubt in her mind. She said nothing to Marsken, for it was nothing to do with him. But fate and life wanted to give her a gift, personally for her. So she should accept it. At the same time she felt fear. Fear that the world would shrink to the size of her stomach. That the globe should become one with her stomach felt like an outrageous self-centredness which she was ashamed of, even if it could be thought natural. All the same she decided to take on both nausea and shame at nature. Until the day when Li gave her the Look. And in her lazy quiet voice said hardly anything, but enough to kill the child.

"When is your appointment?"

It wasn't time to give birth, but to kill. Li wouldn't stand for anything serious to come between her and Zeste, to whom she had joined her life. Men to her were nothing but frippery and prestige. But a child would be a serious threat.

Marsken said "Oh God" on the telephone, when he heard that Zeste had made an appointment at the hospital. She heard the lord and master in him, the man used to making decisions. But she was afraid he would make the whole thing revolve around *him*. He said he would have liked to discuss the matter with her on a lawn.

"But it isn't your child."

The fact that he was not the father of the child did not seem to affect him. It was rather the decision he wished to change.

"Are you sure? Have you thought it over?"

She was about to vomit: "You're not to interfere, it's nothing to do with you."

She felt the foundations of her own life crumbling. He wanted to use her weakness to bind her to him and she felt how dependence would grow in her like a gigantic octopus and threaten to smother her. Now he wanted to be *good,* that was the worst thing.

"You are not nearly as harsh as you let on," he said and that was just the sort of remark that could make you really weak, ambivalent and helpless.

But then there was no-one like Marsken to make her as firmly decided to free herself from every tie and child. No-one could make her as hard as flint like he could.

"What can I do? What can I do?" he went on asking.

Finally Zeste screamed: "Why must you do anything at all? You must accept the fact that there are situations where you can do nothing."

The summer slaughter was over, the wound healed and the blood washed off. To recover from the rigours Zeste had thrown herself into a new love affair, this time with an impoverished young street poet. It did her good to be free of the oedipal triangle, it felt as if life could start from the beginning. Or simply begin.

But then Marsken called to remind her of an earlier promise, that they would spend Christmas together. Would she prefer Bolivia or Barbados? Oh, boo. She didn't want to go anywhere, she wanted to stay with her street boy. But that would sound so impolite, and she hadn't been very kind to Marsken with his deep hoarse voice.

"Take the whip along," was the last thing he said. And Zeste said no. And nor did she need it. They had only been together for two minutes when Zeste took out her book, and didn't take her eyes off the pages all day and all evening. She happened to knock the orange squeezer off a table and trod on it so that it broke into smithereens. Next day, the day before Christmas Eve, Marsken left Barbados.

*

He didn't shoot himself, and he didn't drown himself. But quite quietly the blood began to ooze out of all his orifices. In the end it poured out in cascades, and then he died. The priest spoke about the old lion and the toll his work had taken, which the family had shouldered. He wanted to develop those who were furthest away, and thereby neglected to develop himself. And he took refuge in the breast and the bottle and asked to be buried at Søllerød, where his mother had lain since he was little.

*

In his time Uncle Otto had described the Løvins as a broad-minded modern family with no sensational stories apart from infidelity and card playing, and whatever else bourgeois families go in for. The main thing was that until the day Orm robbed a bank, no-one had ever broken the *law*. As far as anyone could recall, anyway. Except for Gaus, of course, Palle Gaustrup, who had been in prison several times. But he hadn't *really* broken the law, he had just made use of *holes* in the law, something quite different. Besides, he wasn't strictly family.

Aunt Titta, the tennis-playing beauty queen from Hornbæk, who had taken the first place in the fishing boat for Sweden and later on flirted with theosophy, had had a cerebral haemorrhage and was now in a wheelchair. The attack had destroyed Titta's power of speech, so nothing was left but "yes" and "no". But she didn't say no much, she had become a convinced Yes person, as long as she could be near her beloved husband and wasn't sent away for retraining therapy. Every hospital and nursing home was no, no, and home at the villa in Klampenborg with Otto was yes yes yes yes yes yes yes yes yes yes, so he was being driven crazy.

He was obliged to send her away for a few hours during the day "to work", as he called it, to get a scrap of peace. He called her "the Parcel" because she had turned into a dumb thing, that was carried in and out of rooms and up and down stairs, and who constantly drew attention to herself through indecipherable sounds. He lived in an eternal guessing competition, since he denied having developed telepathic talents. He shouted at her from morning to night: "Don't spill" and "Shut up". Sometimes he was simply driven to stuffing a cloth into her mouth so as not to go mad.

But even here Rebekka couldn't subdue a pang of jealousy. Here was another woman who had got everything she wanted out of life. Not by slogging from morning to night. Not by waiting at a bus stop at half past seven in the morning in the dark to get to the office and getting home just before closing time. Titta had got everything simply by *being* a woman, and that made Bekka livid.

That it could pay to *be* a woman, if you dared to bet on it. Even in her most debased situation, as a dumb animal, she made Otto jump to her tune. He loved the Parcel and even as she in her time had jumped around for him in high heels and a Chanel suit, now he jumped around for her, sitting all withered like a little girl from Auschwitz, because she hadn't eaten properly for many years, because her throat, for unknown reasons, long before the cerebral haemorrhage, had tied itself in knots so that no food could pass through it. Since her youth she had laboriously picked the white dots of fat out of her salami. And for many years she had gone to the doctor regularly to have her throat "widened".

For all of their bourgeois life, pleasure had been the order of the day, with dinners and bridge with friends and acquaintances several times a week, cigars and cognac, summer on the Riviera and relaxation on the islands of Silkeborg Lake. They were each other's destiny in joy as in sorrow. They were a couple, not a pair of gloves. Titta and Otto had always signed themselves Totto. And Bekka, who had always had to manage on her own, found that both beautiful and very irritating.

*

Titta's funeral was a simple ceremony at the Mosaic Chapel. No fuss, soft oriental music. Jews do not take flowers to a funeral, but they like to raise a headstone later. In Denmark the families have gradually become so mixed that at the Mosaic Cemetery they are used to people's ignorance of the old customs and prepared for them to bring flowers. So the tradition has developed of leaving the flowers by the monument to those who did not return from Theresienstadt.

Titta's admirer, the chief rabbi, spoke. And he had chosen feminine beauty as his text, Genesis XII. About the famine and the flight into Egypt and how Abraham gave out that his beautiful wife Sarah was in fact his sister, so that Pharaoh should not take Abraham's life and steal her. The rabbi reminded them that since the morning of time, long theological debates had been held about the right of this story to be included in the Testament, just as the dubious place of the Song of Songs had been disputed. For the question was whether beauty was only a superficial quality or the expression of a spiritual reality, a radiation of spirituality coming from within.

And the battle of interpretation continued after the funeral. For Balder's new wife, Plys, and Li, and for once Rebekka – all three agreed that the rabbi had talked *far* too much about womanly beauty. They all three thought it was scandalous to speak of womanly beauty when what was under discussion was a person's inner qualities. And in her heart Li supposed that it might have been difficult for the rabbi to find anything good to say about Titta's inner qualities. For everyone knew she was stingy with both the butter and the cream in the recipe for bolischer that went back to Mama at Rosenvænget. And Rebekka knew, which was something no-one else had realised, that when you were on your own, you got less food from Titta than the ambassador and "the posh people" did. As a rule, you were invited for leftovers and you weren't allowed to bring the dog.

It was a good thing they had the eulogy to quarrel about, for that gave them a chance to forget the family's insoluble conflicts. Balder couldn't stand his sister Bekka because, as he used to say, "I am a success and she is a fiasco." He went on and on about the television programme he was planning: "The other side of the medal of the welfare state." He wanted to interview a drug addict, an alcoholic and a neurotic, and Zeste said he could well start with his own family. Bekka couldn't abide Plys because she was working class and a "Communist" and – worst of all – married to her dearly loved brother. Myren had run away weeping when Zeste asked her to stay. Without Pierre she was as much at a loss as she had always been. Michael, Bilha's younger brother, was plainly ill at ease in his officer's uniform, having to listen to his sister jabbering in the addict's monomaniac descant beneath her Orthodox wig.

Worst of all, Uncle Otto was more than half an hour late for his wife's funeral. After Titta died he had fallen ill himself and had temporarily moved himself into a nursing home. Ib was to fetch him and drive him to the Mosaic Chapel. But now that his mother was no longer alive, Ib had suddenly become the stepson in more senses than one. Ib had always been made to feel somewhat "in the way". For his part he had seen through Otto's dim-wittedness and despised him – and the name. He had taken the family name. It was never mentioned, but at his mother's funeral the old war flared up again. Ib and his harem had never had a reputation for precision. But Ib almost succeeded in "forgetting" to collect Otto from the nursing home. The entire company sat in the chapel with the body of his dead wife and waited for him. When at last he was wheeled into the chapel he was in a soft hat and pyjamas. Ib hadn't been able to get him dressed.

That was the last straw. After that Otto crossed Ib out of his will and put Balder in his place. The two grown men, Ib and Balder, lived close to each other in Bistrup and couldn't avoid meeting in the supermarket. They didn't acknowledge each other for years. Balder was bursting with pride at being the "chosen one". It meant almost as much to him as seeing his own name on the screen. Now he was no longer the little boy, child of shame, who was sent from Riga to boarding school in Denmark, the betrayed victim. He was chosen.

At the time that Titta died, Tor's wife Emma was expecting her child on the island. Tor had finally got his milk quota from the EU. He had become a full-time farmer, "clerk" of the parish and "eldest brother" in the congregation. But complications arose, the child was in the wrong position and would not be turned. The doctors decided that a Caesarian section was necessary. Tor and Emma and the whole congregation prayed to God for the child to move, and a few minutes later it took up the correct position and Emma gave birth easily. It was a girl, who was called Sarai.

*

In the meantime Rejn had moved to a nursing home on the island to be near his son and his family, the only people left to him in the world. And it was the irony of fate that he was obliged to feed on Jesus as well, but since he didn't have much grey matter left, that didn't matter. No-one had thought it possible for him to go to pieces so fast. He, who throughout his adult life had carried Li and groped around in the dark to find the pea that was unsettling her, had never had a chance to be ill himself. True, he had married a French nurse in Africa. And merely the choice of a nurse perhaps suggests a latent desire to be allowed to go to bed and have a fuss made of him at last. He developed Parkinson's disease, but unhappily the nurse fell ill with cancer at the same time, and although they moved to a luxury villa in Switzerland to be close to the world's best doctors, nothing could save her life. Rejn was alone in the world – with Parkinson. He was barely 60.

For a long time Li had made his life a misery through solicitors, trying to get a larger slice of his cake. Surely it wasn't just that she languished away in a boarding house room while he loafed around in a luxurious Swiss villa with some pygmy. There must be some safeguard to ensure her the standard of living she had been accustomed to when she was married to that zombie. But the zombie slid away from it for as long as he was capable, and when he couldn't any longer, Li received official notice from a barrister stating that her former husband, Rejn Møller, was receiving an early pension because of illness, which meant that all maintenance from now on was to be terminated. Li had to laugh at that. Rejn ill? Not on your life. Can a stone be ill?

For a long time her friends at the boarding house had explained to her that it would be wise to forgo the trivial maintenance contribution from Rejn, because she would be able to claim considerably more from the state if she was destitute. She refused to believe that for ages, but it turned out to be true. When Rejn defaulted on his contribution to Li's support because he was going into a home, Li began to be a consumer. She enjoyed a new independence, something she had never known.

All down the years the prognosis had been clear: Li might die at any moment, she never had long to live. Rejn was the survivor who could cope with everything, but he was now on the island weeping. He wept every day in his hospital bed because he knew that as the days went on he would cease, either gradually or wholly, to be a human being. He had lost his work, his wife and his villa in Switzerland along with everything he possessed. Myren had loaded his belongings onto her trailer, when Rejn still had the wit to see to it that neither Li nor Zeste got their hands on his things. He, who had never before had overmuch empathy with Myren, now found they had a common cause. A shared hatred. Just as it had been for Myren, Li and Zeste had become his inner plague. After the divorce they were fused into a tumour of hate inside him, and it grew as he clenched his teeth and concentrated on all the promising discoveries predicted by information technology.

After a long time he was given a room at a home which was not far from Tor and Emma's home, and had it equipped with the latest personal computer and television system with satellite channel and cable TV. And an electronic, self-turning bed, which could turn Rejn over at night like a roasting chicken, now that he could no longer move himself. From then on he had only to press a button. The single drawback was that he shook so much that he *couldn't* press the button. He lay back and wept. He wept like a little child and wished for nothing but to die or for someone to look after him. Whether it was Jesus or Tor. He tried to reach out to him, but he couldn't control his movements. He was back at the children's home – where he had once been left behind when his parents went to Vladivostok. And all night long he called for the paramedics to come and operate his self-turning bed.

Then Li rang. She just wanted to find out if he really was ill, as they said, or if it was just play-acting. At that point Rejn was so sick that she could barely understand what he said. She didn't believe her ears! The man who had always been so meticulous about all his calculations was nothing but a wailing wreck. It couldn't be possible, even though Rebekka, as the semi-doctor in the family, had told Li about the symptoms of Parkinson's. Paralysis, shaking, trembling, and cramps. Stiffness in the body and facial expressions.

"That doesn't surprise me," said Li, "Rejn has always been a stick."

Bekka overheard her sister's irrelevant comment and went on, while Li closed her ears to Miss Know-It-All's scientific lecture: "It is caused by the dissolution of the area in the brain known as 'substantia nigra', which leads to a loss of the essential chemical, dopamine."

Li put more faith in an article she had read in the newspaper, claiming it was a disease which particularly struck train controllers and tax collectors.

She decided to summon all her strength and travel to the island to see Little Blessing and newborn Sarai with the additional purpose of visiting Rejn for the last time so that they would not part as deadly enemies.

She had brought a present for him. An archaeological find, a soapstone figure from a burial ground in Peshawar. The little sculpture was a votive offering that had been buried with the corpse. On the back of the figure of the deceased, some magic formulae had been engraved in a dead language. Rejn had probably bought it himself on one of their numerous journeys through the Khyber Pass, demanded by the Cat so as not completely to dry up in the Afghan desert. And the Dog had indulged her as always. They had stayed at the Intercontinental with great carpets, gigantic crystal chandeliers and air-conditioning, played bridge and golf for days and shopped for a few carpets and antiques in the bazaar.

At the home, a disabled old pensioner sat in a wheelchair in a stained blue jumper, dribbling. His face was expressionless and he couldn't speak although it was obvious that he recognised her. Li looked around his room. On the windowsill she caught sight of a little olive green Sung bowl with lotus leaves in celadon glaze. As she left she slipped it into her handbag.

13

THE GOLDEN TOURNAMENT

Rejn was dead, and at his funeral they learned of a totally different person from the one known to the family. Somebody no-one knew, a man from the Resistance, gave a eulogy to the bravest man in the group, whom he called The Clothes Peg. He spoke of railway sabotage in Jutland, life underground in Sealand and Funen and eventual flight to Sweden. Many people involved in the Resistance found that those couple of years during the war defined their lives to the end, but Rejn had never breathed a word about it. Li certainly hadn't seen him as a Resistance fighter, only as a Dog. Had he mentioned anything of that experience, it would have been dismissed as Boy Scout games, so he held his tongue, so he was able to keep *that* world at least for himself. A world that now popped up at his funeral and filled everything. And as this hitherto unknown brother-in-arms spoke about Rejn, about the one called The Clothes Peg, the congregation felt more and more in doubt about who they were bidding farewell to.

Li had not been invited and Zeste was in London. When she arrived back at Gammel Mønt a few months later she found a big yellow envelope containing his will. There was barely a mention of her, despite the fact that she was a stepchild and thus equally entitled to inherit with Myren, Orm and Tor. She telephoned Li:

"Why haven't I got anything from Rejn, like the others? I have never done anything to him."

"No more have I," replied Li, as if she too was his child. "I *created* him! When I met him he was nothing. All he had was a room in Peder Skramsgade and a pair of nail scissors."

"And a whale-tooth tupilak voodoo figure."

"He didn't know how to be a father to his sons, for he had never had a father himself."

"Was he ever fond of anyone?"

"He loved me for the first seven years. After that he was in love with you," Li said.

Zeste almost vomited.

*

When Li is about to go down by five, she always has a new card to play. The fact is that on her dying day all her new women friends will turn up out of holes in the ground, and all of them, as one, independently of each other yet in unison, will declare that Li is the loveliest person they have ever known.

It is indisputable that Li attracted other people's curiosity because there was something both mysterious and alarming about her. And she weighed no more than Karen Blixen. But her strongest card was always Zeste. "I CREATED HER," ran the headline. Li said in the interview, "Zeste is exactly as I wanted her to be." The journalist wrote: "It must be wonderful to have a mother with such a lively imagination!" When her friends asked her how she had done it, she said the answer was freedom. "I never brought her up, as such, I never interfered. I always counted on the fact that she came ready-made from nature's hand." And the friends gaped, impressed, because they themselves had met with failure from the same method and not a well-known actor.

Li surrounded herself with admirers, it had always been like that, – she couldn't help it. As a child and young girl she had been fêted for her wicked smile and the yellow cat's eyes. In the meantime her eyes had become quite white, like her stools, but she still compelled admiration because she radiated a silent heroism. When she had been hospitalised for tuberculosis, the doctor said: "You must be very brave to say you feel well. It must be because you have never tried feeling well and so have no idea what that means."

Everyone who came close to her quickly realised that here was someone who had lived in hell. Someone who had only survived with difficulty. Faced with this fact, their own tribulations shrank to nothing. That was the way she healed and helped people. By showing off her scarred, bony arms.

And she hardly *ever* complained. She kept her losses to herself. All the same, she couldn't manage to go to Myren's house the few times she was invited to children's birthday parties with a view to giving presents. For there she saw her entire home and furnishings intact. Everything Myren had dragged home from Switzerland on her trailer, everything Li had collected in the Far East. Li did not feel things to be dead – they were a part of her living life. The smallest pottery fragment cut her to the heart and reminded her of triumphs and high points – her pride.

Like the time when the Indian editor in chief of the *Bangkok Post,* Sam, had invited her for a romantic walk on the pretext of showing her his new offices on the edge of the town. And she had looked down at the dust and caught sight of a shard. She knew at once that it was Sawangkalok. They had walked into the nearest wooden shack where a whole peasant family were gathered. She showed them the shard, and they had grinned. She had asked if they had any more of the same kind. And they had enthusiastically pulled down all their soup plates from the shelf to sell them to her, such a crazy "farang". It was all Sawangkalok. And between the editor in chief and Li there had been a feeling of complicity not unlike being in love.

Together they had known what treasures they had just dug up out of the ground. And there it all was at Myren's house, Sung and Ming, Chinese leather chests, lacquer cupboards with gilding, and rosewood tables. And the beautiful carpets from Kabul with deliberately woven errors, since only Allah may be perfect.

But Myren was also – perfect. For instance, she had telephoned Sotheby's to make sure her efforts hadn't been in vain, and she made her mother a speech: "You can be happy that I have all the things. I'm grateful to you for the sense of beauty you gave me. I think of you every time I look at these things." And she added: "And you can be happy that I am married to a man who also has a feeling for them."

Li too called Sotheby's, like her daughter, and they competed with each other, in a deadly jealousy that burned through *the things*. Myren's appropriation and conquest of her mother's whole life (through the things) reminded Li of her own miserably managed pounds. She could never get over the fact that Myren never so much as offered her the smallest ashtray.

Otherwise she lived without complaining in a cardboard box with the trophies she had won. She had prizes from all over the world. After the Dog's death the Cat spent a few rather good years, even though she spat blood every morning, had a temperature every day and weighed 37 kg. She wouldn't see a doctor because she was going to play in the Golden Tournament. Besides, hospital tests began at eight in the morning, and Li would rather die than get up that early. As the boxing promoter had once said of her legendary laziness: "If she goes any slower, she'll go backwards."

Meanwhile, she stopped being a cat and practised just a little at being a human. She learned to read a telephone directory. She learned to "borrow" when she subtracted figures at the back of her chequebook so she could keep control over her money, which no longer came from Rejn. And most impressive of all: she began to use public transport when she was going to play bridge. And she drove past the churchyards where young people loafed and basked on the graves in the sunshine, with their ghetto blasters deafening the dead.

But what had done most to bring about Li's good years – along with Rebekka's never-failing family feeling – was having her own home for the first time in her life. A one-room apartment in Østerbro.

And her usual luck held good. Everyone queued up to help her, as they had always done. "It's a gift I have," Li said. But like all gifts, it came at a price. Li had constantly to hear about her hanging eye and crooked jaw, and now Bekka also wanted her to have her teeth taken out. Just to help.

"We'll have to be thinking about a little prosthesis soon."

"What do you mean by 'a little prosthesis' – dentures?"

"You may have to start to sell your Chinese porcelain if you want to have some decent teeth and not just standard dentures."

"Out of the question."

"But you can't chew any more."

What the hell was it to do with Bekka, whether she could chew or not.

"You're dying of hunger!"

"I'll never sell the china. Never."

"So you prefer to . . . ?"

"Over my dead body."

*

A lady called Ellen Nielsen caught a bus from Amager several times a week with a vacuum cleaner – to tidy up for Li, without payment, just for the privilege. She was afraid it was a privilege that could be lost, and one day it did go wrong. It happened that Li dropped her in favour of a better partner at the bridge table.

"I am so disappointed," wept Ellen Nielsen, who had danced attendance on Li for more than a year.

But Li said: "The bridge table mustn't come between us. You are welcome to go on polishing my silver cups and defrosting my fridge."

Ellen Nielsen was relieved. She hadn't been totally cast out. That was Li's power. With one foot in the grave herself, she gave meaning to life and other people. Or she removed that meaning.

Li had lived in big houses with a servant on each finger. Now all she had was "A room of one's own". Every morning she woke up and said to herself: "Why am I so happy now?" And then remembered: she had her own apartment. She was no longer dependent on any husband and she didn't have to be at the whim of any landlord. Why hadn't it happened years before? It had always been beyond the limits of possibility. And how in the world did she ever manage by herself? She was barely capable of keeping herself alive by, for instance, eating. The miracle was that there was a collective restaurant in the property with meal tickets and thus a reasonable chance of her eating once a week, maybe twice. Many older women live very well, for example, on red wine, which does contain quite a lot of nourishment. That was how Li came to suffer from two contradictory diseases: gout and anorexia. She had never cared much for eating, but now gout made its presence felt, that special rheumatism for *bon vivants*. Her toes swelled up and periodically prevented her from wearing shoes. And then she couldn't get to d'Angleterre, which was the only place where she really ate. Not for the quality of the food there, but because Zeste treated her. Only Zeste gave her an appetite. And Li made short work of four courses and a whole bottle of wine into the bargain, glllugg, glllugg. You had to be

341

ready to call the paramedics the whole time, because her food might go down the wrong way and suffocate her. She had become like a crocodile, which can manage on a gazelle every four months and otherwise live on air.

The restaurant was full of young people. She hated the youth culture. Youngsters who drank champagne and took a taxi to get their giro because they felt it was their right, and no-one dared to stand up to them or lock the door against them. On the contrary, the microphones competed to catch their pearls of wisdom, the one surpassing the other in fatuous self-regard, because – like Danes in general – they had never been tried or tested. They didn't know a thing: "*Du bist nicht geprieft*," as Bekka always said in Yiddish, although it was absurd to think in Yiddish. Usually, a gallant man of her own age would help her into the bus. When old people disappeared, so would helpfulness. Had anyone ever seen a young person help someone older with something heavy, difficult or dangerous? The only help the young knew was to help themselves to old women's handbags. If a young person had seen her white eyes he would have fallen down dead on the spot. She had once rescued her bag from a rocker on a motorcycle. She had just given him *the look*.

But it wasn't every morning that she woke up thinking: Why am I so happy? Now she took fewer sleeping pills she could dream. This morning she woke from a nightmare in which she didn't have enough milk to feed the children of Romania.

*

Li had been tried by life and found wanting, but she passed the failure with brilliance, without illusions. It was different with Orm. The more life failed him, the more certain he felt he had passed. Especially now, when the goal of his life had been fulfilled. After many years of sleeping in railway stations, refuges and on staircases, and after getting the psychiatric treatment sentence for bank robbery, he too had at long last been given his own apartment.

Outside his staircase lived a drug addict on a mattress with ashes and dried vomit, empty bottles and syringes. When Orm came home at night he usually found several ladies' handbags with their contents spread about on the staircase. Later in the evening the contents would have been gone through again and further reduced. There were several layers in the circle of predators. The jackals came last and went off with the remains.

Orm was now an elderly pensioner of 38. He had new teeth, a cosy sweater and reading glasses. He had actually inherited Rejn's old clothes, which were rather loose on him, but Orm couldn't stand anything tight. He had been on the waiting list for an apartment for many years and at last had found one "suitable". It had piss-yellow wallpaper that had once been white, and was furnished with sofa, chairs and curtains for a total of 235 kroner. Withered plants and candles that were never lit. Some said he had become "bourgeois" – and that was still a very bad word, even though there was hardly any real bourgeoisie left. But he maintained it made him irritable if his clothes weren't clean. He also had a thing about real toilet paper and didn't like wiping himself with the *Nørrebro Avis* newspaper.

If Orm were to take stock, he could list seven or eight of his friends who had committed suicide, not counting those who had died of an overdose. He received 9,000 kroner a month, the highest disablement pension, but was still paying off the debt to the Christians in Korsly he had stung for 50,000 kroner in one weekend. Thank the Lord he was now on antabuse. Otherwise he might well consider going in and opening an account at Magasin and filling a couple of plastic bags with booze for a treat. And then the money would have "shot off some place, unluckily", as he put it. So he tried to keep well away from the bad company in Jesper Brochmandsgade, because he was in debt there too in some cryptic way. The debt was about "getting air". "Through the channels I use sometimes, to get air." What did he mean by channels – cannulas? The thing was that Orm didn't have many possibilities left for supplying himself with nourishment. He vomited every day. He couldn't keep anything down because he had wrecked his stomach with spirits and drugs. He consumed, besides his psychopharmacological medicine, between ten and 20 codeine tablets a day, as they could be bought without a prescription, and smoked between 40 and 60 cigarettes every 24 hours. He couldn't sleep at night. For a long time he had used hash as the last resort. But it had begun to make him melancholy and increasingly desperate. He could no longer find the peace he sought from his pot pipe. He couldn't feel any effect without starting to cry. So his finances were now somewhat mysterious.

Money had been his profession. He knew the clauses and laws of social security legislation by heart, it was a full-time job. He was able to talk any claimants' officer under the table by either a charm offensive or simple by threatening the loathsome bitch.

If other people could live on 9,000 kroner a month, with rent paid and food from the council, Orm should be able to, they maintained at the office. But his record was always very odd. For instance, he asked the social services to pay his telephone bill of 3,000 kroner a month, because he had just come from St Hans. And now he needed 3,000 kroner. But how had the telephone bill got so big? Yes, because he had a telephone that was out of order, which he had bought from a junk shop. It would only ring *out*, nobody could call him because the bell had broken.

"A phone like that is costly to run," said the officer.

Orm's eyes started to flicker irritably at the interrogation. Who should he kill now?

Soon she would ask why he hadn't had it repaired in the normal way, and he didn't care to tell the cow that the phone had got broken in the street, or explain what you used a phone for on a pavement. She didn't need to know he had been on the way to the junk shop to sell his phone in order to get a bit of air, or that he had chucked the phone down in a rage when he found the shop closed.

Orm found it increasingly hard to keep a hold on himself, to keep body and soul together either. He felt his apartment was about to be invaded by mysterious beings who would make demands on him. They came from the bad company in Jesper Brochmandsgade, particularly the man with the pony tail, who threatened to smash Orm's kneecaps so he would be forced to spend the rest of his life in a wheelchair. Orm had changed his telephone number five times for fear of Pony Tail, but for some reason he always ended up giving him his new number. He had stuck a note on his door "No hawkers". But all the same his apartment was full of importunate enquiries. He stuck a note on the door threatening police action, but he was so frightened of it himself that he tore it off. He was trying to keep a whole life away from his door, but he wasn't sure he had the strength to keep it up. And he read in the Gospel according to St Luke: "Which of you with taking thought can add to his stature one cubit?"

Playing cards kept Li alive. It might happen that she fainted at the bridge club from weakness – if she hadn't eaten for a long time – but she still won. And she bought – with her disablement pension – an emerald and a sapphire, which she wore on her skeletal fingers, so she could sit fidgeting with them as she laid down her aces, like the old Jewesses in the ghetto. While her liver and kidneys gradually collapsed and her blood was mixed with urine she hadn't been able to separate out for over a year, she grew more and more clear in the head. She remembered all 52 cards, as if they were her next of kin, and she knew in a clairvoyant way what was in her partner's hand. She played at the Golden Tournament and collected all the golden points she would take with her to the grave. She won, and not only because she played her cards faultlessly. But because all the others at the table knew instinctively that they were playing with death and were doomed to lose.

*

Hardly had Li started on her new life and public transport, before a gale blew her away with a single gust and broke her hips. The gale did that every autumn, so Zeste forbade her to go out. But Li always felt happy in the surgical ward, the only one where there was *action* – for life or death. She lay in clean hospital nighties with the jade cat – which in some supernatural way had come back to her after having been stolen – on her bedside table with pictures of Zeste on the front pages of newspapers or magazines. With Zeste on her duvet she was well protected, just as an emblem or a uniform can protect soldiers against the awareness of their all too human weaknesses.

When doctors and nurses came by Li was able to tell them that Zeste had just had a première in Riga. And for most people that was a newly discovered spot on the map with a heroic populace who had sung the Soviet might out of the country with bonfires in the streets and flowers. They had seen the Latvians on television, their struggle and mutual solidarity, where every church and every apartment had been transformed into a first-aid station or shelter, and everyone gave everything they owned to each other, food, coffee, cigarettes. The Danes had tears in their eyes, for a little country which, like Denmark, only wished for freedom.

That was easy to understand. They quite forgot what up to five minutes ago and for the last 50 years they had insisted on: that the Latvians managed perfectly well as a Soviet republic. The Danes' unerring sense for comfort had always dictated their selective memory.

Zeste was moved to be back in her mother's childhood art nouveau town beside the Baltic, to be able to stand beside the Daugava and watch the river flowing where Li as a child had watched the ice break up. Zeste found the family's first apartment on Kalpaka Boulevard in an old, relatively well-preserved jugendstil house opposite the park and the Orthodox Church with its wide staircase winding upwards with an elaborate wrought-iron railing, up to the university library full of card indexes. The librarian looked incredulously but kindly at her when she explained that she was searching for the room in which her mother's cradle had once stood (she made no reference to the marital bed Katze had ordered to be sawn in two). While the old apartment was fairly intact, the modern buildings from the '30s, which they had moved into in Valdemara – for among other reasons because they had lifts – had in the meantime come a long way down in the world, as so often happens. What had once been madly luxurious was now a slum. After Tobias had been forced to close his firm and leave, his apartment and offices had been taken over by the Central Committee of the Communist Party. Today the premises housed a psychiatric clinic.

Last One Out Switch off the Light was being premièred at the State Theatre, and Zeste expressed her joy to the national press at "coming back". She sang the first verses of the Latvian national anthem which Rebekka had taught her, and told them about her grandfather Tobias, who had brought the oil, and that now she was bringing a new fuel, freedom. She openly admitted that the Danish people couldn't avoid feeling a little sad at the thought of all the Latvians had been made to live through and suffer. She told them that they had truly been "tried and tested" while the Danes had been allowed to go free, with their heritage safe under the interior iron curtains that kept them so warm.

She spoke about the play, which had triumphed everywhere and was about liberation from all oppression, first and foremost that of the family. The Latvians nodded with shining eyes and rejoiced at her message. Through the Tobias connection with the

'30s and thus to Latvia's brief and fragile independence. They showed her the monument to freedom, which, to their speechless astonishment, she photographed with a brand-new invention of a camera, whose pictures came rushing out in minutes. Apparently freedom knew no bounds.

And yet, even as Zeste pleaded the cause of freedom she was smitten by doubt. For she came from a world in which everyone ended up in a grave of the unknown, a shared and unnamed one. She came from a country with an affliction directly linked to welfare. The Danes, unlike the Latvians, no longer had any feeling for their fellow man in pursuit of survival.

Although *Lights Off* was a success thanks to the joys of expectation, the play was never performed in Latvian after it had been translated and people realised what it was really about. That it was not, after all, the world and the freedom they had longed for.

*

Balder introduced a polemical discussion about skull caps in a newspaper concerning the correct use of the Yiddish term *"Hut"* as distinct from the word *"Schäbbes"*. In his insistence on *"Hut"*, Balder turned all the Jewish orthographers against him since he was obviously wrong. That was the worst thing, since his whole life was aimed at correcting the glaring error which had once been perpetrated against him. There was an error in the world, an error committed in the garden of paradise, which pursued every succeeding generation.

Balder made an excellent television programme about immigrants, which provoked an article in a Nazi newspaper which described Balder Løvin as "the Jew, sired by Tobias Løvin, who is buried in the Mosaic Graveyard and is polluting the ground water". The article did not neglect to mention that the family came from lower-class Levins, but had thought it more refined to call themselves Løvin.

Balder instituted proceedings against the Nazi and won. The Nazi was sent to prison for ten days and made to pay Balder 15,000 kroner in damages. It was the first time since the war that judgment had been made for anti-semitic utterances. His former wife, Sharpy, who herself wrote letters to editors and criticised the amount of money spent on AIDS patients, also wrote incessantly to her former husband and hate object (since she no longer had any contact with her children). She wrote that it was nothing more than his passion for publicity at any price which had inspired him to bring the case against the Nazi.

The price was high, for he had assumed the most hated identity in all the history of Europe, that of the victim. Public opinion made him a *Jew*. The man who killed Jesus. Balder, who had been born of a Christian mother, baptised and confirmed, had voluntarily taken on the identity of a Jew, and thereby exposed himself to abusive telephone calls, letters and taunts in the street. He had become a Jew, and in that way had by chance grown close to the daughter with the kosher wig whom he had always kept at arm's length and hardly known whether she was alive or dead. He had, with this gesture, re-created the trauma he had experienced at school when he was teased about his long nose and red hair.

The sticks and stones of strangers did not much bruise him, rather they rained down on him as compliments – "better a bad reputation than none at all" – because he wasn't a real Jew. He was a television Jew. Similarly, he was not a real father. He was a television father who with professional solicitude questioned sick children on their tender points: "How many drinks do you swallow in a day?"

For his birthday, which was a round number, his children Bilha and Michael wrote a song to the tune of "Lili Marlene" about their father, who could not tolerate mother's milk and had never grown up.

His colleagues were receptive to his charm as well. As a surprise and affectionate greeting they had concocted a television news item which was broadcast at the usual news time, in which Balder was seen greeting Gorbachev with the comment that now at last the Soviet leader was having the greatest wish of his life fulfilled. Then Khomeini, who couldn't wait to meet Balder, and the sports stars Boris Becker and Mike Tyson, who only had one thing in their heads, to take on Balder. It goes without saying that Balder won every match, every fight. This was on television news!

When Uncle Otto died, Balder took Ib's place as the son in the will. After that Ib simply refused to tend his mother's grave at the Mosaic, on the grounds that "Otto is buried there as well". There would be no end to the struggle between the chosen and the one cast out.

*

On Balder's birthday it was conspicuous to see how Li was failing. She survived only on nervous energy. Her home help had been for a long time shocked at Li's disgraceful living conditions and her emaciated condition.

One day Li sent for Zeste. There was something she wanted to say. She had been thinking about her life, why things had turned out as they did, and where she had gone wrong.

Zeste took a taxi to Østerbro. Li had once asked to come first in Zeste's will. She had always cherished a dream of inheriting her own daughter. Zeste hadn't seen Li since her return from Riga. Now it dawned on her that Li was going to die – not of any particular disease, quite simply of malnutrition.

She was very weak. But after several recent stays in hospital and – among other horrors – lying all night in the bathroom, where she had fallen, without getting any help because there was no help to get, she wasn't going to hospital again. She had lain on an assortment of dirty nappies, unable to move. So she would rather be in her own apartment, whether she could move or not, and lie in her own shit. She coughed ominously, but smiled at Zeste's photographs from Riga. She didn't understand why it was all so shabby. Perhaps, after all, she didn't want to say anything.

"Mother, you wanted to tell me something."

Li wanted to know if she would meet her father again if she died. And Zeste was about to reply that she wasn't God, but suddenly sensed that she would have to be. To assuage the fear of death. So, like Little Claus who described the delightful sea cow at the bottom of the lake, Zeste said that, yes, Li would meet her father.

"Mother, you wanted to tell me something."

"I wanted to talk about my suicides."

It was the first time in her life she had used the word. Taken the word into her mouth. About herself. About her own life. But a little late. She started to count up the times she had really wanted to die and meant it, and the times she had merely tried to take her life by mistake.

"I wanted to die," she said proudly. "For I had had my children and been happy with Father, and now there was no more to live for."

"But your children were quite small! I was eight, Myren six and Orm just born," Zeste said, suddenly angry. "How could you do that to your children?"

"You could have managed on your own."

"How could Orm have managed, when he had just been born?" But Li could quite simply not hear what Zeste had said. And she announced, with the mother goddess's old authority, that Emma, Little Blessing's wife, was expecting again, and Balder's son Michael was also having a child with his new girlfriend and it was a good thing when babies were on the way. It was nevertheless clear that Zeste must steer clear of the chains of parenthood if she wanted to be a *personality*. Otherwise it would be like putting stones in your pockets and walking into the river. Although Li's wish would then be granted and she could inherit her daughter.

*

One night there was a call from the hospital and a voice of a 14-year-old said: "If she were *my* mother I would come now." And then the voice added: "We are putting your mother on a respirator, so you won't be able to speak to her."

"What does she say herself?"

"She's asking for something to help her sleep."

"Why can't you just give her that?"

"She wouldn't last the night."

*

Li was one of the many who do not wish their lives to be prolonged with treatment, but no-one would take her death on themselves, not now that she was on the point of slipping away. They left her to the world of machines.

Zeste had been with her in the afternoon, quite a different time from usual, almost by intuition. Li had been admitted because of pneumonia. She had actually decided she wanted to die at home, but Bekka found that too unpractical and, more than that, unaesthetic. She would never forget the utterly harrowing scene she had witnessed at the time of Titta's cerebral haemorrhage. A patient reading *Berlingske Tidende* one moment had suddenly got out of bed the next and released a furious stream like the Niagara Falls in the middle of the ward, at least eight litres. The fear of losing all control was so terrifying to Bekka that she spoke in one long furious stream. Do you realise that at the moment of death, bowel control is lost, came in ominous tones from the family semi-doctor. Rather a clean corpse in the coffin than shit in the bed. You couldn't lay that on the paramedics.

Li was in a room by herself – so as not to frighten the other patients – drowning in her own mucus. She hadn't the strength to cough any more. And the more mucus they drained, the more rose up to suffocate her. She had asked the priest when God would let her go away, but he hadn't been able to answer.

A doctor put his head round the door, looked at Li and said: "You're looking fine." And Li replied, from the other side of eternity: "This is Zeste Løvin, my daughter."

She asked Zeste to go to the toilet with her, and when Zeste took her in her arms and carried her bones out to the bathroom, it seemed as if a very old weight she had always carried had suddenly become light.

A nurse came into the room and Li whispered: "I have created her, myself."

Zeste carried her mother's pathetic carcass back to her bed, and then went out to ask the staff how long the patient in No. 7 had to live. The 14-year-old looked at the case record and said it was just mild pneumonia, they would soon have it cleared up.

Meanwhile Li lay drowning. She drowned in the ocean of her mother's tears.

*

When she had been on the respirator for three days, Zeste called the hospital and asked how long they intended to keep on with the "treatment".

"Well, we must just deal with this pneumonia," replied the voice.

"It is not a 'pneumonia'. It is a human being. One who has lived a long life. With a bad liver. And bad kidneys. And brittle bones. Gout and anorexia."

"And there is such a thing as 'a dignified death'," the voice said, as if it suddenly saw the light.

"Respirator treatment . . ." continued the voice into the ether.

"Switch it off!" said Zeste with a different authority from the power in her stage presence. And at that moment she was given Li's power: the ability to create and to kill.

14

MARATHON

"Ruht wohl, ihr heiligen Gebeine,
Die ich nun weiter nicht beweine . . ."

Li wished to have this chorus from the St John Passion sung at her funeral, so that Heaven would open for her and Hell have an end.

This can sometimes happen, in the old stories, if a good person can vouch for the dead. Such a person did turn up at Li's funeral: a man in his prime, about 90, in a Saint Tropez outfit, sun-burned and with a gold ring in one ear. He wasn't necessarily a good man, but he turned up at Li's funeral because he loved her. We do not say he was a man who had anything much to boast about, or whom Li had loved, we are just saying that he loved her.

Zeste recognised her godfather as the man who had once over the font promised to bring her up in the Christian faith, if her parents should defect. Balder and Rebekka recognised Gaus, the efficient businessman who had helped the family during the war and since then had been in and out of prison when he wasn't doing business in Switzerland. A friend of the family, they thought in chorus and straightened up, like the Løvins they knew they were. But God whispered: "That man, who was thrown out of the Handelsbank because he made use of bank secrets for his private enrichment, he loved the deceased. A man who sold non-existent trains, ships, buildings and companies and carried on fictitious business in a fictitious world, he loved the deceased. The little cobbler's son from Horsens, who married into tons of Norwegian money, deceived his wife, and took Li's virginity on a desk covered with share certificates and title deeds, he loved the deceased."

Just as at Rejn's funeral four months earlier, strange people now turned up at Li's. A few anonymous representatives of the nursing home came. They did not usually go to funerals, but their relationship with Li was special. She had always expressed her gratitude, didn't mind dust and was more interested in hearing about the carers' lives. And she really listened.

The other strangers in the company were listed as "bridge friends". Men from inns and women with hidden bottles and sorrows. All of them friends who considered Li to be the loveliest person they had ever known. For in her presence all shame had vanished.

*

Rebekka said: "It's a shame Li is dead, because *Gone with the Wind* is going to be on Channel 2. On the other hand, *Glamour* on 3 is worse than ever, so she hasn't missed much."

Rebekka, who all her life had warned people of the possible disaster of a condom splitting, felt very strange after Li had gone. What was missing? She betrayed her passion by spending more than two months to get hold of the biography of a renowned British courtesan. With Li's passing she had lost her association with the risky, uncertain, marginal life, which after all she could not do without. She reported – to whoever would listen – that virago's reckless escapades, including all the rich lovers she captured – with Bekka's backward-looking interpolation that she came from a good family, her father was a lord and she was red-haired. Madge all over again. After Tobias' own heart. Having satisfied herself there was no question here of a "street girl", she could safely recount the lady's dubious merits, including the happy ending, in which the heroine became, triumphantly, an ambassador. But after Rebekka had thus made the *risqué* life acceptable, she pulled herself together and added: "After AIDS, all that would be quite impossible." And she said it with a certain relief.

There was no responsible man left in the family now and Balder never phoned. Rebekka slid further and further into her own televised dream world, as she nursed her overweight dog through its seventh year; it had to have insulin three times a day, like Balder. When visitors called, they first had to ring the doorbell to be handed a gift of biscuits. Next they must ring again and present the gift to the dog, which would then be happy and unwrap the gift with its nose, after which it would be given an injection.

Rebekka maintained her strict rituals and was therefore extremely surprised when a year after Li's funeral she received an invitation. Contrary to confirmed habit, which forbade her from leaving the dog and the television, she accepted. It wasn't every day she was invited out by a man. Besides, this was the man who had hidden Mama in his holiday house at Asserbo.

On the way into town she repeated Uncle Otto's famous words: "Gaus, we have never judged you, but you do not need to boast."

Rebekka didn't know much about Gaus' relationship with Li, because she had been in Sweden while it was going on. But as the bus approached d'Angleterre the memory of other – unpleasant – relationships came back to her. Rubinstein, whom Li worked for, had, like so many other lawyers, borrowed from the clients' account, but – unlike most other lawyers – he had suddenly to flee to Sweden and so was unable to put the account in order. He was accused of fraud and sent to prison. He was a real patriarch, he was the one Li should have had. If only she had had a husband she could look up to . . . a man who could control her and her destructive forces, she would have had a very different life. Li had also gone to bed with the son, whom she called a fake in relation to his father, when the father was away. According to Li, the son played superb bridge, but otherwise wasn't worth writing home about. He went to bed with his father's young wife while the father was in prison. Old Rubinstein forgave his son. He said: "Well, I wasn't there myself, and she was attractive." And in his old days when he was asked to give a lecture on "The Burdens of Civilisation", he began, to the horror of the audience, by saying: "I want to talk about what it is like to be in prison." *He* was a personality.

Gaus was waiting at the hotel entrance, doing bend and stretch exercises to show off his good form. He was just 90, sunburned, wearing yellow cashmere and his earring. He held himself like a pirate of 60. He told Bekka, without any introductory manoeuvres, that every morning he breakfasted on an Old Danish liqueur and a mixture of yoghurt, egg yolk and garlic. He walked eight kilometres a day.

"*Twenty times* I have been to . . ."

Bekka thought he was about to say prison, but instead he said Bayreuth. He went to the opera all over Europe.

"I am totally free, I float on a little pink cloud," he said. "It was lovely to be free of my wife, so I can really be myself. I'm not dependent on anyone, I float on a . . . little pink cloud," he repeated. "No, I have no hard feelings. That's because I'm quite superficial. I learned from Lady Asquith, who kept a salon in London. She used to say, 'You haven't learned to read before you have learned to skip.'"

He didn't ask how Rebekka was, but since she was never at a loss for words she told him herself: "Dirk Bogarde is the feeble young Englishman who is going to Canada to take over a piece of land he has inherited from his grandfather."

"I have entered an internal competition with myself, which is to be as old as possible," said Gaus. "There are 16 people in Denmark who were born the same year as I was. But there are 300 of a hundred and more."

"But why do you want to be so old, Gaus?"

"I don't really know."

He did a few bend and stretch exercises at the table. And Bekka went on talking about the film: "She is this totally efficient children's doctor who is both exceptional at her job, a perfect mother, a sophisticated lover and a faithful friend. But her son falls seriously ill, and she finds herself with a problem: should she give up her medical career and desert her large circle of hard-pressed parents, who need her, to devote herself solely to her sick son . . ."

Gaus recalled for Bekka the New Year's Eve in 1940, when Tobias most elegantly dropped a whole pile of gramophone records on the floor.

Rebekka suddenly remembered Tobias' disappointment over Gaus: "Tell me one thing, how could you both help the family and cheat us? It's not logical!"

"I'll tell you. There are two different pleasures. It's a pleasure to help other people, and it's a pleasure to cheat them. Why forego one pleasure for the sake of the other?"

*

Opposite d'Angleterre near Krinsen Zeste was sitting with a perambulator. She had all her things in it, all her clothes, dinner jacket with silk lapels, flesh-coloured long nightdress with angel's wings plus two dopey cats. Children passing by looked down at the listless cats and asked: "Why aren't there any children in the pram?" If the curious youngsters had asked Zeste directly and not merely whispered to their teachers, she would have given them an answer: the children who should have been in her pram had all been killed in Rwanda during the April massacres. And the children who had survived the *ragnarok*, which is Armageddon, were staggering around with deep gashes in their skulls or else lying on the backs of their dead parents.

After the death of Li, Zeste had become a free woman. And she began to practise living on her own terms. Not those of the theatre and the audience. That was why she had settled down on a bench as a kind of exercise in Zen. Some people seek for bodies to live in, others only a bench. There she found the opportunity to transcend cold and heat, wind and rain. It could rain and snow on her, she was somewhere else. She was completely present. She was where she was, in a position to transform the noise and muzak of the town into an internal mantra of profound silence, to turn pain into pleasure and pleasure into pain. Now and then she recalled Madame Nui. When Buddha in his time left his father's palace in order to seek understanding, he made his way directly into homelessness.

Now and then she threw herself into a wild, purposeless shopping binge and filled bags and the whole pram with goods. The checkout operator's computer noted without blinking: CAULIFLOWER . . . MERMAID'S CLOTHES . . . PIXIES FOAM RUBBER . . . KNICKERS SATIN. Afterwards she emptied the whole pram-load minus the dopey cats into the nearest skip. And was left with the best thing of all: nothing.

It was a long time since Zeste had last seen herself plastered on the façades and waste bins of the town, her face torn to shreds by the wind. Nevertheless, people did occasionally recognise her.

And people came up and thanked her. They said she had saved their lives. She replied – to their great astonishment – that she had also taken many lives.

It was the end of the month, and panic ruled among the pènsioners and those on benefit, of all ages. They hadn't been given their pills, drugs and bottles. It cost blood. It wouldn't take anything to . . . Orm ran wildly around in an attempt to sell his corneas or one of his kidneys. Otherwise he would have to give up his present lifestyle, and then there would be nothing left but the nursing home at Pilgården, waiting to take away all your autonomy and interfering in everything you did.

On the other side of Krinsen sat Bilha, Balder's daughter, gloating over the fact that in spite of everything they were managing on methadone. If it hadn't been for Judaism, which held on to them and their home, she would certainly have been sitting here on the bench with the ones who were begging for money or selling themselves for a fix.

Bilha was on a short visit to Copenhagen, because she had just buried her latest stillborn child at the Mosaic cemetery. It had been born at full term, she was sure of that, and alive to the last moment. Her child hadn't been strangled with its cord, as they maintained. But Bilha and Elias knew very well that they don't take quite as much trouble over addicts as with other people. They hadn't been offered a Caesarean or pain killers. Addicts must suffer. "We are right at the bottom of the human pecking order," Bilha said to herself. "Well below Communists, whores and murderers." But nowhere in either the Talmud or the Old Testament was it written that you mustn't feel the rushing of the wind.

Her brother Michael had been sent with the Danish contingent to the former Yugoslavia, and they hadn't heard anything from him for three months. Aunt Li had always said, quoting Heine: "*Wo man singt, dort lass dich ruhig nieder, böser Mennschen haben keine Lieder.*" But it was precisely in the musical Balkans where polyphony had resounded as a living harmony, that the song had changed into false notes and mass graves. And it was hardly possible accurately to number the victims: not even the dead from the Second World War had been counted up.

Bilha had no connections with the family any more, since she had a Jewish one. If she and Zeste had seen each other at

Krinsen, where they both sat while the square was dug up beneath them to reveal ancient Copenhagen before King Absalon, it is doubtful whether they would have shown any sign of recognition. Fifteen years had passed since Katze's death.

Zeste took her place on the bench with her back to the Royal Theatre, the factory of death. Zeste had found the *real* living theatre, right there on the bench, with a monkey on her head. And with the full force of her lungs and from her whole heart she intoned: "Every atom demands to be set free!"

The customs officer approached on his crutches to offer her sweets – smuggled goods, as like as not. He called himself "the one-legged ogre-rabbit", because he was well aware that his missing leg filled people with horror. He didn't want to bother with a wooden one. "The crutch is useful for hitting out with." He was no gentleman. He talked of the 60-year-old women with backsides as broad as lorries, who carried ten bottles of Larsen in their knickers. An old lady with breasts down to her knees tried to jump the barrier, but got her paws stuck in the fence so they had to cut her down with the garden shears. She had a plaster over her crutch and three and a half kilos of heroin in her cunt. The one-legged customs man gabbled on and on about his red letter days.

*

Around Krinsen and the customs man and Zeste, Myren drove with her ever-laden trailer. She had just come from Gammel Mønt and had still not recovered from the shock. The scratches on her face and hands were still smarting and the deeper gashes bled. Normally she was not worried by dead people's houses, having become accustomed to them over the years. For she had got to know a number of wealthy old men, and she always saw to it that – to the indignation of the heirs – their valuables came into the right hands. Not for nothing had she inherited her mother's appreciation of beautiful things. To start with she sold them from her oriental boutique, which in the meantime had graduated into a junk shop. But there was no more room in the shop, so she had been obliged to make use of the farm as well. And she had become passionately expert at flea markets and scrap metal yards.

All the same she shouldn't have gone up to Gammel Mønt. But

she had had no suspicions. It was just hard to get the big candelabrum out of her head. She still had her keys from school-days. She rode up to the third floor in the same old rickety mahogany lift. On the mezzanine there was now an office for an HIV and AIDS charity.

It was no surprise, they had had to break with Zeste, it couldn't be otherwise. It was because of the children. For a long time they had intended to start a whole new family, from scratch. Write the story all over again. They didn't want, she and Pierre, to drag on with the inheritance that had been so destructive. And surely it must be a human right: to say no thanks, we aren't going to take part in *that* story!

So of course it was slightly ironic for Myren to be the one to go to Gammel Mønt 14 to clear up after Zeste, who obviously could no longer manage by herself. It wasn't exactly pleasant to have to deal with all that old filth. But when a letter arrived from the council saying the apartment was in a state of advanced dilapidation and infested with beetles and rats and altogether neglected, thanks to one's dear sister, so Mum here had to take a hand.

Myren's thoughts dwelled particularly on the silver altar candlesticks.

It was a peculiar feeling to let yourself into your childhood home, when you hadn't set foot in it since Katze died. As in the old days, it was first the lower key and then the upper one. Strange that Zeste hadn't had the locks changed, but obviously she couldn't care less about burglars! A stench assailed her as soon as she entered the hall, where the crystal mirror still hung surrounded by Latvian winter scenes with snow and sables. Zeste had kept everything which smacked of glamour.

In the middle of the drawing room she had placed a large open camphor wood chest lined with white silk beneath a satin sky. That had been in the newspapers too. Regardless of how much you covered your eyes and ears, as a citizen of the country you couldn't avoid knowing that the well-known actor spent at least one hour a day in her coffin. Exactly like her French exemplar. For you were force-fed with salacious information, which you certainly hadn't asked for, so it was not at all surprising to see a skull staring at you. That too had been in the papers.

She had festooned the walls, ceiling and doors with heavy black

Chinese satin, embroidered with bats and mysterious patterns. In the old dining room stood Zeste's ivory four-poster bed with black curtains and a bedspread embroidered with a large red Chinese dragon with golden wings and claws. In a corner stood a full-length mirror in a black velvet frame. In another corner hung a stuffed bat with outstretched hairy wings. On the dressing table was a pile of Tibetan skulls and in front of the mirror stood the handsome skeleton of a young man with white bones like shining ivory.

She had strewn her robes over sofas, chairs and chaise longues. Long grass-green velvet creations with wide sleeves and amber-coloured drapery with fur borders. Moth-eaten leopards and wolves lay under sparkling pearl necklaces, amethysts and topaz. Newspapers covered the floor, stinking of urine. Here and there the cats had done their business, directly onto the star-patterned parquet, but it didn't smell any longer, the faeces had entirely dried up.

The coffin was not empty! On a closer look, it was full of letters and papers. Letters from admirers and worshippers, or from furious and wronged lovers. Not so remarkable when you think that she had only loved Orm, if she had ever loved anyone. Family letters from all corners of the globe too. Chiefly on account of the last category it would probably be best to save the letters, so they did not fall into the wrong hands or come to public knowledge.

But how could that happen? Suddenly she saw, in the centre of the coffin, Pierre's samurai scarf! How had that landed there? Was it Pierre's – or just identical with the one he had once, in their young days, bought in Japan? Or had she herself put it in her pocket before she left home, and dropped it in the coffin? Suddenly a thought struck her like a shaft of lightning: the Czar's silver salver! Had she really sold it? Outside the family!

How weird, that someone you had once known as a child was now an old woman. Wherever she was, she wasn't registered anywhere. All the same, it felt, in a horrible way, as if she was present everywhere and could appear at any moment. Where was the silver candelabrum? What luck, it was still there! Grandmother had told so many stories about the metre-high floor candelabrum. How she had found it at a Jewish antique shop in Riga, looted from a burned-out Orthodox church, though its twin had ended up as a lampshade in a Hungarian family home. And here it still was, although unpolished and somehow insignificant. It certainly was in need of a loving hand.

But then a mysterious thing happened. The black plastic bag in one hand and the altar candlestick in the other, that much was certain. The lift rumbled down – the rickety one which had always been like that. Give the bag and the candlestick to Pierre and the children, waiting in their station wagon. Then hurry up again for more. Just to get the expedition over and done with, it isn't exactly pleasant to walk around in other people's filth. A number of other things were rescued, among them a collection of Chinese porcelain which Zeste had bartered for with Li. Unfortunately the porcelain couldn't just be pushed into a plastic bag, it was necessary to hunt for a cardboard box. Moreover, she came to think of the jade cat. It would be good to take that too. Myren opened the door of Katze's old bedroom.

Nothing had prepared her for the sight that met her eyes. Was it even to be called a sight, and not rather a sound. And the screaming reek of ammonia, which made her eyes smart. Everywhere she looked: spitting and growling wild cats. Twenty in each armchair, hundreds of cats on the bed, sitting quite still and staring at her, ready to attack. And then cats scratching at the mattress and tearing out its contents. Cats climbing up and ripping the curtains. Cats hiding under tables and chairs. Thousands of cats' eyes glaring at her. Where was the jade cat? The sight of the fouled floor almost made her vomit on the spot. The creatures had tried to open food and packets from the kitchen, flour, sugar and grain. Tea and coffee bags were spread around with their contents dissolved in urine over the mixture of shit, bodies, blood and maggots. The cats hadn't been fed for months. But from the small skeletons that were massed on the floor in lakes and piles of excrement, it was clear the cats had begun to eat each other to survive. They ate the kittens first. Then they ate each other. Raging battles had been fought.

From the bloodstained books in Katze's library, a few amputated paws stuck out like hidden, forgotten snacks. Zeste had left Katze's old dresses. The black Chanel and the Pompeii-red crêpe de Chine lay frayed, torn and befouled. Myren was still searching for the jade cat. She was on her way out the whole time, in flight from the horror, but was held back by a strange voluptuous pleasure. For here she clearly saw what had become of Queen Zeste and her famous liberation message from the underworld. Myren did not think the thought, but she felt a deep satisfaction over the eternally elder sister's annihilation. And she saw the cats with fresh eyes, which still smarted with tears, but eyes filled with understanding. They all fought for their own survival. She saw something pale green shining in the shit, could it be the jade cat? She reached out for the jade, but as she stretched out her hand, killer cats set upon her. She ran out and slammed the door.

She took refuge in her trailer and a packet of Kleenex to wipe away the tears and blood. She would have to console herself with the big candelabrum.

"Yes, I gave it to you!"

"No, you didn't!"

"The altar candlestick!"

"No, surely you gave it to one of the children?"

But the children, who had been occupied with a computer game in the back of the car, hadn't seen an altar candlestick. Myren remembered so clearly having had it in the lift, down past the mezzanine. The candlestick must have dematerialised itself out in the street. Probably stolen by an addict. It was the death agony of late capitalism, said Pierre.

*

Shortly after the trailer had driven past Kongens Nytorv, the marathon runners came by. They came from all over the country, and Tor, "Little Blessing", was among them. He ran for his life. And that triggered off his daily dose of anti-depressive endorphin. The leader of the Christian congregation, Emma and Tor's neighbours, had hanged himself in the back garden. The communal life and the dream of a safe, Christian fellowship had been what first drew Tor and Emma to the island. And now? The feeling of powerlessness had almost brought them to despair. But then they gradually realised that their leader's wife was really a witch, and he had succumbed to her spells. What were they to do now? Tor and Emma no longer knew how to adjust themselves, and talked of moving to Africa to help there, Tor as a farmer, Emma as a nurse. But they had so many children themselves to look after. Tor started to run.

Zeste didn't notice Tor in the crowd, it all happened so quickly.

She had known him as a child. But she didn't know him as a marathon runner. Then an elderly man came walking through Kongens Nytorv, nonchalant, elegant. He did not recognise Zeste on the bench with the pram and the monkey, she was more than 50 now. But she recognised him and the last post in his career. Behind him walked his second or third or fourth wife. She resembled Zeste as a young woman. But he made all the women he married into mothers in order to fulfil his practical and emotional needs. On the other hand, when they had turned into mothers he was obliged to put a distance between them so as not to lose his manhood. Therefore, in front of him he had a young girl of fifteen. But only Zeste knew that Serge de Clerval held her labia together with the aid of two long inches of thread, sewn into her thin, tender skin.

The sight automatically made Zeste start her speech from the bench: "The reason for my sitting here is due entirely to an intrigue, for in this country the innocent are condemned. I had an apartment and everything was going well, but suddenly one day the police were at the door. Without a court order, without a search warrant. I am an idiot, I'm so gullible I expect protection from the police. But they merely drag me along to the station. They interrogate me for four hours. But they've got nothing on me. Late into the night an officer says: 'We know perfectly well you haven't done anything.' Nevertheless they chuck me over to the women's section and tear all my clothes off. That is the section the street women go to. And in spite of everything I am a Løvin and come from Gammel Mønt 14 with the altar candlestick, the Czar's silver salver and the Crown Prince's letter, and suddenly I'm naked there with girls I have only read about in the paper. I cannot possibly tell you how frightful that is. Just the thought of it. That's why I'm sitting here. I think about it every day. Being examined internally with rubber gloves. By repulsive little power-idiots. With middle school exams. But I hadn't done anything. That's why I'm sitting here. I want to tell anyone and everyone that you can't count on this society for anything. Hey, you there, do you hear? No, he doesn't care. He's probably in the police. I want to tell anyone at all interested in hearing the truth, you may as well whistle for any kind of justice here. Who, like me, has had the carpet pulled from under their feet once and for all, when you know justice is a town in Mongolia, then you sit here . . I have talked to my lawyer about it. For everyone who cares to listen, be sure the police plant drugs on innocent people if they have the slightest suspicion. Have you read Gustav Wied? Hi, you there, yes, it's you I'm talking to. Have you read Gustav Wied? No, no-one bloody has. An uncultivated rabble, the whole bunch of them. The masses. Walking around so respectably, thinking how ghastly the masses are just because they're going 'to work'. But they haven't bloody well read Gustav Wied. So what's the point of it all? But what was I going to say, I haven't lost the thread: the isolation cell. That is, what they call 'the isolation cell' today hasn't changed since the time when Gustav Wied wrote about the lock-up in 1800. Have you tried the isolation cell? Oh, you haven't? But I know what I'm talking about. In the isolation cell it's just like being shut into a public toilet. It's like being famous! 'Cell' may sound like a room of the kind you see on television with a bed, table, chair and TV. Co-o-o-sy! But in the isolation cell you sit in old urine with shit up the walls. In Paris they have taken away the litterbins and dustpans because of bomb threats. So rubbish and shit are everywhere. You can choose between living in a bombed town or a sewer. Shit, shit, shit. I can see why all the people are full of it. They hurry down the street, full of their own garbage. They haven't a clue what to do with it. They walk with twisted arms and tight lips and huge pupils. But it's not drugs. People always think it's drugs. But it's garbage. They can't get rid of it. That's why everyone is jealous of me. For I sit here and shit on Kongens Nytorv with the monkey on my head. The dream of freedom and happiness. And I'll shit here whether or not I have exhaust gas right up my bum, because I'll wipe it off on the king's envelope. Denmark is nothing but a little frightened land of fantasists who don't dare to look reality in the eye. Poor little Denmark, pathetic Emmanuel Hansteds, the lot. They wander around with their heads right up in the clouds, while they do away with their own children . . ."

ORM'S BOOK

Dedicated to every Human Soul, Hornbækgade, 5.vii.1990

Well, at last I've managed to get some peace and quiet (my words!) here in my first apartment. It's great to know this is going to be (with luck) my permanent home.

The question is this: Can I get myself together enough to write my memoirs?

To start with I'd like to take back all my gall, all the evil I have thought and said, for my life has taken a happy turn. I have been saved countless times from suicide, fire in my bed, etc. etc. So I direct all my gratitude to Christ.

Have just smoked a small pipe of hash; and Ydde doesn't like me doing that. Tolerance is the key word, if we are to go on. Let love lead and carry us through all the difficulties. And we have music to help and comfort us!

Oh, where shall I begin my story? Yes, LSD decided it. It was hard to experience and come out of it again and hash doesn't do me any good. Preferably a little controlled wine. Oh, yes, my stint in Vestre Prison. I still dream about that.

When you are young, you think: A film is just a film; but then one day it is reality in your own life!

My whole life has always been about this: Coming home.

"Don't want to be a fool starving for affection; don't want to drink someone else's wine." (Dylan)

23.34 19.i.1991
Home at last. No sleep, blues still come to me quite often.
War has raged for days in the Middle East. Outwardly life churns on, as if "everything is normal".
May the earth survive just one more time. Prayer.
The Niikolaj Service says that dreams are a clearing up!

08.51 22.i.91
My birthday today! 39! I'm drinking again. I regret it, but can't control myself any longer. Lord Jesus have mercy on me! I give thanks for life.
Have been put on antabuse, so the party's over for good. Only good, only good.
But what about Ydde?? What does SHE want?
I give up. Still love you, sweetheart. But it's all too complicated.
Anne Dorte: "Confidences are the first to go."
If they go completely, can they be reinstated?
There is "changing of the guards" at 11 o'clock. It's now 21.53.
Heard on the radio: Yes, lover of mine, it surely feels like I am losing my mind. Not funny. Sonny.

23.25 9.vi.91
WIDE awake after hours of sleep; dreams about rows with past enemies. Ah, well; better out than in, with those; otherwise they may develop into things I daren't even dream about.
I hereby renounce ALL sneering, despite spirits; they are conquered for ever; without discussion. AMEN.
Acknowledge JESUS CHRIST is LORD.
I know why I'm "at a standstill" just now. What use can it be to write about the past?
Whatever happens, I stand by the above confession.
Money is like "Golden Rain". Alluring to look at, but deathly in the end.
My intention with my notes is above all to acknowledge that the

66 canonical books of the Bible were, are and will remain God's definitive truth. In my heart I call it: *The Book of Truth*. Genuinely meant. Amen.

Slept well enough last night; neutral dreams. Nozinan often causes nightmare; a woman psychiatrist has admitted that this really is the case.

Self-solemnity, ugh.

But you mustn't lose your self-respect.

04.21 18.vi.91

I'm about to fall again; the struggle between good and evil inside me is sometimes almost intolerable. Have mercy on me, dear Jesus; and make a way out for me as well!

21.17 19.vi.91

Just back from Nicolaj Service. It may be that I misunderstand the man I talked to. But in some way or other I got a bad taste in my mouth: neo-fascism and cynicism are gaining ground everywhere.

The horrors of the Progressive Party. No, people like me are doomed to die on the open street according to their ideology. Today's down trip!

But OK once again: it must be I who misunderstands; I only know my self-confidence has almost vanished, after a conversation like that. *Summa summarum*: Dear heavenly Father, Thy will be done, in the name of Jesus Christ, through the Holy Spirit. AMEN.

22.07 20.vi.91

Dylan: "I saw thousands who could have overcome the darkness; for the love of a lousy buck, I saw them die."

05.28 23.vi.91

The sleep itself did me good; but the dream was bad. Once again was caught by the police and thrown in jail. Ugh, when I woke up. But otherwise feel good, for I haven't *anything* "hidden away". Look forward to going to church!!

21.25 23.vi.91

Midsummer Eve.

After keeping myself bottled up all day, now I feel that the explosion is coming. Well, let it come then.

I can feel someone or several are interceding for me just now. The depression is lifting.

03.54 25.vi.91

Good night; woke with a start; really rested; it's full moon the day after tomorrow!!

05.17. 26.vi.91

Good morning! What's the good of being a "genius" if you're as cold as your fellow men? Not that I'm a genius: No!!

04.52. 27.vi.91

Good morning, Universe!

So we'll have a full moon in precisely six minutes!

About "ambition": learn Modern Hebrew!! The idea came like a flash of lightning from a clear sky! But seriously, if it's going to come to anything, so be it!

10.17 10.vii.91

Realisation: I am left to sink or swim in my own sea; no doubt about it. Well, where people are concerned. But: thank you, almighty Jesus, Your grace is enough for me!

Gary Moore: "I found out the hard way, love is no friend of mine."

23.21 22.vii.91

The above is a lie. I just feel it is true when there's something cooking between Beloved and me.

The day ended well, only unfortunately because of a fix. Of course I know the danger of "playing" with that sort of thing; my safety lies in the fact that my shortage of funds won't let it get the upper hand. Luckily; plus that my "connection" isn't personally interested in it getting the upper hand because he has been through the nightmare of dependency and escaped from it again. So we "warn" each other every time we feel the internal alarm bells sounding off.

05.41 28.vii.91
Karen Carpenter: "All I know of love is how to live without it."
I am disappointed in human love; on the whole in everything.
Christ: "That which is born of flesh is flesh."
By that I mean that there's no point in getting into such a state over sexual matters!!
I *have* come to "journey's end"; but it feels further away than ever.

04.28 13.viii.91
Good morning, everyone!

08.01 26.viii.91
Good morning!
No, I mustn't complain over my isolation; I've chosen it myself.

05.29 16.ix.91
Morning!
Yes; the past will catch up with you, that's a dead cert, now in one way, now in another. Yes and again yes; that's my experience, that holds true even if it takes a long time.
The biochemical processes are real.
Self-obsession leads to madness.

06.28 19.ix.91
Heard in secret: Slave or not slave of passion, that is the question. To which with tears in my eyes and my soul I must answer: Unfortunately it looks as if through the years I *have* become a slave of shit. Free for long periods, yes; but then it just comes

without warning. Well now, old Orm, you thought you could escape?

07.37 24.x.91

No, everything is too late for me now. If only I'd had this opportunity ten years ago; then I might have had a chance of managing life, but it's too late now. Let's just look the naked truth in the eye, namely, that I am an incurable drug addict. And don't go on talking to me about love; it is the most repulsive, disgusting lie of all.

08.23 28.x.91

One of the reasons for it being so hard to write is that I prefer to write positively. So what do I do when in my heart, most of the time, I'm full of bitterness?

I *do* really want to write about everything. Not with a view to becoming a writer, but just to get air air air.

11.xi.91

Play it again, Sam:

Just remember this: A kiss is just a kiss, a sigh is just a sigh, and so a fuck is just a fuck. When it's over, it's over.

21.xii.91

Yes; I'm playing Hermann Hesse's "Glass Pearl" play and paying the price too: loneliness and again loneliness, even though I'm surrounded by people.

Ah well; unfortunately there's something that sometimes in this life runs: PULL YOURSELF TOGETHER. To my regret.

03.28 31.xii.91

Admitted to St John's again; voluntarily, yes, but at the same time out of bitter need. Have decided to stay on in Hornbækgade, even though I may be liquidated sooner or later.

Depression can be lived with, but fear, that's just "too much".

Have learned various new things during this stay. The doctors have begun to use a new diagnosis word: Schizoaffective, meaning several different abnormal states at once.

04.39 2.i.92
Good morning everybody (people).
About the *déjà-vu* attacks; however linked they seem, they are corrupt attempts at attack. I know it's all lies, because it's the first time in the history of the universe that we write the above time and date. So knock it off, man; or whoever it is, who is trying to confuse me.
Yes; it feel as if twelve o'clock has struck in my own personal universe; but I am no longer senselessly afraid, awed, yes absolutely.

05.01
The time that may be left is to be for prayer, prayer and again prayer.

23.00 9.ii.92
Ten days and nothing written. Too bad, man.
Have just fired off and hear Jimi is in a good mood. But still empty-headed where writing is concerned. Hmmm. It has all been written before, all the great spiritual truths!!!

05.02 10.ii.92
Yet another night that never ends! "What am I supposed to do?"
That's what makes you despair about the whole thing: There *isn't* anything else to do. Can't be bothered to throw more dust in my eyes: Orm, pull yourself together, there *is* a bright side.
Learn to think of death as a release instead of fearing it.
And the time, that pig, is *never* what you want it to be.
Stop it, how can a single day be long, not to speak of the night.
Yes; it's 17.15 now. But the thought that there's such a night to come!! Ugh.
Well; from this moment I couldn't give a shit about anything. Life isn't worth the hassle of living.

Human beings let you down, but the bottle doesn't!!
Human beings are vermin, but there's still nothing you can do about them.
Burned-out schizocook, that's what I am!!
My faith in the respective worldly authorities is precisely NIL!
Yes; it's 50:50 whether my internal light is switched off.
I'll never learn patience, gave that up long ago.

12.ii.92

Keep on getting the feeling: "The worst is yet to come!"

13.ii.92

It goes on coming, stronger and stronger: Lesson 1: Keep quiet, as far as ever possible; and if I finally have to speak, then think over every single word very carefully!!

20.ii.92

Is it true? Am I living in a huge self-delusion? If so, what am I doing? Where, when and most of all, how? Understand me rightly, please.

P. Simon: "Answer me, honestly, please, can a man and a woman live together in peace?"

Will this darkness,
   winter
      cold
         never stop?

Can't eat, can't sleep. Really want/wish/hope/pray to get all the problems straightened out. For it feels as if I'm going more and more crazy, with every passing minute.

No, I've no idea about the phenomenon of "hearing voices" in psychiatry. At least not enough to explain it to other people. Anyway, to me it's too horrible to be spoken aloud. Away with pessimism/dejection.

No more lies now; there really isn't much time.

FEAR OF TOUCHING. Yes, that's a large part of the problem. Why fear it? Hardly remember the answer any longer. Megalomania

373

and self-annihilation. Both equally wrong . . . and I have no reason for either.

No, I can't pull through that fear on my own.

APHASIA – difficulty in speaking, or perhaps just no speech?

I'm giving up, giving up, giving up this struggle. It's probably only a question of time before they come . . .

Well, is it just fear of castration I'm suffering from? Why has no-one ever explained it to me?

Hurry up and get it over with, before I commit harakiri or something like it.

Well then, 8.35 at last after an evilly long night.

02.31 22.ii.92

Ugh, no gala!

23.ii.92

Today it finally dawned on me: the party is over for ever; and now I can only take the pangs as they come; one by one; or ten by ten if that's the way it's going to be!!

25.ii.92

Yet another lying dictum: "When need is greatest, help is nearest." NO, when need is greatest, everyone turns their back.

03.33 7.iii.92

Hi world: you have to understand, this is the midnight hour of the evil man.

11.43 7.iii.92

On my own account: the pincer movement uses fear as the driving force to make people toe the line.

11.iii.92

I have always been afraid of Judgment Day, but now I'm looking forward to it!! Yes, and I dare to repeat it.

And it must be true, what Engelhardt says, that Christ has been here for the second time; and what Poul Henrik says, that Satan has come back to take over the planet.

I hope it's not true, but I'll leave the possibility open.

About psychopharmacological drugs: artificial substances give artificial results.

The 300-year-old prophecy is right: love has disappeared from the face of the earth, and people prefer to caress cats!

Jeanne d'Arc is still being burned at the stake, believe it or not.

04.42. 13.iii.92

Have just had a really negative conversation with the Nicolaj Service. I forgive them, even though it was a bucket of cold water over my head. But a staff member like that ought to be fired on the spot. It's a lie when you claim I don't want to. When I know I can't.

16.iii.92

No, Ydde, I won't be a financial milking cow for you. It's gone on too long now!!

10.v.92

As the date shows, I've been "dead" for a long time. Most of the time: who could be bothered to read it?

Dear God, dear reader, dear paper: apologies for all the blasphemy and suchlike, it *isn't* the real me. What I'm trying to say is: can't I have some air, air, air; to clean out what's inside? Am praying it may be OK, I can't stand the pressure any longer.

Tell me, could it be that I'm finally breaking free?

No, good old Charlie Brown: the bad – the rest of your life.

Excuse me for being so vicious, sometimes the hurt is just too much, that's why.

28.v.92

At home again, finally. Wonderful! Only – no more fixes!! Ugh!

31.v.92

So that was that, dear universe!

I am dead!! Hope you're satisfied. Ingratitude is the pay of the world!!

06.40 31.v.92

Almighty God of Israel; I confess: I have sinned grossly; and I can only pray for your forgiveness, which I now do: I repent all my life. Amen.

This Sunday will be one of the bad ones; where I'm concerned; with no medicaments, and so withdrawal symptoms. Very, very funny – – –

OK; then I tried to play *The Glass Bead Game* and realise now I have lost everything, everything, everything for ever. (Because of a woman!!)

31.v.92

This is going to be the longest Sunday I have ever experienced on Planet Earth.

My reality: deserted by all, hated by all; scorned, rejected, alone. Then you first notice that one's thirst for happiness is to be alone.

Authentic poem by a long-term prisoner.

Rather die here at home.

11.15 2.viii.92

I hate people who sleep with their money under their pillow.

All right, maybe I do it myself!!

4.viii.92

No, what is life worth without love? Not a pot of piss.

7.viii.92

The voice from above goes on saying:

ti!!

bi!!
Obey!!

9.viii.92
This is the temporary punishment: silence silence.
The bitterest day since I moved into this rotten apartment.

12.viii.92
Yes, I'm going to die of sorrow. Without God, without love everything everything is meaningless.
50:50, maybe suicide.
And you, woman: I accuse you of murdering my soul; yes, that's what I said.

17.27 17.viii.92
Renewed contact with Beloved! Hurrah!! Really honestly: Hurrah!
Prayer: Lord Jesus Christ, teach me self-control. Amen.
Prayer: help me to get away from misuse. Amen.

06.28 18.viii.92
Almighty God of Israel! Thank you for this new day. Lord: I love you!!
Ydde: this time you can light a bonfire for everything that was ours, for the very very very last time. Goodbye to you. Full stop.

06.46 28.viii.92
World: I HATE HATE HATE you!!

02.58 13.ix.92
Ydde: After my experiences with you, I'll never be able to love another person again. I have you to thank for that.
"Love" is the most deceitful word there is.

05.57 14.ix.92

No, this time I'd rather die here at home once and for all, end finale full stop.

02.10 26.ix.92

Something else inside me died.
Yes, Ydde dearest, our loved drowned; was suffocated; in problems, problems.

02.54 5.x.92

Life is a cruel joke; and then it's not even allowed to commit suicide. NO, I just say, loud and clear: NO.

04.48 7.x.92

Yes, my murderer is a woman!!

04.48 17.x.92

Summa summarum of the Sisyphus myth.
No, you'll never manage the last 1/1 0000000000 millimetres!
Remember that; and use your energy on something else!!

04.17 26.x.92

NO, earthly life is truly corrupt and rotten from cradle to grave. But chuck A and B and Neutron bombs together and please do it as fast as possible. Yes, right now you can light a bonfire to see that I mean it.

03.52 3.xi.92

The doctors/staff can't understand that medicine is only a secondary problem.

04.50 4.xi.92

Yes, by spirit and truth my life really did end in a true tragedy.

06.49 8.xi.92

You yourself have let me down time after time, when I needed you most. (Not to speak of the affair with your Kurt.) That's why the situation has developed as it has.

20.34 26.xii.92

I bear the wounds of Christ on my soul.

03.07 8.ii.93

Like Zeste, I believe that what will be, will be!! Amen.

04.22 17.ii.93

Ydde: Disappear out of my life, the faster the better.

01.45 14.x.93

Be integrated into society?
No, my type would rather be interned in some or other "amusing" place filled with rules, rules, rules, orders and prohibitions. And then they expect me to be grateful!!

19.17 11.xi.93

It's their own bloody fault I lock my door.

13.13 6.i.94

Saw her today. Her signal seemed clear: I got another guy.
May he make you happy!!
Good night!!

6.i.94

Sebastian: "– they could have had my heart, but they hadn't enough room."

15.38

You know, I was actually doing fine eight years ago, until she crossed my path.

18.26

No, Miss Ydde, YOU haven't kept your part of the agreement, namely never to leave me however ill I might become. The Lord of Hosts will judge between you and me. Amen.

01.22 8.i.94

Ydde, sweetheart, I love you in spite of it all!!

22.19 9.i.94

I hereby swear by all living Gods and devils: This time I'm gonna take revenge.

Ydde, I HATE you, you false poison snake. Just leave me alone, and I will surely do the same to you, you bitch.

02.00 11.i.94

<u>Never</u> more a woman (or man), <u>ever</u>.

Lord of Hosts, when will my life end?

11.20 14.i.94

"Doctor" Dalbjørn hates me and is only interested in breaking me. That <u>is</u> true.

But the Lord of Hosts laughs at him, for his time is near. Persecution and hatred from my fellow patients grow day by day.

11.48 14.i.94

Ward P1 St John's Hospital is truly the forecourt of Hell.

Life sentence at St John's, if "they" will even grant me that.

16.44

Prayer: Almighty Lord Jesus Christ: Please bring me back to innocence.

15.33 17.i.94

A wicked evening nurse, this evening, down, down.

11.15 18.i.94

Dear God: how badly I hurt over Ydde, but I accept it in the prayer of THY only son. Thy will be done!! Amen.

05.44

Lord Jesus: Help me not to turn love into hate and vice versa.

14.11 20.i.94

To think: Every morning I start out optimistically, but as surely as AMEN in church the day ends badly. So it's with a heavy heart I go to meet each day.

Often, when you ask the staff something, they reply "very soon" or "tomorrow" and so on.

14.09 24.i.94

I hate people who pretend madness to gain primary or secondary advantages.

09.26 26.i.94

Can't tell the difference between joking and seriousness. The others can't understand this, and many react angrily.

04.44

Yes, I must learn to keep control over my temperament.

02.21 30.i.94

Most of the staff aren't fitted to work with other people; they are wicked and do more harm than good. I feel their envy, hate, suspicion and disbelief. Ugh – you'd think they enjoy being sadistic!! Pseudo-fascists and neo-Nazis.

15.00

My "illness" isn't role-play. Or do I mean I'm just deceiving myself? So is it finally the last day of Planet Earth?
Yes; in some way or other I've turned into some low-down woman hater. I play the game once in a while, but . . . NO!!

04.48

Last night I was transformed into the devil. There is no forgiveness in either this world or the one to come. And I've been cheated out of my inheritance, so yet again *The Book of Truth* is right. For it says: "First you hurry to get an inheritance, in the end it is no blessing."
My thoughts will start a Third World War.

14.30 31.i.95

The Spirit of Mockery is the worst of all voices.

16.58

The Beloved has been lying about medicine. So it has been a bad day today, because she whom I call "Grandmother" from the other ward, is partly cheating.

00.23 4.ii.95

A deep trauma as far back as I can remember: Being deserted. Left in the lurch!!! I mean it!!

5.ii.95

From this moment on I will have nothing whatever to do with any human being at all, only with animals, because they are kinder than people. That is the sad truth.

08.07 6.ii.95
"Everything" normal/peaceful this morning. Slept well.

14.52
I've become deaf and blind with pan-fear.

16.36
Deciding now to go on hunger strike because of the wickedness of this planet! Know it can be done. The situation is intolerable now. I must get away before a catastrophe occurs. My death! I am unnerved. No; dear God. I give up once and for all!!

21.05
Now comes the account for my earlier life, and it hardly hurts!!

11.10 7.ii.95
I am here (P1) because I am mad; sick in mind; because of LSD, among other things; sickly childhood; the evil of the world, mainly.

14.32
Ostracised. Feeling down because I have just talked to an icy cold bugger of a social worker of the worst kind. It shone out of him: "I don't like you."

15.36
I'm sick and dead tired and frightened of being here, because everything gets worse and worse. The evil voices really come from live, existing persons. They can do what they like with their false accusations, they can.

16.49 7.ii.95

What goes on in this ward is called "mobbing". There's back-biting here, with teeth. Nothing but hate in this place.

20.52

Yes, OK: let's say it, then. I'm a victim of my own wickedness! But I still can't cope with the fear!!

10.19

I'm tired of being a "lightning conductor" in this ward. Yes, on the whole.

21.42

I am a victim of corrosive envy, false accusations, assertions of lying, and threats.

21.59

Sometimes I amuse myself being a sado-masochist!!

04.53

I also hate *species vulgares*. Vulgar con men and downright scroungers. That's what they deserve, the pigs, to get as good as they give.
To Ydde Krage Møller: You fill me up with lies, deceit and unfaithfulness, you cheating whore.

05.41 9.ii.95

My mission on this planet is at an end, and now I only want to enjoy my retirement and die in peace. Therefore I am applying for discharge as soon as possible.
No more sex with women/men/hermaphrodites – what a relief!!
The truth now!
I am cured/rehabilitated/well enough to go home and look after myself.

Here I am surrounded by evil sadists, psychopaths, murderers etc. etc.

14.41
Lesson for the day: Daddy is a genius!!!

05.07 11.ii.95
Women and hens – now then!! Best be sexless, or manage on your own. Yes, sir!! Hermit, recluse.

20.20
I will not be copped for "articipating" in anything in the least criminal.

21.21
No, the past can't be changed. No more drugs for me, I can't tolerate them.

03.12 13.ii.95
Wide awake. "Time" gets longer and longer. Shit. I must not fall for the temptation of drugs. Hard. Bored.

08.34
Just waiting for liquidation. Naturally, it will come unannounced, whenever, in whatever form it chooses.

19.53
I am being forcibly restrained for the 35th day, because I am a suicide risk; and they persecute me because I'm a Christian. Thank you, dear Lord Jesus Christ, for conquering them; so that now I can rest/stand firm in faith despite their accusations and threats.
O Lord, help me. Amen.

15.23 16.ii.95

If these notes are published, the book/story has to be entitled: Humility.

04.41 17.ii.95

Doctor: There's no point in forcibly restraining me any longer. Discharge me now so we can all have some peace. I am a danger neither to others nor to myself. I don't want to play your game any longer. I am 100% serious.

Yes, let me sail in my own lawful apartment (Hornbækgade 13, ground floor, right hand side).

23.57

Dear God: I wish you had never created woman. She is the cause of the sad state of the world.

21.45 19.ii.95

Goodbye for now. I had a head-on collision with the star psychopath on the ward. No names, but the staff backs me up: he is barking mad.

01.39 20.ii.95

Tonight's night nurse is the jaunty no-type. She hasn't a clue what she's talking about. Lazy, incompetent.

"The eye would sleep, but the mind will rise." Incredible String Band.

19.28 21.ii.95

I hate being physical, sexually needy!!

09.21 22.ii.95

No depot-injection for me, because I can't stand the needle coming from behind!! But as pills, OK, OK. Hebrews xiii.8. Best wishes, John.

10.41 21.ii.95
My life is slowly ebbing out – taking my own life is the only solution now. 150 codium magnesium and a litre of distilled water; and there'll be one pest less on this earth.

18.50
Verily, verily I say unto you, Universe: It would really have been better if I had never been born; and I tell you now. No thank you to a new life!!
John.

08.52 28.ii.95
Sometimes feelings (all kinds) are so overwhelmingly powerful that I believe I will disappear.

20.24 5.iii.95
Strange day, both good and bad. Fell. Hope the punishment won't be too hard.

08.11 28.iii.95
Swedish radio: "Love is just a loser's game."
What a way to salute the morning!

08.33 12.iii.95
When we have once got across the River Styx, everything will be explained to us.

18.57 14.iii.95
No, I'm no longer afraid of the thought police in *1984*.

19.21
Masturbation is a plague to me!!

11.24 22.iii.95

Fairly good talk to G. Everything status quo. Enervating. But he was positive about Pilgården; I just have to be dead clean for a long time.

02.10 14.iv.95

At home again. Hurrah!! Well, I'm suffering from sleep-defiance!! Because I'm frightened of my dreams.

16.20 21.iv.95

Radio and television do what they can to undermine faith, so far as they're able to.

7.v.95

Oh, slept well, but aching all over because of the mattress on the floor; wish I had a bed!! Johnny invited me to the cinema yesterday; we saw *Søren Kierkegaard* at the Grand, and it was a good film/experience. I cherish our friendship, hope it will last.

19.33 8.v.95

A good day, up at Johnny's twice. He doesn't mind, as we agreed to be honest and just say if it gets too much. We talk about EVERYTHING, from sex, family relationships, the right work, prison sentences (he has tried it too), religion, and then a lot about our stays in SJH.

He is a writer himself, poems and so on for the Mad Movement journal *Amalie*, named after Amalie Skram. The first woman to raise a revolt against established psychiatry about 80 or 100 years ago. The first one to thump the table: "Now, that's enough."

21.56 16.v.95

Feeling bored. But of course it was a real mistake to sell my chess computer.

04.50 24.v.95

Joined The Association of Oppressed and Frustrated Artists.

17.56 24.vii.95

Have just found out that Ydde (ex-wife) has been admitted again. What now, dear God?? I'd like to have her back, if she will come! Love certainly is complicated!

07.02 25.vii.95

If she comes looking for me, I will open the door, but I'm not going to visit her – although I love her still.

10.56 30.vii.95

I seldom go to church, partly because I'm frightened of people. But I listen to and take part in the radio church service on Programme 1. People, we included, have to learn to help themselves in Denmark nowadays. That's how it is.

?? 31.vii.95

Hurrah, I'm eternally lost.

Deathday is better than birthday; the end of something is better than the beginning.

31.vii.95

I believe the Muslims will win the Third World War; and that everyone who holds to another faith will be slaughtered, one by one.

1.viii.95

I have no friends, only enemies. I won't have any more to do with any religion. No, from now on I'm going to be a practising atheist. I am in hell now; it's only a question of time before the flames are visible.

Ydde doesn't love me, but she still plays tricks on me.

Dear Jesus, won't you wipe the past out of my mind? Please??? Like Dylan, Harrison and Paul Simon, I too have outlived all the others!! It's good to be stubborn. Poor all of us.

07.48 2.viii.95

I repeat: Here, no affectionate mother helps in the house of the rising sun.

It's psychological warfare to live here, one is more salted than the other is smoked. And if you complain, you'll be lynched at dawn.

There's a half-wit going around with a bib and forever a cigarette in his nicotine-stained hands. The least they could do would have been to give him a bath.

I keep hearing hateful slander: they say I'm gay and a child abuser. Every time there's a sex criminal on the loose, it's thick with rumours here.

20.17 3.viii.95

What shall I be in my next life?? A drug addict, man!

04.04

It's been a long hard journey to get so far, but OK, I'm here now!! Should I re-read Carson McCullers, *The Heart is a Lonely Hunter*?? No, I can't read books any more, my concentration's gone through having taken so much medication.

19.14

I hate the new wave of pietism that's invading the western world. Have rushed into an endogenous depression of hitherto unexperienced proportions.

20.35

Today I've discovered that there is no God, no Satan, no Heaven, no Hell. It's all a big bad joke.

04.04 29.viii.95

43 years old and in a home for the chronically insane; well done.
One of Johannes V. Jensen's most intricate lies (from *The Fall of the King*): God and Satan are one and the same person.
I repeat: an intricate lie. But the fact that war goes on in the world is unfortunately true.
This is an open prison for me. Hope I'm allowed to stay . . . it's a matter of my life . . .

08.00 8.ix.95

I acknowledge defeat . . . there's something from the past I am fleeing from . . .

07.04 10.ix.95

The only problem I have with my teeth is the upper dentures, they fall down every time I laugh. But perhaps that's not a problem, for there isn't anything to laugh about.

06.16 28.ix.95

This is the day the sausage of death is about to come through because:

No money	how sad
No funny	too bad
Sonny	Dad

       Pilgården, 18.xi.95

TOBIAS' BOOK

You might almost think that the Løvin family, polished off by drink and drugs of various sorts, had died out and that there wasn't any more life left to go on with. Unless the story is about to write itself into a matrilinear tradition, in which all Ib's daughters will have to retain their "stolen" maiden name and for the foreseeable future refuse to take the name of any man. Thus the children will have gone back to the mothers, whence they came originally, and the last symbolic remnants of paternal love and influence have finally been abolished.

But astonishingly, Tobias suddenly turns up. A Tobias Løvin, studying architecture at the Academy. We don't honestly know who he is, but no-one can deny his physical existence, although the explanation is rambling. Tobias is the son of that single social worker Else Løvin from Vesterbro, the one Aunt Sharpy, quite by chance, found in the telephone directory. It is the same Else who had an unexpected visit from hr and fru Løvin, Balder and Sharpy, who stood at the door demanding an explanation. Naturally it was Sharpy who took the lead, firmly resolved to get the name of Løvin off Else's door and out of her head. She had no right to that name. Sharpy had married it, for that was the correct way of coming by a name. How in the world did that common Else dare?

But the old Løvins weren't afraid of a tumble in the hay or

rather a *chassé* at the Adlon, lively as they were, so it's by no means unthinkable that down the years not a few women were sent "into the country" to give birth. As had been the intention with Katze. For Else's great-grandmother was born in secrecy and later, as an 18-year-old, was sent to Bremen to study. There she falls in love with an architect she is not allowed to marry, and the couple flee to South America. Regardless of how you turn and twist the story, which according to Else's detailed report includes death in childbirth, Buenos Aires, yellow fever, organ-playing and twelve poor small farmer's sons from Sealand, the name of Løvin went on like an invisible chain from woman to woman, up through the families, in spite of the men. They were perhaps socially inferior, but they had healthy blood in their veins, good sirs.

So one day here is Tobias Løvin, free, undaunted and ready to start from scratch, entirely ignorant of the family's history, incidentally. He thinks only of the future . . .

He has always loved animals. And then one night after closing time at the Benneweis Circus he decides to go in and have a chat with the elephants. There are four of them. The first elephant greets him with its trunk, and Tobias gives the elephant a bottle, which it drinks up in a flash. But the elephant wants more. So Tobias passes it some bread he has brought. Then comes the next elephant. It wants a beer as well. But Tobias hasn't any more beer and instead gives it too some bread. Then comes the third elephant. It gets the last bit of bread, there's not much. And now comes the fourth and last elephant, and it is jealous because there's neither beer nor bread. So it takes hold of Tobias with a strong grasp around his waist and puts him down on the ground. The elephant places its foot on top of one of Tobias' legs and treads down. Tobias' leg is crushed to powder. Then the elephant puts its other foot on Tobias' chest. Tobias holds his breath and thinks he may be the only person in the world who has seen an elephant from below and how big it is. Just as the elephant is about to press down, the other elephants come to Tobias' aid and push his assailant away.

Tobias has a long nail hammered into his crushed leg in hospital. And an amazing thing happens: all the bones and little scattered splinters, they all want to go back to where they belong. For that's what long ago, in the morning of time, they were told they were to be: a leg.

When Tobias had recovered, he married a learned immigrant woman from Gaza. She studied astrophysics at the university and her name – no lie – was Scheherazade. She remembered her grandmother keeping the proof from the bridal sheets, so that all the women of the village knew what had happened. And Scheherazade told many stories from the old days for the benefit of her descendants, terrible stories, for one must do that, she said, if one holds life dear.

> Then unsown seed will sprout,
> bitterness be healed.